SONG OF SUSSEX

Preface

This is a fictional biography based on fact. Authors are advised to write about what they know. My previous books have been set around sailing and farming. But I have always loved music, although as with the sailing I have not been much of a performer.

No single historic character did all the things my Richard Dyer achieves. I have taken as examples the likes of Carl Nielsen, Denmark's national composer, a little farm boy sponsored by the village lord to go to music college; William Walton, a Lancashire boy, whose father, although also a fine musician and teacher felt William had ideas above his station; Gustav Holst, a great composer who could never accept that he was a genius; and Ralph Vaughan Williams withdrawn from the front line to preserve his music. Composers, writers and artists have all had climactic moments when walking in some familiar landscape as inspiration has flooded into the consciousness.

Richard also serves in the wartime RAF as a fighter pilot until the powers that be ground him, not wishing to lose a world-renowned pianist. His Battle of Britain experiences I have shamelessly taken from real life accounts of the time. His tangled love life could also apply to any of the above named musicians. But Richard is also a yachtsman who saves his crew when he takes the wheel for ten hours in a storm. So which musical figure became a keen yachtsman and did this in real life? You may recoil in surprise, but that man was John Lennon a few years before his sad death. My novel is pure fiction, but I hope it is built on a foundation of truth.

My thanks are due to the many people who have read this manuscript and commented; especially East Hampshire Writers Circle, my proof reader Michael Glanister, and Jo Smith who typeset the final book and got it into shape for the printers.

This book is dedicated to *Southern Pro-Musica*

Cover photograph by Michael Turner
Graphic design by Petaprint

SONG OF SUSSEX

James Morley

Song of Sussex

First published 2013

Published by Benhams Sea Mysteries, 1 Fir Cottage, Greatham, Liss, Hampshire GU33 6BB

Typeset by John Owen Smith

ISBN 978-0-9548880-7-7

Printed and bound by CPI Group UK Ltd, Croydon, CR0 4YY

PROLOGUE

The Prime Minister looked at the cabinet secretary. 'I'm puzzled. The Australians are not asking whether we're going to do it. They're demanding we name the day.'

Both men turned as the culture secretary came into the cabinet room.

'Ah, George,' said the prime minister. 'We are trying to make sense of this Australian demand.'

'I know Prime Minister. It seems they regard this man as one of their own; but it's gone further. We've had messages from New Zealand and Canada and the White House, Paris, the Kremlin, and for God's sake, Beijing. They all want to know if we're going to do it.'

The prime minister looked even more puzzled. 'So, this man is a world figure.'

'Very much so. We're talking about the world's greatest composer and whatever the Aussies think, he's English.'

'Prime Minister,' continued the culture secretary. 'I've had a note from the home secretary. She is also concerned. They've had similar requests from all around the UK especially RAF ex-service organisations. There's been huge demands from Sussex. We've had messages from both county council leaders and four south city mayors.'

'Sussex,' said the prime minister. 'There are two by-elections coming up there in a few weeks. You know the other parties are breathing down our necks, and the Greens.'

He turned and addressed the cabinet secretary. 'What should we do?'

'Well, it will be a precedent, but where's the harm? It'll be a nice day out; bring in the tourists. Let's do it.'

'Good, that's settled. We'll need Parliament to approve but that won't be a problem. Can you get onto the Palace? The announcement will have to come from them.'

Jim Marley.

November 2013

PART ONE

CHAPTER 1

Sussex: Summer 1928

The eight-year-old boy ran up the last few yards of the steep grass slope. Beside him lolloped a panting crossbred dog. At the high point of the hill the boy flung himself to the ground and stretched on the short-cropped grass with his dog jumping on top of him, licking his face. Pockhampton Down lay bathed in the hot July sunshine; below, the Sussex countryside stretched unfolding like a map: fields and villages, with the line of the sea shining blue on the horizon.

Both boy and dog loved this spot. For the dog it meant rabbits to chase and trails to sniff. For the boy it meant peace and time to think; time to let the music that filled his mind, morning noon and night flow unchecked. Why did not one of the children in the village school understand this? Why did they laugh when he played on the schoolroom piano, or could not wait to run home to listen to the family's wind up gramophone? He had heard that Mr Tenbury in the great house had just bought something called a wireless that drew music out of the air. He wished he knew how that could happen. Mr and Mrs Tenbury owned the whole village and Dad was foreman of the estate home farm. Mum worked in the great house and they all loved Mrs Tenbury. She was a good, kind lady and it was she who had given him his birthday treat: a fruitcake baked in the house kitchen.

Everyone thought he would go on to work on the farm. He loved the pigs and sheep but did he want to feed them every day when he was a grownup? It was music that he was good at. He already sang treble in the church choir and Mr Locke the organist had praised his, "sense of pitch…". Whatever did that mean? Pitch was that stinky black stuff they painted the barn timbers with. Mrs Tenbury had heard him playing the schoolroom piano. He liked Mrs Tenbury, such a good lady, though he didn't like her little girl Maria who was now at the village school; stuck up, was this Maria. Maria along with her ma and pa never went to the village church on Sunday. It seemed that they were Rooming Clithlicks or something and it was the one thing the villagers did not like. Old Mr Ridge the gamekeeper said that clithlicks worshipped the devil and burned strange scents. Well, Mr and Mrs Tenbury were kind people and surely kind people didn't worship devils. Maria might though. She followed him around and hadn't she tried to scratch his face that time in the playground?

Suddenly he longed to be at home with the piano. He stood up, wiped his hands on the seat of his breeches and started off down the hill to the village. The dog bounded along beside him sometimes diverting to sniff an anthill or examine another rabbit burrow. They reached the dusty village street after slithering and sliding down the last steep slope. The boy paused as he stood in the road. A motorcar was passing, a big'un. It was a Lanchester with a chauffeur wearing a peaked cap. It must be on its way to the big house. The boy ran the twenty yards down the road and turned into a narrow side lane. Ahead was the farmhouse, his home. He crossed the farmyard, his dog panting behind him and splashed through the residue of cow droppings from this morning's milking. He felt hot and sticky and wanted a mug of water.

'Oi!' shouted his mama, Mabel Dyer. 'Get that dog outa' here. I've just washed the kitchen floor.' She was waving a mop in his direction as she stood in the doorway. 'Dickie, you too. Get those boots off and wash your feet in this.' She poured some water from the kettle into a metal enamel bowl and handed it to him. The water was warm and nice to the touch.

He pulled off the heavy leather boots, soaked his feet in the water and scampered indoors. He filled a mug from the cold tap in the kitchen and gulped it thirstily. The old upright piano was in the front room, otherwise called the best parlour. It was kept clean and tidy all year even though it was only used at Christmas or if the people from the big house called. He pulled out the wooden stool and opened the piano lid. He drew in the stool putting his fingers on the keys. By sliding forward to the edge of the stool he could just feel the metal pedals with his bare toes. He began to play that nice little tune that he had heard a dozen times on the gramophone. Mr Locke said it was Mozart's Turkey Rounder, or that's what it sounded like. He could pick off all the treble notes easily, so now he began to pop in some left hand bass notes. It was fun to find he could join the two parts and the sound seemed nice and right. Then there was that piece called Furry Liz. Was Beethoven thinking of his cat? Anyway a few more weeks and he'd have both of them good.

CHAPTER 2

December 1928

Richard picked up his school satchel, left the house and began the five-minute walk to the village school. He could see his schoolmates emerging from their houses in the main street. He waved and called out to them and fell in step with the boys. The girls kept to their own little gaggle some distance behind. This was the last day of term with Christmas a few days away so it was a happy gathering that walked into the schoolyard that morning. Only one pupil had not walked. An open topped motorcar deposited a little curly haired girl at the very spot where Richard was standing.

'Hello Dickiebird ,' she giggled. 'Sing me a song of love.'

'Morning Maria,' Richard grunted in reply. 'I don't do love.'

'Ooh, somebody's got out of bed the wrong side.' Maria burst into a fit of giggles and ran on into the schoolyard.

'Listen to her,' it was Richard's friend Alf. 'My dada says that one's on her way to bein' a tart when she be grown.'

'What's that?' asked Richard.

'Don't rightly know, but dada says them folks as lives in the big houses is loose on mortals.'

The school bell rang out across the playground and the pupils swarmed into the building. Forty children took their places in the main assembly room and stood as Miss Jeffries the teacher entered. With her came the village vicar, the Reverend Davis and with the reverend was another vicar; a scary looking old man in a black cloak.

'Children,' began Miss Jeffries. 'Today we conclude our studies for this term.' She had an odd whining voice that the youngsters loved to mimic. 'This evening, we have our annual carol service to be held in the parish church.' She turned to the vicar. 'Reverend, I think you have a few words to say.'

'That'll be the day,' whispered Alf in Richard's ear. Richard grinned. Everyone knew Vicar Davis's sermons could last for an eternity and were mostly about hell and doom. It wasn't so bad for Alf, he was a Methodist and Richard rather envied them. From all Alf told him their services were mostly singing.

'Children,' said the vicar. 'We are about to enjoy the holy festival of Christmas. We are most honoured that with us in our humble carol service will be Doctor Wandsdale.' He indicated the second vicar. The man smiled and inclined his head politely. 'Doctor Wandsdale is the organist and choirmaster of our cathedral and he wishes to listen to and assess our choir here. So we must of course bring forth our best voices in love and praise of our Lord.' Following this surprisingly brief speech the vicar sat down.

Miss Jeffries announced the start of morning prayers. This was the moment for Maria and another small boy to leave the room followed by hostile stares from their schoolmates.

'Papists,' muttered Alf. 'They didn't oughta' be allowed.'

They all knew that Maria would be standing listening in the corridor, ear to the door, sniggering as the heretics went through their devotions.

Prayers over, the whole school assembled again and split into two classes, senior and junior. Richard, in the under ten group, followed his fellows into Miss Jeffries classroom. It was an arithmetic lesson, and Richard enjoyed arithmetic and he would have looked forward to the hour had not he found Maria tugging on his jacket and then sitting in the desk next to him. The children extracted their slates and stared at the blackboard. Miss Jeffries slapped her pointer down on her desk and the lesson began. Arithmetic was easy for Richard although he found the problems dull: all things about taking batches of pigs to market or how many pounds of flour to make eight loaves of bread. More enjoyable was Maria's complete failure to recite her twelve times table. Richard sniggered and Alf demanded the girl be given the dunce cap, although being highborn saved Maria from this humiliation. She returned to her place and glared at Richard. 'Clever-clogs,' she muttered.

The lesson was over all too quickly for Richard. School break followed and then a further lesson: this time Geography. Miss Jeffries unfurled a huge map of the world with the British Empire shown in bright red. She began by describing Australia, evidently a strange country with great opportunities though founded by criminals. Now the teacher spoke with an expression of strong distaste.

'I'd like to go there,' Maria whispered. Other children heard her and muttered in agreement.

'Silence!' screeched Miss Jeffries. 'I heard that. One hundred years ago, if you hadn't been good you would probably have been sent there; even you Miss Maria.'

Classes over, the children swarmed out of the schoolyard and made for home. Richard hung behind as he made a beeline for the schoolroom piano. He still didn't fully understand printed music scores, but who needed them? He could reach the pedals properly now and knew when to press for loud or soft. More satisfying was his increasing grasp of chords and harmony, not that he really understood these words yet. It was just that his fingers running over the keys could now combine to make melodies and sounds that pleased his ears.

Absorbed with his playing he had not heard the footsteps enter the room until a firm hand was laid on his shoulder. Richard stopped playing and, startled, turned to see the vicar with the black-cloaked reverend he had seen earlier.

'Young Richard, we have been listening to you and Mr Wandsale is impressed, as also am I. We have not heard that piece before. Did you compose it?'

Richard made no reply but nodded. There was really nothing he could think of to say. The black-cloaked man had a kindly smile and no longer did he seem spooky.

Reverend Davis continued. 'Richard, you already know that you will be singing the entry verse at this evening's service. We would like you to sing it now.'

'Sir?' Richard was puzzled.

'It's all right,' said the Black Cloak. 'Let me have the use of your piano. I will give you the key note and then you sing the verse.'

Richard now understood. He was beginning to find a love of performing and the honour of singing alone at this service was something that had thrilled him and his parents even more so.

Black Cloak sounded the note and Richard sang:

Once in Royal David's city
Stood a lowly cattle shed...

He remembered to sing *lowly* and not *lonely*. He finished and felt a bit silly. Had he been showing off?

'That is very commendable,' Black Coat smiled. 'Now, can you sing me a scale in C major?'

Richard knew this too and flung himself into the task. *La la la la la la la-la.*

He smiled as he held the last note for three seconds.

'Very well done, young Richard. You have pitch rare for one so young.

'Is that enough?' asked Reverend Davis.

'Oh yes, I think so. Run along, young man. We will hear you again at your service tonight.'

Only one child was still in the school entrance and Richard groaned inwardly. It was that Maria waiting for her fancy motorcar.

'I heard you in there,' she giggled.

'So what?'

'You sounded sweet. Now, look here. Mamma told me to give you this.' She withdrew a white envelope from under her winter coat and handed it to him.

'What's that?'

'It's got your name on it. Read it. I can't – it's all joined up writing and I can't read that so well as you do, but I know already what it says.'

'Girl, you means as you read it when it's private for me.' Richard glared at her.

Maria grinned. 'I know what's in it anyway: Mamma told me. You're invited to tea tomorrow afternoon. Ganton is going to collect you in the Rolls – so, what about that?'

'It's kind of your mama, but why?'

She giggled again. 'They want you,' she spluttered. 'They want you in that cathedral. That's a very big church with lots of little boys singing.'

'All right, I knows what a cathedral is, but where?'

'Chichester Cathedral. That's the one your church stole from my church, but we've got our own one now at Arundel and it's just as big.' Maria giggled again and then the horrid girl reached over and gave him a kiss on the cheek. Before he could retaliate her motor transport pulled up and she had hopped on board.

'Tomorrow, Dickiebird,' she called. 'Be good.'

CHAPTER 3

For Richard his solo at the carol service was over far too soon. He had thoroughly enjoyed it and would have loved to complete the whole hymn, but after his first verse the choir joined in and they sounded vile. He couldn't actually tell anyone this; he would have landed in trouble, but his fellow trebles were not all in tune and muffed some of the words and Mr Shank, the bass-singing blacksmith, was far too loud and again not always in tune. This was nothing compared with the efforts of the packed congregation. He liked the way Mr Locke played the organ and wondered if he would ever have the chance to try it himself. It was such a baffling thing with its stepped keyboards and all those stops and pedals. It was nice after the service to have praise heaped upon him by his parents and their friends.

Now it was the morning after and the day of the dreaded tea party at the big house. He was nervous and excited. His mam worked in the big house and he had sometimes been in the kitchen and been given a small cup of tea and a piece of cake, but today was different; he was invited to the big house and he would see the inner rooms and eat with the Tenbury family and their friends, or more like with Maria and her stuck up lot and he still didn't know why.

His father came into the room as Richard was struggling into his smart church-going suit. 'They tell as Mr Leopold is back home,' he said.

Richard knew that Leopold was the Tenbury son who would one day run the village, although these days they rarely saw him.

'You knew him in the war, didn't you, Dada?'

'That's right, son. Mr Leopold was our company commander and a good'un. Saw us through some bad times he did.'

Dada rarely spoke about the war, but just now and again he would mention something about it and his face would cloud with a look of pain. Richard's mother had explained how dada's brother, Richard's own uncle, had died in a battle and Father had been there when it happened. She had told him not to raise the matter because his father still suffered nightmares.

Richard hated his smart suit and even more the horrid stiff collar that Mama tightened around his neck plus that silly little necktie. Then he had to put on those highly polished black shoes with the long white socks. 'I looks a right sissy,' he grumbled.

'No you don't,' his mother replied. 'You look a proper little gent. You don't want to be shown up in front of all those fancy people.'

She pushed him into his parents' bedroom and made him stare into the long mirror while she moistened and combed his short blond hair. Richard was not pleased about any of this pansy stuff, but he was still excited about this afternoon's event.

A motor horn was pooping in the road outside. 'Come on, boy, don't keep Mr Ganton waiting.'

The Tenbury's Rolls Royce was parked with the engine ticking over. Richard climbed into the front compartment next to Mr Ganton the chauffeur. The plush rear part was where the family sat when being driven into Chichester or to visit other families of their status. The Tenbury family still maintained a little Model T Ford which Mrs Tenbury drove, somewhat to the scandal of the village. This was the one that brought the tiresome Maria to school.

Pockhampton House lay a mile and a half to the east of the village on the road to Brighton. It was a fine Georgian house: red brick with large square windows. Mr Ganton crunched down into a low gear and turned left through the tall gates and into the long avenue of beech trees. As they rounded the last bend Richard was startled to see the whole front of the mansion illuminated by dazzling electric lights. Mr Ganton stopped the car by the front door with its short flight of stone steps. Never in his short life had Richard entered this house through the front door. With his mother he'd had to go into the kitchen through a door in the side. Richard counted seven other big motors parked in the frontage and more children were climbing out of them and grouping at the front door steps. A dozen other big motors were parked and empty. It was now that he suddenly felt very shy.

'Young Richard, welcome.' It was Mrs Tenbury wearing a heavy fur coat. He hadn't noticed her tripping across the gravel with her welcoming smile. Now he felt better.

'Come on inside,' she said. 'It's cold out here.'

She took his hand and led him past the other children and up the steps through the front door. The house was warm. A huge log fire burned in a massive grate in the front hall. Richard had never seen anything like it. His spirits dropped a little as he saw Maria smirking at him. She wore a pretty little frilly dress with bare arms.

'Hello, Dickie, welcome,' she smiled at him.

Mama had warned him that he must be polite to everyone he met and especially Maria. She had given him a smart slap on his bottom as she said this.

'Hello, Maria,' he replied glumly.

'Come in here and talk,' she said.

With massive reluctance he followed her into the library. He gaped as he saw the shelves from floor to ceiling packed with books. Then he saw the magnificent grand piano in a far corner.

Maria followed his gaze. 'Mamma says you can play that when you're older. It's a good piano, it's a Steinway.'

'Does that mean it's special?' he asked.

'It's very expensive, but nobody here can play it except Leo and he's not much good,'

'Your brother?'

'That's' right,' she laughed. 'Papa's not happy. Leo's studying in a semintry..'

'What's that?'

'It's a sort of school where they train priests. That is priests for our church – the true church.'

Richard was puzzled. 'Why should your dada be worried?'

'Because real priests are not allowed to marry and have children. They have to promise poverty and chaserity for life. And Papa wants a boy child to follow him as heir.'

'A hare,' Richard was even more out of his depth. 'What's a hare got to do with it?'

'No, I said heir, silly. That means a boy to take over when the older ones die.'

She pulled him closer. 'Dickie, what if we got married and then made an heir? You and me would rule this village and all the young ones at our school.'

'Don't make me laugh. Rule the schoolroom. You does that already.'

Now she giggled. 'Have you heard, Fanny Thompson and Billy Briggs are having to get married. It seems Fanny's got an heir inside her when she shouldn't.'

'How d'you know that?'

'Ganton told me. Seems Fanny and Billy had a roll in the hay and Ganton says that's how babies get made.'

'Don't think I was made that way. My mama and dada say they want a sister for me. They does something in the bedroom at night – makes a lot o' groaning noise.'

'That's the trouble. 'Papa can't make more babies because something happened to him when he was shot down in the war.'

Richard remembered that Mr Tenbury had been an air pilot. Now his arithmetic was cutting in. 'Hey, that don't make sense. War was over ten year ago and you're eight same as me. How did you get made? You tell me that.'

She pulled him closer and whispered. 'It's all because of Leo and that priest thing. They wanted another boy heir, so mamma did something very naughty with another man. I heard my Auntie Vi talking about it. They didn't think I was listening, but it seems it's all right for people like us to do that. It's the heir that matters. But they only got me and not a boy and now mamma's too old to make any more babies.'

Music had started playing within the house. Richard's ears pricked up at the sound. He knew this was music for dancing and it was American. It was known as "ragtime" and Mr Locke did not like it. Richard did like it. It had a clever rhythm, that was the word that he had learned, and good rhythm was important for good music.

'Come on,' Maria giggled. 'That's the Charleston. The party's started. She grabbed his arm and dragged him from the room. The music was not in the hall but in the ballroom through the opposite doorway. The room was full of older girls and young men prancing around to the sounds of the four-piece band on a little stage in one corner. Richard could see a pianist, a trombone, a clarinet and a funny looking instrument that he thought was a saxophone. And the trombone player had a black face and Richard had never seen a black man before.

'Hey, let's join in,' Maria squeaked. She grabbed both his hands and began to skip to the music. Reluctantly Richard joined in and gradually he felt the power of the rhythm and within a minute he was enjoying himself. He would have enjoyed it more but for the clumping adults all round them who mostly seemed to have little sense of the timing, and the fog of cigarette smoke that was making his eyes water. Out of the corner of his eye he saw Mrs Tenbury coming towards them. She was wearing a long blue dress, with silvery trimming, the whole thing was held by straps to her bare white shoulders. 'Maria, you silly little girl, you're setting Richard a bad example and you're missing the party.'

They followed her through two further rooms as the music behind them grew fainter. The high ceiling room they entered was full of children surrounding a long table groaning with cakes and buns and biscuits with great vats of orange squash.

'Sit down, you two,' said Mrs Tenbury. 'Start feeding. We don't stand on ceremony here.' She turned and walked away.

Richard pulled up a chair and Maria sat down next to him. 'What was that your mama just said?'

'She means we can eat until we are sick,' Maria giggled.

For twenty minutes they ate in total silence. For Richard much of the food was beyond anything he had ever seen or tasted. Maria indicated that manners required them to eat the sandwiches first before they devoured the sticky cakes and jam tarts. He didn't feel sick, but by the time they had finished he felt bloated and couldn't have managed one more éclair or mince pie. Richard had worried about his reception from these well-bred children. The girl on his right hand side turned out to be French and had a limited grasp of English. But she smiled at him and poured him a huge glass of orange squash. The party ended with the pulling of enormous paper crackers. Richard didn't fancy the silly hat that he won, although Maria had no such embarrassment and pulled a ridiculous mock pirate hat over her head. Then Mrs Tenbury beat the table for silence and announced the arrival of the conjuror: Max the magician.

Max the magician was a little balding man with a drooping moustache. The children watched him as he pulled rabbits from hats, read magic cards and sawed the same little French girl in half. She emerged smiling, while the boys clapped and the girls screamed.

'Did you enjoy that?' asked Maria as she nudged him.

'You betcha, he were real good.'

Maria giggled once more and put on her refined voice. 'Real good? You mean: he was most entertaining.'

'Oh, shuddup.'

Shortly afterwards the party began to break up. Parents and governesses started to arrive as well as unaccompanied chauffeurs. At this point Mrs Tenbury tapped Richard on the shoulder. 'Ganton will run you home shortly, but I would like you to come with me. We have news for you.'

'Go on,' said Maria as she gave him a push.

Richard followed Mrs Tenbury into the entrance hall and then up the wide staircase. Richard had never been in a building like this. At the top of the staircase a balustrade ran around the first floor so that one could look down on the hall below.

'Come on, Richard – follow me,' Mrs Tenbury beckoned.

He followed her along the balcony until she stopped at a door and knocked. She waved to Richard and he walked to the door. The room was a small private study and behind a large desk sat Mr Tenbury. His wife ushered Richard into the room and she followed and shut the door.

Mr Tenbury stood up and smiled. 'Good evening, young Richard. I wanted us to have a little talk.'

'Sir?' Richard felt a tinge of fear.

Mr Tenbury smiled again. 'Can you think why we need to talk?'

'No, sir. Have I done summat? Is it that Maria telling about me?'

Mr Tenbury laughed now. 'You've done nothing to be ashamed of and everything to hope for. I have been in contact with Mr Locke and Miss Jeffries about your musical talent.'

Richard was still puzzled but no longer nervous.

Mrs Tenbury put an arm around him. 'We want you to sing for us. Will you do that? Why don't you sing the first verse of *Once in Royal David's City*? We sing that in our churches as well as yours.'

'I'll give you a key note,' said Mr Tenbury. He stood up and moved towards a tiny piano unlike any that Richard had ever seen. 'This is a harpsichord. Have you ever seen one before?'

'No, sir.'

'It predates the piano and plucks strings instead of hitting them. Bach and Handel composed on it.'

Mr Tenbury sat down at the tiny keyboard. Richard was startled to see that the hand and wrist was most horribly scarred. The man followed his gaze but only smiled. 'War wounds. Keep away from aeroplanes; they burn too well.'

He sounded the note. It had an odd tingling sound but nice. Richard sang the verse as asked. Then to his surprise the adults all clapped.

'Now, Richard,' said Mr Tenbury. 'You sit in this seat and play us a tune.' He left the chair and pointed Richard to it.

Richard sat down and looked at the keys.

'Be gentle with it. It's a valuable antique,' Mr Tenbury laughed.

Richard put his hands on the keyboard and tried a few notes. It was easy and he loved the unusual sound. He began to play letting his right hand run up and down the notes and then began to work in some lower notes harmony. He played for two minutes and then felt a tweak of nerves. He was in a room with all these people and he was showing off. He stopped playing and to his astonishment the adults clapped.

'Mr Tenbury patted him on the back. 'Well done, young man. You are every bit as talented as we have been told. The more so, I would say.'

Mrs Tenbury spoke. 'I talked to your mother this morning and we've arranged to come to your house and talk with your parents, mid-day tomorrow. It's Christmas Eve so we may have a big surprise.'

CHAPTER 4

When Richard reached home that evening he was startled to see the clock in the kitchen said ten o'clock; well past his proper bedtime. His dog, Brownie came running and jumped licking Richard's face.

'I knows,' he said, rubbing the dog's ears. 'You don't like it when I goes and stays out late.'

'Dickie, is that you?' his mother called.

'Yeah, I'm in the kitchen.'

His mother appeared dressed in her nightgown with a coat over the top. 'Dickie, did Mr Tenbury talk to you?'

'Yes, he did, but I don't rightly know what's going on.'

'Well, he's got great plans for you and he and Mrs Tenbury are going to explain to you tomorrow. It's only your father who's making trouble.'

Richard was not surprised to hear that. He guessed that Mr and Mrs Tenbury and mama had some plans for his schooling. That was good and it made him excited. He knew he was good at lessons and top of the class, but dada was set on him working for the farm and Richard knew enough to understand he needed better schooling to get out of that notion.

'Boy, that you?' He heard his father call from upstairs. His mother pulled a face. Ted Dyer, his dada, came clumping down stairs.

'What be you up to at that big house?'

'Well, nuthin'.'

'What you mean, nuthin'? I don't hold wi'it. You should mix wi' your own kind. Them people ain't your class.'

'All right, Ted,' his mother interrupted. 'Mr and Mrs Tenbury are good people. They only want the best for all of us.'

'All right, all right. Now, boy; what did you get up to at that big house?'

'We had a party and there was a magic man come in with lots o' tricks.'

'Did Mr and Mrs Tenbury talk to you?'

'Well, yes, but they're coming over here tomorrow to speak to you, but I don't rightly knows why.'

Ted Dyer gave an exasperated sigh. 'I blames that blasted war. Everything's stood on its head since then. I remembers before the war we stood in church and vicar calls out: *God bless our squire and his relations:* we all replies: *and keep us in our proper stations.* We don't say that no more. Tell you as well. In my young day the Tenburys would never have sent one o' their young'uns to the village school.'

Richard's mother smiled at him. 'Dickie, you get upstairs and go to bed. I'll deal wi' your father.'

Richard sped upstairs to his tiny room and quickly undressed, pleased to be rid of the smart suit, the stiff collar and the polished shoes and white stockings. He slipped on his nightshirt and climbed under the bed covers. He could hear his parents arguing downstairs but could make out none of the words. Anyway tomorrow was Christmas Eve and whatever Mr and Mrs Tenbury had in store for him could wait until then.

Richard woke up the next morning. He had no clock in his room but he could hear the sound of the cows mooing as they came in for milking in the barn across the way. Then he remembered that this was Christmas Eve and no school this morning. Another hour and they would need him to clear up behind the milking. With a bit of luck he might get a ride on the farm tractor. The tractor was an old one now that had been sent to the farm in the war. During the winter they took off the heavy spade lug rear wheels and put on rubber tyres, the stockman drove it with a trailer loaded with hay for the cows.

He slipped out of bed and poured the water from the jug into the china bowl and then washed his face and hands. He pulled on his cotton shirt and work breeches and topped the whole with his rough jacket. He left his room and tripped downstairs to find his work boots. Now he had a shock. In the kitchen his mother was filling the tin bath with water from three kettles boiling on the range. 'Now Dickie,' she said. 'You're not going anywhere. It's bath time for you and then back into your Sunday best.'

'You made me have one yesterday,' he pleaded. 'You said I had to because I was going to that party.'

'True, but now we've Mr and Mrs Tenbury coming to talk to us about you. So, it's clean and decent for today and no mucking about with them cows.'

'Oh, yes, I remembers now. What have they got for me? That Maria said something about a cathedral.'

'Well, yes, that's part of it but not all of it by any means. You wait and see. Now, off with those clothes and into the bath. I don't care what your father thinks. Everyone says you're a clever boy and you need to make something out of your life, not muck around all your days wi' the farm.'

It was still dark when mama finished fitting him into his Sunday best including the nasty stiff collar. Richard grumbled all the time, but at least she let him off wearing the black shoes and white stockings until nearer the time the distinguished visitors were due. Like all the village children he loved to run barefoot on the downs, except Maria of course: she always wore those silly little white button shoes, although even she pulled these off once the adult world was out of sight. Today Richard was told he must stay indoors.

By now his mother was busy dusting the best parlour and polishing the furniture so he couldn't even get at the piano. He tiptoed back upstairs and sat on his bed. The dawn was just beginning to show through the window. In an hour it would be daylight. He was starting to feel hungry and there could be no breakfast until dada came in from work. He wasn't sure he wanted to face his father. It seemed he was to blame for this argument between his parents and it made him feel sad. He loved them both and hated it when they argued.

Richard heard his dada come in from the yard and pull off his boots. He had already caught the delicious scent of breakfast: frying eggs, with bacon cut from the flitch in big fat slices served with wholemeal bread and butter. He waited his moment, ran downstairs and sat in his place at the kitchen table.

'How do, boy,' said his father. 'Seems this is to be your big day.'

'You don't mind?' Richard asked.

'O' course I minds. But there's nobbut as I can do now your mother's invited these big house folk.' Suddenly he grinned at his son. 'Anyway, your ma tells me it's not all going to happen at once. You can always change your mind.'

Richard was still puzzled but he wolfed down his breakfast and asked no more questions.

At eleven o'clock he was packed off upstairs, ordered to don the white socks and black shoes. Once more he had to stand in front of the long mirror while his mother combed his hair and straightened his jacket and tie. He was then taken downstairs into the best parlour and told he could play the piano. He drifted into a different world as his fingers ran over the keys and created melodies that pleased his ear.

His mother tapped him on the shoulder and he came back into the present. 'Come on, Dickie, they're here.'

The kitchen door was open and Richard could see the motor as it parked in the yard. He was surprised to see not the big Rolls but the smaller Model T with Mrs Tenbury at the wheel. And sitting beside

her was her son, Leopold Tenbury.
The two left the car and walked to the door. Ted Dyer suddenly sprang to attention, looking tall and stiff. 'Good morning, sir. Captain, this is an honour.'

Leopold grinned and held out his hand. 'All right, Dyer, we're not in the army now. We're both in civvy street: no ranks, no pack drill.'

Ted Dyer grinned and shook hands with his former officer 'All right, sir. Old habits die hard, as they say.'

Richard had heard much about this man, but recently he had been rarely seen in the village. Leopold Tenbury was a tall man and lean, with a thin face and already greying hair. He was dressed all in black. With pressed trousers and a strange black jacket that buttoned from his waist to his neck.

His mother spoke. 'Mrs Tenbury, Mr Leopold, please come in and I'll make everyone a cup of tea.' She beckoned Richard to the parlour door and whispered. 'In there with you and play the piano. We'll talk to the big folk for you.'

Richard needed no second invitation for this. He pulled up the piano stool and began to play. He had recently found himself able to make different chords in the bass line that harmonized nicely with the treble melody. The tunes came from his head. They were his tunes, but also not his. He really couldn't say where they came from. Music just flowed through his head and out through his fingers. For the best part of an hour he was lost in his own world of melody. He awoke into the real world to find his mother bent over the piano beside him and smiling.

'Come on, Dickie, come and listen to what the lady and gentleman have to say and what we've decided for you.'

He looked up to see that Mrs Tenbury and Mr Leo were both seated in the little-used armchairs a few feet away and he hadn't even heard them enter the room.

Mrs Tenbury smiled and Richard felt a warm glow. How kind this lady was. 'Richard, I've heard you play before, but you've improved with your playing beyond all measure. We are both impressed. Tell me, did you compose that tune?'

'Yes. Maam, although I sort a' made it up as I went along.'

'Now, Richard. We have spoken with your parents and we have agreed that all being well you have a real future in the outside world. So, we have made certain plans for you which I hope you will like.'

Richard felt a pang of worry. 'What about dada?'

'My son, Leo has persuaded him that all is in your and his best interests.'

Richard suddenly understood. Mr Tenbury had stayed at home and sent his son. Mr Leo and dada had been together in the war and he knew dada idolised his former officer. He smiled inwardly. That was crafty.

'Richard,' Mrs Tenbury continued. 'We understand that the authorities in Chichester Cathedral are offering you a place in their choir and choir school, but that will not be available until you reach the age of ten. We could wish that you went to our cathedral in Arundel, but regrettably you are of a different faith and tradition, but I believe that the Chichester choir sings most beautifully.'

Richard didn't know what to say to all this but he felt a little stab of excitement.

'In the meantime,' Mrs Tenbury continued. 'We have spoken to Mr Locke in this village who has a long record as a music teacher and he will take you in hand and show you how to read music scores and to work with you on your playing.' She smiled again. 'So, you will not be leaving us just yet. However we are setting up a trust fund to help you on your way to the choir and to further your education when the time comes.'

CHAPTER 5

August 1929

'Mr Locke, sir. I sight-read that piece you gi' me and I done them five-finger excises. I reckons I does'em good too.'

'No, Richard, think what you say. It should be *I've done the exercises and I believe I've got them right.* You still rush your words. When you go to choir school you'll have to get that right.'

'I know, sir. I'll try, but you don't want me to talk like Maria? If I does that my mates won't want to know me.'

'No boy, no false accents, but you must improve your grammar, that is the way you use words. At the choir school you'll need that. It will be almost as important as the music.'

Richard, with his teacher, was back with the schoolroom piano. He enjoyed these evening lessons more than he could say. Mr Locke was a good and sympathetic teacher and Richard was a fast learner. The arrangement was paid for by Mr Tenbury and suited both parties. Richard learned the basics of music; melody construction, sight-reading and practice, while Mr Locke received a generous fee from the Tenbury funds. Mondays, Wednesdays and Fridays were Richard's music lesson evenings; then Mr Locke gave him finger exercises to practice and pieces to sight-read. To Richard this was no hardship to balance with his school homework.

This evening Richard sat at the piano and played by sight three exercises from the piano method that Mr Locke had loaned him.

Mr Locke was openly surprised and pleased. 'How long did you practice?'

'Not long, and after a couple of goes I found I could play it without the music.'

'Well I never, young man. If you keep this up, then one day you'll make a concert pianist.'

Mr Locke had not confined himself to music. Reading and writing at the village school was basic with nothing to excite a child's imagin-ation. Mrs Tenbury had given Richard a smart new book. It was called Winnie the Pooh and was all about a little bear and his funny companions. Mr and Mrs Tenbury were friends of the writer of the book, Mr Milne. Mrs Tenbury told Richard that the book was really about Ashdown Forest not far away from Pockhampton. Richard read it cover to cover four times. He read it aloud to his friend Alf and then to Maria, with whom he was now on much better terms. They all loved the book. They played poohsticks on the nearby bridge and acted out some of the book's scenes on the Downs. Mrs Tenbury said that Christopher Robin was a real life little boy like themselves and she would arrange for them to meet him. Richard's father grumbled continuously about his son's increasing literacy and education and the more so about the boy's developing use of words.

'T'ain't right. You speaks like the gentry and you ain't gentry.' That said, Ted Dyer made no move to interfere and Richard's mother was fairly sure he was secretly rather proud of his boy. Sometimes he went with his mother to the big house, entering by the kitchen. The joy came when he was invited to leave the servant's quarters and go to the drawing room with Mrs Tenbury. There he was invited to play the Steinway. This was magic. Richard could play several pieces by J.S. Bach and Mozart, or at least those few that his half-grown hands could stretch to. And he enjoyed improvising melodies of his own. The Steinway was professionally tuned and had a tone that his home and schoolroom pianos could never compete with. When Mr Kemp the butler opened the piano lid the music was transformed. The Reverend Davis talked about good boys going to Heaven, but as far as Richard was concerned this was Heaven.

Sometimes Maria and two of her well-spoken friends would sit and listen with expressions of real pleasure. Maria was due to leave the village school at the end of the year and then she would go to the girl's convent school in the nearby town. Mr Leo had been accepted for the priesthood and taken holy orders. Ted Dyer had commented about this. 'God didn't do much for us in them trenches.'

Richard still found Maria a trifle "clingy" as he put it, but on the whole she was amusing company and to be tolerated. One day when he was walking on the downs with Maria and her two girlie friends he had an experience that was to affect his later life although he didn't know it at the time. The sun was bright and the midday air hot. It was Sunday and both sets of children were home from their different churches. All the children loved the downs. The gentle sheep cropped the rough grass and there were flowers and scents, butterflies flitting and skylarks overhead. Now Richard heard a strange, almost musical note distantly but coming closer. He squinted into the sunlight, but it hurt his eyes and he could see nothing. He knew what it was: an aeroplane. He had seen them before but never so close. The four children were near the highest point of the down and the aeroplane was flying low. Now Richard could see it and the aeroplane was going to pass very near to them. It was a biplane painted red and he could see the pilot in his open cockpit and his coat and helmet were both black. The children shouted and waved with excitement and then the pilot raised an arm; Richard could see the wind ruffling his sleeve. 'Cor, I'd like to do some o' that.'

Maria assumed her county accent. 'You mean; I would like to experience some flying.'

'That's what I said didn't I?' But it was the aeroplane that he dreamed about that night.

Three days later Richard and his family were startled when Mrs Tenbury drove into the yard in her Model T. The villagers had mellowed a little bit towards the idea of a woman driving a motor. They knew from the newspapers and from the local cinema that many rich ladies now drove cars. It was one of those developments, including women's suffrage and flapper girls in flaunting dress, that the elder members of the community tut-tutted about. Everyone put these changes, welcome or not, down to the late war.

Richard's mother had brusquely pushed him upstairs while she spoke to the lady. Mrs Tenbury then called him downstairs again.

'Richard,' she said. 'This week in our house we have a very distinguished guest. I have told the gentleman about you and he has asked to meet you. So, at tea time tomorrow I will collect you and take you to see him.'

Richard was worried. 'But, Ma'am, I'm having a lesson with Mr Locke then.'

'Don't worry, Mr Locke agrees with me that this meeting is far more important for you than any lesson.'

She drove away and Richard feeling even more puzzled, looked at his mother. 'Who is this gentleman she wants me to meet?'

'I'm not sure, but he's a Sir and he wants to talk to you. So it's best clothes, best manners and best polite.'

CHAPTER 6

Richard was less attentive to his school work than usual. He tried to figure out why a gentleman who was a Sir would want to see him. They were all hiding something. His parents, Mr and Mrs Tenbury and even Maria seemed to be in the secret. Everyone was, except himself who had a right to know. Miss Jeffries as well. She told him he could leave school before the last lesson of the day. She had patted him on the head and told him. 'Best behaviour today. You're meeting a very big gentleman.'

What did that mean? Was this Sir a giant? Would he be a scary giant? Richard wended his way home and found his mother already boiling the kettles for his bath in front of the kitchen range. Maria told him her house had a special bathroom with taps that had hot water in them. She added that her dada used something called a shower bath because a hot bath stirred up his war wounds. Richard had no idea what she was talking about. Now finally bathed, scrubbed and wearing his Sunday best, he waited for the arrival of Mrs Tenbury. It was a hot and sultry evening; Richard felt sweaty and itchy in his best shirt and the horrid stiff collar felt tighter than ever.

Mrs Tenbury arrived and Richard climbed up beside her in the front of the Model T. This was a very different ride to the one in Ganton's Rolls. The little car sped along the road kicking up dust and small stones. He felt exhilarated. 'This is good,' he shouted.

'Forty miles an hour,' Mrs Tenbury called back.

All too soon they were turning into the avenue leading to the great house. Mrs Tenbury parked the car and led him through the front door. 'Sir Edward is in the garden,' she said. 'He is our guest this week while we all go to the races at Goodwood.'

Richard followed her across the hall and into a long corridor that ended in another room with huge glass doors flung open into a garden of smooth lawns bright with shrubs and flowers. He followed the lady across a wide terrace with tables and cane chairs. A little spaniel dog raced up to them and leapt at Richard licking his hands and scrabbling at his jacket. Richard could see a very old man sitting at a table under a cloth awning.

'Come and meet, Sir Edward,' she said.

Richard followed across the lawn. As they came closer the old man stood up and walked very slowly to meet them. He was certainly ancient but there was something about his face, the curved nose and the huge moustache, that reminded him of Max the magician.

'Sir Edward, this is Richard Dyer our home-grown prodigy.'

The old man leant down and offered his hand. Richard shook it and the old man's grasp was firm and friendly. 'My hosts have been speaking of you, young man,'

Richard was surprised this old man did not speak with the refined voice of their local gentry. It was a soft voice, clear, but with a little touch of country speech. The spaniel had loped back across the lawn and was sitting happily beside the old man. Richard was warming to this person now. He was not as grim as he looked and he had a faithful dog.

'Perhaps we should all go indoors,' said Mrs Tenbury, 'then Richard can perform for us.'

What did that mean? Did she want him to sing or play the piano? Again, who was this Sir Edward? Richard had vaguely seen his face somewhere before. It was in a magazine called Illustrated London News, and now he had a shock. The old man was Edward Elgar, the composer who wrote Land of Hope and Glory that the school sang in their summer concert. So he, nine-year-old Richard was going to perform for one of the greatest figures in world music. Piano or singing he didn't care, he was going to show him his best.

He followed into the drawing room. He felt a glow of excitement as he saw the piano and Mrs Tenbury pointed him to it. 'Richard, would you play for us those two little Mozart pieces and then you can improvise with your own ideas. Richard noticed that Mr Tenbury had entered the room along with Mr Kemp the butler and a little group of house servants. Now he had an audience – famous and ordinary alike. He would show them all what he could do. He raised the adjustable stool to fit his height and still let him reach the pedals.

It always happened when he played. He became lost in his own little world. The music flowed from his head and out through his fingers on the keys. He played the Mozart then Mr Locke's adaptation of Bach's opening of Brandenburg Two and three exercises from the method book including the simplified score of Handel's Harmonious Blacksmith. Richard grinned at this. Their village blacksmith was anything but harmonious. Mr Shank sang bass in the church choir, always too loud and a little off key. Following the set pieces Richard felt free to be himself. He still didn't know where this strange music came from. It seemed his head plucked it from the air and then sent it down into his fingers. He never knew how long he played; probably less than twenty minutes. Suddenly he was conscious that someone was looking down at him. It was Sir Edward as he leaned on his cane watching the keyboard intently. Richard ceased playing and dropped his hands into his lap.

'Your progress is commendable in one so young,' said Sir Edward. 'Tell me; are those melodies your own invention?'

'Yes, sir.'

'And your inspiration?'

Richard looked blank. He wasn't sure what the old man meant but he mustn't be rude. 'Sir?'

'What I mean is, where do these melodies spring from?'

He would tell Sir Edward the truth 'I don't rightly know, sir. They sort of come into my head and then out through my fingers. Sir, they're my tunes but I don't know why.'

Suddenly the great man threw back his head and chuckled. 'That is exactly how I feel. Talking of fingers, yours are made for a pianist. You have good hands and long fingers. So many fail because they are not so gifted.' He turned round to the others. 'If this young man continues to apply himself we may well have a future composer in our midst.'

The others began to clap and Sir Edward joined in as well.

'Now, into the garden again,' said Mrs Tenbury. 'We will record this moment for posterity.'

Again Richard was not sure what she was talking about but he followed Mr Tenbury and Sir Edward into the garden. When Mrs Tenbury caught them up she was carrying her box camera. Richard and Sir Edward stood together and she took three pictures.

'Ganton should be back shortly with Maria,' she said. 'Then I'll run you home.' She laughed. 'I told him to take the Model T and he wasn't pleased. He hates it. The Rolls is his plaything. He thinks my motorcar is beneath him. But in no circumstances will I let him collect Maria with the Rolls. She gets enough inflated ideas as it is.'

'Here they come now,' said Mr Tenbury. Richard could hear the Ford stuttering up the driveway. 'You've been good for Maria,' he continued. 'You've been a good companion. It's lonely for a child here. That's why we sent her to the village school and never employed a governess. Some of our friends and relations disapproved of that but we know it's been good for her.'

Maria raced in through the front door, saw Richard and flung herself at him giving him a kiss. Then giggling she ran upstairs.

'That's nice,' said Sir Edward. 'Childhood sweethearts?'

'What about that, Richard?' asked Mrs Tenbury.
'I wanna' go home,' he spluttered. He worried that he might have been rude.
The adults all laughed.

CHAPTER 7

Autumn 1930

'Let's look at you,' said Richard's mother. Once again he stood in front of the long mirror. This time they had put him in a funny jacket with a strange badge on the breast pocket on the left side. They had told him it was called a blazer and was part of the school uniform. Richard thought uniforms were only for soldiers or policemen and he didn't want to be either. He was going to be a musician and a treble singer in the cathedral choir. For the first time in his life he was going to be away from home for six weeks and all Christmas would be spent singing. He was off to choir school selected as a chorister by scholarship. He understood that this meant the school would pay half his fees and Mr and Mrs Tenbury the other half. He would be living in, so his bed board and meals would cost him nothing.

'Come on, Dickie, downstairs the motor will be here for you soon.' There was a catch in his mama's voice that he had never heard before. She was dabbing her tears with a handkerchief. Richard could not believe it. 'Dickie, oh do be careful, we've such hopes for you; you're all we've got.'

He followed her downstairs. His father stood in the kitchen, 'I still don't hold wi' it,' he grunted. 'They won't be your class, them youngsters. You won't like 'em.'

Richard's mother laughed through her tears. 'Don't listen, Dickie. You'll be just fine.'

'Oh aah,' said his father. 'See how many you invites home in holidays.'

'You'll make good friends, you see,' said his mother.

Richard had already made three trips to the choir school. He had auditioned with Mr Wandsdale the organist and with his younger deputy Mr Ross who ran the school. He sat a written entrance exam, which was no hardship as the questions were easy. Two weeks ago the family had received a letter; Richard had been accepted as a probationer, one of a small number admitted to the choir each year. The examiners had been impressed with his piano playing and Richard was promised professional tuition during his time with the school. In the early afternoon Mr Ganton drove up in the Rolls. Richard hugged his mother and shook his father's hand and picked up the bulky Gladstone bag with his spare clothes and music scores. An hour later they were parking outside the school. By the door were standing two boys of Richard's age.

One of them was a stocky red-headed boy. 'Are you Dyer? We've been told to show you around and see you settled in.'

Richard was relieved that the boy did not talk upper class, but had an accent that placed his as a town bred lad.

'I'm Richard Dyer,' he replied.

'I'm Tom Stacey and this is Michael Brown.' Richard shook hands with each..

'Remember,' said the boy Tom, 'rules say it's surnames only. We're formal in this place. So it's got to be Stacey, Brown and Dyer. Then tutors and clergy are all sir.'

Richard nodded; Mr Locke had already impressed this on him. The boys showed him the whole school: the refectory, the common room, two music rooms and then the dormitories. Richard was shown his own iron bedstead and plumped his bag down upon it.

'Got to keep your bed neat and spruce each day. Matron's a dragon,' said Stacey and he and Brown laughed. 'You'll soon get the hang of the place. We're probationers as well so we don't get much choir time yet, but the music lessons are fun.'

Richard liked his two new friends and he liked what he had seen of the school. It seemed a homely place and nothing like the brutal academy of Tom Brown's Schooldays. He had found that book in Mr Tenbury's library and he had been allowed to take it home. What he read had made him apprehensive. However this place seemed nothing like the mid-nineteenth century Rugby school.

The only sour moment came when Richard was shown the toilet block on the ground floor. A boy, a year or so older than Richard, emerged from the room. He stared at Richard. 'And who is this?'

'All right, Lamingham,' said Stacey. 'This is Dyer, he's a new probationer.'

The boy stepped forward and stared Richard in the face. 'Well, speak for yourself. What's your name?'

'I'm Dyer. What's it to you anyway?'

'Oh, merciful God. You speak like a peasant. What does your father do?'

Richard's temper was beginning to burn. This arrogant fat boy didn't scare him. Mr Locke had warned him about this class prejudice and told him to turn the other cheek. 'My father does an honest day's work with his hands. What does your father do then? Some slimy crooked lawyer I would guess.'

The other boy's mouth dropped open. 'Don't you talk to me like that you impertinent little yokel.'

'What'you goin' to do about it?'

'I am going to treat you to a lesson in manners. You will learn to respect your betters.'

Richard laughed. He deliberately sounded his most mocking guffaw. The other boy advanced gripped Richard's arm and began to twist it. Richard was a village boy honed in minor fights with other boys and he was lean and fit from a month of pitching wheat sheaves; he didn't wait. With his free right arm he swung a punch into his assailants stomach. He felt a surge of satisfaction as his fist sank into the flesh and heard the gasp as the breath expelled. The boy Lamingham staggered away bent double and retching. 'You'll pay for that. You're finished as far as this school goes.' Lamingham took several deep breaths and walked off down the passage gripping his stomach.

The two boys were staring at Richard. 'How did you do that?' asked Brown.

'Who is that fellow?' asked Richard.

'Lamingham? He's a bad lot. Nobody likes him and he's all sour because he's been passed over as choir leader.'

'No surprise that then.'

'Yes,' said Stacey. 'But you'd better be careful. Lamingham won't leave it there. He'll spite you in some sneaky way when you're not expecting it.'

'What we calls a nasty bit o' work, where I come from.'

'Come on,' said Stacey. 'Forget Lamingham. Let's go over to the cathedral. The choir will be singing evensong in half an hour. You'll get a good idea of the sound,'

CHAPTER 8

As the weeks passed Richard began to settle to routine in the school and to enjoy it.

As far as he was concerned life was good with its round of music and academic work. His piano playing advanced as his hands began to cope with the longer stretches. He was supposed to learn a second instrument and although he could make a passable sound with the flute it was the piano that he loved. The singing tutorials improved his voice and he had two outings with the main choir but only at standard cathedral services. And he found he was popular. Most of the other boys came from ordinary backgrounds: Stacey's father ran a shop in the town. The odious Lamingham kept out of Richard's way confining himself to muttering threats. Lamingham's bullying of other boys was ignored by the authorities. Richard supposed that this was because Lamingham had a fine treble voice and an influential father who was a financial donor to the cathedral.

Lamingham didn't play piano; his chosen instrument was the viola. His tutor came from outside the school and was one Mr Willings.

'Keep out of way of that Willings,' Brown told Richard one day.

'Why?'

Brown sniggered. 'He's a homo – likes choir boys. Should be in jail.'

It was a measure of Richard's innocence that he had not the slightest idea what Brown meant. He was just as puzzled after his friends had told him what they had heard.

The cathedral choir consisted of eighteen boy trebles and a male bass, tenor and alto group led by six lay vicars, the term given to the six professional singers. Richard couldn't wait to take his full place in the choir and let his voice loose on pieces like Stanford's choral communion, Handel's Messiah, Stainer, or his favourite, Fauré's Requiem.

The academic teaching was no problem for Richard. It was aimed towards School Certificate, which was a pre-condition of a scholarship to a music college. The one thing that irritated him was the lack of freedom to move outside the narrow confines of the school. With his friends Richard sometimes made an illicit visit into the city. This was not difficult. They would exit through a window into the garden and from there into the street that led to the famous market cross. Just across the way stood the cattle market. Richard had the chance to meet some of his home village friends. He was still happy with school, but sometimes envied his old friend Alf who was now working as a beef herdsman. Fate claimed him on his third illegal visit to the market.

Richard had just jumped in front of a loose heifer and turned it back into the ring. A hand touched him on the shoulder. 'Once a peasant always a peasant,' sneered a voice behind him. Richard spun round.

'Breaking school bounds. Serious offence,' said Lamingham. The boy's voice was twisted in malice. 'Mr Ross will be very interested to hear my report.'

Richard remained calm. 'You are breaking bounds yourself. How about that?'

'I have a legitimate reason. I have been to my music tutor.' Lamingham held up his viola case.

'That Willings. Bit of a funny feller, so they say. Did you keep your trousers on?'

'You miserable little ill-bred yokel. You've insulted a brilliant tutor. You will pay for this.'

Richard spun round, fists clenched. Lamingham backed away. 'Oh yes, turn violent – typical peasant behaviour.'

Richard stared at his enemy who failed to meet his eye. 'You get out of here before I rub your greasy face in that cow shit.'

The boys could see no sign of Lamingham in the refectory at the evening meal. Then the call came. 'Dyer to Mr Ross's study now.'

Mr Ross was sitting behind his desk. Richard knew that this man was kind and fair but did not take kindly to breach of rules. He was frightened now. He was in trouble. Would they expel him and dash all his music dreams? On top of that he would have let down Mr and Mrs Tenbury.

'Dyer,' said Ross. 'I think you know why you are here. School rules are clear. No vacating school grounds without a written exeat.'

'Yes, sir.'

'You were seen by Lamingham and he tells me you accused his tutor Mr Willings of a disgusting offence.'

Richard stayed silent. His hatred of Lamingham intensified.

'Have you nothing to say?'

'Sir, I went to the market because I wanted to talk to my friends there. Lamingham saw me but he was on his own. I was only joking about Mr Willings. I don't know him and Lamingham could have been lying.'

Mr Ross glared. 'Very well, this time you are spared a corporal punishment. I agree that Lamingham's action in reporting you could be construed as a breach of a students code of honour.'

'Thank you, sir.'

'Dyer, you are potentially one of the most gifted pupils I have ever taught. You have a bright future if you will learn to take it.'

'Thank you, sir.'

'So, keep away from Lamingham, obey the rules and be diligent in your studies.'

'Yes, sir.'

With relief Richard returned to the common room. It was crowded with his fellow pupils both probationers and fully fledged choirboys. He was startled when he was greeted with a huge cheer. He grinned and sat down near the open fire. A few minutes later Lamingham stood in the doorway. One boy began to chant, a chant taken up by the whole room apart from Richard. 'Sneak – sneak – sneak – sneak – your trousers leak – you sneak!'

Lamingham's face flushed. 'Dyer, you common yokel. I'll get you.'

The winter term was over all too quickly. The school entered the intense Christmas period when the whole choir was in action with carols, oratorio performances and the Christmas Eve midnight service. Richard loved the whole business. This was what he had dreamed of. When Boxing Day came the boys were released on leave. Richard was collected for home by the Pockhampton House Rolls Royce. Richard was gratified to see Lamingham's face as he climbed aboard the motor. Richard had been untroubled by Lamingham except on one occasion. Richard had told an envious group of boys about his meeting with Sir Edward Elgar. Lamingham had openly mocked this claim and called Richard a liar. Richard had shown them Mrs Tenbury's photograph.

Lamingham snarled. 'Your name's Dyer, that sounds ever so English. I wouldn't be surprised to learn it's really Dio and that you are a Jew.'

'Oh yeah, my dada keeps pigs and we eat bacon at home. So I don't think so.'

Brown intervened. 'Mendelssohn was a Jew, and a good'un.'

'He's dead,' replied Lamingham.

CHAPTER 9

Richard was home again. His feelings were both happy and unsure. He was different. Somehow the world seemed a bigger place. Once he had seen little further than the confines of his village. Now he was on the early rungs of a ladder that could take him to where? At this stage he didn't really know, but he was absorbed in his world of music and that was where he had always wanted to be. His parents had welcomed him home as if he had never been away, his dog had greeted him; so had all his old friends. They laughed at his new speech, something he had hardly noticed.

He had fewer inhibitions about visits to the Tenburys' house. Mrs Tenbury told him he was welcome to come and play their drawing room Steinway. Maria was home from her convent school. The girl had discarded her dowdy school uniform and dressed in a flimsy flapper style dress, she really looked pretty. Richard immediately drove such thoughts from his mind. Maria was Maria and a girl. He was a man or would be in a few years. Girls were stupid and obsessed with clothes and shoes as well as film stars.

'You set to be a nun? he asked.

'About as much as you becoming a monk,' she giggled.

'What are they like, the nuns that is?'

'They're all right. Some of them are French, and they're not as strict as the English ones. The Irish sisters are really scary.'

One huge change had met him at home. His father had bought a wireless. It was a second-hand one and ran off batteries, but it opened up a new world. There had been wireless sets at the school but they had been strictly controlled and reserved for news bulletins and classical music. Now at home he could steep himself in the work of the new dance orchestras. He heard the work of the great bandleaders: Jack Payne, Jack Hylton and Henry Hall. He admired their orchestration and tapped his feet to the catchy tunes. The BBC was a mite stuffy but the wireless could pick up continental stations and these broadcast different music: ragtime and jazz. He couldn't try any of this on the schoolroom or village hall pianos. If he had, Mr Locke would have been horrified. But on the Tenbury's piano he had full range. He learned to play his own versions of Scott Joplin's Maple Leaf Rag and the Entertainer. He found he could improvise and make a dozen different versions of those other tunes that came into his head from nowhere.

Around him the world was changing. Slowly the agricultural depression was beginning to affect everything. Incomes were collapsing and some workers had been laid off. The Tenburys had assured Ted Dyer that his position as farm foreman was safe but he would have to work with fewer hands. Then came devastating news. One of the Tenbury tenants, the Briggs family, had gone bankrupt. A family with a young baby and two workers would lose their livelihoods. The market for grain had completely collapsed; arable fields were being grassed down and contract flocks of sheep were coming onto the land from as far afield as Wales and Northern England. For the first time Ted Dyer agreed that his son was better off out of farming even if he didn't quite approve of the boy's new "gent manners". It did not help that the winter was wet and mild. The livestock in the fields were miserable; everything was wet and soggy and over the way the River Arun rose and flooded some of the surrounding countryside.

Richard was back at school for Easter. He was a regular choir member now with a chance of becoming leader. He had swept through his piano exams and his academic studies were progressing. Then came the first of two life-changing experiences, although he didn't realise it at the time. One Wednesday Mr Ross invited Richard, along with two other boys, Harris and Brown, to come sailing with him. They knew that Mr Ross had a boat on the harbour at a place called Itchenor.

'It's an X boat,' said Harris. 'No motor, just sails and Mr Ross and his wife race her on Saturdays.'

'Can you swim?' asked Brown.

'You bet. I learned in the river back home.'

'That's good, otherwise he'll make you wear a life saver.'

'What's that?'

'It's a great big sort of waistcoat made of cork.'

Mr Ross drove a motorcar called a Morris. It was open in summer but had a hood for wet weather. Harris, the choir leader was allowed to sit in front while the other two sat in the rear. The motor drove off leaving the city behind and taking the road to the West along the south shore of the Harbour. Not that they could see much of the water until Mr Ross turned right along a winding lane that ended in a row of fisherman's cottages and a gravel hard strewn with boats.

'Have to be careful where we leave the motor,' said Mr Ross. 'Can't park it here or the tide will carry it away.' He unloaded an enormous picnic hamper and an armful of yellow waterproof smocks.

'These are oilskins,' he said. 'It's a nice day so we may not need them.'

They left the hard in a little varnished wooden rowing dinghy with Mr Ross pulling on the oars. 'There she is,' he paused rowing and pointed. 'My *Christina.* We named her after my eldest daughter. She was little when we had the boat built but she's getting married now – time flies.'

The yacht looked very small from a distance but gradually grew larger as they came closer. Then they were alongside and Mr Ross grabbed the side and tied the dinghy to a metal cleat on the side deck. He heaved the hamper aboard and then invited them to climb in after it. The hull was painted a vivid blue, but the deck and cockpit were all varnished wood. The wooden mast was also varnished and stood tall above them with ropes that tapped against it in the wind. Harris had sailed before and told them that the rig was a revolutionary one called Bermudan and the mainsail was point shaped without a clumsy wooden gaff. Richard had no idea what any of this meant but it sounded good.

'Come on, crew,' said Mr Ross. 'Let's hoist sail and away.'

For Richard the next three hours were an experience he would never forget. The little yacht sped down the harbour, tacking to windward and out through the entrance. The sun shone, the sea was blue and the wind was enough to drive their ship towards the hills of the Isle of Wight. Richard loved every minute. He could feel the wind and with it a new kind of music. A few miles south of Hayling Island Mr Ross let the yacht idle in what he called the hove-to mode. Then they broke out the hamper and devoured the feast within. Even Brown who had claimed to feel seasick recovered miraculously and joined in. In late afternoon they began sailing again and when Mr Ross let Richard take the helm he was in a dream world. He felt the rhythm of the boat as she lifted over the short waves. Then reluctantly he handed back the tiller to Mr Ross who turned the yacht and she headed back into the harbour.

They picked up the mooring as the sun began to set behind the land. 'Well, Dyer,' Mr Ross asked, 'did you like sailing?'

'I'll say so, sir. Can I go again?'

'You certainly can. Now something else. How are you getting on with the Chopin?'

'Well, it's not easy, sir. But I think I've got it fairly well.'

'Good, I would like you to meet our visitor this weekend. We have a very distinguished guest, an old friend of our cathedral and I would like him to meet you.'

Nothing more was said and Richard didn't probe. His hands were much bigger now but the Chopin preludes were stretching them to the limit. He wondered who this visitor might be. Richard was becoming familiar with a huge range of music but the composers and conductors were just names.

'Please, sir. What's happened to Lamingham?'

Richard's old enemy had appeared at the start of term but had vanished without explanation within a month.

'I understand his family have moved to East Anglia and he was hoping for a place with Norwich Cathedral.'

'Bad luck for them.'

Mr Ross laughed. 'I cannot say that too many tears were shed among the tutors. I doubt you miss him.'

'I never want to see him again.' Richard did not know then that in this aspiration he would be disappointed.

On Sunday he sang the evensong and led the choir in the anthem. Afterwards Mr Ross took him into the music room with the piano and he was introduced to a frail old man who looked around one hundred years old. The ancient fellow was thin, walked with a stoop and clearly had trouble with his breathing. Richard was surprised to be told later that the man was only in his fifties but in poor health. He was Mr Gustav Holst, one of the nation's greatest living composers; the man who had written The Planets. Richard had sung in choir "I vow to thee my country," the hymn tune from Jupiter. Holst listened while Richard played a selection of pieces including the Chopin *Raindrop Prelude*.

'Very commendable,' said Holst. 'But you are a very young man. I remember when I was of an age with you I didn't only play the main classics.'

Richard looked at Mr Ross who grinned. 'Come on – indulge us.'

Richard launched into Joplin's the Entertainer, followed by the Teddy Bear's Picnic, an old melody with new words that had just begun to be heard on the wireless. This was Maria's favourite and she would make him play it over and over again while she warbled the words.

Mr Holst patted Richard on the back before relapsing into a spasm of coughing. 'That was good … very good … I wish you were my pupil.'

‘Be careful,’ said Mr Ross. ‘We mustn’t make this young man conceited.’

CHAPTER 10

Summer 1931

The choir school was on a mid-term break when Richard had an experience that would affect his whole life. He had ridden his ancient bicycle over to the big house with his music scores safe in a satchel around his neck. He was surprised to see an unfamiliar motorcar parked on the gravel beside the front door. The two Tenbury motors were the sort that one climbed up into. This one was low to the ground and shaped for speed. And it looked as if one climbed down into it.

Richard wheeled his bike around the house and went into the kitchen. His mother was there with the house cook. 'What's that motor out there?' he asked.

'That's Major Bell's motor,' said his mother. 'He flew aeroplanes with Mr Tenbury in the war and he's still doing it. He's in an air show at Shoreham on Saturday and they say you can go along with Maria to watch it.'

Richard remembered the red aeroplane that had passed them so closely on the Downs; so close that the pilot had waved to them. That aeroplane had remained in his memory ever since. Yes. He would go to the air show if they asked him.

Carrying his satchel he ran through the house to the drawing room. He stopped in the doorway. Three people were in the room: Mr and Mrs Tenbury and a stranger. The housemaid was serving the three of them with cups of coffee.

'Come on in, Richard,' called Mr Tenbury 'Like a cup of coffee?'

Richard stopped in the doorway feeling embarrassed. Usually the drawing room was empty at this time of day leaving the piano free for him to practice.

'Go on, Dickie,' said a shrill voice behind him accompanied by a smart shove in the back. Maria passed him and tugged him by the arm towards the seated adults.

'Richard,' said Mr Tenbury. 'Come and meet my old squadron CO.'

He stood up. 'Charlie, this is our music genius, Richard Dyer,'

The visitor stood and offered his hand. He was short, with nothing particularly striking about him apart from two sharp blue eyes. 'How do you do, Richard. They've been telling me all about you. I'm not much of a musician but how would you like to go flying?'

Richard shook the man's hand. 'Flying, sir. I would like to do that.'

'Come with us all to Shoreham and we'll see.'

Maria tugged his arm again. 'Come on, Dickie, you can play the piano later.'

Richard followed as she ran into the garden. 'Hey, Dickie, you heard that, we're all going flying on Saturday. Can you come?'

'Yeah, you bet. I like aeroplanes and I'd love to fly in one.'

'Major Bell has his own plane. It's a Moth and he says we can all go for a ride in it. When I'm old enough he can teach me to fly.'

'What? You're a girl. Girls don't fly.'

'You can't say that. What about Amy Johnson? She's flown to Australia.'

Richard knew that was all too true. He had been caught out properly.

'All right then, you can try and fly. I've wanted to ever since we saw that red plane over the Down.'

'Major Bell says the pilot's a friend of his. He was with papa and him in the war. Papa won the MC. Do you know what that is?'

'Yeah, it's a medal. My dada won the MM, but he was only a sergeant. Your brother got an MC, but that's for officers only.'

Maria nodded. 'Leo's a priest now. But he's been put in some place up north called Blackburn. I don't know where that is.'

'It's in Lancashire. Don't those nuns teach you any geography?'

'They do, but it's all about Italy and Spain and places where the Church is strong.'

'Your church?'

'That's the one true church.' Maria smirked. 'But Father Joseph says I can come and listen to you sing in the stolen cathedral providing I confess it to him the next day.'

Richard felt indignant. 'Confess what? Does he say it's a sin for you to hear me sing? You've heard me enough times anyway.'

Maria laughed. 'No, silly. It's only we're not supposed to go inside the stolen cathedral until we get it back again and before that the priests have to drive out heresy.'

'Who says it's stolen? We got it when King Henry kicked your lot out.'

Maria released her most mischievous laugh. 'If you could see your face. Don't take it so seriously. I've nothing against your church. We all pray to the same God anyway.'

'What's your brother say?'

'Leo's broadminded. The war changed him in so many ways. He wants our churches to settle their differences and join together. But he can't say it because he'd be in trouble if he did.'

'Why?'

''Cos, his bishop's Irish and hates everything English, especially your church.'

For a while the two children played happily in the garden. Their attempts on the tennis court were a mutual disaster that left both rolling on the surface in wild laughter.

'Can I use the piano now?' asked Richard. 'I didn't like to with all the grownups in there.'

'That doesn't matter. Come on – Mamma and me want to sing while you play.'

In the drawing room they found that the butler had already lifted the lid on the Steinway. Mrs Tenbury and Maria stood to one side while Richard played his introduction. Then both mother and daughter joined in together. He noted mother's contralto was a bit more in tune than Maria's undeveloped soprano.

If you go down in the woods today
You're sure of a big surprise
If you go down in the woods today
You'd better go in disguise,
For every bear that ever there was
Will gather there for certain because
Today's the day the teddy bears
Have their picnic.

Maria turned to her mother and put a finger to her lips as Richard broke into a series of improvisations on the original theme. Then everyone clapped including the house servants clustered by the half-open drawing room door.

On Saturday morning Richard rode over to the Tenburys. Major Bell had already left to service his aeroplane for that afternoon's display. Everyone was pleased that it was a fine morning with no sign of cloud or rain, so the airshow could go ahead as advertised. This time they all set out in the Rolls driven by Ganton with the two children in front and Mr and Mrs Tenbury in the rear. With five miles to go to the airfield they were to have their first experience of a new twentieth century phenomenon – the traffic jam. Every model of motorcar, motor cycle and a convoy of huge charabancs slowed everyone to walking pace.

'I dunno' what things are all coming to,' Ganton grumbled as he slowed to a halt behind a charabanc. 'Before the war it was only good folk who went to these shows.'

'Ooh, you snob,' Maria giggled.

'Quite right, too, Miss Maria. It's all this equality and that Labour party. I don't hold wi'it.'

They knew that this airshow was an inaugural event on the airfield that had just been refurbished after being abandoned since the war. The municipal authorities in Brighton hoped to develop the site as a commercial airport, and this display was by way of a launch. The car park was reached eventually. The grass field was dry and Ganton found a nice spot away from the charabancs where they could enjoy a picnic.

Beyond they could see the aircraft lined up as for a parade. Richard could see biplanes and a few monoplanes all painted different colours.

'Not much has changed,' said Mr Tenbury. 'I was here in 1917 before we went to France. Our squadron flew DH9s. We had a Canadian squadron with the same aeroplanes.'

They could see mechanics winding the propellers by hand and they could hear aero engines firing. Following a long warm-up period the first aircraft took off. 'That's Charlie,' said Mr Tenbury. He pointed at a slim biplane with a yellow fuselage and silver wings and tailplane.

'How can you tell? asked Maria.

'It's a Gypsy Moth painted in London Flying Club colours. It's the only one on show with that paintwork.'

'Would you young ones like a joyride?' asked Mrs Tenbury. 'Charlie says you can, but it's one at a time in the passenger seat.'

'Oh Mama, can I?' Maria danced with excitement.

'Don't ask me,' said Mr Tenbury. 'Last time I flew I argued with a Boche fighter and he put me in hospital.'

'Will it be safe for the children?' his wife asked.

'Oh, yes. Charles is the best. A circuit and bump on a nice day, no Boche fighters anywhere. They'll be fine.'

She looked at Richard. 'You too?'

'You bet. I've always wanted to fly.' Richard was excited now.

The children had to wait for a couple of hours of suppressed and nervous excitement. They watched as complicated aerobatics were performed and low passes made over their heads. A Moth fought a mock battle with a refurbished German fighter. Inevitably the Moth downed the alleged Red Baron and everyone applauded. Then the moment came. Major Bell walked over to them. Richard didn't recognize him at first, dressed as he was in leather jacket and flying helmet.

'Ladies first, I think,' he said. He fitted Maria with a small helmet and a little fleece jacket. 'I know it's hot here but much colder when we get skywards.'

Maria's flight only lasted a few minutes but long enough for them to pass overhead and her to wave. Now it was Richard's turn. He took over the flying gear from Maria and walked to the aircraft that stood with chocks under its wheels while the engine ticked over. Major Bell and his mechanic helped Richard into the passenger seat and fixed the heavy safety harness around his shoulders, securing it with a metal pin.

'This aeroplane has dual control,' said the Major. 'I'll have the master controls, but keep your hands off the stick and feet away from the pedals. We have a communication system. I can talk to you through this speaking tube. Pick it up when you see this red light.' He pointed to a glass circle among the dials and then ran through an explanation of the other instruments.

Major Bell climbed into his seat. The mechanic pulled away the chocks and the aircraft began to move to the takeoff point. The Major turned the machine to face the wind and opened the throttle. Now they were moving – bouncing across the long expanse of grass. Next was a sensation that in after years Richard compared with a sexual one. They were airborne, and below them the ground slipped away. He could see the cars and aircraft parked below and then the seaport and the long blue line of the English Channel. Next they were turning and the landscape changed to fields and hills with roads and moving traffic. In front of him he could see the spinning propeller and hear the oddly musical sound of the engine. Major Bell had shown him the altimeter, and Richard watched it as the needle climbed in tune with their height. Ten thousand feet – Richard caught his breath. Then he saw the red light on the dashboard. He took hold of the speaking tube.

'Richard,' said the Major. 'Put your feet on the rudder pedals and take the stick in your right hand.' Richard did as he was told. He felt a fresh excitement. 'Nothing can happen because I have the controls, but now she's yours. How do you feel?'

'I'm good, sir. What do I do next?'

'Use the rudder to hold your course. Look at the compass and keep us on a heading of twenty-five degrees. Now watch the altimeter and use the stick to maintain the same height.'

Richard was sunk in concentration, but even now music flowed into his senses. His head filled with music he knew; in this case Wagner the Ride of the Valkyries. He picked up the speaking tube. 'Sir, is that all right?'

'For a first timer you've done well. Now take the stick and move it to the right.' The aircraft banked and began to turn. 'Now gently pull the stick back.' They were turning although Richard felt the master control take over at one point and correct.

Now he could see the airfield ahead of them. 'Good man; now I'll take her,' said the Major. Richard sat back as they came in to land. He felt the light touch and then the heavier bump and they were down and taxiing over to where Maria and her parents stood.

Maria looked indignant as she glared at both Major Bell and Richard. 'He was up there a lot longer than I was. It's not fair.'

CHAPTER 11

Winter 1932

There was little to cheer about that winter. The farm was in the grip of the great agricultural depression. For a two thousand acre estate and a village utterly dependent on farming it was a very grim time indeed. Ted and Mabel, Richard's parents, were also feeling the pinch, particularly as the longed-for second child was now on the way. Ted had had to accept a cut in his pay. Mabel's wages from the big house were more important than ever and they would cease if childbirth prevented her working.

The Tenburys had significant private means apart from the estate whose rents had decreased along with the depression. They did their best to alleviate some of the hardship, but in the long term there was little that they could do in the face of national calamity.

'It's all them politicians,' Ted grumbled. 'Cheap food for all those idle sods in Birmingham and London and such places. And them Germans is getting uppity again.' He glared at the two-day-old morning paper. 'Don't blame the Germans for being German. I remembers in the trenches we saw'em as our opponents. It was the generals and them politicians way behind us that was the enemy. I reckons they saw it that way too, with their people.'

Richard did his best to help out on the farm, now very short-handed, but he was more than ever grateful that he had found his own vocation away from all this. He had passed his twelth birthday and his singing voice was at its treble best. His piano playing was progressing and his tutor was talking about something called an organ scholarship. He loved the singing but he wasn't sure he wanted to retrain his voice when it broke. He had no ambition to join the professional lay vicars. His future lay in music, and if he was to progress then that progress would be in the big city – London. He had never been there and the thought made him a tiny bit nervous.

His parents were excited at the prospect of their second child. It had been a surprise as Mabel was thirty-six and near the age limit for more children. How all this had come about still baffled Richard. His schoolfellows had all sorts of contradictory theories as to how children were conceived and he guessed most of them were untrue. He was still very curious to see what kind of sibling he would have. A boy would be a rival; a girl, however irritating, would be safer.

Then one day Mr Ross had sent for him. Richard couldn't think that he was in any sort of trouble so he was curious. Mr Ross was his tutor and a good friend. That was because it wasn't all music. Richard had sailed in Mr Ross's X boat several times and with Mrs Ross had crewed in a big racing regatta. Richard loved sailing. It was a little bit like flying although less comfortable and wetter. He could never forget his flight at Shoreham and longed to have another try.

'Come on in, Dyer,' said Mr Ross. 'I would like you to meet Mr Boult, and this lady is Miss Cohen. Mr Boult will be conducting the South of England Orchestra in the cathedral next month and Miss Cohen will be playing Tchaikovsky's first piano concerto. Richard was intrigued. He had heard of both these people. Mr Boult was a middle aged, somewhat balding man; he stood and offered Richard a warm handshake. Some of Richard's awe at meeting another famous name seeped away. Mr Boult seemed a nice old gentleman. He was more interested in Miss Cohen the pianist. He had listened to gramophone records of her playing on the Tenburys radiogram. More interesting were the adults whispered comments about the lady. She was apparently rumoured to be a naughty girl and to have shared a bed with several men including the Prime Minister. That must've been a crowd. He was puzzled, but the real significance was lost on him. Maria wasn't much wiser. She said she thought it meant the lady was a "fallen woman".

Well, this lady didn't seem to have done much falling. She was slim with dark hair and the face of a film star, with lipstick and a faint waft of scent. Compared to Sir Edward, and Mr Holst, and even this Mr Boult, she was wholly different from any famous musician that he had seen or met. She took his hand and smiled.

'Dyer,' said Mr Ross. 'This lady and this gentleman wish to hear your musical prowess.' He pointed to the piano. 'How about two Chopin preludes?'

'Yes, sir. I can play those but I'm only a beginner.'

'We'll let our guests judge that.'

Richard sat down and played the preludes. Both were short pieces that his rapidly developing hands could now cope with. The adults murmured and nodded approval.

Miss Cohen spoke. 'That was excellent, Richard. But those were pieces that your tutor nominated. Is there not something of your own choosing that you can play us?'

'Thank you, Miss. I can do Moonlight Sonata. I've just got to grips with that one.'

Richard played the Beethoven and was relieved that it went smoothly. This time all the adults applauded.

'Very good,' said Miss Cohen. 'Now suppose you are at home with other children. What do they like to hear?'

Richard was surprised. He hadn't expected this. Then on impulse he launched into Maria's favourite: Teddy Bear's Picnic.

To his further surprise the adults applauded again. Now Mr Ross spoke. 'Dyer, as I told you next month we are holding our annual Christmas concert in the Cathedral. Mr Boult will conduct the Southern Orchestra with Miss Cohen playing the concerto. We would like you to go away and practice those two preludes and work on them until you can perform them to a standard that I will set. You will then be invited to perform at the concert.'

'Cor'; thank you, sir,' Richard gasped. He hadn't expected this. The adults laughed.

'We're all coming to hear you play in your concert,' said Maria.

'What?' Richard laughed. 'It's in the cathedral, you know. I thought if you went in there you went to hell, or your flipping Pope'll curse you.'

'No, it's a non-religious event so it doesn't count and anyway Leo is coming with us and he can absolve us all at the end.' She paused and kicked a stone across the road. 'Anyway, why are you here? It's Sunday and you should be singing there.'

'No, we've a weekend off. There's another choir been promised a go in the cathedral. They're from...' Richard grimaced as he named a well-known local public school.

If the truth was told, he felt at a loose end. His heavily pregnant mother was finding household chores harder and slower to complete, so Richard's father had conscripted him to help. The piano in the best parlour was hopelessly out of tune and the schoolroom one was worse. His old friends had very little time for him. "Dickie the toff,' they called him. They weren't jealous; he was no longer part of their world.

He glared at Maria. 'Why are you here anyway? You're a boarder at your school as well.'

She laughed. 'I've been suspended for one week. I'm a really bad influence and the nuns are losing patience.'

'What happened? What did you do?'

'Well, there's this horrid little girl called Clara. The nuns love her. They believe she's perfect, but we know she's a nasty spiteful little pig. I called her that out loud and the nuns heard. That's why I'm here in disgrace because I refused to confess and get absolution.'

'What does your Daddy say?'

'Oh he was all right. Mamma and him gave me a bit of a ticking off, but it was sort of tongue in cheek. Papa said something like that happened to him in the Air Force.'

'If I wasn't set on music, I'd join the Air Force.'

Maria looked alarmed. 'It didn't do Papa any good. When that German shot him down he was burned badly. That's why he couldn't have lots of children.'

Richard laughed. 'I'm not thinking of war. I'd just like to fly and when I'm rich and famous I'll learn.'

Maria released her most irritating giggle. 'Rich and famous? That's good; then we can get married and live in our big house.'

'Huh, you can dream all you like, girl.'

Practice, practice, practice. Richard worked ceaselessly on his performance, on the Tenbury piano and back at school on the one provided. He was excited, and of course he was nervous. He was young but not so young as to know he had his whole career riding on this performance and he would get it right. He was still unsure of where his ambition should point him. Did he want to be a concert pianist like Miss Cohen? He could probably be a choirmaster if all else failed, but that was not where he wanted to go. No, he wanted to compose. He wanted to hear an orchestra playing his own creations, both serious and light. Did he want to conduct that orchestra like Mr Boult? Not really, he wanted to make music and he wanted to play music and at just short of age thirteen he made that his resolve. Then without warning it seemed as if his world was upside down and his ambition lost.

CHAPTER 12

Richard was on his way with the other boys to evensong when the message came. He was to go at once to the Reverend Wandsdale's house. This was so odd that he felt that little twinge of apprehension. He had done nothing wrong – of that he was sure. Now he was frightened; a strange intrusion in his brain was telling him that something tragic was happening.

'Come in Dyer,' said Mr Wandsdale. The college head looked tense and his face had a grim set expression. 'Dyer, we have a hire motor car coming to run you home to your family.'

Richard felt as if a block of ice was in his stomach. 'Sir…?'

'We've had a telephone message from Mrs Tenbury, whom I think you know. Your mother is seriously ill. She was delivered of a strong baby early this morning but the ordeal has left her in very poor straits and she has been asking for you.'

Richard couldn't take any of this in. His mother was the centre of his life and he adored her. It was she who had fought for him to go to the choir school against all the grumbling of his father. He loved his father too as he loved both his parents.

'Is she,' he stumbled with the words. 'Sir, is she going to die?'

'That I cannot tell you, but we will pray for her this evening. That I promise you.'

'Thank you, sir.' He could think of nothing else to say.

'Now, young Dyer. Go to your quarters and collect your clothes. You have an exeat to stay at your home as long as you need.'

It was dark when Richard arrived in Pockhampton. It had been a bumpy ride in an ancient motor of uncertain make. He hardly noticed; for the first time in his life he was immersed in prayer. 'Please God, don't let my Mama die, please, please, please.'

To his surprise he saw Mrs Tenbury's Ford parked outside the front of the farmhouse with a second Model T that he knew belonged to the doctor.

'Hey, boy. Who is going to pay me?' It was the driver of the hire car.

'It's all right, Richard. Leave it to me.' Thank God; it was Mrs Tenbury. She went to the driver and passed him the money demanded.

'Please, Mrs Tenbury. Will Mama die?'

For the first time ever she bent down and hugged him. 'Be brave. You have a new little sister but your mother is gravely ill. The doctor and nurse are with her now.'

Inside his familiar home Richard saw his father and the sight of him was a shock. Ted Dyer was almost unrecognizable. His face looked grey and his eyes were bloodshot and heavy with lack of sleep. 'Oh. Son it's good you're here.'

'Oh Dad, is Mama going to die?'

His father shook his head. 'It's a close thing, Son. I saw it in the war. We think you can help her.'

Richard's eyes were moistening. No, I mustn't cry. I don't cry. I haven't cried for years. His father beckoned him into the kitchen. The range was hot and someone had brought in two extra bright oil lamps. But it was none of this that he noticed. A woman he knew by sight was openly suckling a baby. He wasn't sure of the woman's name but she came from a travelling family who lived in a clutch of old army huts on the fringe of the village. Beside her on the kitchen floor stood two little cots. One was empty and one had a sleeping baby with a look of contentment on its face. Richard felt embarrassed. In his eyes the slatternly woman was openly exposing herself and seemed to have no shame.

His father corrected him. 'Son, Mrs McNally has come to our rescue. Your mother is too ill to feed the little one, but Mrs McNally is already feeding her young one and she has stepped in to help us.' Richard had a shock as his father pointed at the tiny baby locked on the woman's nipple. 'Dickie, that baby is your little sister.'

Richard saw the tiny creature on the woman's breast. He was watching a world he didn't understand. His father tapped him on the arm bringing him back into the present. 'Dickie, it's time for you to talk to the doctor.'

Richard followed his father up the stairs to his parents' room. Ted Dyer opened the door and beckoned Richard to look. The room was dark apart from one lamp that gave the place a shadowy feel. His mother lay on the bed wrapped in an odd looking robe that he'd never seen before. In a chair beside her sat the district nurse with Mrs Tenbury and another nurse in a smart starched blue uniform. Richard couldn't help himself. He walked very slowly across the room trying desperately hard not to make the boards creak. His mother lay still. Her eyes were open but she seemed not to see him. He was horrified by the stains of blood on the bed and floor and to smell a disgusting odour. His father touched him on the elbow and indicated another nearby figure. He was the village doctor.

The doctor pointed him to the door and picked up and lit a second lamp. Richard followed him downstairs and into the empty best parlour. 'Richard,' the doctor began. 'Your mother is very ill. She hovers between life and death and you can help her. I want to ask you to do something very unusual; challenging is I think the term. How do you feel about it?'

'Sir, I'll do anything to help Mama get better.'

The doctor looked Richard in the eye. 'Your mother has lost much blood. She is very weak. We cannot use your father's blood because it will not be a match. But there is every chance your blood can save her.'

Richard couldn't grasp any of this. 'I'll do it, sir, but how?'

'You needn't be afraid. We are going to do what is known as a transfusion. Some big hospitals take and store blood but this is an emergency. I want to link a vein in your arm to an artery in your mother's body. Now, don't worry, we're not going to drain you of blood; just short quantities at a time. Your father has given his permission. Do you agree?'

'Yes, sir.'

The doctor walked to the stairs and Richard followed. In the bedroom the doctor opened his bag and withdrew a length of rubber tube with a fat needle at each end. He gestured Richard to his mother's bed. Richard was told to remove his school jacket and to roll up his sleeve while the doctor strapped his arm. The process proceeded for some minutes. It was not painful, but he was relieved when the doctor removed the needle, swabbed the wound and placed on it a piece of sticking plaster. He was told to roll down his sleeve and replace the jacket.

'Well done, young man,' said the doctor. 'We will see what happens, but we may need you to repeat the process. After that I think you should eat some food and build up your strength.'

It was only some years on that Richard learned that they had been pushing the boundaries of medical knowledge with no certainty that their efforts would work. Downstairs in the kitchen they found Mrs Tenbury with the wet nurse and Mrs Tenbury was cooking. For this gracious lady to do something so menial was a shock.

'Here you are, Richard,' she smiled. 'A full dish of scrambled eggs. Eat it up and then a night's sleep.'

'What about Mama?'

'We'll bring you news when we need to.'

Richard found his eyes moistening. 'She mustn't die. We all love her.'

He lay awake in his old home bed and once more he prayed. 'God, don't let Mama die, please don't let Mama die.' In the end he did fall asleep and that sleep was coloured by strange dreams and very odd music.

He awoke well before dawn and the awful horror of his mother's illness filled him with dread. He tiptoed across the top of the stairway and looked in his parents' room. A lamp still burned and now a different nurse sat beside the bed. His mother still lay there in the same position. 'Please,' he whispered. 'How is she?'

The nurse turned. 'You're the son are you?'

'Yes.'

'And you are the blood donor?'

'Yes.'

'Then that's good. Mrs Dyer has had a much more peaceful night. I cannot tell you more until the doctor arrives.'

'Will that be soon?'

'Yes, quite soon. Mrs Tenbury has engaged my services along with my colleague. We'll watch until your mother is well enough to be moved to hospital.'

Dawn was breaking as Mrs Tenbury drove into the yard. Richard ran to the door to greet her and was surprised to see Leo Tenbury with her. Both mother and son were clad against the cold. Leo was dressed all in black with the same sort of white collar worn by the cathedral clergy.

Ted Dyer was on his feet now straightening his jacket and pulling up his breeches. 'Mrs Tenbury and Mr Leo, sir. It's good to see you.'

'Hello, Dyer,' said Leo, 'May I say a small office for your wife?'

'He means a set of prayers,' Mrs Tenbury explained.

'Anything to make her better, though your God never did much for us in the trenches. Our own vicar's coming along this morning as well.'

'I know,' Leo replied. 'Mr Davis is a good man.' He smiled. 'Between the two of us we may surprise you. Mother, may I now have the missal?'

Mrs Tenbury delved in her handbag and produced a small leatherbound book. Leo began to read from it in Latin. Richard knew it was Latin as he had been studying it in class, but he could make little of these prayers. Anyway, who cared as long as it helped Mama.

He felt oddly superior to think of his own cathedral where all was in English.

Mrs Tenbury whispered. ‘Leo is blessing the house and wishing blessing to all living in it. We won’t go into your mother’s presence. That would be for a different reason.’

Richard felt cold. He knew she meant last rites and that mustn’t happen. He began to think his own prayers again. Leo finished, closed the book and made that cross sign that some of their clergy now did in the cathedral. At that moment the new nurse came downstairs and removed the boiling pan from the range. She removed the rubber tube and took it away.

‘Now,’ said Mrs Tenbury. ‘I think I’ll cook us all breakfast. Yes, you too, Edward. You must keep your strength up.’

Despite his worries Richard felt hungry and devoured the eggs and bacon; even his father ate a little.

At eight o’clock Mr Ganton drove up with thc Rolls and took away the first nurse. Minutes later the doctor’s Ford pulled into the yard. It was now time for Richard to give more blood. Was it his imagination, but did his mother’s face have a tiny bit more natural colour? Could he dare to hope that they would win this battle? He pulled down his sleeve once more and put on his jacket. In the kitchen again he saw that the vicar had arrived. With two clergy from rival faiths this was neutral ground. They had greeted each other respectfully and Mrs Tenbury had given the vicar a cup of tea. ‘We must be off now,’ she said. ‘My husband needs a breakfast and Maria is home for half-term. Richard, Maria wants to see you.’

‘Mrs Tenbury, I can’t leave my Mama.’

‘Don’t worry. I’ll bring her.’

Richard was still worried. ‘She’s not to scream or shout.’

‘No, my girl will be all sweetness and light.’

Richard was not at all sure about that but he let it go. Mrs Tenbury and Leo drove away. Now for the first time he wondered where the two babies had gone to. He worried; had that gypsy woman run off with his new little sister? His father reassured him. ‘Mrs McNally’s a husband to care for and both babas need feeding all night. She’s a good woman and we must trust her.’

CHAPTER 13

A whole week passed before Mabel Dyer sat up in bed and pleaded to see her baby. Richard had donated two further blood transfusions and felt a mixture of relief and pride to see his mother beginning to get better. At times he felt a little light-headed but that apart he suffered no ill effects. His mother was still far too ill to feed a baby so Mrs McNally continued to do so for her. The vicar had begun to fuss about a christening. Bringing the family to church was not an option, so one day they had all gathered upstairs and the vicar had mumbled some prayers and then poured a drop of water onto the face of poor little baby Alice, who howled in unison with the prayers.

'Getting' rid o' the devil – that's good,' said Ted.

Richard's father had been badly affected by the whole birth saga. 'Never again,' he had muttered. 'That's the last one.'

Something else was now worrying Richard. Today was Tuesday and on Saturday he was due in the cathedral to play his piano piece. He was horribly aware that he hadn't touched a piano for ten days. For the first time in his short life he began to panic.

'Come to tea and use our piano,' said Maria. 'You'd better or you'll make a mess of your performance and we'll all feel embarrass-sed.'

'You are a bundle of cheer,' Richard grumbled. 'They made you a nun yet?'

Maria released a shriek of laughter. 'I don't think so. Sister Michaela said I was Satan's daughter; said it in front of the whole school.'

'That sounds 'bout right, I reckons.'

Maria grinned. 'You're talking all Sussex again.' She switched on her most irritating accent. 'You meant: that assumption sounds correct.'

'Aw shuddup.'

After two sessions with the Steinway, Richard felt more confident. Mrs Tenbury had let him use the house telephone and he had confirmed with the college that he would play at the concert. Suddenly his apprehension was gone. He was looking forward to the day.

Mabel Dyer was up now and with her husband's support had come downstairs and into the kitchen. 'Son, it seems you saved my life with your blood.'

'I hope I helped,' said Richard. 'But the doctor said he was doing something that no one had ever done before, or not to his knowing.'

'Then there's Mr Leo and the vicar,' his father intervened. 'They prayed over you long and hard. I didn't hold wi' it at first but seems these men o' God can do great things.'

'How is your music?' Mama asked.

'I'm playing the piano in concert this Saturday. It's going well but I need one more practice on Mr Tenbury's grand before then.'

He cycled over to the Tenbury house that afternoon. The grand piano had recently been tuned and sounded better than ever. An hour's practice and Richard was satisfied. He would play in front of all those people and he would make it his best.

Maria's half term break was ending and she was getting ready to return to the convent. Maria was becoming increasingly grown up and worldly beyond her thirteen years. 'Dickie, you're going to be a famous musician. I envy you.'

'Well, you could play music too if you worked at it.'

'It could never happen. I'm for the marriage market.' She suddenly looked sad; woeful Richard thought. 'Oh Dickie I wish I could marry you and look after you while you became famous.'

'Don't think either of us is quite ready for that yet.'

'No, Dickie, darling. In a few years time I will be eighteen and then I'll be coming out...'

'Coming out of where?'

'No, it's the girls of my class become debutantes. We go to balls and the young aristos eye us up like heifers in the market.' Now she laughed and assumed a mock auctioneer's voice. 'Maria Tenbury – what'll you bid? One thousand pounds? Any advance on one thousand pounds? Last time – sold to Lord Fauntleroy.'

'Don't you get to choose?'

'Well, I suppose if the lord is very fat and smelly, but no. You see we need to breed an heir for this place and with Leo celibate, it's got to be me.'

Saturday came and the two Tenbury cars were pressed into service. Ted Dyer wished his son well but didn't feel he could leave Mabel alone. Richard travelled sitting with Maria. Mr Tenbury sat in the rear compartment with Leo and another middle-aged man whom Richard didn't know but looked familiar. Mrs Tenbury drove the Ford with passengers: Mr Locke, the vicar, the house butler and two small friends of Maria's. The roads were all reasonably clear and had yet to reach the crowded rush hour highways of later years. It was not until they reached the outskirts of the city that they were slowed by traffic. And all the traffic was travelling into the centre and towards the cathedral. They could now see that every parking space around the Cathedral was taken and the pavements were crowded with people all heading towards the door of the great building.

Mr Ross with the Dean greeted them and while the others went into the cathedral, Richard was taken to a side vestry. It was here that he was startled to see the same balding middle-aged man who had travelled down in the Tenbury Rolls.

He smiled as he recognized Richard. Mr Ross spoke. 'This is Mr Coates who is conducting his Merrymakers overture.'

'I will be very interested to hear you play,' said Mr Coates. 'Mr and Mrs Tenbury are old friends and Mary Tenbury and I grew up as children in Nottinghamshire. They insisted I conduct at this festival and in fact I have been thinking of buying a house here.'

Richard felt a pang of nervous excitement as he peeped into the cathedral. The pews were full of expectant people and soon he must play in front of them. He could see that the piano had been mounted on a little platform, only a few yards away, to one side of the main orchestral players. These were all in their places and the audience broke into applause as Mr Boult walked onto the conductor's podium. He raised his baton and the orchestra played the overture from the Gondoliers. The audience applauded and the conductor bowed. One more piece and then it would be his turn.
Richard clenched and unclenched his fists as the orchestra seemed to grind out an endless episode of J.S. Bach. In any other circumstances it would be a delight. Then it was over. Mr Boult turned and addressed the audience, or were they the congregation?

'Ladies and gentlemen,' his voice rang loud and clear. 'It is important that we nurture new talent in our musicians. This evening I am delighted to call on a member of our choir in the cathedral here. Richard Dyer aged thirteen who will play two Chopin preludes for us.'

Richard left the vestry and walked up the two steps to the platform. I mustn't trip up and fall was the thought that possessed him at that moment. He reached the piano stool and found to his relief that it had been pre-adjusted for him. Mentally he thanked Mr Ross for that. The audience had ceased their polite applause. Richard took a deep breath and he played. His nervousness vanished as he became swept away by the music that flowed from his fingers. He forgot everything: his family troubles, his friends, everything. Only the music mattered and it consumed him until he was aware of nothing else. The second prelude concluded all too soon and Richard sat back and drew breath. Now the audience applauded; no polite clapping this time but full-hearted enthusiastic applause. Richard stood and bowed as the applause grew louder.

He turned and left the stage. In the vestry all was handshakes and congratulations. Mr Ross clapped him on the back and Mr Coates was grinning with genuine delight. Richard for the first time felt that glow of achievement; future generations would use the term "unwind" and that suited exactly how he felt. He was able to sit down and relax as Mr Coates conducted his Merrymakers overture. The music was filled with fun and happiness far removed from the heavy classical repertoire. Richard was entranced. Could he ever compose work as joyful as this?

Mr Boult returned to the rostrum greeted Miss Cohen amidst warm applause and they performed the Tchaikovsky. Then the concert was over. Mr and Mrs Tenbury were all smiles while Maria, with no warning, put her hands on his shoulders and kissed him full on the lips. He felt his head was spinning. Yes, he had done it: performed in front of hundreds of people and won through.

CHAPTER 14

1936

Richard suddenly found he was in demand as a musician. In the years following his debut concert he was asked some twenty times to perform in churches, village halls and other venues. The local papers wrote articles in praise with photographs, and once a team from BBC Children's Hour visited with a large motor van and some clumsy recording equipment.

'Well done, boy,' his father grunted. 'But don't you be getting above yourself. You be a Sussex boy not a London waster.'

Richard laughed. 'Mr Ross says I'll be off to London anyway. Now I've got my school certificate I can apply for music college.'

His father only muttered.

In reality Richard dreaded the moment when he would part with his family and move to this alien world of the big city. The worst of the agricultural depression was behind Pockhampton, but the political situation was becoming grim. Once more there was the possibility of war with the emerging new Germany. Some of Ted Dyer's concern about his son in London was justified. The papers were full of stories of violence. Communists and blackshirt Fascists were fighting in the streets. It seemed the great city was not a healthy place for his young son.

Richard's little sister, Alice, was walking well and beginning to talk fluently. Richard adored the little girl and would take her for impromptu picnics on the edge of the downs. There was so much that he would miss when he was finally in London. Maria was already there. A confident and increasingly beautiful young lady she was working in a lawyer's office before reaching the age of debutante balls and the dreaded marriage market. Mabel Dyer was always supportive of her son and took his side against his father's grumbling. She knew all too well that secretly her husband was proud of their son. Mabel's health had improved but she was still frail from her ordeal at her daughter's birth. She still coped well with her routine and was immensely house-proud.

The call came one Monday in June. The Tenbury's had arranged for the Dyer household to have a telephone. It helped with coordinating the estate work, but really it was to keep Mabel in touch with the doctor.

'Richard,' it was Mr Ross. 'On Wednesday, be ready for an early start. I'll collect you at five-thirty and we'll catch the train to Waterloo. You are due for interview at twelve.'

At last, the Royal Academy of Music wanted to interview him; yes him, Richard Dyer, a farming son of Sussex. Could he really believe it? His ambition now was to play and compose music. His voice had broken after three years in the choir and he had no ambition to retrain it and join the lay vicars. It might sound conceited but he knew better things lay just beyond the horizon.

Mr Ross arrived driving his Morris. This was a new car, a Morris Twelve: a fully enclosed saloon car and a great improvement on the open rattletrap that Richard remembered.

'I've arranged for you to stay overnight with friends,' said Mr Ross, 'so bring your clothes bag.'

The railway station was familiar as Richard had been there for school trips to Brighton. The local steam train took them to Portsmouth where they changed to the brand new electrified line for London. Richard knew some of the places they passed through. He had already played in the big hall in Petersfield and another concert in Haslemere. They sped onwards through unfamiliar country and towns until they reached the outskirts of London and the drabber streets around Clapham. Now they were at Waterloo station and a world that to Richard was wholly new. Whistles blew amidst a background of echoing shouts and the roar of steam engines on the long distance platforms. He followed Mr Ross to the ticket barrier and onwards across the huge forecourt, then out into the street where Mr Ross hailed a taxi. Motorcars swarmed everywhere in numbers that he had never seen the like.

'Marylebone Road,' Mr Ross instructed their driver.

Richard clenched his teeth and winced as they weaved in and out of traffic and past strange red double-deck buses with exterior staircases. He had never imagined anything like this human anthill of a city. They arrived at the destination and Mr Ross paid the driver. 'Robbery and extortion,' he muttered.

They were standing in front of a huge building such as Richard had never seen before. Redbrick with ornate white stuccos; it reminded him of a giant wedding cake.

'Well, here we are,' said Mr Ross. 'The Royal Academy of Music and my own alma mater.'

They crossed the threshold into the entry hall. A smartly dressed young man sat behind a desk. Mr Ross handed him a card and the man pressed an electric bell. 'I think the examination committee are in session,' he said, 'but I will arrange for you to be taken to the waiting area.'

Five minutes later a kindly-looking middle-aged lady appeared and asked them to follow her. For the first time in his life Richard entered a lift. He felt nervous and couldn't help wondering how they would fare if the cable snapped. However all was well and they arrived on the third floor. Behind them the metal gates clattered shut and the whining lift descended again. Their guide led them along a corridor past rows of doors. They could hear music; violins, cellos, and wind instruments and from behind one door a piano. Richard felt a tiny satisfaction; at least he could play better than that. They ended in a small vestibule where there were sofas and tables with copies of the daily papers and garish London magazines. He began to feel fresh unease. He was out of his home element with a vengeance. What on earth was a Sussex Farm boy doing in this place of urban sophistication?

Two minutes later they were called and Richard, feeling like a condemned man, prepared to face his fate. The room he entered had full sunlight pouring through an open window. Richard could just catch a glimpse of nearby Regent's Park. A fashionable oval shaped table faced him and behind it sat three men. The man in the centre was middle aged with a definite presence. Richard recognized him from photographs he had seen. This was Professor Wood, a man who had graduated from the same college many years ago and was now famous as a conductor of the London Promenade Concerts. As these were intended to give the masses access to serious music, Richard hoped the man might not be too prejudiced against him for his low class. The two examiners on either side of Mr Wood he didn't know.

'Mr Dyer,' the chairman began. This was a shock no one had ever called him that. 'Mr Dyer, your curriculum vitae is impressive. Your academic results are creditable and as a performer you seem to be more than competent.' Mr Wood now looked up from the papers he had been reading and looked Richard in the eye. 'Mr Dyer, have you ambition? What is your aim in life, musically that is?'

Richard held the eye contact. 'Sir, I want to write music and I want to play music and I believe I can do both well.'

'Commendable, but how do you think that we can help you here?'

'Sir, this college is the best in the land, maybe the best in the world. Here I will have the best teachers who can inspire me.'

'Well, Dyer you certainly have the art of flattery. Will you adapt to our life here? Are you a person who will mix well with your fellow students?'

'Oh, yes, sir. I get along all right with everybody at my old school.'

Mr Wood looked stern as he resumed eye contact. 'Yes, we're a friendly establishment here. Your tutor, Mr Ross is a former student of this college and he thinks highly of you.' Mr Wood stood up and offered his hand. Richard shook the hand and the interview was over.

Mr Ross was in the waiting area. 'Well, how did it go?'

'I think I did all right, sir.'

They returned to the lift and back to the ground floor. After another nervous wait Richard was led into a small room with a familiar Steinway piano. The college tutor was a cheerful young man wearing a cricket club blazer. Richard sat at the piano and ran off the two Chopin preludes. The tutor seemed happy, although these were pieces that Richard felt he could play standing on his head.

Outside in the waiting area Mr Ross was with a young man, older than Richard. 'Dyer, this is David Goldstein. David's parents are friends of mine and they have offered to look after you when you come here.'

'If I come here, sir?' Richard felt gloomy now. He was aware again of being a farm boy from Sussex.

'We shall see.'

Richard shook hands with this other boy. 'Are you a student here?' he asked politely.

The boy grinned. 'Yes, I'm a woodwind player and my father plays brass in the Royal Phil and my sister plays flute as well.' He was a cheerful looking lad, taller and a few years older than Richard, with unusually long black hair.

'I play piano,' said Richard. 'But I'm only here for the interview. They haven't accepted me yet.'

'You're coming home with me anyway,' said David. 'Then you can meet my people.'

They walked back towards the entrance and past the lift that had just descended. The gates opened and a young man stepped out carrying a viola case. Richard and the newcomer both froze staring at each other.

'Oh my God,' gasped the newcomer. 'What the hell are you doing here?'

'Lamingham,' Richard stared at his old enemy. 'For that matter what are you doing here?'

'I am studying serious music. You, Dyer are a country bumpkin. This is a college for educated people of good family. You won't be accepted here. When I tell my father he will see to that.'

'You don't change do you?' Richard was scornful.

'Lamingham,' Mr Ross intervened. 'I know for a fact that neither yours nor your father's intervention will work. I am already confident that Dyer will be accepted. He is a talented musician and with that his birth is irrelevant.'

'And I see he's in company with a damned Jew.'

'So what?' Richard wanted to square up to Lamingham but this was not the time or place. 'My friend here has offered me accommodation. I don't care where he goes to pray. What have you got against him and his people anyway?'

Lamingham drew himself up to full height and swapped the viola case to his left hand. 'Jews are scum. They poison our nation!' suddenly Lamingham's right arm sprang into the fascist salute. 'Hail Mosley – death to the Jews.'

David laughed. 'Come on Richard. We've heard all this a hundred times. Let's go.'

Mr Ross hailed a passing taxi and they piled aboard for the short trip to South Kensington. 'Won't be a taxi when you're with us,' said David. 'But it doesn't take long on the underground.' He paused. 'How do you come to know Lamingham?'

'I wish I didn't. But he was at choir school with me for a couple of terms. What is it that's biting him about you people?'

'Look, we're not religious Jews, our family that is. We do our best to mix in and be friendly with everyone. That Mosley character is a failed Labour Party politician, but he's decided to imitate Adolf Hitler and he's collected a following of Lamingham types who go around causing riots and daubing synagogues.'

'The Blackshirts, you mean. We've a couple of them in Chichester – walk up and down the street pushing out pamphlets – people laugh at them.'

The taxi drove through streets and avenues dodging the swarming traffic. Richard had never seen anything like it, although Goldstein, the London boy was indifferent. They arrived outside the Goldstein house in South Kensington. The building was a substantial Victorian design not unlike some he knew back home in Sussex.

David led them up the stone entry steps and pushed his latchkey into the front door lock. They went into a carpeted entry hall with a high ceiling and brightly lit through the windows. Now Richard knew this was a house of music. From somewhere within he could detect the high notes of a trumpet, while in an adjacent room came the trill of an operatic soprano accompanied by a piano.

David grinned and pointed towards the closed door. 'Mamma and my sister Naomi. Mother used to sing with the opera. Nam plays piano but she's really a flautist. '

'That's good,' said Richard. 'I can only do piano.'

David laughed. 'By all accounts you play it better than all of us put together. But Nam's a good improviser. She can do American jazz rather well.'

'Gosh, I'd love to try that, but I'm not sure Mr Ross here would approve.'

Now Ross laughed. 'Why ever not? I may seem an old fuddy-duddy, but even I try a little bit of jazz sometimes.'

'I feel hungry,' said David. 'It's lunchtime. I'll tell those two to stop the warbling and get us some grub.'

Richard was worried. He guessed this being a Jewish family there would be odd dietary rules; certainly no fried bacon.

David seemed perceptive. 'We're not strictly kosher here. We don't eat pork of course; that's strictly tradition, but I think you'll find Naomi's cooking is pretty tasty.'

The meal was served in a spacious dining room. It was an acceptable meal of fish soup followed by cold lamb and salad. Mrs Goldstein was a plump kindly lady who bustled around seeing to the comfort of her guests. Mr Goldstein was a tall, impressive man; an older version of his son. Richard tried not to keep staring at Naomi. She was the most beautiful girl he had ever met. She was slim, with hair as dark as her mother's, but with an elfin face, deep dark eyes, and red lipstick around her expressive mouth. This sophisticated Londoner was a million miles from the dumpy farm girls of his village.

'Now, Richard,' asked Mr Goldstein. 'When will you be joining us?'

'It'll be autumn term, sir. But I don't know if I've been accepted.'

'I think that is a formality. My conductor Mr Boult mentioned you and it seems many more are already well aware of you.'

Mr Ross spoke. 'My friend Daniel is playing a concert tonight with his orchestra. I am going with him, but I understand the rest of the family have plans.' He looked at Mrs Goldstein.

'We're all going to the Meyer's ball tonight and we would love Richard to come with us.' She smiled at him.

Richard felt his mouth drop open. The word ball was alien; he would be really out of his class. 'Thank you Ma'am.' There was nothing else he could say.

'That's good,' said David. 'We'll take you to Levy's and fit you out with a dinner suit.'

'Come on, Dyer,' said Mr Ross. 'If you are to move in this world you'll have to get used to the social side.'

'You can come and listen to my band another time,' said Mr Goldstein.

'Band?' Richard was puzzled.

'I'm a Yorkshire man by birth. Where I come from a collection of musicians is a band.'

'He means a bund, by gum.' laughed David.

The rest of the day went in a whirl. Richard was taken to an outfitter and attired in a dinner suit with a stiff shirt. They explained that it was a hired suit and would go back to the shop the next day. Richard felt less embarrassed by this outfit than he might have. After all, it was the same dress as worn by orchestral musicians. The ball was in a house in Park Lane belonging to a Jewish business family called Meyer.

'Our people don't qualify to hold balls in the London season.' David explained, 'but the Meyers hold an unofficial one and a lot of the same set come to it. Tell you something else. They've hired Joe Loss and his band. I've never heard them, although they've been around the circuit and on the wireless. Naomi says they're good.'

Richard boarded the taxi with David, his delightful sister and Mrs Goldstein. The house in Park Lane looked modest compared with its neighbours until one went inside. It seemed cavernous with room after room opening into a vast ballroom. David began to point our numerous well-known society members although the names meant little to Richard. All ages were present both dowagers and younger family members.

'That thin looking cove,' David pointed. 'That's Viscount Petersfield, he's heir to the Dukedom of Hampshire.'

'Petersfield? That's not far from where I live.'

'It's only a title. Their estate is in Shropshire.'

'I thought you said Hampshire?'

'That's the title,' David laughed. 'I don't suppose they ever go near the place.'

'I think I follow you. I come from Sussex, but the Duke of Norfolk lives near our village. Frankly I'm only a farm boy. I don't go in much for lords although my old Dad is an awful snob. Deferential's the word.'

Richard found himself staring at the girl with Lord Petersfield. The lord was a skinny-looking man with receding hair although he didn't look that old. The girl with him didn't seem over-enamoured but she was striking. She stood some twenty feet away and there was something familiar about her pose. She had her back to them but he could see her hair was fashioned in the modern short bob and she was dressed in one of those blue fashionable and daring, off the shoulder dresses, with no straps. Her trim white shoulders gleamed in the overhead lights. Then she turned and of course he knew her: Maria. He saw her gasp and then her face lit in a smile. Now she tripped across to him on her fashion high-heels.

'Dickie, how did you get here and, oh my, you look so handsome in that suit.'

'I went for interview at the Music Academy and my friends invited me here.'

'So, you're going to study at the academy?'

'If they'll have me. I won't know for a week or so.'

Maria turned to David and Naomi, 'I'm sorry it was rude of me. I'm Maria Tenbury. Richard and I are neighbours in Sussex. Are you musicians too?'

Richard quickly made the introductions that he should have done at once. There were social graces that he must learn. Maria's young man had stalked across to them He looked less than pleased.

'Richard, this is John Petersfield. Johnny, this is Richard Dyer who is going to be a world famous musician.'

The man's handshake was weak. 'I say; how d'you do and all that.' He was clearly suspicious.

Richard found his tact at last. 'Miss Tenbury is a neighbour of ours in Sussex. I wasn't expecting to see her.' Maria looked entrancing but he wasn't going to spoil her chances in the marriage market. Surely there must be more impressive lords around. This man had definite lack of a chin and he had pop eyes. As she turned away with her escort she smiled and winked.

A smartly-dressed butler was standing on the ballroom stage. 'Ladies and gentlemen – refreshments are served.'

Slowly the assembled crowd moved into a further large room. The air was deliciously scented. Richard saw two rectangular tables loaded with food. This was not the sort of tea and buns refreshments at the village fete. This was a quality spread and he was not sure what everything was. As they proceeded into the room the servants were holding trays laden with tall thin glasses. Richard took one and sniffed the contents. 'It's champagne,' David explained. Richard took a sip and grimaced; it was sparkling but tasted like bitter cider. They collected floral pattern plates and began to "tuck in" as David put it. Richard couldn't make out much of the food on offer but it tasted good although it seemed a bit fussy. He tried little pastry things called volovontes, or some such word, and tiny sandwiches with obscure fillings. He would have preferred bacon fillings but in this house it was taboo. Then he had a second glass of champagne and this time rather enjoyed it. The whole party still baffled him but he supposed this would be part of a successful musician's life.

They could hear music pounding away in the ball room. Yes, this was the real Joe Loss band playing their signature tune *In The Mood.* He had to see and hear this. Naomi was beckoning them from the far doorway. She really was the most attractive girl. Was she as attractive as Maria? Well, seeing the two girls in the same room it was hard to choose. The stage was filled with the band, and the music flowed over the company who had now begun to dance. Richard knew that this Mr Loss was a music academy graduate and a classically trained musician and it showed in the quality of his orchestra. David and his sister were already dancing what he understood to be something called a quick-step.

Well, dancing was another mystery of these superior people. He sat on a chair and found himself tapping a foot to the rhythm. He noted with unaccustomed sadism that Johnny Petersfield was not much better at dancing than he would have been. The man was jerking around the floor in an uncoordinated semi-shuffle. Maria appeared to be lecturing him. Richard pulled himself together. Maria was still a friend but jealousy would not do. She had a duty to perform to her family and her upbringing.

Luckily, nobody expected him to dance and he was not going to ask Naomi and then make a fool of himself. He enjoyed the music and the singing by a stylish over made-up girl who sang an intriguing song called *Begin the Beguine;* the beguine he assumed to be another high-class dance. And so it went on for at least four hours. He missed some of the action while he went on a long search for a lavatory, and he found a number of fellow male guests on the same trail.

At midnight the band played the final waltz and the company began to look for their coats. Then the butler emerged on the stage. 'Ladies and gentlemen I regret to tell you that a gathering of undesirables are causing a disturbance in the street. You may care to leave by the rear exit.'

David Goldstein spoke. 'Richard, I want to see this.' While many of the company were being directed to the rear, David led towards the front entrance. The street was brightly lit and filled with one hundred or more; an all-male crowd of weedy youths and young boys throwing the stiff arm salute and chanting:

Yids – yids – we gotta get rid of – der yids-yids – we gotta get rid of der yids

Then Richard heard the singing led by a good clear tenor voice.

'One land, one race, one leader...'

The rest of the words were lost as the rabble joined in. Now Richard recognized the lead singer. It was Lamingham. He was not surprised. Afterwards he couldn't say what it was that drove him down the front steps and across to the mob. For the first time in his life he felt a red mist of rage. It was an emotion that was to grip him a few years later in war combat. He reached Lamingham, seized the man and twisted his left arm until he fell to his knees.

'Why are you with these Jews,' Lamingham gasped. 'You're English, fair hair, blue eyes – you're a decent Aryan.'

'Look, Lamingham, you get this rabble to go or I'll break your left arm and you won't play that nasty little viola for a while.'

'The police are on the way,' it was David speaking.

'Nonsense,' gasped Lamingham. 'They like us, they support us.'

Richard began to feel the mob closing in around him. The eldest was no older than himself. Many were little more than boys and they seemed unsure now that their leader was being so humiliated.

A fresh voice had joined in. 'You people, you are debasing any cause you may hold.' Richard was almost stunned. It was Maria, but not the same Maria, the little girl in the village. This was a voice of a mature woman of authority and breeding. 'Richard, release that man.' She stood over them as he obeyed and Lamingham staggered sheepishly to his feet as Maria stared him in the face. 'You are behaving disgracefully and in an unpatriotic and un-British way. We settle these matters by law and democratic rule.'

Richard could hardly believe he was seeing this. Maria was transformed, she was seemingly charged with some power beyond the capacity of any seventeen-year-old girl.

'Now, I won't say this twice.' The voice rasped. 'All of you – go home!'

The young mob hesitated, paused for a few seconds; looking uncertainly towards the house. In the street in front of the door there stood a line of silent menacing men. In the centre was Colonel Meyer, the master of the house carrying a twelve bore shotgun. The male servants were some that Richard had observed earlier. They were silent and surly and carried heavy wooden clubs. Maria stood directing an icy stare at Lamingham. Slowly Colonel Meyer raised his gun and pointed it at Lamingham's head.

The fascist gestured to his mob. 'About turn, men. We'll deal with these scum when we march.' Slowly the youths slunk away, muttering defiantly.

Colonel Meyer smiled and broke open his shotgun. Richard saw that the barrels were empty.

Suddenly Maria folded and flung her arms around Richard sobbing into his chest. 'Oh Dickie, you are wonderful.' She looked up and began to smother his face with kisses. 'Dickie you are wonderful. I love you.'

He smiled down at her. 'Come on, this is a hired suit and you're making it all wet. Maria, it was you who saved the day. You're the most amazing girl and,' he whispered, 'I love you too, but what about your friend in there?'

The tears had dried. 'Oh, Johnny. Yes, I'll do my duty with him; but it won't affect us and never will.'

CHAPTER 15

Autumn 1936

The letter arrived in early August.

Dear Mr Dyer,

The Royal Academy of Music are pleased to inform you that you have won a place for the Autumn term commencing 4th September. You will study and play pianoforte.

So the Laminghams had failed in their attempt to block his entry. The letter went on to list the things he should bring with him.

It had been a happy interlude back home again. Richard had reconnected with old friends and even given a hand with the harvest. It was then that he found how much his soft lifestyle had affected him. To his delight he found he was in demand as a pianist. He performed another six recitals in different halls and Mr Ross had arranged for him to be paid a fee. After one performance in Horsham he was paid two pounds. Not that he could spend any of this money. Mr Ross had placed it all in a Post Office savings account to be accessed later. He understood that the balance now stood at twelve pounds. That was useful money for a young man in those years.

His repertoire at these recitals was varied within the twenty minutes he was usually given. He played popular Mozart pieces among other short classical preludes. Later, he would improvise his own versions of *Teddy Bear's Picnic* and *In the Mood.* Even though village hall audiences were traditional and staid they always applauded everything with enthusiasm. At that point Richard did not really appreciate that he was their own "Sussex lad"; already a source of pride.

He returned to his village home one evening to hear the sound of an accordion. His father had brought out the instrument and was playing a jolly little jig.

'Boy, you're not the only music man in the family. You've made me dig out this'un after twenty years.'

'You're pa used to play it all the time,' said Mabel. 'Before the war and in the Army, but this is the first time he's tried it again.'

'They want me to play for the Morris men on the green. You're not going to be one up on me, boy.'

Richard laughed. 'So, there is music talent in all the family.'

'Me too,' called a little voice. His sister Alice ran into the room holding a little wooden recorder and at once proceeded to trill a version of: *Early one morning.*

'So, I've got competition,' Richard bent down and kissed Alice on the tip of her blonde locks.

'Me get your room,' Alice squeaked.

'Hope that's all right,' said Mabel. 'She's been sleeping in her cot in our room, but now you're off to the college...'

'I suppose so; times are changing.' Richard suddenly realized he was a grownup and from now on his life lay away from here.

This time Richard returned to London on his own without the support of Mr Ross. He found the adventure easy, even to remembering the correct underground route. He was to find that this autumn he was entering a London about to be in turmoil from two dramatic events.

David Goldstein had lost some of his blasé attitude to the political scene. 'My cousin's been given the sack,' he told Richard one day.

'What's he done?'

'Nothing. He worked at the Palace and the new man loves bloody Adolf and conversely doesn't like our kind.'

'The Palace – you can't mean the King?'

'That is exactly who do I mean. Nasty little bugger.'

'David, you can't say that about the King.'

'I can and I will. You wait and see. My cousin says he's taken up with an unacceptable woman. With a bit of luck that'll scupper the anti-Semitic little sod.'

Richard was happy in his studies, happier than he had ever been before. He liked his tutor. He was a man only a few years older, talented and not in the least stuffy. Richard's piano style was improving by the day and he was venturing into advanced composers like Rachmaninov and in contrast some elaborate jazz improvisation. In his spare time he was beginning to compose. Those melodies that had flowed into his head as he walked on Pockhampton Down he began to grow into concerto pieces for orchestral accompaniment. At the moment he kept these secret and did not show them to anyone.

The wretched Lamingham was still at the academy. The two men kept away from each other. Richard hoped that Lamingham might do something outrageous and get himself expelled. The college had banned the man from wearing his black shirt on the premises and Lamingham, although he had taken the order in bad grace, had complied. Richard, whose interest in politics was minimal, gathered that Lamingham was boasting that some big move by the Mosley people was due in London very soon.

It wasn't all work and study. Richard had joined a sailing club at Ranelagh on the Thames. He had started to crew in an International 14 class dinghy and had enjoyed his first experience of a capsize. And he had started to dance, with hesitation at first but soon he found the rhythms and steps fitted well with his music. He was becoming increasingly fond of Naomi, David's sister and had twice taken her out to the nearby dance hall where he had made a reasonable start with dancing. Naomi was beautiful and intelligent, but he knew deep down she was not for him. Naomi, exactly like Maria, was already committed to her own kind.

Richard tried to avoid Lamingham but this time he failed. He saw Lamingham approaching along the pavement near the Academy. Richard checked for traffic and then crossed the street. Lamingham had seen him and followed. 'Yes, yokel, this Sunday's it – Der Tag. You cringing swine and your yid friends are for it.'

Richard replied. 'I heard you say it. Der Tag, that's German. Show's who your real leader is.'

Lamingham bristled. 'Don't you insult Adolf Hitler. He will cleanse all Europe of Jewish corruption and our leader will do the same here. As I say, it starts this Sunday.' His right arm stiffened in salute. 'Hail Mosley!'

Richard laughed in as irritating a way as possible. 'What's so special about this Sunday?'

'We're on the march. Five thousand of us. We're purging the Jewish quarters and the police, our allies, are with us.'

'That sounds unlikely to me.'

'No, this time the police are with us. They are going to clear the way of reds and yids and then we shall march.'

Richard told the Goldstein family of Lamingham's boasts and was inclined to think them funny. He was soon put right by the grim expressions of his listeners.

'No, Richard,' said David's father. 'It's true. The Fascists are quite open about it. They're going to march through the Jewish quarters in the East End.'

'What about the police?'

'Yes, it's true there is a lot of anti-semitism in the Metropolitan Police. But to be fair this time they're caught in a bit of trap. They are supposed to keep the streets clear and our people are going to block this march. There is going to be big trouble, but we can't let Mosley and his thugs win.'

'I'd like to see this,' said Richard.

'I'm going,' said David. 'Naomi and I are going to watch from an upstairs window.'

'That's in my cousin's house,' said Mrs Goldstein. 'That's Rabbi Greening. Yes, you two can watch but don't go down in the streets and get involved.'

They started early on Sunday. Richard, with David and Naomi reached Shadwell underground station at around nine. Richard was startled to see the number of police already gathered in the streets. Many were drawn up in military formation and one mounted unit was standing by. They had walked only a few yards when they were challenged by two police officers.

'You three. Where d'you think you're going?'

'We're visiting a house just round the corner.' David pointed.

'Names,' said the officer.

David told him

'Thought so. You're Jews. Come to cause trouble have you?'

'I told you. I've come to visit my cousin – Rabbi Greening. We may see something going on but we're not involved.'

'Rabbi is it? Thought you lot prayed yesterday.'

David sighed. 'That's why we have to come today. Can't go anywhere on the Sabbath.'

The policeman grunted and turned to Richard. 'You don't look like a Jew to me. Reckon you could be a communist, a red.'

'You're joking aren't you? I come from Sussex. My mum and dada vote Tory.'

'All right, I've got your names. If we see you on the street then we'll arrest you.'

They walked the twenty yards to their destination. 'That was pretty high-handed,' said Richard. 'Are they always like that?'

'Well anti-Semitism is in their culture, but this time those two looked nervous.'

The Rabbi's house was in a long drab terrace of two floor dwellings. Richard remembered the vicarage back home in Pockhampton: sumptuous and Georgian. Rabbi Greening was a younger man than Richard expected. He wore a black cap and had a bushy beard. 'Come on in,' he greeted them. 'This is a grim day, but I believe we shall win.' He introduced them to his wife and two small dark-eyed children who stared at Richard with undisguised puzzlement.

'Mr Dyer is going to be a famous musician,' Mrs Greening explained. 'And he's a friend of David and Naomi and our people.'

'I'm so sorry,' she whispered, 'but the young ones think every English Christian hates us.'

'No,' Richard was emphatic. 'I'm not a Londoner, but where I come from there's no support whatever for these blackshirts.'

'I don't suppose you've had breakfast?' asked the Rabbi.

'Only a cup of coffee,' David replied.

'Rebecca, breakfast for David and Naomi and their friend,' ordered the Rabbi. Richard was used to the male-dominated world but this sounded like a military command.

David grinned. 'This house is really kosher, but I expect there'll be something tasty.'

By mid-morning a change had come over the household. Rabbi Greening had fitted a heavy cast iron grille to the inside of the front door attached with bolts already fixed in the wall. The whole family began to reinforce this with sandbags. Heavy curtains had been drawn across the downstairs windows that had already been covered with sticky parcel tape.

'Mosley's thugs will already have marked us as a Rabbi's house,' David explained. 'Let's go upstairs and see what's happening in the street.'

For the last half hour they had been conscious of distant rumbling sound that Richard thought sounded like a football crowd. From the upstairs window he saw a sight he couldn't have predicted. The Police had lined across the street, and facing them fifty yards away, was a huge civilian crowd. It was these who were chanting in unison. Most of the assembly seemed poor working people, both men and women. But Richard could make out a smattering of better-dressed middle-class demonstrators. He couldn't quite make out the rhythmic chant.

'Nil passéran,' David explained. 'They shall not pass.'

'Looks like a confrontation's building, but where are the blackshirts?'

David pointed up the street to the right. 'As I understand, they'll be coming down our road from that direction and the police are committed to clearing the demonstrators out of the way.'

Richard leant forward to the window. The crowd had grown in the last ten minutes a solid block going all the way to the far junction. 'Not a chance I'd say. If that lot sit down the police will never shift them.'

'Well, it's started now,' said David. 'Come on you workers – smash'em!'

Richard was startled. He had been brought up to respect the police but David had a gleam in his eye and Richard saw his friend change in that moment into a very different man. The police, both foot and mounted, were on the move towards the anti-fascists and the latter were responding by surging towards them. The police walked into a hail of stones and bottles. They paused briefly as the crowd closed to within a foot or so and then they responded. Wooden truncheons were drawn and wielded without a thought to the consequences. Within seconds Richard could see heads bleeding and arms broken. The crowd shrank back and the police ranks opened to let through a mounted charge. The horses thundered into the mass of people, rearing up and crashing down as their riders wielded batons. As the wounded staggered aside, the crowd's ranks closed and surged again. There were loud screams from the nearby houses and Richard saw chamber pots being hurled down on the luckless policemen. These, and of course their contents, seemed to be more effective weapons than the bottles and stones.

'I've gotta' get out there and fight,' David yelled.

'No!' his sister screamed. 'You'll get hurt.'

Richard was alarmed. 'No, you promised your mother and father. Don't be a damn fool.'

'I've gotta go out there.' David had a twisted expression almost as if he was going to cry.

Richard physically grabbed the man and forced him into a chair. 'David, David. Listen to me. You are a professional musician. If your arms are broken out there you may never play again.'

'All right, I know.' David was breathing heavily. 'I'll do as father tells me.'

A relieved Naomi knelt against her brother and wept.

They watched as the battle below raged. The police had the advantage in discipline and weaponry; the crowd had the advantage in numbers. The fight surged back and forth up and down the street but the police failed to clear a way and there was still no sign of the Blackshirts. Finally a police vehicle appeared with a huge trumpet-like instrument on its roof. It hummed and then issued a series of announcements. Richard caught the word “abandoned”. The crowd were stilled but stood where they were. The police made no further moves against them. Rabbi Greening had appeared in the room.

‘The police say that Mosley has abandoned his march, but I think our people do not wholly believe it.’

Richard could see both sides standing motionless while each ones’ wounded were attended to. Then suddenly the police closed ranks turned about and marched away. A mighty cheer rang around the streets. The enemy had not passed.

CHAPTER 16

Lamingham was still studying in the academy but both David and Richard went to lengths to avoid him. By all accounts the man was surly and disgruntled by his leader's humiliation. Richard was making progress with his piano studies to the point where his tutor had nominated him to perform at the academy's concert.

He met Maria again at Pockhampton on a weekend at home. It was Maria who had some disconcerting news, not this time about her, but about a sensation in the wider world of which the public at large knew nothing. 'It's the King,' she said. 'They've kept this out of the papers, but they say he's trying to marry an unsuitable woman and the government won't let it happen.'

Like most people not in the know, this was news to Richard. 'My friends the Goldsteins don't like the King, they say he admires Hitler and he's thick with Mosley.'

'Yes, I've heard that too.'

'Maria, are you sure you've got this straight?'

'No, Dickie it's true. Johnny says it's common knowledge in society.'

'Who's this woman you mentioned?'

'She's a Mrs Simpson. She's American.'

Richard was not impressed. 'Is that so bad? I mean that lot have been marrying each other for years. An American might bring in some fresh blood.'

'No, you see she's been married and divorced twice and both your church and my church won't allow divorce.'

Back in London it seemed David had heard the same rumours. 'This could be the best thing that's happened. The little sod will have to go.'

'Steady on, old chap,' Richard was shocked. 'I know you don't like him but he is the king.'

'But it's true. Your lady friend gets her gossip from high society. We get ours from inside politics. The man's turning stubborn, but he's got no support except Mosley and, for some reason, Churchill's supporting the King. Well, he shouldn't. He's one of the few that see Hitler for what he is, so he should be with us.'

'What do you think will happen?'

'Well, we hope the little swine'll dig in his heels and marry the woman. If that happens he'll have to go.'

'David, I still don't like this. I mean is that the end of it? Will there be another king?'

'Yes, his younger brother will take over. He's a decent chap, not over bright but his wife keeps him in order and they've got a couple of sweet little girls, so the succession is there.'

Richard spent many happy evenings scoring his own unperformed work and also variations of famous themes, and what he believed to be improvements to some of the popular dance band tunes of the moment. It was Naomi this time that gave him the idea.

'Dickie, Daddy met Harry Malburg the other day…'

'What, the band leader?'

'Yes, that's him. He's looking for a bright young lad to score music for him. Says he'll pay you well.'

Richard knew that Malburg was another gifted musician, but he'd heard that the man was self-taught.

'Yes, that'd be rather fun. How can I meet him?'

' Daddy can fix that. You are interested?'

'Rather.'

'Very well,' said the piano tutor. 'Rachmaninov Three and you say you can play that in concert with full orchestral accompaniment?'

'Yes,' Richard replied. 'I'll need to work hard on it, but I can do it. I want to do it. If I don't set targets I won't succeed.'

'If you make a mess, my reputation will suffer as well. However, at a risk of making you conceited, you are the best prospect I've taught since I came here. So yes, go away and practice Rachmaninov, then come back to me and prove it.'

Richard left his tutor's room humming part of the Rachmaninov refrain.

In the entry hall he saw a brightly-coloured poster on the notice board that hadn't been there earlier. It showed a Royal Air Force roundel. Richard walked across and read it and as he did so his pulse began to race.

LONDON UNIVERSITY AIR SQUADRDON.

Potential flying training recruits are invited to attend Northholt Aerodrome on Saturday November 16th.

Richard noted the times. He understood he would need to attend a medical examination and to bring his school certificate with him.

'Dick, if war comes you'll be committing yourself,' David was doubtful.

'I don't care. I've always wanted to fly and anyway it's a cleaner warfare in the air. I'd sooner be there than in some trenches.'

'I know, up to my neck in the trenches. That's where I'll be.'

Richard knew his friend expected war – maybe almost hoped for it. But David had a real cause; to defend his people from Hitler's hate.

'Another thing,' Richard added. 'My old Dad was in the trenches in the last war and he's never recovered; still can't talk about it.'

Richard arrived at Northholt on the appointed hour and was directed to a drab redbrick single-storey building. Inside were gathered six other hopeful student fliers. He reported to the desk and handed in his academic papers. Shortly after that a bulky man in an RAF sergeant's uniform appeared. 'Doctor's 'ere. So, all o' you take off all your clothes except yer jacket and trousers.'

Richard exchanged embarrassed grins with his fellows but all complied. One by one they were summoned into the next room. Then it was his turn. The doctor was a cheerful middle-aged man in a spotless white coat. On request Richard handed the rest of his clothing to the sergeant and found himself naked and very self-conscious.

The doctor looked mildly bored but was thorough. Richard had his heart listened to, his blood pressure taken, his reflexes tested, he coughed on command and then was told to read a multi-lettered and numbered card pinned on the far wall. As with the other candidates the ordeal was over in little more than ten minutes. They put their clothes back on and were given a series of bizarre tests such as blowing into rubber tubes attached to columns of mercury. Richard was told that the tests were to check his lung capacity. Lastly he was asked to raise a metal rod balanced on a ruler to shoulder height and back again. These seemed more like party games than a medical examination.

Then they were all marched to another office where an RAF wing commander conducted interviews with each in turn.

'It seems you are a musician,' the wing commander sounded less than impressed. 'Why on earth would you want to fly?'

'Sir, I've always wanted to fly.' He thought rapidly. 'I've done a bit of dual control, with Major Bell in his Moth.' Not exactly a lie but a mite exaggerated. 'I just love flying and I think I would do it well.'

'If war comes, and it may, you will be a Royal Air Force Reservist and you will be called up to fight. As you are a musician how would you take to service discipline?'

'Just the same as everyone else, sir. I learned discipline at home from my father. He fought in the last war.'

The wing commander gave his long stare and then nodded. 'Send the next one in.'

Richard obeyed and wondered how he had done. He was told he would be informed of the result by letter within a month. 'Reckon you did all right, boy,' the sergeant had muttered to him on his way out.

Richard returned to the South Kensington house. He felt pleased with the world. Everything he had ever hoped for was coming together. But could it last?

David met him indoors and took him into the family sitting room. Standing there was a little man in smart blue suit and a striking red bowtie. 'Richard, meet Harry Malburg.'

'Pleased to meet yer, young feller. I've 'eard lots about you.' Richard shook hands. Harry was every inch the East End Cockney made good. 'I've 'eard you can do a bit o' orchestrating, you know, scores on paper like.'

'Of course, that's what we learn at college.'

'Let's see you then.' Harry handed him a blank sheet of lined score paper and a propelling pencil. The man sat down at the piano and began to play a syncopated melody: treble clef and bass. Richard had by now cottoned on. He grabbed a chair and sat down at a nearby table. It seemed that this was a day of tests. He listened to the music and then scored the two parts on the paper.

Harry picked up the paper and stared at it. 'That's good. That's very good. You see, I make music but I don't write it that well. If you would come in with me on this I'll pay you. Pay you well if the results are good.' The East End twang was still there, but the man was speaking without the dislocated vowels. It was clear that this Harry was a showman.

'Right, now I'll play this next number once. Then I'll go away and let you score by memory. Maybe you'll improve it,' Harry laughed and played another short piece.

Harry Malburg clapped Richard on the back and bustled away cheerfully. Richard turned to see his friend staring at him in astonishment. 'Scoring a strange piece by memory? Can you really do that?'

Richard laughed. 'Why not, Mozart did it all the time.'

David joined in the laughter. 'Mozart? Someone around here is developing a bit of a swollen head.'

The Academy's concert was due for late January. Richard had satisfied both his tutor and the college authorities that he was competent to play the Rachmaninov Three. This was a piece that would challenge a long experienced performer let alone a seventeen-year-old student. The composer had permitted several cuts in the more complicated second and third movements. Richard had tried both versions and had come down on the side of a full performance with no cuts. Both his tutor and the group of professors had been very dubious, but after Richard had played they were all smiles. Then he had a talk with the American conductor for the night.

'Your performance is second on the bill just before the interval, OK? Now this is your show. Me and the boys are your accompany-ment. So don't let any asshole push you around. You do it your way and we'll follow.'

Richard couldn't help smiling. This Yank really was a breath of fresh air compared to the staid college professors. In contrast he was beginning to revel in his work for Harry Malburg. The Tenburys paid the balance of Richard's college fees plus his board and lodging, but he felt a lack of pocket money. All he had for this were his concert earnings back home in Sussex. Harry's payments had changed that with a vengeance. Richard would meet the band and its leader two evenings a week and would work with them on a score. Then he would go home and do a fair copy for Harry to make photographed copies for the band. Richard was able to make several embellishments to some of the original themes and Harry had been delighted. Then Richard had started writing his own dance tunes and Harry had been happy to use them.

The news plastered in every headline and all the billboards was about the King and his possible marriage. This had brought the surly Lamingham out of his shell. The idiot had taken to standing in the street with a huge sandwich board demanding *Save our King*. His school bully attitude was back and he was prone to corner the weaker members of the college and force them to sing *God save the King*. Richard understood that the government had now banned the wearing of military-style uniforms by political groups. This had badly affected the morale of the Mosleyites much to the pleasure of the Goldstein household. Then on that December the eleventh they had sat around the wireless and heard King Edward's abdication address to the nation. David and Esther Goldstein had broken open the champagne that they had kept on ice.

CHAPTER 17

One day while sitting in the academy's common room Richard started to browse the current number of Country Life and almost immediately he was in for a shock. There was a portrait of a young lady in the traditional girls in pearls spot, and she was Maria.

Maria Tenbury, only daughter of Mr and Mrs Tenbury of Pockhampton Manor in Sussex.

He was stunned by how beautiful she looked; so very far away from the cheeky little schoolgirl of his youth. He suddenly realized how fond he was of this girl. He remembered her beauty at the ball and her demolition of the Mosley rabble. He remembered that she had told him "I love you". Perhaps he really loved her too, but Maria was destined to marry into an aristocratic family – to put it crudely, to become a breeding machine. She was not and never could be for him.

The Academy orchestra's concert would take place in Queen's Hall not far from the BBC building. Richard had been there for two concerts as a listener but this time he would be playing to a potential audience of a thousand. A week before the event the orchestra had assembled in the empty hall for a run through of their programme. He was excited, and of course nervous. He only wished that Lamingham had not been present playing in the viola section. The man was a competent musician even if his views on music were as warped as his views on race and life.

'Rachmaninov is a bloody Slav,' Lamingham had hissed.

Richard had laughed. 'Perhaps we'd better do some Mendelssohn.'

'Excellent idea,' said David who had arrived on stage with his oboe. 'Finest music in the repertoire.'

Lamingham had snarled and walked away.

Richard felt nervous and he knew he should feel nervous. The finest performers in the world felt nervous before going on stage. But it was strange that as soon as he sat down and laid his fingers on the piano keys the fear vanished and he was in a world of his own alone with the music. This time of course he was playing a concerto in partnership with the orchestra. Whatever the conductor had told him he knew he needed to blend in with the others and to watch the conductor's baton.

The rehearsal run through was certainly hard work but he enjoyed it. Richard had played solo to audiences but working with an orchestra was so very different. That was the problem – not the piano technique. During a break the American had pulled him aside. 'Second movement, with the long intro before you come in; you hesitated waiting for me to wag my goddam stick and I was waiting for you, boy. You nearly put the brakes on the whole wagon. Remember what I said; it's your show.'

He was relieved that Lamingham made no further intervention. The man took his place with the other players and performed faultlessly. Richard had to admit that Lamingham was a good musician even if he was mildly insane. If the man would only curb his insanity then he might too become a soloist.

The following day the letter came. On Saturday Richard was told to report to Northolt airfield for initial pre-flight training. Reaching the airfield was less of a problem this time. He had arranged to take a lift with a fellow student, a London science undergraduate with a very battered Austin Seven. They arrived to be joined by eight other potential recruits. The instructor summoned them into a small lecture hall. Before commencing their flying they were told they would be required to take part in some ground exercises.

They were all issued with a hefty manual for which they were required to pay ten shillings. To Richard and most of the others this seemed exorbitant but he paid up. The ground exercises consisted of aerodynamic theory, navigation and, for some reason, Morse code. The instructor had a battery linked to a buzzer that was almost musical. Some of his fellows struggled but Richard found assembling strings of dahs and dits into words not unlike scoring music. In the lunch break everyone grumbled about the Morse and wondered what it had to do with modern warfare. Richard remembered Mr Tenbury telling him how in the war he had ranged artillery barrages from the air directing the guns with Morse. Surely by now spoken radio would have removed this antiquated method. By the end of the day everyone was satiated with wing lift, vector triangles and the aforesaid Morse. They all longed for the day when they would climb aboard an aircraft and fly for real.

January the tenth was Richard's seventeenth birthday and he was allowed to obtain a break from college and take the train home to

Sussex. Seventeen, yes he was seventeen. Old enough to take his driving test, old enough to take the controls of an aircraft and, amazingly, old enough to perform one of the most demanding piano concertos. Life wasn't bad, old boy, he grinned. Then he saw at least two of the other passengers in the compartment were looking at him in an odd way. He hastily stared out of the window at the passing scene. After changing trains in Portsmouth he reached the nearest station to Pockhampton, no more than a country halt. Having arrived there he walked the last two miles. That would have been a short stroll in his schooldays but now his London life had made it a tiring ordeal.

Arriving home it was almost as if he'd never been away. To his mother and father he was still their small boy even if he had run away to the dark city.

'Mr and Mrs Tenbury are doing something for your birthday,' said his mother. 'We was baking your cake in the kitchen.'

'Mrs is going to fetch you in the morning,' said his father.

'Their Maria has been asking about you,' said Mother. 'What a beautiful young lady she's become. End of this year when she's eighteen she's getting engaged to be married.'

Richard tried not to let this news upset him. He had told himself so a hundred times. Maria was a friend but not a wife for him; wrong birth, wrong religion, wrong lots of things. Little Alice had run to greet him and had seized him by the hand and led him to see the little garden patch she had made. The day was cold and raw but a few daffodil heads were showing. 'You'll grow lovely flowers come the summer,' he said. She really was a pretty little thing and in a few years time would certainly turn heads.

Alice had long ago taken possession of his old room. 'I'd like to eat here,' he told his mother. 'But tonight I'll put up at the pub.'

'No need,' she smiled. 'You're honoured. 'Mrs Tenbury wants you to stay with them at the Manor. But don't tell your father.'

Richard laughed. 'I know, he's still all "keep us in our proper stations".'

'Yes, he'll never change, so this time it's a little white lie. He thinks you'll be at the pub.'

'He won't see me there if he goes for a pint.'

'Leave that to me.'

Richard greeted his father while Mabel fussed around her son as if he was still an eight-year-old. The Pockhampton Dyer family didn't really go in for eating lunch; breakfast and two-course afternoon tea were the meals of the day. It was past midday so Richard's mother cooked him a huge late breakfast. After weeks in the Goldstein house it was a joy to sit down to fried bacon and eggs. The morning was cold with a white frost and a light crust of snow on the summit of the Downs. Richard went to search the outbuildings for his bicycle. He found it and wheeled the machine into the yard just as a car drove in. It was another boxy little black Austin Seven, but shiny and new; and the person behind the wheel was Maria.

'Hey, where did you get that motor?' he greeted her.

'It's mother's shopping car. Ganton hates it.'

'Have you passed the driving test?'

'I'm practicing for it. But I can't go into the towns without an adult who's passed.'

'I've a friend who's got the same, but it's not as smart as yours.' Now he laughed. 'You may be learning to drive but I'm learning to fly.' He explained.

Maria gasped. 'Oh you are lucky. But won't it be dangerous?'

His mother had asked the same question. Now he had to reassure Maria. And the girl looked more beautiful than ever. She was dressed for a winter morning in Sussex enveloped in a heavy coat with riding boots and a woolly hat, but her face was filled with such an enticing smile. Once again he told himself; Maria was destined for another. She was not for him.

'Come on,' she said. 'Grab your things and then hop aboard.'

'I was going on my bike.'

'No need, I'll drive you.'

He went indoors and told his mother and then collected his overnight bag.

'I suppose that young lady is safe,' his mother scowled.

'I'll soon find out.' He kissed her and left. What did his mother mean by "safe"? He wasn't sure she was talking about driving.

Maria's driving was a mix of extreme caution around corners and foot to the floor acceleration on the straight sections. In no time it seemed they had entered the long avenue leading to Pockhampton Manor. Maria slammed on her brakes and the little car skidded the last few feet on the gravel by the front door. 'Come on,' she said. 'Let's get indoors in the warm.'

He picked up his bag and followed her through the front door. The house was quiet apart from the whine of an electric Hoover not far away. 'Come on,' said Maria. 'I'll show you to your room.'

Richard followed her up the grand staircase and along the passage past Mr Tenbury's study. 'Father's in London for an Air Force reunion,' said Maria.

They turned a corner and now they were in a corridor. Maria opened a door and led him inside. It was a large room with a single bed, a wardrobe and an ornate washstand.

'There you are,' she said. 'Our best gentleman's guest room and I promise it's not haunted.'

'I'll hold you to that,' he laughed.

'Next door on the left is the bathroom or you can use Father's shower bath as he's away.'

'No, a hot bath before bed will be fine.'

'Did I ever show you the nursery?'

Richard shook his head. 'No, this is only the second time I've been upstairs in your house.'

'Come on then. I want to get rid of this coat anyway.'

He followed Maria back along the corridor and around the balustrade that overlooked the entrance hall. Maria led along a further corridor and into a large room in the corner of the house with square Georgian style windows. This was a very different room compared with the rest of the house with a well-worn carpet on the floor and a battered leather sofa. There were pictures on the walls, some religious and others with nursery rhyme themes. She pulled off the overcoat and threw it across a chair. Richard was struck by her beauty. Under the winter coat she wore a short dress of a high-fashion that defined her shapely body.

'They've taken out most of the furniture from here,' she said. 'When Leo was a little boy he had a model railway all round the room.'

'How is your brother?'

'He's hoping they'll give him his own parish. Poor Leo, I had a silly row with him and I wish I hadn't. I upset Mummy as well.'

'What was that about? I mean I don't want to pry where I'm not wanted.'

'No, I'd like you opinion. You'll never believe this, but it was about politics.'

Richard was puzzled now. 'I don't really have strong views. I hate Mosley but the political parties don't inspire me much. We don't get votes, neither of us, for a few years yet. Anyway you were telling me about your row.'

'It's this war that's going on in Spain. The Army there and that man who wants to be a dictator.'

'I know, Franco. My friend David Goldstein gets really worked up when you mention him.'

'Well, I hate what's going on there. They have a democratically elected parliament, all right it's a bit socialistic but that's what the people choose. But it seems these generals are killing people; not just men but women and small children.'

'I know David's been following it. But why your quarrel?'

'It's the Catholic Church. They are all behind this Franco. They can't see that the man's a monster. Leo can't see it. He says the Pope loves Franco and so must we all or we're not true Christians. I told Leo outright, he's blinkered – can't think for himself.'

'Now when he visits he won't speak to me; or not until I confess my evil thoughts.'

Richard was baffled. Maria was talking about a world he could never understand.

'My friend David's Jewish but I don't think his religion is like that.'

They were sitting on the well-worn sofa. 'Dickie, is there going to be another war?'

'David says it's a certainty. But let's hope not. It'll mess up my musical career.'

'Will you be flying?'

'If it comes to that, yes.'

'You've met Johnny, you know – at that ball in London.'

'Yes, if that's the one you were with the night you destroyed that oaf Lamingham and his Blackshirts.'

'Dickie, you sound a bit jealous. Look there's no need. I'm doing a duty by my upbringing, but there's only one love in my life and has been always.' She had snuggled against him. 'Look, Johnny's ever so considerate and he's very sweet, but I don't love him.'

'But you're going to marry him.'

'Yes, when I'm eighteen, but that's just something our people do. We need continuity. But it won't affect you and me. Dickie, listen to me.' She had flung her arms around him and was kissing him full on the lips. He responded and they clung together passionately for all of five minutes. 'Dickie, listen. I love you!'

Gently he pushed her away. 'But you're marrying that chap. Once you've done that you'll be untouchable. I mean there's rules.'

'Oh you're all stuck in that middle class morality. Our class also have rules. Look, we never went for all that Victorian moral stuff. I told you, my mother conceived me with another man, but she will never tell anyone who that was. But to me my father is my father – legally and for real. Johnny's lot the Courbailiers, are a very old Catholic family. Johnny is an only son although he has his sister. The Corbailiers need an heir and we need to preserve the estate here. Look, think of it. What will happen if the Pockhampton estate was to be broken up? What would happen to the people here; to your mother and father?'

'Yes, I hadn't thought of that.'

'You should. When I marry Johnny, he will promise to keep the Pockhampton estate just as it is. Anyway we've lost the thread. Johnny's a Guards officer. He thinks a war is a real possibility.'

'With the Germans again?'

'Yes, that crazy man Hitler could well start one.'

'Then I'm glad I'll be flying. I don't want to go into any trenches. My Dad's never got over that in the last war.'

Maria clung to him again and they kissed. Richard felt his whole body becoming warm and responsive. Both of them were sliding their fingers into forbidden parts. Then Maria drew back. 'No,' she whispered. 'Not now, not today. Not until we're really ready.' She sat up and regarded him with a smile. 'Maybe I'm entitled to be jealous. Who is that pretty dark girl you were with at the ball?'

'Naomi, don't worry about her. She's Jewish and they have rules too. She's got to marry inside her own lot. A bit like your situation.'

'As long as we won't be sharing you, I don't mind.'

He put his arms around her again and whispered. 'No, I only love you.'

CHAPTER 18

David Goldstein almost ran into the room and he was spluttering with mirth.

'Who was that on the telephone,' asked Richard.

'It was the lady who organizes our outside events. You won't believe it but she's just confirmed they've changed the programme and we, the orchestra that is, have to go in for two more rehearsals.'

Richard was alarmed. 'What about me and Rachmaninov?'

'Don't worry, you're still on. No, it's our last item after the Beethoven. They warned us while you were away that it might happen. You'll never believe it but they've changed the final concerto from the Bruch to the Mendelssohn,' David spluttered with laughter.

'Do you want a slap on the back?'

'No, but you should have seen Lamingham's face when the news broke. You see it's not just the Mendelssohn, the guest soloist is a chap called Menuhin and he's also Jewish. I thought Lamingham was going to bust a gut. He's going to ask the academy authorities if he can be excused from playing.'

'What an idiot.'

'I guess he's going to be taken ill suddenly and they'll hire another viola.'

'I suppose that's better than having the fool standing up in the hall and shouting, hail Mosley.'

This surprising news had broken with only five days to go to the performance. Fortunately the orchestra was familiar with the Mendelssohn, and Menuhin the soloist had played the concerto many times. The concert was to be a huge step in Richard's career and he had been practicing for hours. As well as this he had just learned that in ten days time he would be taking his first hour of instruction in a Tiger Moth aircraft at Northolt. His life's ambitions were coming together and he was still only seventeen. Not even his love for an unattainable girl could spoil this.

It was the evening of the concert. Richard pulled on a hired dinner suit and stiff shirt and a bow tie. He still wasn't sure why musicians had to dress in this formal way but he accepted that was the rule. Was he frightened? Yes, deep down he was scared. He had waited for this day but could he do it? He, Richard Dyer, farm boy from Sussex would have to walk onto that platform and play one of the most complex works for piano ever composed in the classical repertoire; a work that should be wholly beyond a seventeen-year-old unless that player was especially gifted. He was that player; his tutor, the conductor and his fellows believed in him and he was not going to disappoint them. An audience of a thousand or more had come to hear the music and they hadn't come to see him. So bury your conceit; the music is far more important than you. Let the music speak.

A bulky coach had arrived to carry them all to the hall. Richard and David boarded it together and looked around. 'No Lamingham?' said Richard.

'Apparently his father has been taken ill and he's taken a train for Norwich,' David replied.

'What a fool that fellow is,' Richard sighed. This flippant speculation helped him bury the ordeal ahead.

'I agree,' said David. 'You see, I don't understand why he connects music in that way. I mean Wagner was a nasty anti-semite. I wouldn't want anything to do with such a man, but his music is wonderful.'

'Adolf Hitler's banned Mendelssohn,' said Richard. 'And as far as Lamingham is concerned that's final. Or I assume that's why.'

'Well he's really missed his chance to hear Menuhin. That man's only a few years older than us but he's set to be one of the finest violinists.'

'In that case Lamingham loses the chance to learn something.'

The motor coach arrived at Queen's Hall. Parked near it was a black van with long cables sprouting from it and into the hall. On its side were the letters BBC. A man in a sports jacket had just climbed out of this van and was writing something on a message board. Richard raced over to him

'Is this a broadcast?' he asked.

'Spot on,' replied the cheerful engineer. 'Easy one for us – just round the corner.'

'I didn't know anything about this. I mean I'm playing in there tonight.'

'Lucky you. The whole nation'll hear you.'

Richard felt as if a block of ice had emerged in his stomach. He felt mildly sick. He turned back to join the others who were carrying their various instruments into the hall.

'What, the BBC?' said David. 'Didn't you know that? No, you were away at home when we learned they were going to broadcast us.

Instead of just this audience we're going to be heard by a million or so.'

Oh, God, thought Richard. That'll mean my mum and dad and Maria and her mum and dad. I must do my best. If I flunk it tonight, I'll never live it down.

Inside, the hall looked more cavernous than ever. The performance piano was now on the platform. It arrived delivered by a haulage team who had handled it as if it was made of eggshells. The piano was another Steinway, and just about the most expensive model in existence. Richard approached it nervously and lifted the keyboard lid. Without sitting down he ran a few chord and trills. No doubts, the tuning was perfect. Suddenly he felt a tiny bit of confidence. He pulled out his watch; still an hour and a half until doors opened. How he wished he was sitting in one of those tiers of seats and waiting for someone else to perform.

'Want a cup of tea, Dick?' It was David carrying a tray of cups. Richard took one and gulped down the contents.

'Where's the lavatory?' he asked gloomily. This apprehension was a new experience for Richard. It was one that was to live with him in war when his life was at stake and not his reputation.

The orchestra were taking their places and starting to tune. Richard glanced at the viola section and saw Lamingham's replacement, a rather pretty girl. This was a first in a largely all-male world and that was pleasing. She had a shapely face and fair hair. That at least should satisfy Lamingham. The conductor arrived with the violinist. This Menuhin was a young man, maybe in his early twenties. He seemed on the face of it to be serenely confident. He shook Richard's hand and gave him a few words of reassurance. 'You'll do it. Everything I've been told about you says you'll be brilliant.'

The orchestra had left the platform into the adjacent waiting room. The conductor and the two soloists followed them. The audience was beginning to enter; flowing in a steady stream until the hall was filled and echoing with a rumble of subdued conversation. Then the orchestra, with the violinists and woodwind players carrying their instruments, began to file out into the hall to be greeted by mild applause. The leader with his violin entered to longer applause and once more the orchestra went through its tuning ritual. Last of all, the conductor followed with prolonged applause. Richard couldn't see the point of any of this when none of them had delivered a single note. He picked up the printed programme.

Schumann Symphony 1. The scherzo.

This was the introduction piece short and popular.

Rachmaninov Piano Concerto 3 in D minor.
Soloist Mr Richard Dyer.

Well, there it was in cold print.

Interval

Beethoven Symphony 5 in C minor.

Mendelssohn Violin Concerto.
Soloist Mr Yehudi Menuhin.

The orchestra and the wretched American conductor had raced through the Schumann in less than ten minutes. Now it was his turn. With a fixed smile and a supreme air of fake confidence he strode onto the platform and bowed. He sat down on the seat, placed his fingers on the keys and watched the conductor's baton. He played the beginning of the lovely melody that weaves its way through the first movement. And now the miracle happened. The music enveloped him. He needn't worry that he might miss or forget a note or phrase. This was music he'd practiced and practiced; music he'd heard since childhood. He didn't need a mental photograph of the score. The work was burned in his memory. Gradually, as the concerto evolved, it possessed him. The music came from outside him and fired in his brain. Every nerve and fibre in his body was alert as the music flowed from his brain and through his arms and fingers. They were no more than a conduit that carried every beautiful passage to the piano and projected it to the listeners both in the hall and further afield.

Next began the second movement: the Intermezzo: adagio. He would not repeat the mistake that he had made in rehearsal. He waited and absorbed the lovely romantic orchestral opening. He joined the theme and played through to the cadenza that completed the movement.

Now the Finale: the third movement. He was riding on such a wave of emotion now. Here was one of the most complex works for piano and he was performing it in concert. He knew this was not wholly true; some power outside him had taken over. He was aware of the nearby orchestra, but the hall, the audience and the outside world were no more. He smiled; he could feel his eyes moistening but not enough to stop him seeing the piano keys. He reached the final climax and his performance was over. He sat back and closed his eyes.

What on earth was happening? He could hear applause, wild clapping joined by shouting and cheering. The conductor took his arm and almost lifted him to his feet. The audience was not politely applauding; to a man and woman they were standing. The clapping was joined by more cheering. A group of uniformed schoolgirls near the front were squealing and jumping up and down. Beside him the orchestra was applauding. The applause doubled as the conductor raised Richard's right arm as if he was a victorious boxer. He bowed to them and bowed again. Then the conductor's pretty little twelve-year-old daughter came onto the platform and presented him with a bouquet of flowers. He bent down and accepted them and bowed again and again. Only then could he escape into the offstage to be greeted by more congratulations and handshakes. It was over – he had succeeded better than he could ever have hoped.

The next morning Richard, for the first time in his life, allowed himself to oversleep. His hosts were happy for him to do so and it was almost ten o'clock when Naomi knocked on the door and brought him a cup of tea.

'Oh, Dick, you're a star, you're my hero.'

He sat up and smiled. 'Don't lay it on too thick or I'll be really bigheaded.'

'Breakfast's still ready for you and we've a stack of telegrams all saying you're wonderful.' She gave him a mock glare. 'One of them's from a girl and she says she loves you.'

'All right, clear out and then I can get dressed and come down.'

He slipped out of bed, put on his dressing gown and made his way to the bathroom. He washed his hands and face and plied his new safety razor. Keeping his face free of stubble was a relatively new experience; a sign of adulthood. He returned to his bedroom and noticed the dinner suit and stiff shirt on a wooden hanger. He had better get that back to the outfitter pronto or face an extra payment. Then there were the presentation flowers. He'd better ask Naomi to put them in a vase with water.

He had to admit he felt no anti-climax, more a glow of warmth. He had succeeded last night, but why? He had set out to play a challenging piece of music, but then that same music had possessed him, but how and why? He finished dressing, this time in sports jacket and flannels. Then downstairs and eat breakfast, no bacon this time of course, but a nice dish of hot porridge and a plate of scrambled eggs.

Naomi and her mother brought in the telegrams on a silver dish. There were eighteen of them. Some came from people he hardly knew, but then:

Richard you excelled. We are all so proud of you. Peter Ross.

Heard streets of Sussex deserted while you played. Magnificent. H. Locke.

Richard, we loved your performance. Mary Tenbury.

Dickie. I cried listening to you. I love you. Maria.

He read the last one again and again. He tried to imagine Maria and her mother sitting around their radiogram listening to the concert. One thing worried him. Had Mrs Tenbury seen Maria's telegram? If so would she be shocked? He hated the thought of the Tenbury family being offended by his innocent friendship with their daughter.

'You really stole the night,' said Naomi. 'I can tell you that audience was buzzing like a beehive after you'd finished.'

'Don't put it all down to me,' Richard protested. 'You saw David play his oboe. I was watching him all through the Beethoven and he was magical.'

CHAPTER 19

'Is your old man feeling better?'

Lamingham glared. 'Really, Dyer. You are still a common yokel. What you mean to say is. How is your father, Sir Rufus Lamingham? You should learn to be respectful of your betters.'

'Your Mosley is a sir and I don't respect him.'

'Just because you pound away at a piano rather well does not give you a right to insult your betters.'

'Lamingham, you lost a chance to learn from one of the best violinists in the country. Menuhin was inspiring.'

'You lodge with a Jew boy, so I suppose that's warped you. Where is your patriotism?'

'Patriotism,' Richard pronounced the word in his most irritating tone. 'Patriotism, I'm starting flying training with the RAF. They're the best, so your Hitler had better watch out.'

'You are hopeless,' said Lamingham. 'When Hitler marches we should march with him.'

Lamingham's hostility was his own. Richard was still basking in the aftermath of his success. Congratulations poured in from every source. Ernest Newman, *The Times* music critic had been complimentary.

A refreshing, sensitive, interpretation performed by a young pianist from whom we may expect much in the future.

Richard had been excited to be invited back to Langham Place, this time to take part in a BBC interview. In the end this had been a disappointment. Richard had not been allowed any spontaneous views. The whole interview was delivered from a pre-written script and sounded wooden and contrived. Well, that weekend he would be cut down to size with a vengeance. He was due at Northolt for his first flying session. He could forget his prestige. This time he would be a tyro, a nonentity. Nobody would give a damn about his music. Could he really fly? Time would tell.

Richard was up at five-thirty in the morning. The rest of the household were asleep, so he made himself a cup of coffee and some bread and marmalade. At six o'clock he heard the beep of a car horn in the street. It was his friend with the battered Austin Seven.

They arrived at Northolt for their first serious day's training. Three smart looking Tiger Moth aircraft were lined up in the dispersal area. First they were due for a morning's classroom instruction. Richard was clutching his copy of the Flying Training Manual. He had been pouring over its pages ever since the initial class. The morning session was an intense course on airmanship theory and all the technicalities of flying that they would have to put into practice. It was explained that all training was set in a pattern laid down by the RAF Central Flying School and auxiliary units such as the university squadrons received the same basic instruction.

At the lunch break all present were almost too excited to eat anything. Next they were called in alphabetical order to don their flying kit. This was bulky and awkward and complete with a helmet containing earphones. A parachute was also provided. Richard was wary of the latter but was told that it was there mainly for the pupils to acclimatize to their full kit. Now he was called to meet his instructor. The man was a stout genial character who laughed a lot, but Richard knew the man would not be in his job unless he was a pilot of exceptional standard.

'I'm Philip Rendell, Squadron Leader – and your name?'

'Richard Dyer, sir.'

'Where have I heard that name before?'

Richard had an idea where the man had heard his name but he was not going to boast. 'I don't know, sir. Dyer is quite a common name.'

'No, I've seen you as well, but no...it'll come back. Right, follow me.'

They walked slowly across the tarmac, slightly encumbered by their flying gear and the parachutes they carried. A Tiger Moth was standing with its engine ticking over and heavy wooden chocks beneath the landing wheels. Richard was helped into his parachute harness and then into his seat in the aircraft. The Sutton harness was next secured to hold him in place. He knew that this was by way of an initiation flight, rather like the one he had flown at Shoreham those years ago. Squadron Leader Rendell taxied the Tiger Moth to the takeoff point and turned into the wind. The experience was just as Richard had remembered from his trip in Major Bell's Moth. The takeoff vibration ceased as the runway vanished beneath them. As the aircraft climbed Richard saw the panoramic view of North London on one side and the fields and trees of the countryside on the other. Just as before he could see roads with traffic on them and villages and bigger groups of buildings all set out like toys. He felt at ease and he could not help himself smiling as relaxing music flowed in his head in sympathy with the aircraft's engine.

The aircraft performed a steep turn. His headphones crackled. 'Right, Dyer, we return to base now.' Richard looked around he had temporarily lost all sense of direction; then he saw it again. Northolt airfield was straight ahead and the instructor was beginning to throttle back as the Tiger Moth descended.

'All right, Dyer, how was that?' They had left the aircraft and were divesting themselves of the bulky parachutes.

'Wonderful, sir. I can't wait to start learning properly.'

'No qualms, no air sickness?'

'No, sir.'

'Good, we now take the rest of your friends and then it's back in class for the de-brief.'

The three Tiger Moths took off again with three more trainees. Two hours later they were all assembled in the briefing room. Squadron Leader Rendell, as Chief Instructor, told them that they had all satisfied their instructors as far as the initiation flights were concerned. The next session would be a real flying lesson.

Richard was preparing to leave when the Squadron Leader touched him on the arm. 'Dyer, I've remembered where I've seen you. Would you come with me to our mess for half an hour?'

Richard was puzzled. 'My friend is waiting with his car to run me home.'

'Don't worry. We'll arrange transport. Follow me.'

Richard followed his instructor along a series of pathways to another building with a sign outside denoting it as the RAF officer's mess. He worried that he might have done something wrong and couldn't think what. The flight had been exhilarating. He had loved it. The instructor ushered him into the building. Inside was a room with comfortable armchairs a closed bar and through a doorway, he could see another room with a table laid for a meal. Richard felt his spirits sink as he saw the other instructors were already in the room.

'Mr Dyer,' said Rendell. 'I know where I've seen you before and heard your name. My wife and our daughter went to your concert. You are Dyer the piano player? Your papers say you are music academy.'

What a relief. 'Yes, sir. My career is in music but if a war comes I want to fly.'

'When you get to your squadron you could be the most popular man in the mess. Tell me, do you only do the classics?'

'Oh, no sir. I do arranging for a dance band and I like playing modern but it's not encouraged in the college.'

'Would you honour us with a few numbers on our piano here?'

'Yes, sir. I'd be delighted.'

Rendell pointed to the dining room and Richard followed him. In a corner was a somewhat battered upright piano. 'We had a fellow here who could play that, but he's been posted. Would you give us some real music? We've got a wireless of course but that's not the same.'

Richard certainly could give them music. It seemed music would smooth his path, so music they would have. He had already guessed that in the Air Force he would be asked to play on all sorts of pub pianos and worse. He sat down on the very battered leather top stool provided, opened the lid and began to play. In fact the instrument could have been worse. It made quite a pleasing clakkety sound with only two high treble notes missing. He ran off his versions of: *Sunny Side of the Street, Exactly Like You, In the Mood,* and finally *Teddy Bear's Picnic.* This one had a poignancy that made him think of Maria and he must not think of her.

His audience applauded warmly and even the white-jacket steward leaning through a serving hatch grinned and gave him the thumbs up.

'Well done, young Dyer. Whatever squadron you end up in they'll be crazy for that. Now we'll see about getting you home.'

He reached South Kensington in an Air Force car, a real return in style. He walked up the front steps and plied his latchkey. The house was surprisingly quiet; not a note of music could he hear. He stood in the hallway and called out. Someone was crying – no sobbing inconsolably. What on earth? In the sitting room was Naomi her face distorted and wet with tears.

'Oh, Dick, you're here.'

'Naomi, what on earth has happened?'

'It's David. He's gone.'

'Gone where?'

'To Spain. He wants to fight the Fascists but they'll kill him. They kill anyone Jewish.'

CHAPTER 20

'When did this happen?' Richard was trying to grasp the enormity of this news. 'I know David has been going on and on about Spain, but are you sure he's gone there?'

Naomi handed him a flimsy piece of paper.

Today, I've had my marching orders to join the International Brigade.

We must win in Spain or the future of our people and our religious faith will be lost. I cannot sit in idleness and comfort here and watch disaster happen.

I have told the music academy that I am leaving them. My flute and oboe are in my bedroom. Please guard them safely until the day I return.

I wish Dick every success. He is one of the youngest and greatest pianists in the world.

Father, Mother and dearest Sister I love you. Please forgive me and wish me well.

Your David.

Naomi had flung herself against him and buried her face in his chest as the tears flooded again. Very gently he lifted her and sat her in an armchair.

'I don't know,' he sighed. 'Can you stop him?'

'Father has been to the police. You see, it's illegal for a British subject to fight in a foreign war. He could face prison.'

'A lot of people have gone already. They say this war is the prelude to the big one.'

'I know. It's worse for us. If that man Hitler were to rule all Europe there's no knowing what he would do to our people.'

'Where's your mother?'

'She's gone to her sister, my aunt, in Poplar. The whole family are shocked.'

Richard shook his head. 'I do wish he'd spoken to me. I would have done anything to change his mind. But he never spoke about actually going to fight. He was forever poring over newspapers and talking about it.'

'He wouldn't bother you when you had that big performance

coming up.'

'I know; I am too bound up in my own selfish world.'

'No, Dick, you mustn't blame yourself. It's difficult for you. We like you but you're not one of our people.'

Life at the academy had returned to something like normal, but Richard found himself almost in limbo. His piano teacher had told him that he had reached a standard of playing that the tutor couldn't really improve. His tutorials were mainly the two of them playing gramophone recordings of the great names of the day and analyzing their work. He resolved to do everything he could to fit in with the other students and not in any way to be accused of boasting his triumph. He and Lamingham avoided each other, which was a relief. That was until he literally bumped into the man as he emerged from a practice room.

'So, your Jewboy friend is a communist. Gone to help the reds in Spain.' Lamingham jeered.

'He's gone to uphold democracy.'

'Democracy is dead. There's a new order in Europe now. We're going to sweep away that deadwood, purge the bad races and be a pure society.'

'Lamingham. Give it a rest. I want to play music.'

Lamingham leered. 'Oh, yes. I've heard all about your rendering of that Slavic stuff. Clever finger work by all accounts and the expressions on your face while you played I've heard. Like someone doing some dirty sex. Have you been fucking with that little Jew girl?'

Lamingham had been backing away as Richard red-faced charged at him. He seized the chubby little Fascist by the throat and pinned him to the wall.

'No,' roared a detached voice. 'No, this will not do.' The voice was the college principal. 'Both of you – my office now.'

Richard released his enemy as Lamingham breathing heavily addressed the head. 'Sir, this man is mad. He attacked me with no provocation.'

'No provocation indeed. I heard every word of that exchange. Follow me.'

The pair of them followed the principal along the corridor and into his office. The head shut the door and ushered them to stand in front of his large desk. He himself sat on the edge and glared at them. Richard wondered if the man would or was allowed to deliver a caning.

'It is fortunate few persons were around the building. Your behaviour was disgraceful. First you, Lamingham, I am telling you to collect your instrument and your other things. You are disruptive, you let us all down by refusing to play in our concert, and your tutor tells me you have not only made no recent progress but your standard has slipped.'

Lamingham looked appealingly at the principal. 'But sir, I wanted to play in the concert, but my father was very ill.'

'On the contrary, Sir Rufus was seen by witnesses at his place in the City of London all day on the date in question. We are not interested in politics, only in the quality of our music. Your insulting a fine musician like Dyer is the final straw. You are expelled.'

The principal looked at Richard. 'Dyer, you were provoked but we cannot tolerate violence in any form. You are suspended for seven days.'

Once again Richard walked the two miles from the railway halt to Pockhampton. This time he was despondent. He felt a burning sense of injustice. There were still five days until his next flying lesson, but in the meantime he preferred to be home in Sussex. London had lost its appeal. The morning was cold and damp, typical of February in the country. He pulled his Macintosh coat more tightly around his waist.

A car was coming up behind him from the direction of Chichester. He looked round in surprise. It was Mrs Tenbury's Austin Seven but the driver was Maria. The girl applied the brakes and the car slid a few yards on the road surface.

'Dickie, you're home,' Maria shrieked with excitement. 'Get in the car quick and I'll take you the rest of the way.'

He climbed into the passenger seat and Maria let the gears in with a jerk and then they were on their way. 'We didn't expect you,' she said. He glanced sideways at her. She looked beautiful. She had donned some little gold earrings that shone against her lovely soft complexion.

'I'm in disgrace, that's why I'm here.' He told her about Lamingham.

'But, Dickie that's all wrong, after all you've done and that wonderful concert you gave. What did this Fascist say?'

'I told you, he made a disgusting suggestion,' He wasn't going to tell Maria what Lamingham had implied about Naomi.

'What, you mean he's a homo? That fits with a lot of what I've heard about those people. Anyway, I've something you can do for me.' Richard gritted his teeth as the car swerved while she reached into the back seat. She held up a heavy shopping bag.

'What's that?'

'You'll see when we get home.'

'I must call in and see my mum and dad.'

'Of course, anyway we're nearly there.' They were now in the outskirts of Pockhampton and another hundred yards would bring them to his parents' house. This was a moment of real apprehension. His mother and father were so proud of him. Even old Ted his father had become reconciled to his son moving in society above his station. What would they think of their son being involved in a sort of pub brawl?

He walked across the yard to the door. He was aware that his smart patent leather town shoes were spattered with cow dung.

'Dickie,' little Alice greeted him all smiles. 'Mama, she screamed. Dickie's here.' Alice caught his hand with her tiny fingers. 'I'm going to school soon.'

Mabel, his mother, came down the stairs and stood staring open mouthed. 'Son, we didn't expect you.'

Rapidly he explained what had happened, leaving nothing out.

'You did right. You're father would have done just the same. Come on in, the kettle's on we'll have nice cup of tea.'

'Maria's out there in her car.' He pointed across the yard to the road.

'In that little car. I sometimes wonder if you're safe with her.'

Now he laughed. 'Safe in what way?'

'I wonder. No, bring the young lady in.'

Richard stood in the door and waved to Maria and beckoned her inside the kitchen.

They were back on the road again heading for Pockhampton House. 'How are you?' he asked. A silly question and not what he really wanted to know. 'How are things with your fiancé?'

'With Johnny? Fiancé is a bit strong. The engagement isn't until November when I'm eighteen.'

'But you're going ahead with the wedding?'

'Dickie,' her tone was severe. 'You're being jealous again. I've told you I'm doing my duty but you are my love.' She turned to him with such a sweet smile. The car swerved again.

'Hey watch out. My mum says you're not safe to be with.'

Maria giggled. 'I wonder what she's thinking.'

They reached the big house and Maria hustled him inside. He followed her up the stairs into the nursery. She was still carrying the shopping bag. They reached the nursery and Maria tipped out the contents onto the table. Richard could only see a heap of little leather bound books. What on earth?

'I went to my old school this morning. A lot of my younger friends are still there. These are their autograph books and I've promised to make you sign them.'

Richard was aghast. 'But, why me?'

'Oh come on, Dickie. Why do you think? We all heard you play the Rachmaninov concerto. Don't you realize you're famous?' she looked at him with such an enticing expression that momentarily he was lost. How he loved this girl. Despite all the insults he'd heaped on her in their childhood he knew he always had loved her.

'Come on,' she said pushing one of the books towards him. This one belongs to Polly and then there's Bernadette, and Francesca, and Lucia and...' Now she giggled again; that seductive sound that he remembered from their childhood. 'I can't believe it but Sister Assumptia wants your autograph as well.'

'A nun?'

'That's right; at times she's almost human. But she was swept away by your playing.' She paused. 'Me too, I told you I cried. I couldn't help it you were wonderful.' Now she had her arms around him smothering him with her kisses. The little autograph books scattered onto the floor. The two of them rolled together on the old leather sofa and he kissed her and she him for several minutes. 'I love you,' he whispered. 'And I don't want to lose you.'

She licked his ear. 'You will never lose me.'

Gently she pushed him away. 'Come on, you've all these autographs to sign.' She delved in her little fashion handbag and produced a fountain pen. One by one Richard signed the books.

'I wonder how much Beethoven's signature would fetch in an auction?' she said.

Richard laughed. 'I'm not Beethoven.'

He completed the task and then Maria ran downstairs to find her mother.

'Hello, Richard,' Mrs Tenbury greeted him. 'I saw you two arrive. Wonderful to see you; you will stay to lunch?'

'Yes please.'

'Good, my husband is in London today. He's at the Air Ministry.

They're interested in employing him there if a war comes.'

The lunch was served in the main dining room; the same long room where Richard remembered seeing Max the magician. He still felt a little bit out of place in these grand house surroundings and he couldn't help worrying about Mrs Tenbury's reaction if she knew about his intimacy with her daughter. In fact he needn't have worried. Mrs Tenbury sent Maria out to buy a newspaper from the village shop and then took Richard upstairs into the little study, the one with the harpsichord. He felt apprehensive and he had a nasty suspicion about the reason for this "little chat" as Mrs Tenbury had termed it.

'Please sit down, Richard,' she pointed to an armchair near the fireplace. 'We listened to your wireless recital. I think it would be fair to say you were inspirational. The effect it had on Maria was a surprise to say the least. I think she told you she cried.'

'Yes, she told me in the telegram she sent me.'

'It was a bit more than that. She confessed to loving you and did she have to go through with her engagement to the Corbailier family.' Mrs Tenbury stared at him and Richard remembered that time as a small boy when Mr Shank, the blacksmith had caught him scrumping apples. He looked back at Mrs Tenbury but said nothing.

Now she smiled. 'You and my Maria have been close friends almost since birth. I will tell you something in the strictest confidence. I was brought together with my dear husband as a family arrangement. I belonged to an old Catholic family in Nottinghamshire. We always marry like for like. I had a rich inheritance that helped save this estate here from financial trouble. But I wish to make this clear. I love my husband and once we had been introduced I knew he was right for me. Our son Leo is following his vocation and that is a vocation that bans marriage and children. Maria is the only heir and she must marry into her own kind and have a marriage that will preserve this estate and all the people who rely on us.

'I think that John Petersfield will be good to Maria; he is gentle and kind but I foresee problems. Do you follow?'

'I'm sorry Mrs Tenbury, but honestly I've never pestered Maria for anything wrong; we're friends…'

She held up her hand as he stuttered into silence. 'I said I foresee problems. That is why I want you to stay close to Maria. In the modern phrase I think you are soul mates and young as you both are there is a bond between you that will last.' Now she smiled on him with a smile so like her daughter's. 'Your friendship has our blessing.'

CHAPTER 21

Richard's daily yearning for the unattainable girl was the only thing that blighted his life that spring. Public excitement in the year of 1937 was growing as the date of the Coronation drew near. It seemed this new king would be a safe pair of hands, so different from his elder brother.

Richard had buried his regrets in his music and his flying. He had given a second performance of the difficult Rachmaninov and had even had a short complimentary telegram from the composer in America. In his spare time he had composed seven advanced dance numbers for Harry Malburg. Richard loved performing but his long-term ambition was to compose. His tutor suggested he might like to be a conductor, but Richard was uncertain about that. To sit down with an orchestra and play was one thing but to stand up in front of a full orchestra and hope that they would go with his interpretations; well that was a different matter entirely.

He lived for his music and now he also lived for his flying. His instruction days at Northolt were the great events of the week. With Squadron Leader Rendell's guidance he learned not just to turn and bank but to loop and roll, recover from a spin, sideslip and finally to make well-judged descents and landings. It hadn't all been plain sailing. The Tiger Moth was a docile aircraft but it had some tricks that found out the inept students.

One afternoon in May, Richard and his instructor had made a number of circuits and bumps. Latterly Rendell had very little to say, which surprised Richard as the Squadron leader could be acerbic at times if things were not performed to his satisfaction. Richard performed one of his better landings to date and brought the Tiger Moth to a halt near the flight sheds. To his surprise the instructor undid his harness, climbed to the ground and walked round to Richard's cockpit.

'Dyer, that was good. Now you take her up, do one circuit and let's see a good landing. So, off you go.'

Richard was excited. He was going for his first solo and only the second in his group to do so. Very gently he opened the throttle and pulled the stick back to keep the tail down. He taxied the Tiger Moth to the end of the runway and carefully turned her to face the wind.

This was the moment. It was almost as if he was sitting down to play to an audience although this time his only audience was a highly critical instructor. He lined up the aircraft opened the throttle and he was away. To his surprise he left the ground a good deal quicker than usual. Without the corpulent Squadron Leader the Tiger was lighter and a great deal more responsive. He watched the altimeter and climbed. He was heading away from the airfield and it was time to make a turn. The Squadron Leader was a stickler for neat turns so he had better do a smooth one. The airfield was in his sights so now the descent. He pointed towards the far end of the runway and eased back the throttle. A gentle descent and well clear of stalling speed. He pushed open the throttle an inch and then back again as the Tiger sank gracefully onto the runway. She was so much lighter without the instructor and he failed to touch down at the spot he had chosen but the landing if not perfect was not over bumpy. He was a little apprehensive, wondering what his instructor would say about that. He taxied back to the flight sheds and Squadron Leader Rendell was standing there with a huge grin on his face and a thumbs up.

'Well done, young Dyer. And did you enjoy that?'

'Yes, sir. When can I go again?'

'Very soon. Now follow me into the office for the de-brief.'

Rendell looked at Richard with a searching expression. 'Dyer, you are a talented musician and you can fly well, but I don't see you as a team player.'

Richard had no sensible reply, so he kept silent.

'I mean no insult,' Rendell continued, 'but I do not see you as the captain of a bomber crew should we, God forbid, have another war. So I am directing your training towards fighter aircraft. What do you think of that?'

Richard's face lit with delight. 'Oh, God, sir. That's what I've dreamed of. Thank you.'

'Good man. Now I think a rendition on the mess piano is the next item.'

This time it was the Squadron Leader in person who drove Richard back to Central London.

'Right, more solo flights next time,' said Rendell. 'And then we'll discuss future progress.'

Richard almost ran up the steps of the South Kensington house. Inside things were almost normal. He could hear Daniel Goldstein's trumpet and Esther and Naomi were singing a duet in the kitchen. He was bursting with his news although it was doubtful it would mean much to his friends.

'We've heard from David,' said Naomi. 'He's in Barcelona.'

Richard was now concerned for his friend. 'Has he been fighting?'

'Not as far as we can tell. He sent an international telegram and just said: *I've arrived and all is well.*

'Let's hope they find him an admin job behind the lines.'

Naomi looked gloomy. 'No chance of that, I'm afraid. He'll want to fight the Fascists. That's why he went there.' She changed the subject. 'How did the flying go?'

He told her with a glow of pride.

'I'm not sure about any of that,' said Esther. 'If God had meant us to fly he'd have given us wings.'

Richard laughed. 'Well, I had some pretty good wings today.'

'By the way,' Naomi gave him an odd look. 'A girl telephoned here asking for you.'

Richard was alert now, 'Who was that?'

'I don't know. She didn't say but she sounded a bit hoity toity.'

'Did she give a number?'

'No, she said she'll try again. You look a bit glum. Do you know who she is?''

'Yes, I've a good idea.' Well-spoken girl; there could be only one of those looking for him. He sat down at the piano for half an hour and lost himself in melodies from Mozart to Gershwin. Then the wretched Naomi appeared her face lit by a half-smile, half-smirk.

'The girl's on the telephone. I said I'd fetch you.'

Richard closed the piano lid and followed her to the telephone in Daniel's study. As of now he only wished Maria would let him forget her while at the same time he was desperate to see her again.

'Hello, Dickie, what are you doing on Coronation Day?'

'Well nothing really. We're going to listen to it on the BBC. I want to hear the singing.'

'We're going to listen to the wireless but Dickie, the Corbailiers have a town house overlooking the procession route. Mummy wants you to come with us and watch.'

'I suppose your fiancé will be there. He won't want to see me or me him.'

'No, Dickie darling. Johnny is parading; riding with his Life Guards in the procession, and afterwards they'll go to the officer's mess for a drinking session. Johnny's father the Duke will be in the Abbey sticking his coronet on and swearing allegiance. But Mummy wants you with us watching it all go by. And, Dickie, there's going to be a guest who wants to meet you and say sorry.'

'Who on earth?'

'You will have to wait for that. But, it's a once in a lifetime. I want you to be there.'

'That sounds better.'

'Oh, Dickie, you will come, won't you?' Her voice was musical and seductive.

'Put like that, girl. Yes, I'll be with you.'

Naomi was now spluttering with laughter. 'Go on, Dick. Tell us. Who is she?'

CHAPTER 22

May 12th 1937

The Corbailier family had a medium-sized town house nicely situated on the return route of the Coronation procession. Richard had dressed in his only smart suit and had taken the underground. He now had to walk the final five hundred yards. Already crowds were gathering and some people had obviously slept outside. Richard had only mixed feelings. He wanted to see Maria – in fact he longed to see her – but this was a daunting assignment. An aristocratic town house was a new frontier to cross. He was only glad his father knew nothing about this visit. He reached the house and stared at the stone steps leading to the portico and the square front door. For a moment he wondered if he shouldn't go round the side and knock on the servant's entrance. No, Maria would only laugh. He walked boldly up to the door and pulled the bell.

Instead of a haughty butler, he saw a rather pretty maidservant. She smiled at him and then curtseyed which made him feel even more out of place. Next the butler appeared. He was tall, austere, unsmiling, grey-haired and immaculately morning suited. He pointed to a silver card dish on a sideboard. Once more Richard had ceased to be the rising musician but had become the little Sussex farm boy again. 'I'm terribly sorry but I haven't got a calling card but I am expected. The name's Dyer...'

'Indeed, Mr Dyer. You are expected.' The man spoke with a refined Scottish accent. Then a little smile flitted across his deadpan features. 'Perhaps you can oblige.' He spoke in a near whisper and pointed to the maidservant. 'I think Miss Muriel here wants your autograph signature.'

The pretty girl smiled and nodded and held out a notepad that hung around her slim waist. Richard took the pencil she offered and wrote his name. The girl took her notepad back and curtseyed again.

'If Sir would follow me,' the Butler ordered.

Richard followed him up a wide stairway. He felt rather like an obedient Labrador. The Butler knocked on a white door and then opened it. 'Mr Richard Dyer,' he announced.

Although it was beginning to rain outside, the room was brightly lit by daylight through large glass French window doors leading onto a balcony. Within the room stood a group of people and nearest to him was Maria. She ran to him and took both his hands in hers. 'Come on,' she said. 'I'll introduce you.'

Richard had already seen Mr and Mrs Tenbury. There were two strangers; one was a woman. She was attractive, tall and blonde haired but with interrogative blue eyes and a severe expression. 'Richard, may I introduce, Lady Sylvia Corbailier. Lady Sylvia is John Petersfield's elder sister.'

The gracious lady smiled and Richard felt he was the farm boy again. 'So you are Maria's Richard. We have heard so much about you and your music.' She offered him a tiny white hand and Richard shook it politely. He wondered if he should bow.

Maria was next pushing him towards a man standing by the open windows. He was smartly suited, late middle-aged and silver haired. The man held out a hand. 'Mr Dyer, I am deeply sorry for the rudeness and persecution you have suffered at the hands of my son.' Richard was baffled. 'Richard,' said Maria. 'Remember, this is a happy occasion and we are guests of these kind people. Please meet Sir Rufus Lamingham.'

The man held out a hand and his pleading expression was one Richard could not politely reject. He took the proffered hand. 'Mr Dyer, I have sent my son for medical help. His mother and I do not share his views. I believe Mosley to be a deluded scoundrel and Hitler to be an uncouth Austrian.'

Richard shook the man's hand. 'Thank you, sir.'

'My son, Michael, is a talented musician but he has thrown his career away. You are a fine musician, Mr Dyer. My son insulted you and me when he said I was ill and he couldn't play at your concerto.'

Richard could see the sincerity in the man's expression. 'It's not your fault, sir. These things happen.' Suddenly he found he liked this man.

The day went as planned. They all crowded round the radiogram to listen to the service in the Abbey. The singing was beautiful, although secretly Richard felt his Chichester cathedral choir would be just as good. He loved the stately Crown Imperial march.

'That's composed by William Walton,' said Lady Sylvia. She stared at Richard. 'I've heard that Mr Walton wants to meet you.'

'Really,' Richard replied. 'I'd be honoured if it's true.'

'Of course it's true. I heard it from Alice Wimborne, his mistress.' Richard looked around embarrassed, by this revelation, but no one else seemed to notice.

The service on the radio over, the company sat down for lunch. Richard wished this Lady Sylvia would not keep staring at him. He guessed he needed to watch his carefully-schooled table manners. They could now hear the sound of distant cheering and all went out through the window doors onto the balcony. The butler hustled around setting chairs for them to sit on. Below, the streets were lined with soldiers and spectators crowded behind them. Now the procession was here. Soldiers, sailors and airmen marched by, along with troops from Australia, red-coated Canadian Mounties, turbaned Indians and an array of other colourful forces from the far-flung dominions. As the climax drew near the cheering increased threefold. The household brigade were passing with their drawn swords and shining helmets. Their balcony was protected with an awning, but down below the streets were soaking in rain.

'Johnny,' Lady Sylvia shrieked. 'Sit up straight, man. Go on, sit up!'

'It's no good,' Maria giggled. 'He can't hear you.'

'God, that brother of mine, a little bit of rain, big occasion and he hunches up like that.'

Then came the state coach and everyone stood. 'The little girls are with them,' said Mrs Tenbury.'

'Good experience,' replied Sylvia. 'The eldest one'll be crowned herself one day.'

'What do we know about this new king?' Mrs Tenbury asked. 'I mean; Sylvia, you've met him.'

'Bertie: he'll be all right. Strong marriage, nice children. He'll do much better than people expect. He's a decent man, not like that elder brother who ran out on us. When he was around we classed him as a nosit.'

'A what?'

Maria giggled. 'NOSIT – not safe in taxis. I know one or two of those already.'

'Not your friend here, I hope,' Sylvia stared at Richard.

'What Dickie?' Maria giggled. 'He's a bit too honourable for his own good sometimes.'

Richard wriggled as the women laughed.

'Come on you ladies,' said Mr Tenbury. 'Have mercy, the poor boy's gone red.'

With the procession and celebrations over, Richard's overwhelming desire was to escape and go home. He felt ill at ease among these high-class people and Maria did not help. She was supposed to be promised to that man who had passed them on a horse, but she was all over Richard and twice kissed him in front of the company. And he really liked Sir Rufus, a man with no resemblance to his odious son. At last the party broke up. 'It's still raining out there,' said Maria. 'Did you bring a mac? No I thought not.'

'I'll be all right. It's not raining as hard as it was.'

'No, you won't. Ganton's got our car round the back. I'll ring downstairs and fetch him. Let's hope he hasn't drunk too much.'

Another disconcerting moment came when Lady Sylvia called him over to her in the entrance hall. She held him by both shoulders and stared him in the face. 'Yes,' she muttered. 'Right hair, right eyes – you'll do.' Richard wondered if the lady, to coin a phrase, was mildly batty.

Twenty minutes later Mr Ganton brought the Tenbury Bentley round to the front of the house. He stood beside the car like a child with a prized toy, waving away the dispersing crowds who stopped to finger and admire it. Maria walked down the steps with Richard.

'What's biting that Lady Sylvia?' he asked.

'Sylvia is the guardian of her family. Everything has to pass her inspection and that includes you of course.'

'But why me? I mean it's you that's important.'

Once again, regardless of onlookers, she kissed him. 'It's the future – you'll see.'

CHAPTER 23

Summer 1938

Financially Richard was finding his feet. He had a steady income now; enough to pay tax. His scoring and composition for Harry Malburg paid well, and suddenly his piano playing was in demand. During the latter months of 1937 he performed five recitals in different halls and was well paid each time. He was now an independent musician and no longer a student. He had thought to move into a flat of his own but the Goldstein family insisted he must stay with them while David was away. News from David was sketchy. They knew he was in Madrid, caught up in the desperate defence of the city against the besieging Nationalists. In contrast, the younger Lamingham had been arrested and charged with arson, having been caught pouring petrol through the window of a synagogue. Fortunately he had been stopped before he could fire the building. Following his influential father's intervention Lamingham avoided prison but was sectioned under the mental health act and placed in an asylum.

In October the Times announced the engagement between: *John, Viscount Petersfield, elder son of the Duke and Duchess of Hampshire of Manningley Park Shropshire, and Miss Maria Tenbury daughter of Mr and Mrs Tenbury of Pockhampton Manor Sussex.*

Richard felt both fatalistic and bereft and yet he kept in touch with Maria who behaved as if nothing had happened. Her marriage was due in the Arundel Catholic Cathedral in June of 1938. She repeated to him that she was doing her duty. Johnny Petersfield was sweet but he, Dickie, was her love. Then, on one climactic evening he took her home to her flat after one of his recitals. The girl had produced a packet of Durex and in her apartment she deprived him of his virginity. They were breaking every rule of his upbringing and her religion, but they couldn't help themselves. The experience was something wonderful and it didn't seem wrong.

'What was it your Mother said about me?' Maria whispered as they snuggled to one another.

'She said I wasn't safe with you.'

'Now, I wonder why she thought that.'

'I've got a good idea now,' he replied.

Richard had never been a follower of politics but, like everyone, he knew war, if not inevitable, was a possibility. The dictators were showing off their armed might. Hitler, Mussolini and Stalin all held menace. The Spanish republic was resisting the fascist takeover but for how long? Richard's flying training ceased to be a big game but was becoming serious. He didn't mind too much. If there was to be war he knew where he would sooner fight.

His flying instruction was becoming more intense. He made solo flights and for longer. He was absorbed in navigation and finally the toughest test: blind flying. This meant taking control of a Tiger Moth with an instructor, but the pupil sat in a cockpit covered with a hood. The trainee pilot had only his instruments and his compass to help him. It was easy to think the instruments were wrong; that the turn and bank indicator was not level and the aircraft was near to a spin, that the compass was reading south when it was really northeast. Some pupils panicked under this stress and once or twice Richard nearly did so as well. On two occasions he was taken to a nearby RAF base and did time in a link trainer, consisting of a cockpit linked to an instructor's console and all safely on the ground. Eventually he was able to do some real cross-country flights using classroom navigation and observation of the ground features below him. He had now completed the basics, and having passed the set written exams. he was declared competent. Squadron Leader Rendell had congratulated Richard and told him to go away and wait for the call for advanced training.

'And now, I think a last rendition on our piano.'

June came, and on the 10th Maria and John Petersfield married. Richard had not been invited and he would have made some excuse if he had been. A week later he forced himself to look at the lavish wedding pictures in *The Tatler*. Neither bride nor groom looked ecstatic. Petersfield was in his full Lifeguards uniform ex-the helmet while Maria wore a laced wedding gown and a little frilly cap. Both sets of parents standing behind the couple seemed moderately happy, but the formidable Lady Sylvia looked hard-faced and grim.

Richard threw himself into performing. He had been booked for three recitals and another concerto, this time the Tchaikovsky One and once again in the Queens's Hall. He was surprised to see the same girl viola player who had taken Lamingham's place when he played the Rachmaninov. Her name was Stella and she was an Australian. Stella was a fine player, not frightened by performing in a man's world. She was pretty, and she was outspoken, very like Maria had been. But now he was free of Maria he was drawn to Stella.

'I don't know much about your country,' he told her. 'What part do you come from?'

'Me, I come from Melbourne. It's a great city, better than Sydney.' She took a sip from the wine he'd bought her. They were in a wine bar; a new fashionable venue among a number opening in London. 'All my family are from Melbourne. But we were free settlers a hundred years ago, not convicts.'

Richard couldn't help smiling. He remembered Miss Jeffries in the village school and her disdain for the penal founders of Australia. 'Well, you're a good musician and you've plenty more from your country; there's Melba and Grainger.'

Stella giggled; she really was very like Maria. 'I'm only a rank and file player – don't think I compare with those.'

'I wasn't sure I'd make out as a soloist until I tried. You need ambition.'

She laughed again. 'I like playing in the orchestra. I'm not sure I want to stand up in front of a load of people.' She stared at him. 'Is it true you're taking up flying?'

'Yes, it's true. But I've qualified and I'm an RAF reservist now.'

She grimaced. 'Some of our friends say you're being stupid. If a war comes you'll be made to fight.'

'Well, that's what it's about. Nobody wants a war, but if that crazy Hitler starts one we'll be drawn into it. And I'd rather be flying than in some trenches like my poor old dad was in the last one.'

Stella fixed him with a woeful expression. Once again he thought how like Maria she was. 'Richard, you are such a talent, everyone says so. I'm sure you could give just as good service as a musician.'

'Too late now. I'm committed, but there's no certainty we'll be in a war. There's millions signing the peace pledge and I would say our government would rather talk to Hitler than fight him.'

Richard and Stella went out together on a number of occasions. Richard was still uncertain as to how deep a relationship he wanted with this girl. He found, to coin a phrase that she was on his wave-length. Theirs was an easygoing friendship, but he could not delude himself. He still yearned for Maria. According to Mrs Tenbury, Maria and her new husband had honeymooned in Cannes and on returning to England had gone to the family home in Shropshire. From Maria herself he had he heard nothing. He lay awake at night thinking of her.

The thought of his Maria copulating with that chinless idiot made him feel sick.

One evening he returned to the Goldstein house to find a very wan and haggard man sitting in the dining room drinking a cup of tea. The man was thin and looked ill and his hands shook. Richard looked at him then looked twice and gasped, 'David, you're home.'

'Hello, Dick, yes, I'm home.'

The jolly one time oboe player had changed. He was emaciated and his face was both suntanned but with a tinge of yellow. Richard knew he must be cautious. Here was an old friend who had been in hell.

'Dick, it's so good to see you. My war's lost I think. The International Brigades are no more. I reached Barcelona and got out on a cargo boat.'

'David, I'm so sorry. But we must get you back on your feet again.'

David poured out his story. He would never regret going to this war. He had fought hard and seen some terrible sights. Physically he felt he would recover but he was tormented by nightmares. 'I don't like to talk to Naomi about it, but Dick – it's such a relief to get some of this off my chest. It was such a dirty business. Our airforce was no match for the bloody Germans. Hitler and Mussolini have poured weapons and equipment into Spain. We couldn't win against that. The Russians supplied our side but they are just being cynical. Now I'm really frightened. Will we resist Hitler?'

'Well, I'm a qualified reserve RAF pilot. If Hitler tries any funny business in our skies he'll get a shock.' Richard spoke with a confidence that he hoped would reassure his friend. He knew the country and the population at large were weary from economic depression and the grim memory of the previous war. But everything he had learned from Squadron Leader Rendell and his fellow officers told him that an advanced home air defence was being assembled in secret. New fighter aircraft were already in service. Richard remembered his excitement only a few weeks ago in seeing one of the new Spitfire fighters flying over Sussex. If war came he would likely be flying such an aircraft and that was better than being in some muddy trenches with Johnny Petersfield.

For Richard it was a happier summer than he might have expected. He had no news directly from Maria, but Mrs Tenbury had told him that the new couple had moved into a house on the Corbailier estate and that Johnny was heavily involved away with his army duties. He saw more of Stella and twice went to see her play in the orchestra at the Promenade Concerts in Queen's Hall. In both cases the conductor had been Mr Wood, the professor who had interviewed him when he joined the Academy.

Stella was fun to be with. She was jolly and didn't mind him laughing when she tried to refine her Australian accent. Her father managed a Melbourne bank and her parents owned a house on the outskirts of the city. She loved sailing and that was another bond between them. In August that year the pair of them had spent a happy week at the Cowes regatta crewing for Mr Ross.

The newspaper headlines and the BBC news were filled with gloom. Adolf Hitler had his eyes on the German-speaking province of Czechoslovakia, the Sudetenland. Unless the British and French governments conceded his right to this land he would invade it anyway. The talk was now all of war. This would not be a clean-cut shooting war. Cities would be bombed and gas masks were being issued. Richard was called up with many others to take his first steps in advanced flying. This was initially in a Miles Magister, a monoplane low-wing training aircraft but similar to a fighter and a different proposition to the Tiger Moth. He was piling up flying hours and that would serve him well should war come.

He was dancing with Stella at the Hammersmith Palais to the music of the Harry Malburg orchestra. Stella lay back in his arms and smiled, she really was an amazingly attractive girl. 'This tune they're playing – guess who composed it?' he grinned at her.

'I like it but I don't think I've heard it before. Is it one of Harry's?'

'Yes and no.'

'You're not making sense,' she smiled.

'Well, that tune was composed by Richard Dyer, and strange to relate, he's me.'

Stella laughed and snuggled even closer. Richard knew he had a decision to make about this girl and he must make it soon. They went out and found his car. Richard had passed his test and his newfound prosperity was enough to buy a second hand Morris Twelve. He dropped Stella home to the flat she shared with two other girls. Then he headed for the basement flat that he had taken for himself. It was in South Kensington, a street away from his friends the Goldsteins. He let himself in, turned on the wireless, poured a whisky and settled down in his armchair. The doorbell was ringing; at this time of night?

Who on earth?

He stood up and opened the door. There stood Maria.

CHAPTER 24

'Dickie, don't stand there staring, I want to come in.' Maria had her sweetest smile. 'I went to your old address and they sent me here.'

Richard was worried. Would the Goldsteins keep their mouths shut?

'Come on in,' he said. 'Why this honour?'

'Why do you think? I wanted to talk to you,' she smiled again. 'I've really missed you.'

He was excited to see her. He led her into his sitting room and took her coat. Then he caught his breath. Beneath the coat she wore a dress, or what passed for a dress. It was a light shift, and almost transparent. He found himself grinning. 'What do you call that dress?'

She put her arms around him. 'It's Paraquois of Paris. It's the height of fashion.'

'But if you take it off. I mean what's underneath?'

'Oh, come on Dickie, you've seen me naked plenty of times.'

'Eh?'

'Not just our last run around in my flat. I mean years ago.'

'Oh yes, but we were only children. That was different.' He remembered now; the dozen or so six to eight-year-olds in the August heatwave; splashing around happily naked in the stream by the bridge, with clothes lying on the grass nearby.

'Anyway, come and sit down. Like a drink, gin, sherry?'

She smiled again. 'A sherry would be nice.'

Now, ask the inevitable. 'How is married life?'

'If you want the truth, it's bloody awful.'

Richard was shocked. 'I'll pretend I didn't hear that.'

'I don't care. As I told you once; Johnny is sweet and kind but as a man he's useless. I'm just an ornament.'

There was nothing he could say to this. He waited for her to go on. She smiled in her most seductive manner. 'You seem to be doing well. You've bought a piano.'

Richard felt relieved at this turn. 'It's a baby grand but it's a nice tone and it fits in here just right.'

'That's rather well put. Le double entendre.'

'Sorry, I don't understand.'

She laughed; that same old Maria laugh that he remembered so well. 'Can I look around your place here? It's rather nice: Victorian high ceiling – tasteful.'

He stood up. 'Come on, I'll show you.' He led her into the kitchen. 'Have you eaten? I'm becoming quite a hand at cooking.'

'No, I had a good tuck in at the Corbailier's house about an hour ago. That's not what I'm hungry for.'

'Explain.'

'I am hungry for love – real love.' She put her arms around his shoulders and kissed. 'A girl has certain needs and just now I need love from the real man in my life.'

'What about your Johnny?'

'What about him?'

'Does he love you?

'No, he does not. Johnny loves his batman – one Corporal Stoppings.'

Richard halted in his tracks really shocked. 'You mean – he's a…'

'Yes, Johnny is a homo; the typical product of a titled family and a superior public school.'

'But that's illegal.'

'For everybody except the likes of Johnny. Remember how Oscar Wilde was put in jail while his aristocratic lover went free?'

She walked to the bedroom door. She glanced inside and gave him a sharp look. 'That's a very nice double bed. Is that for the little Australian girl?'

'No it is not. It came with the place. Who told you about Stella?'

'Dickie, get used to the fact. You are a personality – you are fodder for the gossips.' She smothered him with more kisses. 'I love you, Dickie, and I always have.'

Now he was lost. 'I love you too.'

She giggled. 'We sound like Clarke Gable and Vivienne Leigh, or anyone in the films.'

'Richard gasped as she kicked off her shoes, slipped off the flimsy dress and stood in front of him completely naked. He stared at her as he took in her pert breasts and erect nipples and looked on down the lovely shape of her body and slender legs. Her little shock of blonde pubic hair, he remembered, and it proved that her head hair was not dyed.

'Well go on,' she giggled. 'Must I turn my back while you get undressed?'

'No.' He loosened his tie and ripped off his shirt. Two minutes passed before both lovers fell naked on the bed. They kissed and embraced and then, as he entered her, Maria squealed and seemed to explode. For a whole glorious evening they loved and loved with short periods when both collapsed in sleep. After six hours neither had any ardour left and lay together in a happy contentment.

'Maria,' he whispered. 'You are wonderful, but will you have to go to confession?'

She sat up abruptly on one elbow. 'No, of course not.'

'Surely your church would say we've sinned.'

She laid her lovely soft face and hair on his chest. 'No, no – you are the one I was meant for. I believe God is smiling on us.'

It was daylight when the pair awoke the next morning. Richard was suddenly aware that it was far too late for Maria to walk up the steps from his flat and not be noticed.

They both dressed hastily and Richard made a pot of coffee. He put his worries to Maria. 'You're a high-society lady, you might be recognized.'

Once again her giggle. 'And you are a noted musician; what scandal! All right, I'd better leave in disguise.'

'How are you going to do that?'

'I'll be the cleaner. You know – the daily woman.'

He was doubtful. 'You don't look like one and hardly, in that apology for a dress.'

'Can you find me anything tawdry to wear?'

'Not really, wait, I've an idea. I expect the lady upstairs will lend me something shabby, she's an artist with a studio.'

'How are you going to bluff her as to what's it's really for.'

He thought and then snapped his fingers. 'I'll tell her my cleaner has burnt her dress and needs some new cover, anything will do.'

Maria laughed. 'Oh, thanks for the compliment.'

Richard left his own apartment and ran up to the street level. He knocked on the actual front door of the house. A middle-aged lady in a long dressing gown opened it. This was Margery McGraw, well known as a painter and society eccentric.

She looked Richard up and down. 'How is the young lady this morning?'

'What?'

'The young lady with whom you and she were pleasuring each other, or I hope you weren't murdering her.'

Richard's mouth hung open in shock.

'I assume it was pleasure; the young lady's screams sounded definitely more pleasure than murder.'

'Oh no! Were we that loud? I mean there is an explanation.'

'Not needed. Young Richard, this is an artistic community. You play music, I paint and the young man upstairs writes novels. We are what is called broadminded.'

'If you say so.'

'Well, I do say so. What can I do for you?'

'We were wondering if you could lend my friend something to disguise her when she walks out of here. Make her look like a cleaner.' He hesitated. 'You see she's known and I'm known in our own worlds and we need to be discreet.'

Margery spluttered with laughter. 'Why, is she a film star?'

'Something like that,' Richard felt it was better to go along with this.

'All right, wait here and I'll see what I can find.'

CHAPTER 25

War was now a real prospect in a world that was seemingly going mad. Adolf Hitler was still demanding the secession of a large chunk of neighbouring Czechoslovakia. His attitude had hardened. France and Great Britain must accept this or he would invade and take the territory anyway. After that he would turn his attention to them. The newspapers and wireless reports were filled with doom and gloom. Air raid precautions were being increased and more gas masks issued.

One morning a small gaggle of Mosleyites marched down the street outside Richard's flat. They were shouting for *Peace in our time. No war to save Jews.* Leading this mob was Michael Lamingham. It seemed the tiresome fellow must have talked his way out of the mental asylum. Richard wondered if his own RAF recall was in the post. As a reservist officer he could be recalled at any time. Reluctantly he cancelled a recital he was to give in Colchester. In the future he was to regret the huge relief he felt when he and Stella sat in the newsreel theatre and watched Neville Chamberlain wave his little bit of paper at the airport. Normal life could begin again, or so he thought.

In this uncertain world Richard's private life was tearing him in two. Following his night with Maria he saw little of her. She would ring his telephone and engage in long heartfelt talk that must have been costing a fortune. He only hoped the wretched Johnny would not check the bill, nor her fierce sister-in-law be listening in. Johnny's regiment had been put on high alert, but following the peace deal they had been stood down. He wondered, would Johnny be charging into battle with horse and armour? It seemed not. He and his like would find themselves in the mud and grime of modern warfare.

Whatever Maria might say, she was not his. She was not attainable apart from these occasional secret trysts. He did not understand this division in Maria's mind between duty in marriage and their private love. She did not seem particularly jealous of Stella. She had referred to her with no obvious female malice. Maria was wonderful; their lovemaking was out of this world. She was closer to him than anyone else that he knew, but she could never be his wife. She was his mistress. Dozens of well-known figures in music, art, the stage and literature had mistresses, or the women, lovers. Margery upstairs thought nothing of his and Maria's affair. She hadn't even asked who the girl was.

Then there was Stella. He was so fond of her. She was a fine orchestral musician and she made him laugh. He felt relaxed in her company and she would be the ideal wife and companion. Stella herself had hinted that with precautions she would share his bed, but that was firmly Maria's place. Anyway he had better forget about girls for a few days. That Saturday, the first in October, he was due in Bournemouth to play the Rachmaninov again with the local symphony orchestra. He yawned and began to pack his overnight bag.

Richard parked his car outside the little boarding house and drew breath. It was a warm late autumn afternoon and he felt relaxed. London with all his emotional problems seemed a thousand miles away. Next he signed, in, found his bedroom and unpacked his things. He owned his own dinner suit now, which he placed carefully on a hanger in the wardrobe. This was Friday: his performance was tomorrow evening, so he had twenty-four hours to relax and enjoy the sea air. The orchestra was to assemble in the Pavilion the following morning and he would then get a chance to run through his piece and get to know them. Sir Dan Godfrey, their famous conductor had retired and Richard had been delighted to learn that his bluntly-spoken American was the guest conductor. But he had better put on a good show because his old tutor Mr Ross would be in the audience with his wife, daughter and son-in-law. The Ross family was taking part in a late autumn sailing regatta on Poole Harbour. Richard half wished he could sail with them, but it was music that called him first and foremost, and anyway he was being pretty well paid for this concerto.

He glanced at his wristwatch. Dinner was not due until six thirty. He had plenty of time to stretch his legs. He left the boarding house and never saw his landlady reach for the telephone.

Richard strolled on the beach and drew in a delicious breath of sea air. What a contrast from the smoke and fumes of London. The sand was almost literally golden, and across the water he could see the distant hills of Purbeck. He felt some more music coming on.

'Hey, squire,' a voice was calling. He turned to see a man in an ill-fitting pinstripe suit with a trilby hat. He reminded Richard of Tommy Trinder. Beside him was a little chap wearing a jacket and flannels sporting a toothy grin and an ill-fitting cloth cap. Round his neck was a press camera.

'Squire, are you Mr Dyer the famous piano player?'

Richard was startled. 'Some people might call me the infamous pianist.' Why should he recall Maria? 'Why do you want me?'

'Because you are celebrated. You're performing in our town and our readers would like to know.'

'Readers?'

'Sorry, Mr Dyer, I should have said,' he held out a card. 'Sam Shortman from the Echo.' The well-named Mr Shortman had produced a tiny notebook with a pencil attached. 'Mr Dyer, what do you think of our town and are you pleased to be playing here?'

Richard felt like laughing but fought to keep a straight face. 'Well, I've only just got here but I like what I've seen.'

'Do you like our symphony orchestra?'

'Well, I know them by reputation and I'm very happy to play with them.' Richard stared at the man. 'Mr Shortman, why this interest in me?'

''Cos they like the classic music around here and you are a big name.'

'If you say so.'

'Not me, Mr Dyer, everyone we talk to says so. Tell me – is it true you're an air pilot?

Richard was really taken aback now. 'Well yes, I'm an RAF reservist. How did you know that?'

'A reliable source.' Mr Shortman looks solemn.

'Well, all right. Yes, I enjoy flying and I've been lucky to qualify for the Air Force.'

'Mr Dyer, you come from Sussex. I worked for the Brighton paper and I can tell you they all rave about you in those parts.'

Richard grinned. 'You're trying to tell me I'm a country boy. Well that's true; born on the farm, bred on the farm and very proud to say so.'

It was a relief to escape from the comic newshounds. To conciliate them he posed for three pictures. This fame was starting to worry him. He was still only eighteen. He had achieved more than he could have dreamed of when he started out, but would this success last? He was young and resilient. He could take the mental stress of playing but would he be able to do so when he was much older? Music had long since taken over his life and he was still ambitious. Yes, he enjoyed being a soloist but long term he wanted to compose. Tomorrow he would perform the concerto and then he was due a break. He would drive over to Sussex, say hello to his folks and then lose himself with a long walk on Pockhampton Down.

The Bournemouth performance was not Richard's best but the audience seemed not to notice. He knew it was always going to be difficult to replicate the Queen's Hall performance.

'Aw, boy, you worry too much,' said the American. 'All sounded good to me. Say, you got an agent?'

'A what?' Richard was baffled.

'An agent, a guy to do your business. Fix your performance dates. Do the goddamn paper work.'

'No, I've been doing all that myself.'

The conductor sighed. 'Boy, you're heading for the big time – you need an agent. Believe me; I couldn't function without my guy.'

'What does he cost? – and would he do it for me?'

'Yeah, I'll talk to my man, but it won't really cost you. In fact you'll be in pocket. Sure, the agent takes a percentage cut, but he'll more than make that up for you in takings and bookings.'

Richard left the matter in the conductor's hands and drove to Sussex. It seemed there was a complex business world out there and he had better start understanding it.

He arrived in Pockhampton and booked in at the village pub. Some of his old school friends were in the bar. Clearly they regarded him as a bit of an oddity. His smart clothes and shiny motorcar were symbols of a world they couldn't aspire to. They didn't envy his fame themselves, but were rather pleased to see one of their number achieve it. He did his duty and bought the assembled company a round of beer. Then he put some coins in the pub's telephone and called home.

His parents greeted him in the farmhouse as if he'd never been away. His father did grunt a bit when he saw the smart suit and shoes that Richard wore. Mabel, his mother overwhelmed him with chatter about the family and village gossip. Yes, it was nice to be back in a world of sanity. Little Alice caught his hand and pulled him into the tiny garden to see her new swing suspended from a branch of the oak tree in the corner. It was a liberation and delight to push her and hear her joy and laughter.

Later he took the whole family for a drive in his car. He drove away from the village in a direction that took them nowhere near Pockhampton Manor. He worried whether Mrs Tenbury had found out anything about his illicit nights with her daughter. Much as he liked the lady he was anxious not to meet her.

His parents enjoyed the ride, evidently a rare experience and treat.

They asked him politely about his career although that was clearly an alien world for them. They brought him up to date with village news. He heard how old Albert Shank, the un-harmonious blacksmith had died that week and that his funeral was the next day. It would be a big occasion for the whole village. This was sad news, for in spite of his appalling bass singing Richard still felt a fondness for the old fellow.

To tell the truth Richard was feeling increasingly downhearted. Tomorrow he must attend the funeral of an old man he had always respected. It was more than that. This was his home village and he felt safe here. London was waiting for him and London was going to mean trouble. He loved his music and burgeoning career in it; but it was bringing so much worry in its wake with all this talk of agents and booking tours. He was not sure he really wanted to tour if that meant night after night away from home, living from a suitcase in a string of shabby hotels. London meant doing something to sort out his tangled private life. He loved both the girls he was involved with, but he never doubted that Stella would walk out on him if she ever found out about Maria. Maria could never be his, but Stella could be a soul mate for life.

Maria had only succeeded in driving a wedge between him and her family. He would see Mr and Mrs Tenbury at the funeral tomorrow and he would try and avoid them. But if he did that he would feel dreadful and ungrateful for all they had done for him. He clenched his fists in anguish and he felt the tears flow down his face. He downed two pints of beer in the pub and stumbled upstairs. He fell on his bed and slept fitfully invaded by surreal dreams and no music.

Richard overslept that next morning. He walked slowly downstairs and the landlord invited him to eat breakfast in the kitchen. He did so and felt slightly better for munching a sausage and a fried egg. Once again he had dressed in his best dark suit instead of the casual jacket and flannels. Everyone in the pub and out in the street was attired in some form of black. He felt depressed again. The church bell was tolling. What was it that poet wrote? *Ask not for whom the bell tolls. It tolls for thee.* Somehow he almost wished it did.

The coffin was outside the church on a farm wagon draped in black ribbon. The mourners were gathering; representatives of every family, including the gentry. He could see Mr and Mrs Tenbury standing a little apart, and with them stood Maria.

CHAPTER 26

Maria smiled directly at him and Mrs Tenbury waved. Thank God, she didn't look angry, so with a bit of luck she knew nothing about his nights with her daughter. Maria was beckoning him urgently, so he couldn't in politeness ignore her. He walked across. Mrs Tenbury gave him a dazzling smile and held out her hand. Maria leant up and gave him a chaste kiss on the cheek. The funeral cortege was moving into the church. Richard wondered if the Tenburys would actually enter the building, it being an Anglican church, even if Mr Davis had high-church pretensions. In the event they entered and settled in a pew near the entrance.

Mr Locke was playing the organ. While they were waiting outside he had given a fair rendering of Pachelbel's Canon. Now as the coffin proceeded up the aisle, he moved into Elgar's Nimrod. Richard was a better pianist than an organist although he had taught himself to master the keys, stops and pedals. Mr Locke was a good organist and a good musician as Richard already knew. The sombre service started, the prayers were said and Mr Davis delivered a moving tribute to old Alfred. The choir and congregation sang the hymn: *Abide With Me* and the coffin was carried out into the graveyard.

Outside, the soft October sunlight shone down as the coffin-bearers lowered their burden into the open grave amidst respectful silence. Mr Davis spoke the committal, Alfred's daughter and grandchildren wept. Then it was over and the congregation made their way slowly to the village hall for the wake. In the hall lay a huge spread of tasty food prepared by the women of the parish. Richard found much of his depression melting away. He was with old friends in the community he loved. He was happy that Maria attached herself to him and, thank goodness, avoided any open display of affection. Maria leapt on the food as if she was still a ten-year-old. Richard was more restrained; he still didn't feel like celebrating. He had just seen an old man whom he had liked and respected laid in a grave.

Someone touched him on the arm. It was Mrs Tenbury. 'Richard, we were hoping you will come to dinner this evening.'

He mumbled acceptance. There was nothing else that he could say.

'Good,' replied Mrs Tenbury. 'We'll be off now, but Maria will bring you in her new car.'

Maria tugged at his sleeve. 'Come on.'

Outside the hall was the same little Austin Seven that Richard had seen Maria driving, but this time it was Mrs Tenbury who settled in the driving seat and drove away. 'Shall we take my car?' he asked.

'No, have a ride in mine,' she replied. Maria pointed at a smart and shiny MG Sports car that Richard had already noticed parked outside the hall.

'Is that yours?'

She smiled. 'Yes, I've only had it a month but it is rather fine, don't you think?'

'Did your husband give it to you?'

'Now, Dickie, you are sounding jealous again and that won't do.' She laughed. 'If you must know yes, he did give it to me.'

'Where is he today?'

'Where d'you think? He's somewhere having a high old time with his lover.'

Richard grimaced. 'What – his batman?'

'Not any more. They've had a tiff and Johnny is enamoured of a young lieutenant. An officer – much more suitable.'

'Oh, Maria, I am sorry.'

'Who cares – I've got you.'

Richard settled himself in the passenger seat of the MG. He felt as if was sitting only an inch above the road surface. Maria fired the engine and they set out for Pockhampton Manor. Richard gritted his teeth as she hurled the car into the corners and pushed the accelerator to the floor on the straights. She sped up the avenue and skidded to a halt on the gravel by the front door. A relieved Richard followed her into the house.

'Come on in, Richard,' said Mrs Tenbury. 'Come in the drawing room and have a drink.'

Maria suddenly turned unsteadily and staggered into the hallway.

'Are you all right?' Richard was concerned.

'I'm just a bit queasy,' she replied. 'I'll be fine in a minute. He watched her run across the hall and through a far doorway that he remembered led to the downstairs lavatories.

'Is she well?' he asked.

'Take no notice,' said Mrs Tenbury. 'She'll be all right in a minute.'

'She did eat a lot at that wake party,' he said.

Maria returned ten minutes later and she was smiling again.

Richard enjoyed the dinner at the Tenburys, but Maria's presence was disturbing. She came to dinner dressed in the same high-fashion evening gown with the strapless top. She'd worn it that night at the ball in London. He could only think how totally wasted it was with Johnny. How he adored this girl – his girl – and yet tomorrow he would return to London to meet Stella and have to pretend that Maria did not exist. At least Mrs Tenbury treated him she always had, or perhaps not. She evidently suspected nothing of his affair with her married daughter, but at the same time she was going out of her way to be indulgent. A good hostess would do that but this was almost as if he was a trusted member of her family. It was up to both Maria and he to keep their mouths shut. Later he had sat at the Steinway and entertained them with a medley of the latest dance band numbers. Then Maria ran him back to the pub in her MG.

'Are you feeling better now?' he asked. 'You looked rotten when we first arrived at your place.'

'Oh, that was nothing. I just felt a bit queasy.'

The next morning Richard drove back to London. He felt depressed again. He had spent a restful few days in the community that had raised him and that he loved. Problems seemed to be growing and looked almost insurmountable. He would have to make career choice about this agent and he would have to face Stella. He wished he could do another course of flying. He was a registered RAFVR pilot awaiting advanced flying training, but now the danger of war had faded, so had his chances of going for the next big leap in his flying.

He wended his way through the West London traffic, reached his home street, parked the car and walked down the steps into his empty flat.

CHAPTER 27

1939

The next morning Richard awoke and tried to put the tangled dreams of last night behind him. He sat down at the piano and worked solidly for an hour and a half on standard exercises and then a big slab of Tchaikovsky followed by his medley of dance band tunes. He concluded, shut the piano lid and made himself coffee and a boiled egg. At least his brain seemed to be working and his fingers still agile.

The telephone rang and it was Stella. Her voice was high-pitched with excitement and her Australian accent extra vivid. 'Hey there, Dickie mate, I've news, you'll never believe it. I didn't think it, not wi' all those poobah Poms running the show, but it's true…'

'Darling Stella, would you please translate into English and not all this outback shrieking?'

'Yeah, sorry. It's just that I'm going to do a concerto. Going to be a front player just like you. I need some tips.'

'That sounds good, tell me more.'

'Hector Berlioz, Harold in Italy; it's a viola concerto. The Academy are doing it and they want me to solo.'

Richard was familiar with this work. It was a nice visual piece with a composer's programme explaining the story behind each movement. It was not a particularly demanding work for the soloist; no comparison with the Rachmaninov, but it was a nice step up for Stella. No wonder she was excited. For the snobbish academy to invite a girl, and a colonial as well, to a main role was quite a progressive move.

'There's another thing,' her voice broke into his thoughts. 'They asked me if you would play at the same concert. They thought some Choppin would go down well.'

'I think you'll find Chopin is the correct pronunciation.'

'Yeah, all right – Showpan if he was an Aussie.'

Richard didn't see why not. It would give some moral support for Stella and it would be nice to play on the same stage. Thank goodness he had not committed himself to this agent. The man would probably think of a dozen reasons to stop him.

'When is this and where?'

'August in the Brighton Dome hall.'

'I know it. I've been there but never played there.'

'Dickie, would you take me to the flicks this evening? The Odeon round the corner from me are re-showing Fred Astaire – Top Hat. Have you seen it?'

'Yes, it's got some good Irving Berlin music. Yes, I'd like to see it again.'

'Good, pick me up at my place – six thirty.'

Richard felt a glow of anticipation. It would be wonderful to see Stella. He felt very happy for her with her solo playing assignment. It was no more than she deserved. Girl or not she was a fine viola player and a good deal better than the wretched Lamingham whom she'd replaced. It would be a lovely evening for both of them. He could forget all about Maria and enjoy the company of this lovely volatile girl. He enjoyed all the Astaire and Rogers films. They had energy in the dancing and Berlin's music was bright and tuneful. Top Hat was his favourite; he was not so keen on Damsel in Distress. Its theme of aristocratic forced marriage was a bit too close to home even if the film was a comedy.

He met Stella at her flat and escorted her for the short walk to the cinema. They both enjoyed the film with its music, dancing and crazy storyline. Afterwards they went to a little Italian restaurant popular with the performing music set.

'Evening, Luciano,' Richard greeted the proprietor. 'How's Mussolini?'

'He has the pox, I hope,' the Italian made a throat cutting gesture.

They found a quiet nook in a corner of the restaurant and ordered their food.

Stella was smiling at him in a new and disconcerting way. 'Dick,' she began. 'I think I should know. Is there someone else? I mean are you seeing another girl?'

Richard felt as if his stomach was going down in a lift. 'What makes you think that?'

'A girl's intuition.' She leaned forward across the narrow table. 'You seem uncertain and I want to know our future. Dick, I can't hold it back. I love you, we're both in music; we have so much in common. I would like to spend the rest of my life with you, but there's something that's hidden and I think it's another girl.'

There was nothing for it. He had to clear the air with a modicum of truth. 'Yes, there was a girl I was fond of, but she married someone else.'

'Do I know her?'

'No you've never met and you won't now.'

'I would hate it if I was the girl you caught on the rebound.'

'Well, you're not. You are your own person and you are very different from the other one.' He looked her in the eyes. 'Stella, I was bowled over the first time I saw you, the night you played in the orchestra at the concerto.' Richard made a sudden impulsive decision. 'Stella, darling, I haven't got a ring with me, and I don't think this is a place to get down on one knee. I'm still not nineteen so it won't be tomorrow, but one day will you marry me?'

She smiled and laughed with delight. 'Yes, of course I will.'

He leaned right over the table and kissed her. 'I adore you and I won't let you down.'

Richard had made a decision, crossed the Rubicon. Stella was right for him. Maria could still be his long-term friend, but Stella was the person he would spend his life with. Of course tradition would require him to take her home to Sussex to meet his parents, but in that case he would see that was on a week when Maria was safely with her Johnny. The real problem that overwhelmed everything was war on the horizon again. Adolf Hitler was not playing cricket. Rules and treaties seemed to the mean nothing to this man. His armed forces were threatening more than ever. Hitler had set his sights on Poland, a country with a German descended minority. He had already annexed the Sudetenland and overwhelmed his birth nation of Austria and, latterly, the rest of Slovakia. It seemed more and more likely that Britain and France would have to fight Hitler and in that case Richard would be flying in battle. That was a dark shadow that he pushed into the background. In the meantime he had found a life partner and he had a career to follow in music.

Stella had suggested both of them settle in Australia. Richard suspected her motive was to remove him ten thousand miles away from Maria. All the news from her home had been about the terrible Black Friday when over seventy people had died from the bush fires in Victoria. Her parents had abandoned their holiday house and fled back to the home city. He had one letter from Maria that he took care to hide from Stella. The contents were harmless enough. Her brother Leo didn't like the new Pope and he had applied to become an army chaplain in the event of war. Johnny had told her war was inevitable. He was now a major and his regiment was training flat out for war. Her father had been advised that he would be called up by the Air Ministry.

Then Richard had received a visit from the man appointed as air raid warden for his street. It was all very depressing. He threw himself into his concert dates and tried to forget the gloom and doom. His old friend David Goldstein had recovered from his Spanish horror and was now playing oboe in a London orchestra. David had become very serious and had started to practice his religion on Saturdays. Franco's victory in Spain had saddened him in the most personal way. Reports of the revenge atrocities being carried out on Franco's orders had deeply affected David. Then there was the news that shiploads of Jews fleeing Europe were being turned around and sent back to whatever fate Hitler might have in store.

Richard heard the telephone and ran into his front room to answer. The clock said eleven pm, so who on earth? 'Hello, Dickie, it's me – Maria.'

'Maria, it's so nice to hear your voice,' he replied. That was true of course but he wasn't sure what this was about. Now he had a shock.

'So, you're thinking one day of marrying the little Australian girl. Am I right?'

There was nothing for it but the truth. 'Yes, I am but how the hell did you know?'

'I keep telling you. You're famous and people gossip.'

'Oh God, well maybe it's for the best. Maria, I'm still very fond of you but you're spoken for and married.'

'No, Dickie, I don't want either of us to be jealous. We're linked together now for ever.'

'Sorry, I don't get you.'

He heard her old familiar giggle. 'Don't get you; you're back talking Sussex again. Anyway when's the happy day?'

'Not just yet. We're both busy and there's all this talk of war,' he paused. 'I hope we can still be friends.'

'We'll always be friends. As I said. We'll be linked for ever.'

'I still don't understand.'

'I'll tell you when I see you. Bye-bye, Dickie, be good.'

End of Part One

PART TWO: WAR

CHAPTER 28

1940

If this was war it was becoming a bit of an anticlimax. It was cold and damp when Richard climbed into the service transport sent to meet him and half a dozen other advanced trainees from the local station. After weeks of instruction this was going to be the great moment when they would come face-to-face with a Hurricane.

Anticlimax was the thought in his mind because, after three months of declared war, nothing had happened. No Luftwaffe bombers had ranged overhead despite the apprehension in London and other big cities. Even sleepy Pockhampton had its share of evacuee children. How prepared the allies were for Hitler was uncertain although Richard knew that RAF Fighter Command had a sophisticated defence system shrouded in secrecy.

Back home, his girl Stella had been told there was no chance for her to return to Australia so she had joined the WAAF. Maria seemed to have vanished off the planet which was probably a good thing as far as he and Stella were concerned. Mrs Tenbury had told him that Maria was an ATS commissioned officer and involved in something top secret. The idea of Maria keeping a secret was a novelty, but then this was war. The lorry bounced its way over a potholed road. Richard felt under his jacket and fingered the pilot's wings now sewn on his uniform. He was Pilot Officer R. Dyer. RAFVR and that felt good. He would be flying an advanced aircraft and he had been told he would be in high demand with his piano playing. Things could have been a lot worse. Johnny Petersfield was holed up somewhere in Northern France with his brigade. Very soon that aristocratic dandy would be up to his neck fighting in a muddy trench.

Soon, but how soon? What was this Hitler up to? He had ruthlessly conquered Poland and, by all accounts, he was committing atrocities among the innocent population. His ally Stalin had occupied another slice of that unhappy country. Some Poles were defiant. Richard had met several pilots who had escaped and were serving in the RAF. Sooner or later this phoney war must end and the killing would begin. Well, please God, he would be ready.

The lorry slowed and stopped. Richard could just see a pole barrier lift and now they were driving along a much smoother roadway.

Speeding by, through the tail of the lorry he could see workshops and huge hangars. Finally they stopped in front of a redbrick HQ building. 'Gentlemen this is it, you may descend.' The corporal's respectful voice had a sardonic edge.

Inside the building they registered their names with a bored-looking sergeant. Then a rather pretty WAAF was ordered to show them their quarters. They were designated two-bed cubicles with the most basic of facilities. The WAAF shook her head and smiled at the ribald comments then left them to it.

They all drifted back to the entrance hall. Richard was feeling hungry but no one had told them when or where they would eat. A grey-haired man with a wing commander's uniform entered from a door at the side. The assembled trainees sprang to attention and Richard saluted. The Wing Commander glared at him in an unfriendly way. 'Pilot Officer, why the salute?'

'You're a senior officer, sir and we're all new here.'

'May I remind you. I am not wearing a hat and you are not wearing a hat,'

'Sorry, sir,' Richard was contrite, while sincerely hoping that this pompous blimp was not typical of the service.

'Very well,' said the blimp. 'Initial briefing is at eighteen hundred and after that there is dinner in the mess.'

In reality the Wing Commander was not a blimp. After a few days Richard found he respected his new commanding officer as a fine leader. It was an exciting time. The trainees were instructed in every facet of their new aircraft. The Hurricane was one of four RAF fighter aircraft and by far the most numerous. The slightly more modern Spitfire was faster, but the Hurricane was stable and war damage easily fixed. She had eight .303 machine guns arranged to fire in a converging arc. Any aircraft hit by this blast would be devastated. It was also important for pilots to avoid the defensive rear gunners of a bomber, as it was eliminating the Luftwaffe daylight bombers that would be the Hurricane's primary mission. Finally the day arrived that they had all been waiting for: their first flight.

'Right, are you ready?' asked the instructor.

'Yes, sir.' Richard was excited. He could see the Hurricane with its engine ticking over on the tarmac.

'She's a very forgiving aircraft. Just remember careful checks, prop in takeoff pitch and radiator open and keep the nose up.'

Richard knew all this; it had been ground into him the previous week.

'Good show, she's yours for half an hour. Have fun.'

The mechanic vacated the cockpit. Then Richard, lumbering his bulky parachute, climbed into the narrow seat, fixed the harness and pulled on his helmet and oxygen mask. Next came the pre-takeoff checks. Yes, all in order. Let's go. He waved the chocks away and slowly opened the throttle.

'Able one, able one, you may scramble,' came the radio call.

He was aligned now at the take off point. He pushed the throttle open and felt the surge of power far greater than any aircraft he had flown to date. He must keep the nose up; too much tilt forward would destroy the propeller on the runway.

They speeded along the runway and now they were airborne; he was flying a Hurricane towards the skies above. Next, undercart up, propeller set to cruising pitch and climb. The speed of that climb took his breath away. This was a million miles from the dear old Tiger Moth. Once again the same music, *Ride of the Valkyries* surged through his mind and took him over. He was on such a surge of happy adrenalin. He dived and watched the speed rise to over three hundred mph. He completed turns to left and right, imagining a Messerschmitt behind him. He swept around almost blacking out with the g-force as he shot down his phantom enemy.

'Able one, able one, return to base, return to base.'

Richard searched for the airfield and yes, there it was dead ahead. He changed the propeller pitch, lowered the undercart, lowered the flaps and throttled back. The ground was approaching at a horrific speed and the huge engine in front of him was blocking visibility. Then, miraculously, they touched down and rolled along the runway. Richard taxied towards the point were the instructor stood. Brakes on, throttle right back – he had done it.

'Good man,' the instructor grinned. 'Did you enjoy that?'

Richard nodded. He was exultant but lost for words. Cold as the outside air was, his body dripped sweat. He hadn't felt this way since his famous debut concerto.

There followed more weeks of intense practice: more flights and exercises in formation-flying, gunnery and fighting tactics. It was Christmas: the phoney war seemed to have settled into a permanent state. The RAF regular full time fighting squadrons were based in France. Richard must wait for the call to his own future squadron. In the meantime he was awarded ten days leave. He packed his meagre possessions and headed for Sussex.

Richard arrived at Waterloo station and took the underground to South Kensington. For the next stage of the journey he needed to recover his car. As war had become inevitable he had taken the precaution of filling the tank to the brim before the stringent petrol rationing came into force. London was unrecognizable; the streets were semi-deserted and no lights shone. Only a tiny slit of light was permitted through the painted out headlights. He was relieved to leave the capital behind and head south. He left the Portsmouth road at Petersfield, the town that the drip Johnny was named after. Now he was on a twisting cross-country route that would take him to a point just north of Pockhampton. Having reached Arundel he stopped and caught some sleep sitting in the rear seat of the car. It wouldn't be fair on his people if he turned up at two o'clock in the morning. Ted, his dad, would be up at six. He aimed to arrive home around then.

Richard knew he wasn't expected but his family's welcome was overwhelming. Soon a cluster of neighbours was round to meet him. All admired his smart blue uniform and the pilot's wings. War had left a shadow on Pockhampton. None of his friends of his age group were still in the village. All had faced call up to military service. The fact that he, their village boy made good, had returned as an officer was an extra excuse for gossip. Little Alice was sharing her bedroom with a tiny evacuee girl called Kathleen who seemed without speech as she stared dumbly at Richard. Several other houses had evacuees and his mother told him that three more were placed at Pockhampton Manor.

The news of his return spread fast and at midday the telephone rang. 'For you,' his father grinned.

'Dickie, it's me, Maria.'

'Maria, how are you?'

'Oh, I'm fine. I'm on leave like you. Please, can you come to tea?'

'Yes, all right – when?'

'Well, right now. I've big news for you. Do you want transport?'

'No, I've still got my car. But there's lots of people here wanting to speak to me.'

He heard her old laugh that he remembered so well. 'Come as soon as you can. We've lots to catch up on.'

He reached the avenue leading to the manor a little after one o'clock. The roads were quiet apart from a few military vehicles and a platoon of soldiers marching away from the village.

As he drew up in front of the house Maria ran down the front steps arms outstretched. In full view of the house and the distant road she hugged him. She was also in uniform as a lieutenant in the women's ATS. She stood back and admired him. 'Oh you're a pilot – so glamorous.'

'You look pretty smart yourself and you're senior to me in rank. Should I call you ma'am?'

'Not unless you want a clip round the ear.'

He laughed. 'Not today. Tell me what are you doing in the army?'

She made a grimace. 'I can't really tell you. I'm working at a secret establishment in Buckinghamshire. It's based on a big house, bigger than this one and even I'm not entirely sure what's going on in there, but they've recruited a whole lot of we upper-class girls to do the secretarial side. They seem to think we keep secrets better than the mob. Lots of the girls have brought their horses with them. The local stables are making a fortune.'

Richard laughed again. Her presence was so infectious. 'Well let's hope the Gestapo don't interrogate you and then learn the place is experimenting in the latest method of producing corned beef.'

'How is your flying? I worry about you. Flying is so dangerous.' Again she clung to him.

He was worried. 'Watch out, people can see us.'

'No they can't. All the servants have been called up. Daddy is in London with the Air Ministry. Mummy runs the place with daily helps now. Your mother is a star. Mummy's taken the evacuee kids to a pantomime in Chichester. Only Hilda's in the house and she knows the score.'

'Who is Hilda?'

'You'll see in a minute. Come indoors.'

Richard feeling mildly bemused followed Maria up the steps and into the entrance hall. 'Hello, Hilda,' Maria called. 'Can you come down and bring James as well.'

'Hilda's Dutch,' she said. 'She's James's nanny.'

'James?'

'Yes, you are about to meet, the Honourable James Leopold St John Corbailier, son and heir to John Viscount Petersfield.'

Richard was genuinely shaken. So, Johnny must have held his nose long enough to conceive this brat.

A woman came down the stairs. She was a well-built dark-haired girl, maybe mid twenties. With her was a child: a small boy of around one-year-old walking and half crawling secured by a light body harness. He was a funny little chap with already a shock of blond curly hair not unlike his mother's but also not unlike…! Richard stiffened in shock.

'Yes,' said Maria, 'You've guessed. This little chap is your son and mine.'

CHAPTER 29

'Oh, God. It was that night wasn't it – eighteen months ago, at my place.'

'That's right. Oh Dickie, it was so wonderful and look what we've been given. Isn't he a little darling?' She took the baby harness from the nanny and carried the little boy over to Richard.

The child was chubby, with chubby bare legs and chubby arms, and Richard felt a mix of deep pride and real alarm. 'Maria, what does your Johnny say about this?'

'Oh Dickie for God's sake, Johnny is relieved. He's got an heir to the Dukedom, and making that heir was beyond him so obviously it was down to me.'

'But is it legal? I mean he's not Johnny's blood.'

'And a damn good thing too. That family have been marrying their cousins ever since the Norman Conquest. You and me have injected some good honest Sussex blood and now the whole clan has a future which they wouldn't have had if it was down to Johnny.'

Richard was torn in two. The little boy was so obviously his. He mirrored the pictures that were taken of himself when he was one-year-old.'

'What about the village? Who knows about all this?'

'The village don't know because they haven't seen him. I'm only down for a few days leave. They know I've a boy born but that's all. Anyway it was announced in the Times and in the Tatler. I thought you might have known.'

At last Richard could laugh. 'Not my usual reading, either of them.'

'Well, I hope you've had a lovely surprise.'

'Yes, I have, but it's the future. Can I see him if I keep our secret?'

'Yes, of course you can. From now on you are Uncle Dickie and you can spoil him and teach him to play the piano.'

Richard was far from reassured. 'What about Johnny's family? They must know there's been some funny business,'

'They don't mind. Oh, Dickie, you're still stuck in Victorian middle class morality. Great families have never bothered too much about all that. The lot down the road are descended from Nell Gwynne and there are dozens of others, not just us. In fact I know they've guessed about you and me already.'

Richard groaned. 'That only makes it worse.'

'No it doesn't. You are a famous musician. They're pleased.'

'Yes, but Maria, darling. There's a bloody great war coming and I've only a fifty-fifty chance of coming through it alive at the end.'

Maria clung to him. 'Don't say that.'

'It's something we all have to face. This phoney war won't last and when the real war starts people are going to die.'

'But not you, darling, I can't bear to think that.'

'Well, cheer up. I'm not going to throw my life away and what you've shown me today will make me a lot more careful. Anyway, I want to play music and compose music once this catastrophe is over.'

'I know. It would be a terrible loss to music if you didn't survive.'

Richard took her in his arms and now he kissed her full on the lips. 'We're all vulnerable. What if the Germans decide to bomb your top secret place into oblivion, I could lose you then.'

Now she was sobbing into the front of his uniform. 'Oh God, I hate Germans and I hate that horrible little Hitler.'

'We're all going to beat him.'

Richard nodded towards the nanny. She was standing no more than ten feet away at the foot of the stairs.

Maria shook her head. 'Hilda knows the score, as I said. She's Dutch and very broad-minded. A British nanny would be shocked, and as I say, there's really nothing to be shocked about.'

'Shocked! Oh Maria, if my old dad ever finds out he'll be more than shocked. He never took to me mixing out of my social class. You know it's: *God bless our squire and his relations and keep us in our proper stations.*'

She laughed. 'It's time he woke up. This war is going to bring a social upheaval such as we've never known before.'

'Don't let my mum see this little chap or the secret will be well and truly out.'

'Oh Dickie, remember how you mother used to say I wasn't safe. I'm pretty sure she's guessed already.'

'You're talking about woman's intuition.' Suddenly he couldn't resist laughing. 'If my old dad ever knew his grandson was the heir to a dukedom. I guess his head would explode.'

Maria placed both her hands on his shoulders. 'How is the little Australian girl? Have you married her yet?'

Richard had a spasm of guilt. For the last half hour he had completely forgotten Stella. 'Oh, she's been posted to somewhere up North around Newcastle way.' He hesitated. 'Look, Stella keeps asking me about you, or rather she doesn't know who you are and I've told her you've married someone else. We're not married yet but the plan – that is her plan – was for us to settle in Australia. Once there the rival girl will be out of reach. But now it's war. I'm in the Air Force and she's been told there's no way she can get home. So any wedding is on hold until this blasted war is over.'

'Oh, Dickie, I'm not jealous. I want you to marry your girl and be happy. You'll make fine music together.'

Richard made no reply. Maria's attitude to life and love was beyond him.

She released him and stood back. 'Where are you staying tonight?'

'In the pub I suppose. Can't sleep at home. Alice has my old room with a little evacuee.'

'You are not going back to the pub. You are our guest tonight. Have you got your things?'

'My overnight bag is in the car.'

'Well go and get it and I'll show you your room.'

'Here you are,' Maria pointed through the bedroom door. 'Our number one guest room. This is where Sir Edward Elgar slept that time you met him.'

Richard liked the room. It was bright with the late afternoon sun and contained a double bed, wardrobe and dressing table. He placed his bag on the bed and yawned.

'Right,' said Maria. 'It'll be me cooking dinner tonight. We're short on staff.'

'You, cooking!'

'Don't look like that. I'm getting good at cooking. How do you fancy steak, onions and mashed potatoes?'

'Well, that sounds safe enough.'

'Good, and Johnny left a case of French red wine.'

'Will your mother be with us?'

'No, she's with the evacuee kids. It'll be you me and Hilda.'

The three of them spent a happy hour playing with little James. Richard felt a sense of pride such as he had never known in his life. The little boy gurgled and laughed as he rolled on the drawing room carpet and the adults took it in turn to lead him around the room in his harness. It was a happy experience for Richard although he knew he had better relish the moment before he was swept into war.

Hilda took James upstairs to the nursery where they both spent their nights and when she returned they ate Maria's dinner. This was an event that Richard had to admit was something of a triumph. At ten o'clock Richard yawned and said he was ready for bed.

'Can't offer you a hot bath,' said Maria. 'There's wartime restrictions on hot water.'

'I didn't know that.'

'No, you can use Daddy's shower bath. It's just along the passage from the guest room.'

The shower was certainly soothing. He could understand why Mr Tenbury preferred it. He winced a little as he remembered it was the burns the man suffered from and those had come about as a shot down airman in the last war. The shower cubicle was hot and steamy and it was impossible to see through the condensation on the glass door. So he was caught out when a sharp burst of knocking came and he could see a shadowy figure on the outside. Then the door swung open and the figure revealed itself. It was Maria and she was stark naked. Somehow he was not surprised. If the girl had planned this trick then one way or another it seemed meant.

'Here's your towel,' she smirked. 'Turn those taps off and I'll dry you.'

In a seeming dreamworld he wrapped the towel around himself and then followed the girl as she skipped happily down the passage to the guest room. Inside she walked to the bed and picked up the pyjamas he had laid out and threw them into a corner of the room.

'Pilot Officer Dyer. I am your superior officer and I say this parade will be birthday suit order.'

Once again, as they had those months before, the lovers fell on the bed. Richard was aroused and he felt his face redden. For five minutes he pleasured this lovely girl with his fingers and tongue before he entered her. Once again she screamed and seemed to explode like a volcano. It was perhaps fortunate that in his ecstasy he never knew that Maria's mother had stopped outside the door and listened to her daughter's squeals of pleasure and delight. Mrs Tenbury's face filled with a smile as she nodded her approval.

CHAPTER 30

Once again they lay in each other's arms, exhausted and exhilarated as well. 'You said this was Elgar's room,' Richard whispered in her ear. 'What would he think of all this?'

'Oh, he wouldn't mind. He had a loyal wife and a nice young mistress. Good combination.' Maria tightened her arms around him and they kissed. 'I think I've sown more trouble for you,' she said. 'Your Stella will be even more suspicious. You know how to please a girl in the bedroom and she will wonder where you learned.'

Now he laughed. 'Perhaps I'd better play the blundering idiot the first time.'

'Maybe, but I don't see that happening.'

Richard closed his eyes and he slept. He woke twice to find the girl slumbering peacefully by his side. A green tin alarm clock was ticking loudly on the bedside table. He was beginning to panic. The time said six o'clock in the morning. Pockhampton village would be awake but Maria was very much asleep. Was Mrs Tenbury home? What would happen if his mother arrived and wanted to clean upstairs? What if she or someone wanted to make the bed and saw the damp patches that betrayed their mad night? He sat up, slipped out of bed and quietly opened the bedroom door. The house was quiet, not a sound to be heard either inside or out.

'Hello, you're awake. What a surprise.' He jumped with alarm but it was only Maria standing behind him her hands on his shoulders.

'I'm worried,' he said 'Really worried. We're completely compromised. You're still here, our bed is a mess. I can't risk my mum seeing it and as for your mum. I tell you I'm scared.'

'I've told you, you worry too much.' She leant up and kissed the back of his head and he could feel the line of her lovely bare body against his back. 'All right, I'll go to my proper room.' Without warning Maria, still naked, sprinted along the passage and then pattered down the stairs, incredibly whistling an off-key *sunny side of the street.* Horrified, Richard watched her vanish through a second-floor doorway. Thank God there was no sign of her mother. His thoughts turned to his baby son in the nursery with the nanny Hilda. He hoped he could see James again before he left Sussex. He returned to the dishevelled bed and slept.

In the end, strangely, not a single repercussion came back to embarrass Richard. He spent an idyllic day playing with his little son. He returned to his parents' home to find a forwarded communication from the Air Ministry.

Pilot Officer Dyer,

You have been assigned to Fighter Command at 13 Group RAF Bracksby Whitby North Yorkshire. You are ordered to report by Thursday A.M. 25th January 1940.

The mail was signed by some civil servant in the Air Ministry.

Richard was pulled back into the real world. This was war and he must be mentally adjusted and ready to fight.

The further north the train travelled the colder the world became and the more snow could be seen by the trackside. The carriages were filled with uniformed soldiers and callow youths on their way to Catterick and other such places. Eventually, with a second change of train, he arrived at Whitby and was told a bus to Bracksby would not be available for two hours. Richard found a convivial pub and ate a fish pie sitting at the bar. The bus arrived twenty minutes behind schedule but at least he was on his way. In the event, RAF Bracksby in darkness was a depressing place. Richard could just make out hangars, a control tower and a village of Nissen huts. At least the officer's mess was a brick building. He reported to the adjutant who seemed a relaxed sort of chap and was directed to his quarters. He was informed that he would be allotted his aircraft in the morning. Then, the unbelievable happened. A uniformed WAAF walked into the room and both stared at each other in shock. The girl stiffened and almost dropped the clipboard she was carrying.

Richard gasped. 'Stella'!

'Are you two acquainted?' asked the adjutant.

'She's my fiancée,' Richard replied.

'Well, congratulations I suppose,' said the adjutant. 'You're not married.'

'Not yet.'

'Just as well. You see officers on active duty are not allowed to have wives on the station. Bad for morale.'

Richard knew he was looking blank. Later he understood this man was being tactful. The service did not want the distress of having serving wives on the same base when their husbands were lost in combat.

'Can I show Mr Dyer to his quarters, sir?' Stella asked.

'Yes, go on then, that will be fine.'

Richard followed Stella out of the building and across to a row of Nissen huts. He felt uneasy. Of course he knew that Stella was based in the north of England but her letters had a postal address in Whitby. He guessed she had been forbidden to give the base as her location. Suddenly he knew he was pleased to see her. She was the girl he could make a life with, whereas Maria, for all their secret trysts was out of his reach.

Stella saluted and opened a hut door. Inside was a space with four single iron bedsteads. 'This is it; you'll be sharing with three other guys.' She turned and now she was smiling at him in her old loving way. 'Oh, Dick, I saw the name Dyer on the new pilots list and I thought it might be you.'

'Stella, I love you. When can we get married?'

She was clinging to him now. 'Oh, if only we could but it's not allowed. We're different ranks and they don't allow wives on husband's stations.'

'Why does that matter?'

Stella was crying now. 'It's because the men go into battle and they get killed. I just can't think of it happening.'

'I'm not planning to get killed, or not that easily anyway. Why did my letters to you go to somewhere, not here?'

She laughed through her tears. 'We girls are not allowed to live here. Not overnight; they ship us all out to local places. They don't trust us with all these men.' Stella wiped her eyes and laughed again. 'I'd better go or they'll be asking questions.' They kissed and she left him to it in the gloomy hut.

'I'm David Sutton and you've been posted to my flight.' The Flight Lieutenant was a fellow not looking much older than Richard, but he had been told that the man was a regular RAF officer of long experience. 'I've your flight record and I understand you've completed ten hours on Hurricanes.'

'Yes, sir.'

'Don't bother with the sir. We don't stand on ceremony here, or not unless some big noise is visiting. Right, you may wonder why you've been posted here.'

Richard made no reply.

The Flight Lieutenant continued. 'When Jerry starts attacking he'll expect to draw all fighter command to defend London and the South Coast ports. If we allow that to happen we'll leave Tyneside wide open for him to demolish unopposed.'

'I did wonder,' Richard replied. 'Personally I'd rather be defending my own people down south.'

'Well we're all the same now it's war. Right, down to basics. Forget all the Fighter Command standard attack drills. They're balls, they don't work. It's one to one; select your target and never fly straight and level for more than three seconds. Watch your tail and be prepared for some bastard to sneak up behind you. Shoot down one enemy and you've justified the expense of training you, shoot down two and we're in profit. Any questions? All right, let get in the air.'

On the tarmac was his new aircraft. It had been delivered from the factory two days earlier and it looked magnificent. No battered training mount this one. The Hurricane was his: his battle steed. He met his mechanics, a cheerful pair, one Irish and one a Geordie. The general public might glamorise the pilots, but Richard knew these were the men who would keep his aircraft flying fuelled and armed; then repair it when damaged. And they would do this while the bombs and bullets fell around them.

Soon he was in the air. How he loved this Hurricane. It was smoother to fly than any training aircraft. It climbed faster, turned tighter and in front of his eyes was the most modern reflector gun sight. He turned and climbed while his flight commander tried to get on his tail. Richard was happy that this experienced flyer only succeeded twice.

Three flights were completed that day and Richard gained in confidence. If the Germans were planning to kill him, they would not find it so easy. That evening in the officer's mess he had a further surprise. In a corner of the room was a smart baby grand piano. Squadron Leader Jones, his commander waved him towards it. 'Local business mogul heard you were with us so he's donated that. So, go on, lad, give us a tune.'

CHAPTER 31

May 1940

Now it really was war. All was confusion. What the hell was happening in France? First the papers were full of talk of success, but then it was all retreat and withdrawal. Why couldn't the French defend their country? It seemed Britain had a new prime minister. He was Winston Churchill, an odd choice; a maverick who at least sounded more like a leader than the willowy Chamberlain. The army was falling back to Dunkirk though all was still quiet in Sussex but, Richard guessed correctly, not for long. Maria was away on her posting. She had left him a contact address in a Buckinghamshire village called Bletchley, wherever that might be.

The RAF in France had had a torrid time. Hopelessly outnumbered they had scored victories and taken appalling losses. Richard's squadron commander and his flight leader had lost friends confirmed dead and other comrades unaccounted for. Everyone in his unit wanted to get involved in the fight and seethed with frustration in this northern outpost. The news on the radio was worse and there were graphic pictures in the daily papers. Some sort of miracle had occurred and thousands of British troops had been rescued and brought home. It seemed the whole nation was alone and faced possible invasion and extinction. Not if the Air Force had any say in it.

News good and bad affected Richard personally. Maria wrote and told him she had encountered David Goldstein who was working at the same brain-box secret establishment as she was. He worried about David's parents and little Naomi. If Hitler's forces invaded what chance did the Goldsteins have before the odious Lamingham directed the Gestapo to their door?

For Richard the war was becoming personal. The news came back via his music colleagues. Jehan Allain the brilliant young French musician and composer, whom Richard had briefly known, was dead, killed in action having returned to France after being evacuated. Richard had a vivid dream. He saw a German military patrol surge up the lane to his old home and drag out his parents and little sister. No, war wasn't an exciting game. There was no chivalry. He had discovered hate. He would avenge his friend and no Nazi would touch David, Naomi or Mr and Mrs Goldstein, nor would they defile his family.

He and Stella had never been so close. He took her out every evening after the squadron stood down. They found a sturdy northern pub within walking distance of the base where they could sit in a quiet corner of the snug bar and talk and talk. Talk about their future, perhaps in Australia. Stella, thank goodness, no longer seemed suspicious of his other life. When they married and had children, would those children ever know that they had a secret sibling with an exotic title? The title wouldn't mean a thing if they were Australians, but the ructions could be disastrous. In the meantime they both had a war to fight.

August 1940

Richard, along with all his comrades, suffered alternatively rage, frustration and boredom. Isolated in the north of England, they had to watch their fellow pilots and their ground crews fight the battle of their lives a hundred miles to the south. While they scrambled in pursuit of a dozen false alarms, old friends were fighting and dying. It was hinted that if no raiders attacked their sector they would be needed to relieve a hard hit squadron from the south. On the fifteenth of August their day came. Hermann Goering, confident that all of Britain's reserves had been drawn into the main battle dispatched his Luftflotte 5 from Scandinavia to attack Tyneside. It was true that no single-engine fighters could make the distance from Norway and Denmark, but then in Goering's estimation his bombers would have no fighters to face.

Richard awoke at six o'clock that morning to see a misty airfield. That didn't concern him; the sun should burn that off shortly. He had spent a relaxing evening the day before. He had played the mess piano with a medley of dance numbers, some of his own composition. Then he had walked Stella to the pub and they had talked of their future and he had listened to her nostalgic tales of childhood in Melbourne and how she wished she had more time now to practice her viola.

Richard could see the ground engineers beginning to start the Hurricane's engines. The engine fitter would sit in the cockpit while a battery accumulator on a trolley was connected to the starting system. The engine fired and two ground crew would sit on the tailplane while the engineer pushed the throttle to full power but not past the boost point: another fruitless patrol on the way. Richard yawned and snatched a cup of coffee from the urn in the crew room. He went outside and saw Stella helping to pull the trolley acc away. He waved and she blew him a kiss.

Now came the shock. The tannoy crackled. 'All units, all units scramble – scramble. Attack imminent.' This was different – no practice session this one. Richard sprinted to his Hurricane lugging his parachute and pulling on his helmet. The engineer vacated the cockpit and helped him climb aboard and strap in. Richard connected his oxygen and fixed the mask across his face. 'Squadron scramble,' he heard Jones his commander's voice in his headphones. Whatever happens don't mess up on takeoff was his abiding thought. He must keep straight and level with his comrades on either side. They were all airborne; every aircraft from both squadrons was in the air and climbing.

'Calling blue leader, large formation of bandits approaching from east. Vector one zero. Breaker.'

Breaker from ground control meant full throttle and maximum climb. Jones, the leader, altered course and they climbed to twelve thousand and then fourteen thousand feet. Richard knew that Jones was taking them eastward and up sun. Hopefully they would see the enemy long before the enemy saw them. Yes, there the bastards were. Two huge formations, the leading one all Heinkel 111s, looking like ugly black slugs and behind them a second group: ME 110 twin-engine jobs, thank goodness no 109s.

Jones voice crackled in his ears. 'Tallyho, go get'em.' His squadron needed no second invitation. Richard, along with the others swung round on the same course as the enemy and dived. The speed was exhilarating and as he dived music flowed into his mind – not Wagner this time but Brahms 4th. Richard remembered the drill and turned the gun button safety ring to action. How many Heinkels? They were like a swarm, there must be rising one hundred and almost as many 110s. He set himself at a bomber on the far left of the formation; if he dropped slightly below its line and far enough back, he could rake it with all eight of his guns. The enemy must have divined his intention – it broke away while tiny red flashes came from its rear gun. Richard heard a crack in the cockpit behind him and now a current of cold air. In that split second he saw a pattern of holes in his right hand wing. But the Heinkel had made a basic error by moving away from the combined strength of its formation. Richard knew he had got it. He remembered to keep swerving side to side as he closed again, and this time the bomber was fair and square in his sights. He pressed the firing button; short bursts no more than three seconds. He broke away and stared at his prey. One engine was smoking and then the lumbering aircraft rolled over and plunged. Within thirty seconds it had hit the sea. Three more Heinkels were falling and he could see two parachutes. He pulled away and climbed. As he did so he saw more holes in his wing and a cracking noise behind him. He swerved and pulled up as an ME 110 powered past. No match for a Hurricane that one. He picked it out again and latched on to it. 'You are not getting away,' he muttered. The music had ceased and once again he saw the storm troopers kicking in his parents' front door and now an evil bastard pulling the clothes off little Alice. The 110 tried to turn tightly but Richard could turn tighter. It was in his sights and this time he gave it all his ammunition until his guns ran empty. His enemy exploded and Richard winced as he flew through the debris unscathed.

'All right, ammos running low. Spits are on their way to finish. Re-gather – we're going home.'

Then came the reaction. His body was soaked with sweat and his nose ran. He shook with the aftermath of the fight. He should feel triumphant but he only felt very tired with an overwhelming desire to lie down. He tried to get to grips with what he has just done. He had destroyed two aircraft and he had killed. During the fight he hadn't seen the enemy aircraft as filled with fellow men. He only saw them as evil sinister machines. He knew that this time they had faced no opposing fighters. If they were sent to the main battle down south things would be very different. But if they were sent to the battle down south he would be defending his home and Maria's home and the landscape he knew and loved.

CHAPTER 32

September 1940
Fighter Command: Long Heath, Dorset.

They were all tired. With four missions flown every day in good visibility they were taking casualties. Friends and comrades who had been together for months were gone. A few in were hospital wounded or burned but most dead. The squadron had moved south: swapped with a damaged and battered unit who had fought the first stage of the battle over the English Home counties. They had been posted to the tiny grass airstrip at Long Heath, well placed to defend the south coast ports and conurbations.

The twenty-year-old Richard had come of age. He had started this battle a callow youth but now he was hardened and aged beyond his years. He was a Flight Lieutenant, promoted to flight commander following the death of his leader David Sutton. He had doubled his number of kills to four and still the enemy kept coming.

The ground crews had travelled with them and they were magnificent. Hurricanes returned day after day with damage. A few were beyond repair but, for most, the ground engineers worked through the night to restore them to fighting fitness. Three ground crew had died and one young WAAF when the airfield was bombed. Richard had been sickened by the sight of the mangled body of the poor girl. Richard's engineers had laughed off their experience but he knew that they were both hardened and strangely glad that they were sharing their pilot's danger.

Richard was relieved that Stella had remained in Yorkshire. She had clung to him weeping and pressed a little lucky charm into his hand. He wore it around his neck at all times. Maria had written and told him she was immersed in work, little James was talking and that her brother Leo, the priest, had said special prayers for Richard. He wasn't sure how much this would help, but he had to remember that Leo had been in battle far worse than anything Richard was seeing. Leo and Richard's own father had gone over the top in the trenches of 1917 France. It was strange that he was continually thrusting away an illusion that he would survive; that he had a planned future in a post-war world. This was not the case with a few of his comrades. Some, mostly the older members of the squadron, were visibly cracking.

They expected death every day and it seemed some were looking for it.

He himself had survived a few narrow squeaks. His beloved Hurricane was not the machine she had been when he first sat in her. Five times her wings and fuselage had been riddled with bullets and needing overnight repair. By some miracle he had remained unscathed. Every night he and the boys had walked to the village pub. The appreciation of the locals was uplifting. They never had to buy a drink; that was always on the house. Richard entertained everyone on the battered upright piano with versions of *Blue Birds Over etc* and *We'll Meet Again...*while the assembled company bellowed the words in a discord that made him wince. The pub air was almost unbreathable with cigarette smoke. Richard had never smoked, it had never appealed to him. His friends were hardly ever without a cigarette in hand. But those evenings he drank too much. Alcohol was a balm after the horrors of the day. He knew it was dangerous, but somehow when they scrambled the following morning the hangover vanished.

Then very early one morning, still dark, something happened that was to be the defining moment in his life. What followed was to burn in his mind years later and to be the spark that lit his greatest achievement and was to elevate him to world status. Three new pilots had just arrived to be greeted by Squadron Leader Jones. Richard felt a guilty pang. These chaps had no idea of the battle they were getting into. He walked towards the group and then stopped short. One of these new arrivals he knew from way back. 'Hey, you're Tom, Tom Stacey.'

'Dick Dyer – Chichester,' his old friend sprang forward hand outstretched. 'Gosh, I've followed your career and I love your music. I still try and play sometimes but I'm a solicitor in civvy street.'

'Tom, it's good to see you after all these years.'

'Dyer, can I be in your flight? The CO says you're a man short.'

'How many hours have you done on Hurricanes?'

'Four.'

Richard's heart sank. 'All right, you'd best come with me.'

Tom looked little different from the small boy in the choir. He had the same spotty complexion and red hair. Richard launched into a stream of advice. Today would be the day little Tom was thrown into combat and he could not be more unprepared.

'My orders are follow me, watch me – do what I do – all right?'

Tom nodded and smiled. Oh God, this boy had no idea. Boy, Richard had to think twice. Tom and he were of the same age, but he was a flyer hardened and cynical, so in that respect he was the man and his old schoolmate still a boy.

An hour later they scrambled. It was a relatively quiet sortie; the main Luftwaffe thrust was fifty miles to the east. A lesser formation of Dorniers was heading for Southampton but turned tail and vanished when the squadron challenged them. They returned to base for once unscathed. Another surprise was in store for them. During the morning standby a police car, accompanied by a section of Home Guard, had pulled up outside the mess.

'We thought you gentlemen might like to see a Jerry. Little sod used his parachute yesterday and we ran him to earth an hour ago.'

Several pilots shook their heads but Richard and a few others peered through the glass into the rear of the police car. A little man in a Luftwaffe officer's uniform sat in the back with a burly police constable.

'He's pilot Ernst Litten,' said the first policeman. 'We gather he was in one o' they Messers and you chaps shot 'im down yesterday.'

Richard, who had pictured his enemies as red in tooth and claw, couldn't reconcile this with the poor unhappy looking specimen in the car. Well maybe Ernst Litten was one of the lucky ones. In a POW camp he might just survive this war and he couldn't do any more damage to them.

He walked back to where his flight was on standby. Tom Stacey was there with his parachute and helmet obviously trying to look nonchalant. Richard spoke to him.

'Remember we're here to take care of the Hun bombers. Don't tangle with the 109s – the Spit boys'll cope with them. Follow me, do what I do. Whatever happens don't fly straight and level for more than seconds – keep swerving.'

The call came twenty minutes later. Then they were airborne and heading towards the Isle of Wight. Another squadron had taken off from north of Portsmouth and a third from Middle Wallop in Wiltshire. So, thought Richard, they had a decent size force to tackle whatever was coming in. Jones, directed by ground control, took them to sixteen thousand feet and yes, there they were: Junkers 88 bombers with a screen of 109s. The radio order given they dived. The Hurricanes were there to take the bombers, the Spitfire squadron was there to cover them.

'Tom, Tom,' Richard called. 'Stick with me.'

He turned the gun ring to fire and tested his guns with a very short burst. The Junkers were in a tight defensive formation. Richard kicked the rudder side to side as he swerved; nothing appeared in his rear mirror, but that wouldn't last for long. A Junkers was falling in flames, but so nearby was a Hurricane. He hadn't time to see if the pilot baled out. An ugly great Junkers swam into his gun sight. He fired and dived beneath the target to avoid ramming it. Now he saw it: ahead of him the spectacle that was to haunt his dreams for the rest of his life. A Messerschmitt was locked on the tail of a Hurricane and the machine was Tom Stacey's. 'Tom, behind you, break man – break!'

It was too late – the Hurricane turned to the left and was stricken, the forward fuel tank had blown and the aircraft was on fire. He saw Tom climb from the cockpit and slide off into the air. Thank God, but oh no, no! The boy pulled his ripcord seconds too early and the canopy shrivelled in the flames from his aircraft. While the inert body plunged earthwards Richard saw the Messerschmitt soar skyward in triumph.

For what happened next Richard had only a faint memory augmented by other people's witness. He was enveloped in the much talked about *red mist.* Music surged in; Ride of the Valkyries burned in his mind. He pushed his throttle to boost and climbed after the 109. He knew he would never outclimb the other. The 109 was faster. His Hurricane would never catch it. He pulled the stick back and took a wild deflection shot. It was against all the logic of air combat but it worked. The converging blast from all eight of his guns shattered the 109. It exploded and fell. His blood was up; his ears were filled with the music as he went for two more 109s. He was bent on vengeance. He would kill them both even if he had to ram them and die himself; he didn't care. From that point onward he had no memory. Only when a hammer of bullets slammed into the armour behind his seat and more bullet holes splintered his left wingtip did he return to the present. He turned as his opponent surged past him. Richard threw his aircraft into a spin. Beneath him the sea shone blue in the sunlight. He recovered seconds before he also plunged into the water. He tried his guns but they were empty. Could he fly back to base? He supposed so. For some reason he was alone down here and he could no longer see the battle above him. He was weary and mentally and physically exhausted. He saw a vision of his home village, of his parents, and Maria and their little James. He felt around his neck and found Stella's charm. No he hadn't finished his war. He swung round towards the distant coast and tried to pick out a landmark. Good God, yes he had one now, the Needles at the west end of the Island. He only had to climb a few thousand feet and he would see Chichester and the Sussex countryside. No, not this time: he turned and took a compass course for base.

He knew now that his beloved Hurricane was a sick beast. The rudder must have come apart in the spin. It had little positive effect and the aircraft was sluggish. Worse, he was carrying minimum fuel. He crossed the coast at Poole and changed course for Long Heath. Minutes later there was; the airfield. He tried to call control but his radio was dead. Good – the flaps lowered as normal. And now, for God's sake, the undercart wouldn't go down. He tried again and again but it was stuck. He screamed in frustration and banged the control panel with his gloved fist. Don't damage your fingers – you are a musician said the voice in his head.

Well, nothing for it. He aligned with the airstrip pulled back the canopy and felt the fresh air surge into the cockpit. The grass floated before him and now it raced closer. He throttled right back and the Hurricane hit the ground and slid grinding and grating across the surface stopping as it tilted forward on the shattered propeller. For a moment he feared they would pitch right over, then relief as his aircraft settled back on her tail wheel.

He punched the release button on his harness and stood up; dragging his parachute behind him he leapt to the ground twisting his ankle as he did so. He remembered that joke; how no one moves faster than a pilot leaving an aircraft about to catch fire. This time it didn't catch fire, it just lay there, an old friend wounded and broken. Richard turned and hobbled towards the buildings and a little group of people watching him.

CHAPTER 33

Squadron Leader Jones looked less than welcoming although Richard could see the trace of a smile that faded instantly. 'Hello there, Dickie boy, we thought we'd lost you. What kept you?'

'I got in a bit of a fight.'

'Huh, I'll say you did.' Jones's smile returned and vanished. 'Are you all right – not wounded?'

'No, I'm fine. Hurt my ankle getting out just now.'

Jones grinned. Could he really be relieved? 'Dyer, go get a shower, best uniform and put some cardboard in your pants.'

This last puzzled Richard. 'Why, sir?'

'Sorry, public school parlance for a caning. Group Captain Woodward wants a word with you. So best bib and tucker and best behaviour. As soon as we've got the film from your guns you can debrief.'

That meant report to the intelligence officer. This poor man was the butt of everyone's jokes although in fact he was a university graduate and genuinely intelligent. Only appalling eyesight had prevented him flying with the rest of them. Anyway, he would soon be analyzing the shots from the film camera installed with Richard's guns and if he'd done any damage to the enemy they would see it.

Group Captain Woodward was the senior officer on their base and also the adjacent fighter airfield. He was a genial man most of the time and a veteran fighter pilot from the last war. To Richard the man seemed old and grizzled although he couldn't be a day over forty-five. Richard, now in his most spruce uniform entered the station commander's office and remembering his hat was still on he saluted.

The Group Captain did not return the salute, his hat was still on his desk and his look was none too friendly. 'Dyer, can you possibly recall your flight orders?'

He wasn't sure where this was leading. 'To engage the enemy, sir.'

'Be specific, man. What part of the enemy?'

'Well, the bombers, sir.'

This time Woodward's face had a flicker of a smile. 'Well, the Spitfire squadron are highly offended; they've complained about a raving lunatic in a Hurricane getting in their way.'

Now Richard began to understand; the Spitfire squadron were covering the Hurricane's attack on the bombers. He rather envied them. The Spitfire was a more elegant and faster aircraft and he hoped one day to fly one himself.

'All right, Dyer, why were you mucking around with all those 109s and ending by wrecking your own aeroplane, which on first sight looks hors de combat?'

He had better tell the truth. 'I'm sorry, sir. I admit I lost it when I saw my old friend's parachute on fire. But I think I got the 109 that did it.'

'Hmm, yes, Dyer, you did a bit better than that. We have analyzed your camera shots. I can tell you that confirmed you have killed one Junkers 88, and two 109s and a third a possible. I calculate that you to date have seven confirmed kills. In my day, in the last war, that would make you an ace. Bloody good show, but what do I tell those Spitfire boys?'

'I don't know, sir.'

'Well, I don't know either. Jones, take this idiot away I've got a mountain of paperwork and some of it concerns him.' Woodward now had a broad grin.

Richard saluted and with Jones he left the room. 'He's not getting me posted elsewhere is he?' Richard could not stand the thought.

Jones laughed. 'No he is not. He's filling in an application to get you a gong.'

A medal, thought Richard. Stella will like that.

'Immediate punishment,' said Jones. 'You've no aircraft now so you are stood down until some pretty little ATA girl delivers you another.'

Richard had one more kill – a Junkers 88 on September 15th. None of them knew that this was culmination of their fight; the day that Hitler and Goering had to admit that they had taken a crushing defeat. The Luftwaffe had suffered nearly three thousand casualties of their elite aircrews, either dead or held prisoner. Not even they could stand losses like this. Neither Richard nor his companions knew the significance of that day. It was just one more fight, a bigger one than usual, but just one more tough fight. Richard's own nemesis took place in early October. The squadron scrambled to intercept a smaller enemy formation than usual heading for the Navy base at Portland. Richard lined up to fire on a Junkers, but this time he was careless he steadied his aircraft long enough to receive a full charge of bullets from the Junker's rear gunner. One moment he was flying and the next his engine was smashed dead. Richard's first reaction was to yell a torrent of obscenity. Then the truth screamed in his brain. His aircraft was finished. He had a full fuel tank in front of him and he could smell hot metal. Get out – bale out. He looked down. He must not land in the sea and drown. But his aircraft must not fall on the town of Weymouth and kill innocent people. He was six thousand feet over the island of Portland heading south and descending fast. Go on, man, before it's too late – get out!

He was alone, no sign of the battle. He had that horrible recollection of Tom Stacey's death. No, this one would be copybook. He pulled back the canopy released his harness and rolled upside down. He fell from the cockpit and gave it a final push with his left leg. He counted three whole seconds and pulled the ring. The canopy opened with a crack above him and suddenly all was amazingly peaceful. Below him were the Portland stone quarries. He could see one with a lorry and some small dots of men. He pulled gently on the rigging lines and floated towards the spot. Slowly at first and then faster and faster the land approached. And that land was filled with traps. Huge lumps of grey granite. He began to panic. He put his arms above his head and held the rigging lines. You are a musician, not a fighter, first and foremost you are a musician; the only thing that matters is to protect your hands. He could see the men in the quarry goggling at him. He aimed for an empty spot but the wind caught him and he slammed into a lump of rock shattering his pelvis and breaking his right leg.

CHAPTER 34

'It's all right, he's not a Jerry, he's one o' ours,' an unshaven red face was crouching over him and the man's breath smelt of tobacco and beer. 'You all right, lad?'

The whole of Richard's lower body felt numb. When he tried to sit up he nearly fainted with pain.

'You'd best sit tight and we'll fetch help.' His burly looking rescuer stood up and shouted. 'Joe, they've a telephone in that house up there. Go tell'em we needs an ambulance.'

Richard began to flex his arms and, thank God. he could wriggle his fingers and they seemed normal. The one called Joe who seemed no more than a small boy was running up a narrow track out of the quarry. Richard lay back and closed his eyes. Later, he never knew how much later, he heard footsteps crunching towards him. Four rather elderly men carried a stretcher and in front walked a dapper middle-aged man in a dark suit and carrying a black bag.

'I'm Doctor Hardcastle,' the man said. 'You've taken a bit of a knock it seems. We're going to get you to hospital, but first to ease things – a shot of morphine.'

Gradually Richard was consumed by a strange peaceful floating sensation. He was not in an aircraft; he was defying gravity, floating on a cloud.

He could hear voices, cheerful voices. 'Doctor, seems we'm in luck. There's an ambulance just down the road. Old lady's died and they're fetching her body.'

'That's good fortune. Our pilot hero will have to share the thing with a dead body, but he's not likely to mind that.'

'Doc, do we take his parachute off 'im?'

'No leave it. He's seriously damaged and we don't want to make it worse.'

Richard drifted in and out of consciousness as the four men huffed and puffed carrying him up the steep track with his parachute bundled up behind him. Then he was vaguely aware that he was in the ambulance with the doctor sitting beside him. Now they were on the move with the loud bell clanging. The journey seemed endless before the ambulance stopped. A blanket-covered object was removed on another stretcher and then they were on the road again. Finally they arrived at a hospital.

‘Dorchester County Hospital,’ explained the doctor. ‘Good facilities here; so don’t worry – they’ll fix you up.’

Richard was conscious enough to see that he was being carried into a door in a muddled complex of buildings old and new. He could hear Dr Hardcastle explaining to someone in subdued tones: ‘Single room, this man is special. I think several breaks but the X-ray will confirm it.’

By this time he had been separated from his parachute. He was too woozy to feel embarrassed when a couple of nurses began to cut his uniform away, skilfully and very gently until he wore only his underwear and, bizarrely. his boots and socks. He could see that he was now on a hospital trolley in some room lit with dazzling light. A man in a surgeon’s gown spoke to him. ‘How do you feel?’ A nurse was holding his forearm working up a vein.

‘Try counting to ten aloud,’ said the man as he inserted the needle.

Richard reached number four and then all was oblivion.

Waking wasn’t quite the right term. One moment Richard was as good as dead to the world; the next moment he was awake while a nurse withdrew a needle from his arm. He was flat on his back on the same or similar trolley. He could see his leg heavily plastered with two filthy toes showing. He closed his eyes again.

‘Do you feel any pain?’ a female voice asked. He opened his eyes and saw the nurse, or rather a superior nurse in a blue uniform. He tried to move and he felt a spasm of pain that shot through his whole body. ‘Yes,’ he gasped.

‘Right, you can have another shot of morphine but we won’t let it be a habit.’ The nurse had a clipped upper class accent that was cold and functional. She reminded him of Sylvia, Johnny Petersfield’s sister.

Now the trolley was being wheeled along corridors until they reached a room with a single bed. Three people followed into this room: a rather pretty nurse and this time two more elderly men in white coats. Very slowly the whole group lifted Richard onto the bed. The surgeon appeared still dressed in gown and white cap.

‘I’m afraid you’re pelvis is broken in two places as well as your broken right leg. You have excellent chances of recovery but we cannot guarantee your walking will recover to your previous state. You are held in a heavy cast around some of your lower body and it will speed your recovery if you stay still, or as still as you can.’ The surgeon nodded and the nurse administered the morphine. Once again he lapsed into another world.

Richard felt depressed. A week before he had been engaged in battle, his life on the line every time he flew. Now he was a prisoner laid flat on his back in a hospital bed unable to move. Basic toilet functions could only be performed with the aid of nurses wielding chamber pots and urine bottles. He was nearly driven round the bend by the sound of aircraft overhead. These were not always the healthy rattle of a Merlin engine. At night he frequently heard the rhythmic moan of the engines of the Luftwaffe night bombers. To be fair to the medical staff they did their best to cheer him up. Nurses brought him library books and one of the girls came in with music scores. On the evening of the third day he had his first visitors. Squadron Leader Jones and Group Captain Woodward bounced in full of cheer.

'Young man,' said Woodward, 'when you're out of this place you've got a date with royalty.'

Richard knew he looked blank.

'Yes, DFC, Distinguished Flying Cross and, funnily enough, the King wants to pin it on you himself. So you won't have some old air marshal coming in here instead.'

Richard couldn't get his mind around any of this. 'Why should the King want me more than anyone else?'

'I wondered that myself, but it seems you've got some influential friends at court and they like your piano playing,' the Group Captain laughed. 'We rather miss your playing as well.'

Richard was pleased about the medal but he had more important things on his mind. 'Sir, do my family know what's happened to me? I don't want them to think I bought it out there.'

'Rest easy, Dyer, they know, and there's a rather pretty little WAAF waiting outside in the corridor and she's coming in here when we've finished.'

Jones grinned broadly. 'Your fiancée, from Bracksby, but she's wangled a posting down these parts to be near you.'

'Stella?' Richard sat up in shock and then felt the pain and slumped back again. 'I didn't want her to see me like this.' Of course it would be wonderful to see her and hear her voice. 'Sir, what's been happening? Have we lost anyone else?'

'Yes, sorry to say one of the new lads got downed,' said Jones. 'He was caught by two 109s – never stood a chance, but it's been much quieter of late – seems the Hun has had enough of daylight and he's switching to night bombing.'

Richard's own nights had been affected by the memory of Tom Stacey's death and he'd been troubled by dreams. He only wanted to get fit again and fly. The men said farewell and left. Stella came in. She tiptoed across the room and smothered him with kisses. He hugged her and showed her the little charm still around his neck. 'You see, darling, it worked.'

'It never stopped you ending in here,' she replied.

'That was self-inflicted. I made a complete balls-up of my parachute landing.' He told her how he was only thinking of saving his hands.

'Quite right too, you're a world famous pianist and you've lots more music to play once you're fit again.'

He relapsed into gloom. 'Will I ever be able to walk to a piano?'

'Yes, you will. Your surgeon says so.'

'Will I ever fly again?'

'Dickie, darling. I think you've more than done your bit. No more flying for you, mate.' She spoke the words a few inches from his face and her Australian accent was vivid.

He sighed. 'They say I'll always walk with a dodgy limp.'

Stella smiled as she kissed him softly on the cheek; then she quoted.

He that shall live this day and see old age
Will yearly on the vigil feast his friends
And say tomorrow is St Crispian
Then will he slip his sleeve and show his scars
And say – these wounds I had on Crispin's day.'

'Yes, you guys saved this country from invasion. You'll carry that honour for the rest of your years.'

For the first time in weeks he laughed. 'Tell me; how many Australians have enough culture to quote Shakespeare?'

She spoke within an inch of his ear: 'Thousands more than you may suppose, mate.'

Richard forgot how many books he read and how many music scores he performed in his head. Stella's regular visits were the one thing that cheered him through the long days. Seven weeks passed, and finally the X-ray was positive enough for the casts to be cut away. They had become intolerable and the continuous unreachable itching was torment. His muscles, strong once, had shrunk and his attempts to stand ended in a spasm of giddiness. Slowly with support on either, side he hobbled to a room fitted with a set of parallel bars. Half an hour working out on these and he was exhausted and faced the humiliation of being pushed back to his room in a wheelchair. More visitors came. His mum and dad and little Alice had faced the ordeal of a long cross-country rail journey. They fussed around him, told him how proud they all were of him and that he must not do any more flying. Richard wanted to fly again, he recalled every minute of his time in action, that strange mix of choking fear and exhilaration. He wanted to fly again but he knew from everything the surgeon told him that his days in action were over. If he was to contribute to the war effort then why not through music: millions of overworked and worthy people toiled in the services and in the factories. Would not music cheer them?

He was sitting in a chair reading one morning when the nurse appeared. 'Flight Lieutenant, there's visitors for you.'

Richard looked up and there stood Mr and Mrs Tenbury with Maria and little James. Mr Tenbury was dressed in a Squadron Leader's uniform with the last war's wings and Maria wore her smart ATS order. Maria sped across the room and planted wet kisses all over him. Then she took James from her mother and set him on Richard's lap. It was a moment that would live long in his memory.

Mrs Tenbury smiled. 'You see, Richard, we know and it's all right.'

Richard was both embarrassed and wholly relieved. He had been living a lie and now that was over.

Richard looked up at Maria. 'How's your husband?'

'Johnny, he's waiting to see if he's to be sent to North Africa. His sister Sylvia gave me this. She handed him an envelope. In it was a neat card with the handwritten words:

To Richard, we are all very proud of you. May you have a speedy and happy recovery.

Sylvia Corbailier.

'I know, Sylvy is a bit formidable,' said Maria. 'But she means well.'

Mr Tenbury threw back his head and laughed. 'Formidable? That woman is terrifying.'

'We've spoken to the admin here,' said Mrs Tenbury. 'You should be discharged before Christmas but they will want you to recuperate at home. Your parents haven't room at home, but Pockhampton House has been designated as a recovery hospital and we want you to stay with us. Then in February there's a medal presentation at Windsor Castle and you will receive the royal command.'

'I expect you've heard the news,' said Mr Tenbury. 'London's a mess. The bloody Hun is over every night dropping bombs. People dead and wounded everywhere and buildings smashed. From all I've seen the spirit's good. Hitler won't break us that way.'

Maria kissed Richard again. 'You stopped them – you did it! They're too scared to come over in day time so they sneak in at night – cowards!'

'And we're hitting back,' her father looked grim. 'I can't give you too many details, it's classified. But Bomber Command will be a force to be reckoned with in the future and we'll give back a lot better than they're handing out to us.'

'We'll leave you now,' said Mrs Tenbury. 'The nurse out there told us no more than twenty minutes or you'll tire.

Maria kissed him full on the lips. 'We've a surprise for you at home.'

'What's that?'

She stood up and shot him a malicious grin. 'Wait and see.'

Richard watched all four of them leave and felt a sensation of joy and emptiness.

CHAPTER 35

March 1941

London was a shock. As the train ran onwards towards central London Richard was appalled by the devastation. The poor districts around the Elephant and Castle were filled with rubble and smashed buildings. More devastation was revealed in the approaches to the terminus. Having arrived in the capital he took the underground for South Kensington and his reunion with the Goldstein family. He felt a little chastened by the hostile stares his uniform produced in the underground station and on the train. He was glad he hadn't yet received his medal and didn't wear the ribbon. He understood, and in some ways he could relate to this reaction. But there was little the RAF could do to stop the night bombers. Richard had thought of applying for night-fighter training but he had been told no.

His recovery was almost complete, or as complete as it was ever likely to be, but he still limped and leaned on a stick. Richard had spent a happy leave recovery period back home in Pockhampton. The whole village, his parents and the Tenbury family welcomed him as a returning hero and that had felt both pleasing and embarrassing. Ted his father was in uniform again patrolling with the Home Guard. The old man had received a definite new lease of life as he and his fellows stalked around the lanes at night hoping to find a German spy. Apart from this, Ted Dyer was immersed in the agricultural war effort. He grumbled a lot about the War Agricultural Committee who supervised everything on the estate's farms and directed what should be grown and where. This had meant the arrival of more tractors and such devices as milking machines. All things that Ted "didn't hold with". As far as Richard was concerned the machinery made sense. The labour shortage had resulted from all the village's young men and many girls being away in the forces. He knew that with his stumbling lameness he wasn't much use anymore on the farm.

On the third day Maria arrived having somehow worked a forty-eight hour leave pass. With her came her promised surprise, or rather an earthquake of a shock for Richard. With Maria was Hilda the nurse with James and another child: a three month-old little girl, with the same blonde hair and round face as her brother.

Richard gasped. 'Is she…?'

'Oh yes,' Maria spluttered. 'You should see your face. Yes, the Honourable Julia Corbailier is our little girl.'

'And nobody minds?'

'Why should they? I've told you before. Our people don't follow your middle class morality. We want a healthy succession and now we've got it.'

'It was that time at Christmas a year ago wasn't it?'

'Yes, it was a glorious night and what a reward we have,'

'Who knows?'

'The family.'

Richard knew warmth and happiness as he held both of his children, but the happiness was mixed with an undercurrent of anger. He was fond of the Tenbury family and he still had feelings for Maria, but there was no doubt these haughty Corbailiers had used him. All this could poison his relationship with Stella and that would be unforgivable. If only this war would be over, he and Stella could leave all this behind and settle in Australia.

South Kensington seemed relatively untouched by bombing although even here an unpleasant acrid smell blew on the wind. Richard saw plenty of damage from the train in the above ground parts of the route. He walked through familiar streets until he reached the Goldstein house. He was standing two streets from his old basement flat where he and Maria had spent that wild night when James was conceived. Would James have a talent for music? Who could tell?

Richard was to spend the night as a guest of the Goldstein family, and at ten tomorrow morning he would travel to Windsor and meet the King. He had come a long way from his Sussex childhood and he found that rather frightening. To think of it: the little farm boy Dickie Dyer an internationally recognized pianist and a top-scoring fighter pilot. The two things seemed at odds. Here he was as well; engaged to a lovely Australian girl who must never know the truth that he was already an illicit father of two.

'Oh, Dick, come in, come in,' Esther Goldstein was all smiles as she hugged him and then suddenly she was crying; tears streaming down her face. 'Dick, you're our hero, you've saved us. You and all you RAF boys saved us and all our people.'

'We've stopped the daylight attacks, but there's a long way to go.'

'No!' said Esther. 'You've stopped the Germans invading and if they came here they would kill all Jewish people.'

'She's right.' It was her husband, Daniel. 'We've information from our communities in Europe. It's confined to ghettos and slave labour and we've heard there's been killings.'

Richard could believe this. He wondered where the crazy fool Lamingham was. In custody if there was any justice. 'I'm glad you like what we've done, but I got some dirty looks on the way here.'

'Some people think you should be stopping these night bombers,' said Daniel.

'I know,' said Richard. 'I think the Air Force are working on a solution, but our day fighters can't do anything at night. Even with a bright moon the Jerries can avoid us.'

He had a happy evening recalling old times. Daniel told him that he was still playing with the one orchestra in full commission even though it had been stripped of all its young players. At night he was an ARP warden. Richard knew that David Goldstein was working at the same top secret establishment as Maria. He had wondered about that. David had been tested in battle in Spain, but with the danger to his people Richard would have expected David to be in the army.

'No,' said Esther. 'He's been called up to some high-security place. We've no idea what they're doing but it seems David discovered something in Spain and they want him there. He told us there's a girl in records or something who knows you.'

Richard wondered how to play this. 'Yes, I had a letter from the lady. We were at school together in Sussex.'

That night sleep had been broken by two air raid alarms. The household had gone down to the cellar, but in the end, apart from a rattle of anti-aircraft guns and distant explosions, nothing happened.

The next morning Richard dressed carefully in his number one uniform. Mr Tenbury had loaned him his Air Force sword and belt. He could see why the army might like swords but the thing would hardly be much use in a Hurricane. He grinned to himself. He would have to attack everything from the left to keep his sword arm free. Much better, an Air Force car was due to fetch him and three others for the ceremony. With his lameness Richard hadn't felt up to the long walk from the nearest station to Windsor Castle.

They arrived at the castle and were greeted by a pompous major-domo who would have made the Corbailier's butler look a clumsy oaf. They were shown into the grand hall and took their places on the plush red-cushioned chairs. Richard saw five other RAF men: three from Fighter Command and a pilot and navigator from bombers.

The national anthem greeted the King; then the ceremony began. The King was handed a sword with which he knighted a general. Following this the medal winners were summoned one at a time.

Then the call: 'Flight Lieutenant Dyer.' Richard was not really nervous but he was interested. He limped as smartly as possible up to the monarch. The man was shorter than he appeared in photographs. Richard snapped to attention.

The King looked him in the eye. 'Flight Lieutenant Dyer. It is a great pleasure to see you here.'

'Thank you, Sir.'

'You are multi-talented. You are a successful fighter pilot and a talented musician.' Not a trace of the rumoured stammer. 'Yes, the Queen has a gramophone record of you playing, and I believe you compose for the Malburg band.'

'Yes, Sir.'

'My daughters have a gramophone recording of that band. They dance to it.'

The King took the medal from a tray 'Dyer, will you be doing more flying?'

'I would like to, Sir.'

'No Dyer, you must not – you have done more than your duty.'

Then came the shock. 'I understand you know the Corbailier family?

'Yes, Sir.'

'Lady Petersfield has a fine son. My younger girl, Margaret, went to his birthday party. It seems he is a boy for any father to be proud of.'

The King smiled and dropped the medal onto the hook on Richard's jacket. Richard replaced his hat saluted, and limped back to his place. He felt as if he had just been punched. Oh my God, that conspiratorial, male-to-male, grin, near wink, gave the game away. The King knows. If the King knows how many other people know?

CHAPTER 36

The music returns

What in hell was he to do now? Richard had applied for night-fighter training and been brusquely turned down. He had made a painful journey to visit his old squadron and, although welcome, he no longer felt part of anything. Squadron Leader Jones was still in command although he was waiting for promotion and a new posting. Richard's complete failure to climb into a Hurricane cockpit was his greatest humiliation to date. He laughed along with his old comrades at the attempt, but inwardly he felt depressed. Here he was; the supposed fighter ace, who was incapable of even boarding his aircraft. He was further mortified to learn that his squadron was to be equipped with new Spitfires and would be crossing the Channel to take the fight to the enemy

It was Jones who gave him the sound advice. 'Dickie, you are a headstrong young fathead. You have more than proved yourself with us, but first and foremost you are a music man. You're still on recovery leave, and let's face it our lords and masters won't let you back in aircraft cockpit. So I tell you straight. Your duty to your country is to play music.'

That sounded wonderful, but how and when? There was a war on. The solution came a few days later in London and was wholly unexpected. He received a letter of command to attend an office in outer London. It was a sub-branch of the Information Ministry that had been evacuated from Central London to a seedy office block in the relatively safe suburbs. The black and white painted signboard read MOI Entertainment. Richard checked his watch; the service had conditioned him to be punctual. He was shown into an inner room and there seated were the two unlikeliest people he could have expected to see. One was Harry Malburg and the other was the top classical composer William Walton. He had already met Walton on a couple of occasions pre-war and he had scored music for Harry. William Walton, like Richard, had started life of insignificant birth.

'Good to see you, Richard,' said Harry; the little bandleader gripped his hand. 'Good to see you and you're all in one piece.'

'Dyer,' Walton was also smiling. 'Am I correct to say that the Air Force have grounded you? That is the term I believe?'

'Yes, I don't welcome it but they have the last say.'

'No,' said Walton. 'I understand that the powers that be have decided that we cannot have you getting yourself killed. You are a fine musician. I compose but I never could play anything. Never in one hundred years could I play the piano like you.'

'I do my best.'

'Now, to business. The Government has conscripted a lot of us with the aim of cheering the nation. I have been hired to compose film scores. We already have the ENSA concert parties. The armed forces are mandated to recruit dance bands. Harry here is involved in this.' Walton nodded to Harry.

'Right,' said Harry. 'The RAF band is called the Sky Blues but we want to create something with a bit more class than a wind blowing ensemble. We want someone to create a light orchestra that plays the whole range: popular song and dance through to classical with an established pianist leading and conducting. Right, boy, it's yours if you'll do it.'

'Morale of the nation,' said Walton. 'We've all got to do our best even in a field that isn't our first choice.'

Richard felt that odd sensation that he had known during the battle, the conviction that somehow he was destined to survive although to what end he couldn't say.

'Very well, if I can't fly I'll play music. Yes, I'll do it.'

'Walton held out his hand. Good man. Wait the call but there's nothing to stop you recruiting your players.'

'Is there a gender ban? I mean can we use girls as players?'

'Yes, indeed girls will be very welcome,' Walton smiled. 'The more glamorous the better. I understand you know a rather fine string player.'

'Stella Barnes, yes we're engaged. She's a really good viola player and she was a soloist with the Berlioz concerto.'

'Jolly good, give the lady the call. We can let you know who else is available. Even the old ones will need to wear Air Force Blue.'

Richard then braced himself for a duty that he would prefer to avoid. He left the train at Chichester and walked through the town to the ironmongers shop. He stopped outside, paused to take a deep breath and then walked inside.

The shopkeeper saw him and raced round from behind his counter, arm outstretched. 'Richard, oh, it is so good of you to come and see us.' Robert Stacey called out towards the back of the room. 'Vera, come quick, Richard Dyer's here.' Robert called a shop girl and told her to man the counter; then he led Richard into the living quarters at the rear of the shop.

Vera Stacey, Tom's mother, greeted him. 'Oh Richard, I'm so pleased you've come.' She lowered her voice. 'Poor Tom is buried in the cemetery. You must go there.'

'I'm so sorry, but he was a brave man,' Richard replied. This was easier than he had dreaded. The Stacey's were bereaved, but it seemed not inclined to blame him.

'Poor boy, he was found in the sea. He got out of his plane but drowned.'

'I know, I was there.' He wasn't going to tell them that Tom had died from the impact of a ten thousand foot plunge with no parachute.

'We miss him terribly, but we're so proud of him. You boys have been wonderful, all of you. We are all so grateful.'

'Did you have much enemy damage? I mean with Tangmere just up the road.'

'Yes, we caught a few bombs but it's not like what's happening in London every night. I hate that Hitler. We've got to beat him. Got to kill him. Then Tom won't have died in vain.'

Richard said goodbye to the Staceys and made his way to the cemetery. He found the grave with its new headstone and stood quietly. There he found serenity, an inner peace. No one else was around as he laid a bunch of flowers he had bought in the town.

It was poignant here so close to the places that he and Tom had shared. His friend lay within sight of the cathedral where they had both made their music; near the park where they had played and the pitch where they had kicked footballs. He bowed his head and said a prayer. He knew it could so easily have been he who had died in that battle. 'Goodbye old man. Sleep well.' He turned and walked away to find the bus for Pockhampton and home.

The new orchestra was coming together nicely. Richard had recovered his own piano from storage and it was in a village hall just outside the little Surrey town of Farnham.

He now had twenty orchestral players billeted in and around the town and he had found a nice family in the village with an unused cottage where they had let Stella stay for a peppercorn rent. Life felt much more secure with the arrival of the Canadian army who occupied the nearby heathland and took over the neighbourhood, the pubs, the girls and everything that moved or shook.

It was a joy to have Stella with him every day and she was happy in her turn to have him and to have her music back. Stella also had seen grim sights. A young bomber crew had died on the airfield with her last posting. Five young men burned to death in a crashed aircraft on the runway; all lost in spite of the efforts of the fire crews. Stella had seen it and it had affected her as much as Tom's death had affected him.

One of Richard's problems was to pacify the villagers. Their commandeered hall was now an official RAF facility with a name board and a flagpole. He explained his orchestral practice sessions would be confined to mornings and early afternoon. Once they were ready and running they would be away on tour or broadcasting and then the locals would have their hall back again. The twenty players recruited were overwhelmingly strings players, including Stella. He had a Polish refugee girl who was a useful flautist and an ex-Salvation Army girl trombonist. Two ageing timpanists were found for him by Malburg. A full woodwind and brass section was promised. The girls were young and attractive but the male players were all elderly and some had been retired for a few years. Once the whole band was assembled they would have to be kitted out in Air Force blue.

Some of the rank and file string players were distinguished men who had once graced the desks of the major symphony orchestras. Richard was at once in a fight to make them take him seriously. In their view, how could this callow boy compare with the great names that had wielded the baton in their day? War or not they grumbled at the sub-standard rubbish they were being asked to play. One day they were honoured by the arrival of no less a figure than William Walton. Walton told them in no uncertain terms who Richard was, about his background in music and his record as a pilot. Then Richard sat at the piano and led them in a good burst of the Rachmaninov Third.

Following this he was grudgingly accepted, and as the days went by the men began to like him and like his interpretations of the classics. They also accepted the short pieces he composed himself. The three girls never caused him pain; Stella was always supportive even if she ribbed him in private about the situation.

He enjoyed the experience but he would enjoy it more if he were not torn in two. He was safe on the ground and had a good chance of seeing out this war in one piece, but he still missed the adrenalin of flying. His walking was improved and he was not sure that he couldn't one day fly again. He suspected authority knew that but they needed him to create music.

His relationship with Stella was growing; they were closer every day and so much on the same wavelength. But he missed his son; the little boy he was so fond of but whose existence he could never admit and his little daughter whom he hardly knew for the same reason. He had been angry with Maria and her family for the trick they had worked with him. Now he could see there was a cool logic to their plan. Poor Maria with her deviant husband was starved of physical love, and he had given her both that and the children she longed for.

Now Stella and he had begun to sleep together. They were still unmarried so they were careful, but to Richard their lovemaking became a revelation. With Stella the physical act was her showing her man love. That was in strong contrast to Maria's desperate carnal energy. For the first time since his disablement Richard wondered if a happy future might be possible.

CHAPTER 37

1945

For four years music had taken over Richard's life. The Sky Blues were an institution. By 1945 they had expanded to forty players half of whom were women. Richard was only interested in quality musicians He was infuriated by prejudiced bureaucrats who made problems with his recruiting black players. Surely that's why they were fighting this war. The band's unique rendering of rhythmic dance music had swept the nation. Their live broadcasts on *Music While You Work* had genuinely cheered an exhausted people. The band spent hours in recording sessions with such artists as Ann Shelton and others, including the lively little twelve-year-old Amanda Verriman who was to make a name in adulthood singing after the war. The Sky Blues had no inhibitions about their work. The orchestra played modern big band swing and sometimes Jitterbug. Then the band would play waltzes before breaking into the *Merry Widow overture.* Richard's signature tune, one from his *River Thames Suite,* was played and whistled throughout the land. Sometimes in a full ballroom they would play a musical joke such as the time when a swing quickstep was in full flow. Suddenly the orchestra opened new music scores and began to play Delibe's Coppelia Mazurka. The dancers continued in the new rhythm and then often stopped to applaud.

Richard lost himself in his composing of song melodies and wrote in partnership with WAAF driver Marianne, a member of the support team who was a talented lyricist. Marianne had lost her fiancé; a bomber navigator he was shot down and killed over Germany. Sad and distraught Marianne penned a beautiful poetic tribute to her man: *My Love is not Lost*. Richard promptly set it to a soft haunting melody and the resulting song became what in later years would be called a hit to be performed long after the war.

Richard had met many influential persons including Churchill, who had praised him. The wartime censors had tried to ban *My Love is not Lost* from being played by the BBC on the grounds that it would spread "gloom and despondency".

'Never heard such bloody nonsense,' said the PM. 'My wife loves the song.' Needless to say the song had the opposite effect. For many families who lost loved ones it was a comfort. In the sad post-war world *My Love is not Lost* was translated and played in every European language.

General Montgomery had complimented him for raising soldiers' morale. The melody of the song *You Sparkle in my Dreams* was reputed to have had different, sometimes ribald versions sung by all the combating armies in Europe on both sides. Richard had met and influenced other musicians who had in their turn influenced him. William Walton was working composing film scores including the song *All Over the World.*

Richard had a short but rather frosty relationship with the American Glen Miller. He suspected that Miller saw him as "an upstart Limey..." Then there had been those magical moments when the band had launched into a Tchaikovsky concerto with Richard on piano. It was magical in the sense that the dancers had frozen awestruck as they turned to the stage and listened intently.

He and Stella had still not married. Stella as a player and he as conductor and arranger hardly had a spare minute. Apart from this, Richard's pre-war savings had diminished and both of them were only on a standard war service pay. Whoever was making a fortune from their recordings it wasn't any of them. Stella had met Richard's family in Sussex and his parents had been delighted. 'I remembers the Aussies in the last war,' Ted his father had said. 'Grand lads the Aussies, they never lets you down.'

Maria and he met sometimes when she had a leave break in London. He felt better about this now. He and Maria met as old friends; he was committed to Stella and Maria accepted that. Maria's husband Johnny was no more. The man had met a heroic death in the North African Desert leading his men against an enemy position. He was already rated a brave officer with an MC. The year before Johnny's father had also died in his sleep so little James was a Duke. Richard could not quite get his head around this last news. Both James and little sister Julia played with their "Uncle Dickie". The three of them had a natural rapport, but obviously neither must ever know why.

Maria's brother, Leo was in the thick of the Army's fight across Northern Europe. As an Army chaplain he had witnessed horrors when he was among the first to enter the Belsen concentration camp. Leo, a veteran of both world wars, still retained his unbroken religious faith. Maria had become more and more secretive about her own work. Richard guessed that something very big indeed was being hatched in this Buckingham top-secret retreat. Then out of the blue came a shock. One day some idiot of an MP asked a question in the House.

"We are all familiar with the music band called the Sky Blues. It appears that the conductor of this band is a qualified Royal Air Force pilot. Can the Minister tell me why this man is having an easy life and not serving the nation in the capacity for which he is trained?"

The government minister had assured everyone that the conductor of the band was a badly wounded pilot who was serving his country in the best way he could. The minister had delivered the rebuke in scathing tone to a supportive House.

Richard felt mentally and physically sick. That day he applied for a fitness test. For more than a year now his walking had improved although still a long way short of normal. He had spent hours standing in front of the orchestra and he had painfully climbed a ladder to fix a drainpipe at their Surrey cottage. His old squadron commander Jones was now a Wing Commander in charge of a training base. Richard called in old favours and bullied Jones into giving him a trial flight in a Tiger Moth. It was unofficial but it proved he could still fly. In fact nothing seemed to have changed from his last disastrous escapade four years ago. 'I don't think you can ever fly on ops again,' said Jones. 'But I know where there's a vacancy for a test pilot.'

'I'll do it,' Richard was definite.

'Nothing too exciting but Westland have a strange machine that they've built. It's a top secret project, a very safe and stable craft, but almost certainly come too late for this war.'

Richard went home and formally applied for the posting. It was distressing that the storm had not died. The Beaverbrooke press had taken up the story and they were openly hostile to Richard. Stella was tearful and outraged. Richard comforted her but did not tell her of his plans to return to flying. The Air Ministry was on the defensive now and that must improve his case.

The telegram arrived at breakfast on the morning Stella and he were due to give a performance in Kent. Richard was unable to intercept it before Stella.

'What the hell is this?' she glared at the telegram and then at him.

To acting Squadron Leader Dyer: you are ordered to report to

Westland Aviation Yeovil Aerodrome Somerset not later than 12pm Friday 27th April 1945.

'Oh, darling!' Richard was appalled by the expression on her face. 'It's not a fighting posting. They want me to be a test pilot.'

Stella screwed the telegram into a ball and hurled it at him. 'You deceitful bastard,' she screamed. Her Australian accent was vivid and now she was crying. 'Why, why…? The bloody war's almost over.'

'I know but I have to go back to an active role. You know what all the papers are saying…'

'No! It's only one paper and that stupid MP. Dick, everyone loves your music, our music.'

'Stella, darling. We can still make music when the war's over.'

'Oh yes, after you crash and kill yourself? I don't think so.'

He stood up and hugged her. She pushed him away and fled the room sobbing.

He left her to it. This had been their first real quarrel and it had horrified him. This was far more than Stella's suspicion of her suspected rival. Once more he was torn in two. He realised how much this lovely girl meant to him. He loved his time with the Sky Blues orchestra and he had plans for after the war. But he must justify his flying training; must justify the medal ribbon on his chest. He drew a deep breath and followed Stella into the cramped little kitchen. Stella was peeling potatoes to roast with the miserable bit of ration beef. She was still crying with no restraint.

'You're making those spuds all salty,' he smiled.

She continued peeling.

'Stella, darling – darling. We're going to be married in a few months.'

She turned on him with an expression that recalled a snarling farm cat. 'Why should I marry you – selfish bastard?'

'Because we love each other.' He caught hold of her and held her until her struggles subsided. Very gently he took the potato knife from her hand and then turned her to face him. 'Whatever you say and whatever I do, I love you and nothing will ever change that.'

She sobbed into his chest. 'Oh, Dick, love, can't you see if you go back to war you are playing into those horrible people's hands. They'll say you were never wounded at all.'

'How will they know? I am going to help a top-secret project. If any nasty little reporter blabs he'll be in breach of the law. Likely be shot at dawn.'

'What about our band?'

'Now that has been a worry. Why don't you take the baton? As far as I know my assignment will end when the war ends and that can't be long now.'

Stella gasped. 'What me? Me take the baton? I'm a girl.'

'No, you are fully trained orchestral musician. You, of all people, understand music and interpreting scores. Whatever you think, I won't be away long.'

Stella laughed through her tears and punched him hard in the chest. 'God, bloody men. You all are primitive; wanting to prove yourselves in battle. You stiff-arsed Poms are not as bad as Aussie men. Ours want to flex their muscles and fight all the time – bloody men!'

'But you are a lovely woman and you will support your man.'

Stella seemed to finally accept the situation but Richard was still troubled. He sat at the piano and ran through a new piece, a love ballad that he was pleased with. As yet it had no lyrics. He had been going to pass it to the poet Marianne, the WAAF girl who organised the band transport. No, not this time; Richard was no poet but he would try.

This would be Stella's song and he would write it. He never guessed at the time that this lovely ballad, *I Live for your Love,* would be played and sung in a dozen languages well into the next century. The Sky Blues too would be remembered long after the end of the war.

It was evening when Richard arrived at Westland Yeovil airfield. He had managed to board a bus that took him within a few hundred yards of the entry post. He felt in his overcoat pocket for his pass. His other things, spare clothes, shoes and letter writing paper plus of course his ration book had all been lovingly packed by Stella in his overnight bag. This was a classified top-secret aircraft development base and he needed his papers in order if he was to be allowed past the gate. The place looked drab, a typical base with buildings and a huge hangar. Here and there he could see relics of bomb damage. Not any more though. The Luftwaffe was engaged in a last desperate defence of the Fatherland, now caught in a pincer from east and west.

'You can pass, sir. But there won't be anyone around at this time. Night shift's due in an hour.' The guard commander was friendly enough.

'I've been asked to see Doctor Cotan. I assume he's not a medical doctor?

'Naah, he's a boffin. Clever bloke by all accounts. Would you like me to ring through and see if he's still on base?'

'Oh, please.'

Richard did not have to wait long before a rather battered Austin drove up to the gate. A cheerful little man emerged. 'I'm Frank Cotan,' he smiled and held out his hand. Doctor Cotan was a jolly character dressed in a white overall coat beneath which Richard could see a spotted bowtie.

'Mr Dyer, climb aboard and I'll show you something.' Cotan bowed Richard into the passenger seat in a way that reminded him of Ganton the chauffeur. 'Well, I know you're not a spy. Seen you before.' The little man chuckled.

'Really?'

'Yes, first time, Queen's Hall 1937. That was your debut, I understand.'

Richard was startled. 'You were there?'

'You bet I was. I love that concerto but you put a whole new life into it that night. Recently I've seen your picture in the papers.'

'Yes, I was unfit to fly for a while and I worked with this band.'

'Band – yours is a bit more than a band. Finest light orchestra I've ever heard.'

Richard was warming to this character. 'You like music?'

'Good music, yes. Never could play it myself.' The man shook his head mournfully. 'We're nearly there and I'll show you what we've got.'

The car pulled up beside the blackened hangar. In the darkness it seemed enormous.

'Come on,' said Cotan. 'Mustn't hold the door open too long – blackout's still in force. Waste of time. No Hun bombers around these days.'

Cotan led him to a side door and they passed through it into the hangar. Richard shut his eyes against the overhead lights that dazzled him. In the hangar there stood three of the oddest aircraft that Richard had ever encountered. The fuselage, tailplane and cockpit looked much like any twin-engine fighter. It was the wings that startled him. The wingspan was the widest he had ever seen. These wings reminded him of the gliders that used the updraft on the Sussex Downs in pre-war days.

'That's our baby, she's been named Welkin. These two,' he pointed, 'are high-altitude interceptor fighters. They can fly at forty-five thousand feet plus. The government has commissioned them to deal with any high-altitude intruders the enemy may send over, but so far they haven't produced one and with a bit of luck they can't now.'

Richard had walked over to the nearest aircraft. 'The pilot will need oxygen but what about cockpit pressure and heat?'

'Ahh, you are already ahead of the game, that's good.' Coton looked pleased. 'We have developed an automatic foolproof pressure adjustment and heating system. The pilot can fly in his everyday clothes,'

Until the system fails, thought Richard.

'Now, it's this third aircraft that concerns you,' Cotan continued. 'Those two,' he pointed. 'Those two are single-seaters. This new one has a navigator's seat and that is the one that we are developing for high-altitude photo-reconnaissance. That is the one you will be working on.'

Richard now found himself in a very strange world; a mystery world of engineers, draughtsmen, temperature control scientists, and a cheerful supporting workforce. Remembering how Stella was far too perceptive, he reluctantly ignored the doe-eyed looks of the girls, their flattering comments and giggling groups when he was around As April turned to May a feeling of exhausted relief spread through the factory and the surrounding community; six years of hell was drawing to a close. But the cost had yet to be counted.

Richard was now finally told what was expected of him. 'This aircraft is way ahead of its time,' said Cotan. 'However, civilian test pilots are not allowed to fly over enemy territory. We needed a service pilot and a service navigator. There is a man in the Air Ministry who has a rather high opinion of you, Dyer. He recommended you to us.'

'Who was that' asked Richard.

'I can't say, but only that he has known you for many years. Because you are a musician it is believed that you have an ordered mind and will report accurately on the aircraft. We really wouldn't want a young glory-seeker.'

Mr, or Wing Commander Tenbury must be the man in the Air Ministry. Perhaps he would like me buy it over Germany and not come home. Richard expunged such an unworthy thought. Mr Tenbury was not like that. He and Mrs Tenbury had long ago accepted his relationship with their daughter and approved the two illicit children.

Cotan broke into his thoughts. 'Our aircraft has had twenty three test flights and we know she's in amazing good fettle. We would like you to undertake a high altitude reconnaissance over northern Germany. She's fitted with the latest three-dimensional cameras. The aircraft is reliable and no Hun can get near you at forty five thousand feet plus.'

Richard felt the mental juices begin to flow. The war was almost over, unlikely to last more than one or more weeks. He only had to fly the plane. He would have a navigator to work the cameras and to put him on the right course. 'I'll do it, it'll be an honour.'

In the early hours of May 7th 1945 Richard was assisted to climb into the cockpit of the Welkin. He had already performed two test flights with this unique aircraft and loved it. His navigator was a cheerful Canadian Wing Commander. The difference in rank only mattered on the ground; in the air all differences in rank were forgotten.

He powered up the engines. The Merlins were nothing like the version he had had on his Hurricane. These were top-secret classified units designed to operate on minimum oxygen in the stratosphere. The take off was smooth. This was a large aircraft compared with anything Richard had had handled before. She was a delight to fly. In spite of the weight of two crew and extra fuel tanks, he marvelled as they climbed: ten, twenty, thirty, forty, forty-five, forty-eight thousand feet. Richard could see the curvature of the earth and the cloud base far below them.

Now once again Richard heard music; not the savage Wagnerian themes that had entered his brain in combat, but the glorious sound of Beethoven's ninth symphony. Yes, *Ode to Joy,* it fitted with the relief that he detected everywhere. Six years of strife and slaughter were nearing their end. The navigator gave him his course and they headed for Germany. The cameras were primed for their mission to record the final destruction and to identify any fighter airfields that might still be operating. First they had to fly the width of England to reach the East Coast then cross the North Sea and reach the Dutch coast. They had been airborne for two hours when the navigator called Richard. 'Skipper, we're ordered to abort the flight. Seems the war's over. We've flown the last mission of World War Two.'

PART THREE: PEACE

CHAPTER 38

1948

For Richard, like millions of others the post-war world was baffling. Peace had certainly not brought prosperity. The regime of controls and rationing had tightened even further. At the peace Richard had been sent on leave. Finally he had been discharged from the service and awarded his demob suit. The suit was an indifferent fit, but at least he had survived and could once again live a life of music.

The Sky Blues were still performing. Richard had recovered the baton from Stella and had enjoyed conducting a number of concerts to celebrate victory. These included a great open air performance on Hampstead Heath. The enlarged orchestra had performed Tchaikovsky's 1812 overture with real gunfire and a firework display. His old friend Harry Malburg had suggested the Sky Blues re-form in civilian life. This offer was tempting, it would give him an occupation and recoup his diminished funds, but it was a dead end and a dead end did not suit his ambitions. Instead he signed up as a mature post-war student to study composition.

Stella and he were now in a position to be married. Richard rented a London flat for them and also a small cottage a mile out of Pockhampton. The couple could not live together before the wedding; the village and their families would certainly not approve. In the end they compromised with a low-key registry office ceremony in London and agreed to tie the knot later in Pockhampton church. The Reverend Davis had retired but was living not far away near Crawley. The new vicar was happy for the old one to preside.

Richard had set about his piano practice with a new zeal. He worked intensively for hour after hour with exercises, short etudes, popular numbers and then the Rachmaninov that had made him his name. He mastered all the other concertos, working through the whole recognised repertoire. Now he felt confident to perform and ambitious to compose. Stella who had signed up with a London orchestra was fitting in well and was popular. It was a happy period only marred in Richard's eyes by one disquieting incident. Buskers held regular pitches in the approaches to many of London's underground stations. Some were competent students; others were bumbling no-hopers plus a few sad war veterans. One evening Richard heard the sound of a viola played with a genuine quality and sweetness. He walked over to investigate and had a shock. The viola player was his old enemy Lamingham. The man was older, less well fed and sallow cheeked. His suit was shabby and by his scuffed shoes stood a hat with a meagre few coins.

Lamingham lowered his instrument and glared. 'Dyer the yokel, I suppose you've been busy winning your war.'

'I served in the Air Force, yes.'

'To what end. All you've done is let Stalin's red Russian swine into Europe and destroyed a valiant new order. And now we're governed by reds ourselves. I suppose low class as you are you voted for them.'

Richard laughed. 'I voted Labour, millions did. I haven't dared tell my old dad.'

Lamingham grunted and glared again.

'Why are you doing this Lamingham and how was your war?'

'My war, my war! Two years locked in Pentonville jail for no reason whatever. Then they made me work on a farm. Clean pigsties. Think of that – me an educated man of good family.'

'Well, you shouldn't have backed Hitler.'

Richard was startled to see the expression on the other's face. 'Adolf Hitler was the greatest man for hundreds of years; I loved him.'

'What about the concentration camps – you must have seen the films and pictures?'

Lamingham snorted impatiently. 'Yes, but they were only Jews.'

Richard gave up.

He later learned that Lamingham's prison sentence had been the last straw for his family who had disowned and disinherited him. Richard knew he shouldn't feel this pity for the deluded fool, but he couldn't help it.

Richard's plans for his future life were coming together. He recovered his car that he had mothballed for the duration. He was not surprised to find that someone had siphoned out the petrol tank. He had just enough petrol coupons to reach Pockhampton and with luck find some black market fuel thereafter. When he reached the new cottage he set about furnishing it. He still had a few hundred pounds left from his pre-war savings and he put this to work to buy tables, chairs, a bed and, a huge luxury, an Aga stove. With good luck this would heat the place in winter. He cleared the overgrown garden, and lastly he obtained a sloppy Labrador called Sam. Sam was his new friend and companion in the long days when he was away from Stella. She was busy in London playing in the symphony orchestra. If he could obtain bookings for his recitals he should reimburse much of what he had spent. It was while he was home that there came the moment that was to change the course of his life.

His new tutor for the composition course had given him a stack of blank orchestral score paper and sent him away to compose a work echoing Richard's war experience. One morning, with Sam running beside him, Richard walked to the summit of Pockhampton Down, just as he had so many times in his life and childhood. It was now that it happened. His consciousness filled with pictures. A dying man is said to see his whole past life spread out before him. Richard was very much alive, but so many other men women and children alike were not. As he climbed the hill he remembered the times, young days, when he could have run this path: not now. He had led a sedentary life, as well as having his war wounds, and it was showing.

The pictures in his head were real. He saw Maria; not the nubile twenty-year-old temptress, but the mischievous little eight-year-old schoolgirl. He saw the farm as a boy, his father and mother. He re-visited the trauma of his mother's near death in childbirth and a vision of pretty little sister Alice. He was visited by other pictures: his dear departed friend Tom at choir school, the Goldsteins and the Mosley riots in London, flying in a Tiger Moth. Music began to pour into his head. To the end of his life he could never say where that music came from, only that it was recorded in his mind and he couldn't have expunged it even if he had wanted to. He did not want to; it was music that took over his soul and burned in his brain.

Now he was at war. So many men had died before his eyes; Germans that he had killed; his friends and comrades who had not survived. On the airfield the pretty little WAAF and the three ground crew blasted by that bomb. He tried to block the final revelation, the one that had haunted his dreams for all those years. Sadistically, the replay took him back to that day he saw his friend Tom die so horribly before his eyes. The music intensified as Richard staggered the last few yards to the top of the hill and fell to the ground. Now he wept, wept as he had never wept since childhood. He lay on his back shaking while the music, fortissimo now, pounded into his brain. His dog, Sam, lay on top of him licking his face. The music reached a crescendo and died away to silence. He saw a vision of Stella staring at him with a puzzled expression, and then little James and Julia. He gave Sam a cuddle, staggered to his feet and set off unsteadily down the hill for home.

All that night and the whole of the next week Richard scored the music. It was easy, so vividly was it burning in his mind. He was being ambitious beyond anything expected of him. He felt more driven than even in war combat, taking only short breaks for food and sleep. He couldn't help it as he created a full symphonic work in three movements. All of it was recorded in his brain and it hurt, but the final movement was agonising. He could only relieve the pain by extracting it to the paper scores. He worked fluently, penning all the orchestral parts on the score sheets. He knew he must set the work down exactly as it had been delivered to him. It would be his tribute to Tom and all who had died in that grim battle. At the end of six days and nights he was exhausted and delusional. He slept for a further twenty four hours and was only woken by Sam pleading for his daily walk.

On the following Monday, Richard drove back to London. He carried his new score to his tutor and left it for him to comment. His reaction would be interesting but Richard did not think he could alter anything. He was still unsure where this music had come from. Was it really his? He was at a loose end. Stella was in rehearsal until midday, so he called on the Goldstein house. Daniel was in the same rehearsal as Stella, but David was home, preparing to leave for an orchestral post in America. David would never talk about his war service. He had been recruited to the same top-secret place as Maria. All Richard knew was that his friend had found some piece of German secret equipment while fighting in Spain. Although it was bulky David had brought it home as his war trophy.

The existence of this box had thrown the security services into an ecstatic tizzy. David was a musician but he was also a graduate mathematician. The secret services had co-opted him for the duration of the war. Goodness knew what these people had discovered but David had a smug look when he claimed he had helped shorten the war. Richard ate lunch with the Goldsteins and then made his way home to his and Stella's furnished apartment. He had hardly walked through the door when the telephone rang. He picked up the receiver and heard the voice of Professor Hankins, his tutor.

'Dyer, your score has aroused a lot of interest, real interest. I have to ask; is it an original work?'

'Yes, I worked on it all last weekend.'

‘Jolly good. Now, please drop everything tomorrow morning and join me at the college at eleven thirty. I want you to meet someone.’

CHAPTER 39

Professor Hankins had a second man with him: Sir Thomas Beecham. Richard instantly recognized the world-famous conductor. His first thought was that he had intruded on a private meeting.

'Come on in, Dyer,' said Hankins.

'Come in, young man,' said Beecham. 'I don't bite.'

Richard wasn't sure. This old man had that reputation.

'Yes,' said Beecham. 'Hankins, has shown me your score.' He held it up for Richard to see. 'Most interesting and original. What was your influence?'

Richard knew he must tell the truth. 'I don't know. The music just seemed to come from my mind.'

'I daresay Beethoven would say the same if he were around. Let's have a look.' Beecham laid the score sheets on the desk.

'Hmm, if I remember, you made your name with Rachmaninov. You ever meet him?'

'No, but I'd have liked to'

'I knew him in America. Yes, I can see his influence here; Sibelius too.' Beecham grinned. 'I met him once – miserable bugger, but then he's a Finn. Section here in A minor, Mahler perhaps? But my goodness this is amazing stuff. I don't know how you do it, young man, but you've taken inspiration from these masters and made something new and unique for the present century.'

'Will you do it?' asked Hankins.

'Yes, I will conduct this work. It will be an honour – but young man,' he held out his arm and gave Richard a firm handshake, 'I warn you, your life will never be the same again. Hankins says you're getting married.'

'Yes, next month.'

'Yes, that and your new fame will be a big shake up.'

Richard was surprised. He had never expected this. His first symphony had been an ambitious work but never in a hundred years would he have anticipated a debut by the Royal Philharmonic and their famous conductor. It was exciting – but first he had a wedding to look forward to, and a new life.

The wedding that should have been Stella and his greatest day had pitfalls. They had already performed the simple registry office ceremony so they were married in the eyes of the law. Now it was not long to the real event in Pockhampton parish church. Here arose the problem. The Tenbury family insisted that the reception be in the manor house. Richard's father didn't like this. 'What be wrong wi' village hall then, boy?'

Well, nothing wrong with that, but either way Stella would meet Maria. What would happen then? He doubted Maria would be looking for a confrontation, but Stella was a girl with startling intuition and she would be meeting not only Maria but their two children. If Stella added two to two literally when she met James and Julia...

Oh, God, what a bloody mess. On top of this his parents, he supposed, had never seen the children. They were old-fashioned traditional folk. What would happen should old Ted with his rigid views on class discover he had a grandson who was a duke? Richard could laugh were he not on such very thin ice. Stella had invited her own folks from Melbourne and they were on their way by sea. The final date for the church wedding was set for the week following their arrival. If Stella had her way they would both be on the ship to Australia with the return trip. Richard was not having that, or at least not yet. He had a symphony waiting to be performed by a great orchestra under a great conductor. Stella was, in her turn, contracted to an equally prestigious orchestra and making her own musical career.

On the weekend of the wedding Richard drove down to the cottage. Stella was staying with her parents in the hotel nearby. Stella's father, he knew, was a Melbourne bank manager. Even allowing for the man being an Australian, Ray was nothing like Richard's mental picture of a bank manager. The man was genial, casual in dress and did little to hide his amused disdain for Poms. Richard liked him and was pleasantly surprised to find his future mother-in-law, Grace, was a very nice lady who had once sung opera. 'Had to chuck it when the kiddie was born. Liked your piano work, boy. Gotta gram record of you before I knew you'd hooked up with Stell.'

Richard's best man was an old comrade from fighter squadron days. The two men spent an hour in the pub before returning to the cottage to cook a meal. Other survivors from those desperate days were on the guest list and included his old leader Jones, and the now Air Marshal Woodward. Then of course there were the Tenburys including Maria. He had met Maria the previous week. 'All right, all right,' she had the same girlish giggle of old. 'I'm not jealous. I won't spoil your great day and Sylvia is going to keep the two children in order. The governess is hopeless.'

'Your Sylvia could keep anyone in order,' he grumbled.

Once more he felt torn in two. He wanted to see his children and play with them. But on this day he could only hope the authoritarian Sylvia would keep the pair out of the way.

The June weather was perfect, typical of that year's hot summer. Richard and his best man arrived at the church, both smartly suited with medals jangling below breast pockets. They were greeted by the ageing Reverend Davis who had emerged from retirement for this day, and Ted and Mabel Dyer. Little Alice was preening herself in her bridesmaid dress. More guests arrived and Richard endured the ribald comments of his old squadron comrades and also his onetime schoolmates. It was sad that so many from both of these groups were missing, having failed to return from war. Richard found a real sense of proportion in meeting his old village schoolmate, Alf. Captured at Singapore, Alf had spent three and a half years as a Japanese captive and had only just survived.

The Tenbury family arrived in their pre-war Bentley driven this time by the Ganton son. Mr and Mrs Tenbury greeted him and Maria gave both Richard and best man a chaste kiss on the cheek.

Inside the church Richard could hear the organ playing Handel. The quality of the music surprised him.

'The organist is one of your guests,' Reverend Davis explained. 'He's a Professor Ross from Chichester Cathedral.'

Of course; Richard had already spoken to Ross's wife and daughter and had guessed his old tutor was not far away. Now came the moment to enter the church and await the bride.

Thankfully, the ceremony went without a hitch. The best man produced the ring on cue, both Richard and Stella spoke their vows without a falter, although Stella declined to say the word "obey", then it was outside in the sunshine to face a surprising number of photographers, most local, but for some reason two from London newspapers and, incredibly, a newsreel camera.

The pair boarded the hired car and headed for the reception. The Tenburys had worked hard in spite of rationing to produce a wonderful spread of food and bottles of real champagne. The village ladies had pooled their ration flour, sugar and butter to make a fine wedding cake. Maria's behaviour was impeccable while Sylvia Corbailier brought in James and Julia. Richard wanted to hug and kiss both but knew he must not.

A string quartet played and Stella's mother sang an aria. Richard played a piece of Chopin and then a medley of wartime dance band hits accompanied by his bride playing her viola. The time arrived for the couple to leave for the four mile drive to their cottage. The following day they would board train for a honeymoon in Devon. The wedding guests grouped on the gravel drive to wave them away.

'Happy?' Richard smiled at his bride as he held her in his arms. They were safely in their new home with a life ahead of them.

'Of course,' she smiled in turn. 'I've got my man and I ain't letting him go.'

'Let's hope the rest of our life is as smooth as today.'

Stella had that mocking expression. 'I rather liked Maria, but tell me; she's the girl you couldn't marry. I'm right aren't I?'

He had dreaded this moment. His wife had too much female intuition for her own good. 'Oh darling, Maria is an old friend. We were at school together, but marry her – never! Look I'm only a village boy. She's from a great landed family and married her own class. What's more, her family are Catholics and mine are Anglican. We're very old friends, but that's all.'

'We don't have class where I come from. I'll swallow that if you really say so, but where's her husband?'

'Johnny, he was killed in North Africa. During the retreat from Tobruk he led a crazy charge against an enemy position. He was a Guards officer and that's what they do. He'd already won the MC.' Richard guessed the effete Johnny had little to live for.

Stella was carefully folding her wedding dress having already changed to a stylish going away outfit. 'I can't make out the way your classy Brits treat children. Christ, that snooty Sylvia bitch and a governess. Dickie, if we have kids I'm looking after them myself. Those poor little mites of Maria's; what chance do they have of a normal life?'

Richard felt overwhelming relief. His secret was still secure.

CHAPTER 40

This honeymoon really was an idyll. Both husband and wife grew to know each other. They had never been so close both physically and spiritually. Their lovemaking was magical, and they began to find they shared their thoughts as they lived and breathed their music. They had taken a holiday cottage near Salcombe for the ten days. They spent happy times walking with their dog Sam, exploring the coastline. The month was enveloped in a searing heatwave. Stella took the Australians love of casual dress to new extremes. In the privacy of the cottage she went completely naked. On their trips to a nearby beach she wore a costume, not a modest two piece but something called a bikini, a French import. Richard was amused by the covert male glances all around them and the corresponding disapproving scowls of the women.

For two days they chartered a little sailing boat and explored the estuary from end to end. Richard promised Stella they would have their own boat on Chichester Harbour as soon as he earned enough to buy one. In London he had already completed two piano recitals and hoped for many more. With the war now gone an exhausted nation was beginning to emerge from its shell and crave entertainment.

On the fifth evening they did not eat out but between them they cooked a three course dinner. Richard had done his best to share the household chores. "Start as you mean to go on" his old mother had advised him. The evening was hotter and more humid than ever. Stella and he stood at the sink washing the dishes. Richard was wearing only a pair of trunks; his beloved wife was nude.

'What was it you said about Beecham?' softly he ran his hand down the valley line of her lovely bare back and stroked her bottom. She squeaked with pleasure.

She turned to him. 'Willy Harris, who plays in that orchestra, says Beecham has sworn them all to silence and they're going to rehearse your symphony in secret.' She sniggered. 'It can't be that bad.'

'That's a puzzle I must say. What does Willy think of it?'

'That's it; none of them have even had a look at the score. Yours is part of a programme of orchestral music by living composers. That's all they've ever been told, except yours is to be the last item.'

'Well, it seems old Beecham likes it. I just hope it doesn't flop on the night.'

Stella put down her dishcloth and smiled. Then she flung her arms around him and pressed the whole line of her lovely body against his. She released her hands and slid the trunks down to his feet. He kicked them away and gently lowered her to the tiled floor where they made long and passionate love.

Ten days was the most time they could afford to be away from reality although both would have been happy to continue their honeymoon for a month or more. But Richard had performance dates to fulfil and Stella was due with her orchestra to play a tour of midland cities. They returned to London in time to show Stella's parents the sights. London was still bomb-damaged and weary, but Buckingham Palace was as stately as ever and the Big Ben tower still stood guard over Parliament. In that building great reforms and changes were afoot. A National Health Service was being constructed and that would be a boon for elderly couples like Richard's parents. Food rationing which had been more relaxed in Devon was in force to the letter in the capital. Richard had managed to scrounge a supply of eggs and bacon from the Pockhampton home farm and a couple of pints of milk to store in the flat's tiny fridge.

To increase their income Richard had started to take piano pupils. They had managed to squeeze his own baby grand piano into a corner of the flat's living room and it was here that he was able to take lessons for advanced players who were not involved in any of the music schools. His pupils' ages ranged from twelve to sixty; from talented but horribly spoilt little children, to a grizzled dance band veteran who wanted to convert to the classics. One pupil stood out from the crowd: Laura Seydon was just sixteen. She had never been to a music college but was at least as advanced as Richard had been at her age. Laura was not only a pretty girl, she had impressive parents. They were happy to let her relax and enjoy her talent. They had no wish to be over ambitious for her. She was to enjoy herself.

Richard had tried and tried to find out more about the first performance of his symphony. Beecham was never available and his secretary was always noncommittal when he telephoned. All he knew was that the performance was to be in the autumn at the Albert Hall as part of a programme of contemporary music. Oddly enough it was little Laura who gave him a clue. It seemed her father worked for the ex-service charity sponsoring the concert.

'Mr Dyer, they're rehearsing your symphony in secret, but Daddy says it is a corker. He's heard the last movement and he says it sums up the feelings of millions of people who knew the war.'

'Yes, I was asked to compose something that did that.' He knew there was no way that Laura could comprehend the shattering memories that had inspired the work.

'That's why Daddy is so proud that I'm learning with you. He says that you're going to be famous.'

'Well, that's nice of him to say so, but the proof will be in the pudding as they say. Right – come on now, back to Mozart. I want to hear the whole of this section.'

Richard was earning again. He had completed three more solo recitals in London including a much-praised one in Wigmore Hall. Copyright of the Sky Blues had been released and royalties from his dance band compositions were building up nicely in his bank account. He did not tell his ageing father that he had a bank account nor did he tell him that he had been elected to membership of the Royal Air Force Club in Piccadilly. He really had left the little village boy a long way behind. Yes, "keep us in our proper stations…" Well, it was new world out there now and he had carved a little place in it for himself.

Everything would have been perfect had he not longed to have a part in his young children's lives. While Stella had been playing in Birmingham he had met Maria in one of those Lyons Corner Shops. She brought both children with her and later he had a happy hour playing with them in Hyde Park. Maria was rebuilding her life as personal assistant to a City of London solicitor. She was happy earning her own living and had no ambition to marry another aristocrat. Richard and she still felt close but neither had any longing for a physical relationship. She asked him many questions about his service in the Air Force and in the great battle of 1940, but was still tight-lipped about her own war service. He gathered that this had been in a covert intelligence centre called Bletchley and that all concerned were proud of a contribution which had gone a long way to winning the war. He reminded her about David Goldstein.

'Oh yes, I remember David, but he was one of the inner circle, really hush hush.'

'He won't talk about it either.'

'No,' replied Maria. 'Nobody there will ever talk about it. Our work is classified for a hundred years.'

Suddenly her face clouded in that way he so well remembered. 'Poor Johnny, he was very kind and sweet, but I think you know we never shared the same bed.'

Richard was tactful and made no reply.

Maria continued. 'He was so brave. You know, his commanding officer put him forward for a VC, but there were too many being awarded.' She smiled in a dreamy way. 'I'll never forget our love making, yours and mine, and I'm so grateful for my two lovely little ones.' Her face had clouded as she looked him eye to eye. She was so beautiful. 'Fate meant us be together, but the same fate forbids it. It's so cruel.'

'Yes,' said Richard. 'You and the children will always mean the world to me. But can you tell me how many people know our secret, apart from their Auntie Sylvia that is?'

'I can't say that, Dickie. But it's very few people and they are all in the titled set.'

'I'll tell you who does know. The King told me when he pinned on my medal.'

Maria released her signature giggle that Richard remembered so well. 'I think that was in the war when that little Margaret came to James's birthday party. She's very like me when I was that age.'

Richard laughed. 'What a dreadful thought. Anyway it's the elder girl who'll get the top job.'

Maria looked across the grass. 'Hey, James, leave her alone you big bully. Both of you come and say goodbye to Uncle Dickie.' She turned to him. 'We'd better go, but remember what we have is special.' Once more she gave him a soft kiss on his cheek.

In spite of everything he looked wistfully after her as she and the children walked away.

CHAPTER 41

Financially it was a productive summer. Stella had established herself in her orchestra; Richard was in demand as a performer and a piano tutor, plus the royalties from his wartime band music had restored his savings. Stella and he were able to buy their Sussex cottage and Richard bought a little sailing cruiser. Stella had lived sea and sailing in Australia. Richard had no ambition to fly again, but he loved boats and the escape route from the busy world that they offered. Their little boat was a twenty-five foot sailing cruiser with a cabin. She was a Hillyard built in Littlehampton on the coast not far from Pockhampton. She was named *Dragonfly* and it was a happy day when the pair sailed her along the coast to her new home on a mooring in Mengeham Rythe by Hayling on Chichester Harbour. *Dragonfly* was no luxury yacht; she had no frills apart from an auxiliary petrol engine and a compass. The cosy little cabin was lit by a single paraffin lamp and they cooked on a two-burner primus stove. *Dragonfly* was their retreat from the world. On their third trip they took Richard's little sister Alice, equipping her with a new-style life jacket. Ted Dyer, now retired, grumbled loud and long about his son owning a "yacht", apparently as big a class betrayal as his "mixing wi' them London folk".

'Don't you start getting ideas as well,' Ted had glared at Alice.

She smiled sweetly. 'I'm going to be a poet and a top fashion model.'

Ted groaned.

A Concert of Contemporary British Music. So read the advance notice. The date had been set for Saturday October 4th in the Royal Albert Hall to be performed by the Royal Philharmonic Orchestra conducted by Sir Thomas Beecham. The programme comprised works by major composers and others little known. One of these was Richard Dyer with *Symphony in Three Movements.*

Richard had been warned that traditionalist members of the music establishment were not happy. They accepted that this man Dyer was a competent pianist, but why should he be given a performance of a new work of three movements? The whisper was that these were die-hards who dismissed Dyer as a man of low class birth and worse: a dance bandleader. Post-war Britain was changing, but institutional snobbery was far from dead. Beecham told Richard to ignore everything but asked him to write a programme note setting out his thoughts for each movement.

This was easy. Movement 1. *A peaceful countryside in sunshine with happy children playing cricket.* Movement 2. *A young man hears rumours of war and feels apprehension.* Movement 3. *Dark memories of war in the air. The young airman walks alone on the hills amidst memories and visions of his fallen friends.*

This last was the music that haunted him morning noon and night and it appeared that Beecham liked it. Richard was not so confident. Would the audience relate to it or would he give the snob element ammunition to damn him.

The day came and Richard felt real apprehension. Not even waiting to go into combat compared with the paralyzing fear that consumed him. Stella had heard through her orchestral colleagues that the evening's concert was a sell-out.

'Don't worry, you'll be fine,' said Stella. 'Anyway I'll be there; I ain't working that night and I want to hear this work myself.'

'It could still be disaster.'

She leaned up, placed the tips of her fingers on his shoulders and kissed him. 'If so we'll take refuge in Australia.'

Richard reached the Albert Hall an hour before the first work was due to play. Already the doors were open and crowds of concertgoers were filing inside. They seemed a mixed collection of humanity; both genders and all ages. The orchestra was assembling in their backstage area. Many of them he knew from pre-war days and some were old friends from the music college. Their cheerful greetings did nothing to soothe his nerves. He knew he would have to sit through an hour and half of other works before his own symphony was played. The orchestra was almost ready to go out into the hall and he had a decision to make. And there coming towards him was Beecham.

'Please, Sir Thomas. Will it be all right if I go for a long walk and not come back until my bit is over?'

Beecham looked shocked. 'Indeed, it most certainly will not, as you say, be all right.' He walked to Richard and stared him in the face before he delved in the pockets of his dinner suit. 'Young man, here is a five pound note.' Beecham pointed. 'Go down that corridor; at the end is a staircase. Climb that staircase and you will reach a bar. You will enter that bar and buy yourself four double whiskies and then you will take your seat and enjoy your triumph.'

Richard had taken Sir Thomas's advice up to a point, in that he had only drunk two double whiskies. Now he felt a little bit like those days in 1940 on the evening before another day's combat. He entered the auditorium and was shown to his seat a few rows from the front and next to the gangway. He did feel more relaxed and he was able to listen to the early programme and appreciate the performance. There was no doubt that the controversial Beecham really was the finest of conductors. The orchestra played three short, but popular pieces; then followed a twenty-minute interval. Richard took the opportunity to refuel in the bar with another double. For the tenth time he read the printed programme.

Memories of war. A new symphonic work by Richard Dyer. A musical journey from the composer's past recollections of peace and war.

There next were printed his programme notes for each movement.
Peace. Apprehension. War.

Richard Dyer is a noted pianist. He served as a fighter pilot in 1940. Later he led and composed for the Royal Air Force Sky Blues light orchestra.

He returned to his seat feeling pleasantly fuddled. He was no longer nervous; this was the moment when one was seated in the cockpit ready to take off and fight. The second to last work was finished, the audience applauded and now it was his turn. His music was playing and for some reason he now felt he could relax. He shot covert glances at the listeners around him. They were not bored; they were not whispering among themselves, they sat still, genuinely wrapped in the music. He listened to the two movements: *Peace* and then *Apprehension at the approach of war.*

Once more he saw the pictures in his mind: his home village, his mother and father and Alice, his friends and school playmates, the Tenburys and then Maria, once young and cheeky, then a sultry temptress. In the second movement he was transported to the Mosley riots, he saw the demented face of Lamingham, he felt the exhilaration of flying a Tiger Moth. All too soon the second movement was over. Now he must sit and hear and feel again the pain of the third.

Beecham had turned and was looking at the audience. On his face

Richard could read a sardonic half-smile. Then the music began. To sit and hear his score performed in reality by a great orchestra was an experience such as he could never have dreamed of.

He felt it all again. The stricken German bombers, the carnage from that bomb blast, the mutilated body of the pretty little WAAF. Finally, he was taken to the horror of his friend Tom and saw again the body plummeting earthwards. Was this really his music? Where had it come from? He would never know. The climax; the slow diminuendo and the last two chords. The audience seemed to react with an audible gasp and then to Richard the world around him went mad. The audience stood and they applauded as if they would never stop. Why, Why? These were people, men and women of his generation, the wartime age group; some looked ecstatic, others both men and women were dabbing tears. Oh, God, what have I done?

The orchestra leader had discarded his violin and was walking towards him. 'Mr Dyer, Sir Thomas is anxious that you come to the podium.'

Richard followed him down the gangway and then onto the wide orchestra stage. Sir Thomas stood waiting with a genial grin. He offered his hand and Richard shook it. Sir Thomas turned and held up an imperious arm. Gradually the hubbub of applause subsided. 'Ladies and gentlemen, once long ago, the Germans called our nation the land without music. I say damned impertinence. I think we have discovered tonight a young composer who has stuffed that lie down their throats.'

CHAPTER 42

'You'd better read this,' said Stella. She handed her husband a newspaper cutting. They were home in their Sussex cottage and had recovered Sam their dog from Ted and Mabel. Richard's father had been indifferent to his son's new fame but Mabel had told them to ignore him. She knew that he was proud of his boy.

Richard was already feeling so overwhelmed he was not sure he could take any more compliments. It was stupid, but almost he would welcome some damning critics. 'Oh well it seems the audience liked it,' he said to his wife. 'I had this privilege seat, but did it sound all right from where you were?'

'What d'you think? Stop being all bloody Brit – all stiff upper lip modest. Your music was a sensation.' She gave him a mock glare. 'I'll tell you who did enjoy it. I was sitting two rows behind your girl, Maria and that stuck up Pom sister-in-law. I tell you your little girl cried her eyes out.' She gave him a meaning smile. 'I tell you she cried and…and if you must know, I cried too.'

With a sigh he picked up the news cutting. It was a critique of the concert, but goodness, the writer was no hack. He was the famous French conductor and no mean composer.

This symphony in three movements with a programmed note was outstanding. The first two movements were expressive and I knew we were hearing something significant. The final movement was a revelation. I listened in awe, every nerve and fibre of my being engaged. Suddenly I was hearing music, great music, page after page of beautiful music that I believed to be amongst the finest work ever to come from the Anglo Saxon race.

Richard handed the cutting back to Stella. 'Never knew that bloke wrote such good English.'

'I would guess he wrote in it in French but this version had a translator.'

'Stella, darling, this is mad. What do we do now?'

Once again she kissed him. 'How say we run away to sea.'

'That is the most sensible suggestion I've heard this month.'

Dragonfly cleared the entrance of Chichester Harbour and set a course westward. It was autumn now and the summer heatwave was but a memory. Stella and Richard were well wrapped in wool jumpers as they sat in the cockpit of their little yacht. The wind was a moderate breeze from the west and they were happy to work to windward and not use their motor.

Richard was in a state of bemusement. It was exciting suddenly being recognised as a composer. He would be less than human not to feel a glow of pride. But could he ever create another piece of music of that quality? All he had done was set down that amazing movement that had flooded into his mind as he walked surrounded by memories. That music would be attributed to him forever, but could he repeat the success?

'Wow, look at all those ships,' Stella pointed. They were heading for the forts off Portsmouth and passing the anchorage in Spithead. The water was thick with anchored warships including the giant aircraft carrier *Formidable.*

'Would you have liked to fly from a carrier?' asked Stella.

'No, I would not. Bloody dangerous – the Navy are welcome to all that.'

'What are all these ships doing here?'

'Well, it's sad but I guess they're all for the scrap yard. No war now.'

It grew dark and Richard lit the paraffin navigation lights and set them in the rigging. 'We'll sleep the night in Beaulieu River.'

'What a funny name.'

'It's medieval French. There used to be a monastery and later on they built ships for Nelson at Buckler's Hard.'

Just as the last of the light was failing they dropped anchor inside the sand spit that guarded the estuary entrance. Richard replaced the port and starboard lamps with a single white riding light. It would mark their position if any vessels entered the river at night. Below in the cabin they lit the hurricane lamp and settled down for an evening meal. Stella sat the little portable radio on a corner of the cabin table. It was a battery-powered set called a *Double Decca.* It was still tuned to the BBC Third programme with a rendering of Beethoven's Fifth in progress. The reception was adequate considering their location and the fact that their ship was settling lower on the falling tide. The Beethoven concluded and now came a weekly revue of the current serious music. Richard listened as a pedantic reviewer, one Professor Fillingbroke, with a strangulated Oxford accent began to comment on contemporary composers and then launched into a critique of

Richard's symphony.

'We were impressed and we were most surprised that a work of such depth came from such a source...a composer who appears to be a product of the lower classes and known for a dance band... That good music should spring from such an unlikely source need not necessarily be judged an aberration...'

Stella was outraged. 'Who the fuck is that pompous bludger Pom? If I ever track him down he'll know about it.' She turned on her husband. 'And OK, why are you laughing? It's you the plum-mouthed little bastard is getting at.'

Richard was still spluttering. 'Sorry, darling, but this isn't Australia. These people don't count for anything as much as they did. They're an endangered species. Ignore him.'

She looked plaintively at him. 'I wish we could put this rot gut country behind us and settle in Oz.'

'All right, I've promised we'll go out to see your folks, but don't rubbish my country. It's been good to both of us.'

She laughed now. 'Oh God, you should see your face when you said that.'

'Trouble is,' said Richard. 'I've got a bit of a block. Will I ever compose anything half as good again?'

'Of course you will. I will see that you do.'

He laughed. 'That's a threat I can't ignore.'

'When we do go to see my folks...' Stella hesitated. 'It would be lovely if we had a little kiddie to take and show them.'

'Yes, that would be good. It'll make us a family.'

'I'll hold you to that. Two week's time; I should be about ripe for a try.'

'No good trying it right now. These bunks are not made for two,' Richard replied.

He knew she was right. They needed a child to complete their life. Stella must never find out that he already had two healthy children that he could not acknowledge. He loved James and little Julia and felt a pang whenever he thought about them. A little boy or a girl that he could be close to and proclaim to the world would be something new to live for.

Early next morning they made sail and headed west down the Solent for their final destination – the beautiful secluded Newtown Creek.

Richard had been here before with Mr Ross in his X class boat. It was not the easiest creek entrance to navigate in these immediate post-war days. They took the precaution of lowering sail and feeling their way in under the limited petrol in their engine. Richard handed the helm to Stella while he climbed stiffly onto the foredeck with a lead line to drop in the water and read the depth shallow or safe.

'Darling, do be careful,' his wife called.

'Don't worry about me. Will you just steer as you're told!'

She smirked back at him. 'They say every man becomes a brute as soon as he boards a boat.'

Richard remembered the safe channel from old times. It had moved slightly, so he was glad they were being careful. He found the final turning and then they were entering the magical little harbour where they anchored.

'This is lovely,' said Stella. 'I didn't know such a place could exist today.'

'It's special because you can't get near it with a car. You either walk or come by boat.'

'Oh, such a sense of peace.' Stella took off a layer of sweater so warm was the air even in the weak autumnal sun.

Richard pointed to the nearby shore. 'This was once a major commercial port until the French burned it in the Middle Ages.'

'What did they do that for?'

'In those days we didn't get on and there was no Fighter Command to make them piss off.'

Richard went down in the cabin and put the kettle on the primus stove. Now at last he could put aside the excitement his symphony had produced and the sneering comments of that reviewer. Yes, true, he was Dickie Dyer the Sussex farm urchin and by God he'd come a long way. But how much higher must he climb before a fall? One thing that symphonic movement seemed to have done was purge the worst of the nightmare memories it had recorded. There had been no further visitations since that first performance. He relaxed and closed his eyes. 'You, know, Stell. I feel some music coming. How about a piece entitled Newtown Creek scored for viola with orchestral accompaniment?'

Stella shot him a mischievous grin. Oh how he loved this girl. 'Who is the soloist?'

'Who do you think? I'm looking at the finest viola player in the land right now.'

'Oh, you are so full of bullshit sometimes.'

He changed the subject. 'What's on the wireless?'

'We don't want the third programme and that nasty little smart-arse. But on the other side there's Much Binding In the Marsh.'

'That's more like it. Two funny Air Force chaps and lot's of in jokes that we get and the populace at large don't.'

Stella slept that night the sleep that refuses to be disturbed. Richard went on deck at tide change, time to check the anchor. A bright moon shone across the water with just a shimmer of breeze to ripple the surface. Yes, it was a fact; he heard fresh music.

On an impulse Richard pulled in the line of the little wooden dinghy that towed astern of *Dragonfly*. He slipped quietly aboard, picked up the oars and rowed ashore to the shingle beach. He wished now he had put on an extra waterproof; the night was cold and the breeze off the sea colder. This delightful spot was full of music and he sat as it flowed into his mind. This was not the emotional music of the symphony; this was gentle, reflective music that so fitted this tranquil place and his present mood. He had a right to be happy. He had his music, a career he loved, his beautiful volatile wife and the prospect of a child. He still loved his secret children and was fond of their mother but his life lay with Stella. He had proved himself in war but he never wanted to go there again. He would work at his music, encourage Stella with hers and support his parents in their old age. He pushed the dinghy down to the water's edge and quietly paddled it across the falling tide to his little ship.

CHAPTER 43

1950

Stella played the Newtown Creek concerto in three movements for viola and chamber orchestra. The critics said nice things about *this charming husband and wife collaboration...*The work was part of another concert of new work played at Wigmore Hall that March.

'That's a bleeding miracle,' said Stella. 'I expected a sneer about the common farm boy and the uncouth Aussie.'

'No', laughed Richard. 'It's only that Professor Fillingbroke who's got it in for me and I told you he's an endangered species.'

Life was good. Stella and he spent as much time as they could at their Sussex cottage and now they had the company of their little son Tom born in July. With Sam the Labrador, the family was complete. Richard still suffered pain from his war injuries especially in cold weather, but after ten years he had learned to live with it. Looking after Tom had restricted Stella's earning power to guest appearances. She could no longer accompany an orchestra on tour. Richard was so much in demand now that he had had to give in and hire an agent. He hated being parted from Stella and Tom, but his commissions were taking him from Southampton to Edinburgh and all places in between. He was still composing but it was the piano recitals that brought in the money along with recordings and royalties from the Sky Blues. Life was hard work but it was good.

One happy and intriguing day both Stella and he had gone to Abbey Road studio to hear Beecham and orchestra record Richard's War Symphony. The third movement still brought memories but no longer sparked nightmares. The world loved it, but he knew he had other work for the future. Like so many composers, both serious and popular, he could never really say where the music came from. He was credited and praised for his symphony, but he still felt that he was only a conduit for something beautiful that came from outside himself.

While Stella was at home in Sussex, Richard had been living in the London apartment while he fulfilled recital engagements. It gave him an opportunity to see his two illicit children. It was winter now and cold, but he was able to meet them when Maria brought them to his apartment and he treated them all to tea in the nearby Corner House café. As far as the world was concerned it was a meeting of old friends. Even if someone saw him he would take the risk that Stella would not find out. Even if she did find out what did it matter if he took tea with an old school friend and her young children? He loved all his children and was saddened that the three of them could never meet as brothers and sisters. Then there was the problem of his sister, Alice. She had shown up on his London doorstep in tears.

'It's not fair,' she sobbed, the standard complaint of an eighteen-year-old.

'Come on then indoors and tell all,' he waved Alice inside.

'It's just not fair – not fair!'

'All right, take it easy. What's the problem – boyfriend?'

'No, it's Dad.'

Richard began to see daylight. Alice had turned out to be another bright young child. She had won a place at the grammar school and passed her school certificate. One would think these were things of which any parents would be immensely proud. Mabel Dyer was proud of her little girl, but Ted had shouted at her and accused her of "having ideas, just like that brother o' yours". Inwardly Richard sighed. Two world wars and a massive social shake up and his old man was still striving to put the clock back to nineteen hundred.

'Dad doesn't want me to go to stage school. He says that's immoral and I'll be corrupted, and it's not true. They're ever so respectable and we girls are supervised.'

Richard already knew that Alice had set her heart on acting. For different reasons he shared his father's disquiet. Acting was a very uncertain profession. So of course was music but he had been lucky; he'd always been in the right place at the right time. Would Alice have luck? She certainly had the talent but that might not count for much in the real world of stage.

'It's not fair!' she was tearful again. 'It's my life. Acting's what I want to do, not marry some sweaty farmer. He blames it all on you.'

'You want me to talk to him?'

'I don't know that it would do any good. He says it's you that gave me ideas. Ideas, for God's sake! He so stuck in his little world he thinks ideas are bad.'

Richard sometimes wondered what the neighbours thought of his visitors. His London apartment was now in a leafy street, a modest little flat in an otherwise expensive neighbourhood. Curtain twitching was a way of life among the bored housewives and here was this bohemian musician being visited by pretty girls; teenage was the word now in fashion. They would be disappointed if they knew the truth, that one was his sister and the other Laura Seydon, the very talented piano student, whose parents paid him to advance her work. Sometimes the two girls did stay late but that was only to purloin his wireless so that they could listen to Dick Barton – Special Agent.

He wasn't sure he could help Alice. If the girl was over twenty-one she could up sticks and away legally. He loved his parents, but he knew that trying to persuade his father would be as good as talking to a brick wall. No, this was another task for poor Mrs Tenbury.

'You should look at this,' said Stella one day as they sat on the sofa with Tom on her lap. 'It says in this article that they're building a new concert hall on the South Bank near Waterloo station. It's part of this Festival of Britain that's being planned. They say there's going to be a competition to compose a musical work for its opening.'

'It says there's a five hundred pound prize,' Richard grinned at her.

She gave him a playful slap. 'That sounds mercenary. A composer should be unworldly.'

'I dunno', Mozart was pretty worldly and he would have dashed off a winning entry in ten minutes.'

'It might be worth a go.'

'Stell, it's not that easy. You're right, a composer needs a spark, an inspiration and I don't see much in a new slab of concrete by the Thames.'

The doorbell rang. 'That'll be Laura,' said Stella. 'I'll go let her in.' She put little Tom down and went to the door.

Laura Seyden appeared clutching her music scores. 'Sorry if I'm late.'

'You're only a few minutes. Stella will make us all a pot of coffee.'

'I have my orders,' Stella laughed. 'Watch out, Laura. Men are men.'

'And girls will be girls,' Richard laughed. 'Right, Greig, how is he going?'

'To Norway, I would guess,' Stella called.

Laura adjusted the piano seat and rattled off Greig's *Wedding at Troldhaugen.*

Stella appeared with the coffee tray. 'Where in Norway is Troldhaugen?'

'No idea, I've never been further north than Aberdeen, but I do have that booking for Copenhagen. It's Greig again – Concerto in A minor.'

'Wow, I know,' Stella shrieked. 'Can I come along? My Mum's part Danish and she'd love that.'

'Won't you be playing that weekend?'

'No, we're off for three weeks. I was going to suggest the trip anyway.'

'That's a great idea. How say we fly out a few days early and then explore Copenhagen.'

Stella clapped her hands. 'You're on.' She turned to Laura. 'You want to come too?'

Laura looked gloomy. 'Can't, I'm afraid. I'm working now and I can't get away.'

'Don't worry,' said Richard. 'It won't be forever. You'll be playing the Greig yourself in a year or so.'

'Flying?' Ted Dyer growled. 'Ain't you done enough o' that in the war?'

'Oh, come on, Dad, We're going to Copenhagen in a very safe and solid airliner. Won't be a single 109 in sight.'

'Aeroplanes is not natural. If God'd meant us to fly we'd've had wings.'

'Ted, that'll do,' Mabel shouted. 'Your boy fought the Germans in that battle. They saved us all.'

Richard changed the subject. 'Is Alice around?'

Mabel grimaced at her son and jerked her head towards his father. 'She's staying with the Tenburys at the manor.'

'That's it,' said Ted. 'Her own folk's not good enough for her no more. That's what comes o' them ideas you've given her.'

Mabel pulled at Richard's sleeve and led him out of the kitchen. 'Alice is helping Mrs Tenbury and Maria. Maria's little boy is a bit of a tearaway and Alice reads him books. You know your father; he doesn't like books.'

'I know, they give us ideas.' He paused. 'Alice came to see me in London. She wants to go to stage school. Acting is very insecure, but I think we ought to let her do it and see what happens.'

'I know, Mrs Tenbury came over the other day and says Alice should do it and she'll find a safe place for her to live in London.'

Richard felt relieved. Once again his dear mother had had the last word. He wasn't sure he approved of Alice looking after little James, but he assumed that his parents knew nothing of the boy's origin.

'She'll come back here today.' Richard reassured her. 'She's promised to help look after Tom until we get home.' He picked up the telephone. 'I'll give her a call.'

Richard's mother caught his arm. 'She can bring that little James with her if she likes.' She glared at him. 'There's something about that young'un that's not right.'

My God, he thought. She's guessed.

Richard and Stella stepped off the plane at Copenhagen airport to be greeted by the manager of the national orchestra. His name was Peter Nielsen and he spoke perfect colloquial English. 'I was in your country in the war. Like you I flew, but in my case I was in bombers.'

Richard shook hands again warmly. 'That's wonderful. I was in Fighter Command for a while until I put myself in hospital. But you guys went through a hell of a lot worse than we did and you never got much credit.'

'We know all about you, Mr Dyer. You flew a Hurricane in the 1940 battle. Tell me – was that the inspiration for your war symphony?'

'Yes, for the third movement anyway, but I've no doubt you have similar memories.'

Nielsen took them on a tour of the city. They were both impressed by the beauty of the architecture, the waterfront with the Langilenie park and the little mermaid on her rock. They were drawn to a group of sleek-looking sailing yachts.

'Those are Dansk folkboats,' said Nielsen. 'I'm told you like sailing boats. Would you like to try a folkboat?'

'You bet we would. I've seen pictures of them and they look exciting. Better be after I've played your concerto.'

'I will arrange it.'

Peter drove them to the suburb of Hellerup and introduced them to their hosts in a little bed and breakfast residence near another yacht harbour. The hosts were a young couple who showered Richard with compliments about his music and once again his war service. 'There are a hundred good restaurants in the town,' Nielsen advised. 'But don't go into a Kro, that's a sort of pub. The locals are not too bright and sometimes mistake English people for Germans.'

'You don't like Germans.'

'We hate them. Look what they did to us.'

'I know,' said Stella. 'We've sort of forgiven them, but then we were never invaded.'

'Maybe we too will forgive them one day, but not yet.'

Richard spent the rest of the day sightseeing. Nielsen had told him that he would be having a run through of the concerto the next morning when he would have the chance to meet the conductor and orchestra. Nielsen also told him the concert would be broadcast live and relayed to Norway and five other European countries including Britain. Richard recalled his near panic years before at his first performance of the Rachmaninov, when he saw the BBC van.

'I'll never forget that night,' he told Stella. 'And who did I see playing the viola in the orchestra? A lovely little Australian girl.'

She smiled at him. 'I'm never going to forget that day either. You moved everyone with that performance.'

'I've got to do as well with the Greig. It's one of the most popular works of all. Everyone can relate to it, even if they're not into serious music.'

Stella giggled in a way that recalled Maria. 'Just you keep your eyes on that keyboard and don't go looking for any little Danish girl in the band.'

'If I'm to pull this off I can't go looking for little Danish girls even if I would like to.'

'Just don't; I've got you and I'm not letting you go.'

When Richard reached the concert hall he had a pleasant surprise. The conductor was his old pre-war mentor, the no nonsense American, though much older and greyer now. In dealing with both soloist and orchestra the man never pulled his punches. He always came over as a sort of Mid-West Beecham.

'Gee, Richard. Good to see you again. Say, you played this piece before?'

'Yes, I played it in Edinburgh a few months back and in Birmingham last year.'

'Great, Mr Greig would've liked you playing it in Edinburgh; they say his granddad was a Scotch guy.'

'So I've been told.'

Following two practice runs, both the conductor and Richard were happy. The orchestra was enthusiastic and a few wanted his autograph. Ironically these included a very pretty red-haired cello girl who cheekily stole a kiss. That information he would keep to himself. He found a taxi and returned to the lodgings. Stella was there having been on an excursion to Helsingor or Hamlet's Elsinore.

'That Hamlet, right ditherer if you ask me. Anyway how did it go?'

On the night of the performance Richard and Stella arrived at the hall. He was nothing like as nervous as he had been at his pre-war recitals. Maybe war had hardened him and given him confidence. Not too much confidence; he needed some pre-performance nerves if he was to give of his best and send this audience away happy.

Someone gave him an English language translation of the printed programme.

Richard Dyer is noted as a performer and composer. His War Symphony has been applauded around the world. Mr Dyer is not only a fine musician, he served in the late war as a fighter pilot and fought in the great air battle of 1940 that ultimately led to victory and our freedom.

Stella of course was delighted, but Richard couldn't see the relevance to his music and to Greig's music. His was the last item on the programme and once more he was taken over by that strange force that poured the music from his mind through his fingers. He forgot everything: the audience his tangled life, only the music counted. And this was wonderful music; music that he remembered from childhood, that lovely first movement that he had first heard on Mr Locke's gramophone. He felt his eyes moisten, his expression reflected the music and then it was over.

The same scene that had happened so many times still baffled him. The audience stood and applauded and then cheered. School children in the front waved little Danish flags and Union Jacks and amazingly little RAF roundel flags. He stood and bowed and bowed again and again. It was gratifying that he had been the giver for such joy. Then it was over and he was able to retire to the dressing rooms and down a welcome glass of the local Aguavit.

'Richard you always amaze me,' said the conductor. 'How do you squeeze that new emotion from a piece we've all heard a thousand times?'

He couldn't answer that because he really didn't know himself.

CHAPTER 44

1952

A February day that enveloped the nation in gloom. The King had died in his sleep. Still a relatively young man, the strain of an office he had never sought finally destroyed him. Richard had such vivid memories of his one meeting with the man at the medal ceremony. He would never forget the grin – almost a wink when the King revealed that he knew of Richard's involvement with Maria. Not a sovereign ruling a subject, but a simple man-to-man moment. For that reason alone Richard felt the national grief. Stella as well was oddly subdued. The British monarchy was ambivalent for many Australians, but Stella only saw the sadness as they felt for the new Queen, one of their own wartime generation. Of course there was another side to Richard's own problem. It seemed that an incautious remark at a birthday party had been overheard by the King's younger daughter and found its way back to the palace. But then all polite society knew about Johnny Corbailier's sexual predilection, even if few knew that it was Richard who had solved the family's problem.

Only the month before Stella had announced that she was expecting their second child. Amidst the national sorrow they at least had something to look forward to.

'My Mum's on our national music committee,' said Stella. 'There's a new post in Sydney. Professor of music and composition; good pay and a house near Bondi.'

'That's pretty tempting. What facilities do you have out there? I mean sorry, Stell, but we Brits don't associate your country with advanced culture.'

'Oh, come off it. We're not all outback and sheep. Sydney and Melbourne have great music scenes. Sydney's got a concert hall. They played your War Symphony there.'

Certainly this sounded very tempting. He would be taking a step up in his career and Stella would be happy to return to her home country after nearly fifteen years. Also her new baby would be Australian by right of birth. He knew there was a huge reverse side. The chances were that he would never see his elderly parents again, as well as being parted from James and Julia. However, sad as that was, his secret would be safe from Stella. It seemed she suspected nothing. She had even entertained Maria to tea in their London flat, although Maria had left the children at home with the governess. Richard adored his wife but he still felt sadness every time he met the ebullient Maria.

Richard was moving in refined music circles, although the snobbish Professor Fillingbroke never ceased to denigrate Richard's lowly birth. Well, Elgar, a shopkeeper's son, had a pretty ordinary background, as Richard's supporters were at lengths to point out. His wartime music mentor William Walton, had approached him not long after the royal funeral. 'Richard, next year there's going to be a coronation. They've commissioned me to write the processional music for the Abbey service. Would you write symphony in honour of the event? It could be performed in the Festival Hall.'

'Go on, Dickie,' said Stella. 'You'd be brilliant.'

'I've had an idea for one for sometime. Yes, I'd love to have a go.'

Once again Richard walked alone followed by his labrador Sam. They walked the old walk to the summit of Pockhampton Down. It was a perfect June day with the sun high in the sky and the sea a brilliant blue on the far horizon. Once again the music flowed into his being, as it had at this spot throughout his life, from exactly where he never knew. That night, and the following weeks, he worked on what was intended to be the Coronation symphony, but became known throughout the world as the Sussex Symphony.

'Stella wants us to go to Australia. It seems there's a job for me there.' Richard announced this to his parents and sister around the dinner table at the farm.

'Yes, we had been half expecting that,' said his mother.

'That's a long way from England,' said his father. 'But I daresay as your girl is homesick. I never lets a woman push me around though.'

Richard burst out laughing, He couldn't help it. 'Dad, you've let mum take all the decisions as long as I remember.'

'Yes, she pushed me around when you and Alice got ideas. Look where that's got you both.'

Alice looked indignant. 'Oh come on Dad, I've just got my first big role and Dick's world famous.'

'Maybe, but both of you go poncing around with them London folks. I never did hold wi' it.'

'Dad,' said Richard. 'Can we get back to the point? Will you be upset if we spend some time in Australia?'

'Well, we'll miss you, both of you and the young un'. But you do what you think's right for you. You've always done that any road.'

His family's reluctant acceptance was a relief but Richard still felt uncertain. England was his homeland, the land he'd fought for in battle, the land from which his music sprang. He knew so little about Australia although he loved his wife and liked her parents. Stella assured him he could earn a good living in her country; both in teaching and performing, but would he find the inspiration to compose music? That was where he believed his future lay.

The supposed Coronation symphony was complete by the end of the summer and Richard passed it to William Walton for submission to some committee. The score was returned within a week condemned as, *unsuitable for performance around such a great national celebration.* The committee consisted of five eminent persons of whom only two were connected to music, and of course, one of those two, the chairman, had to be Professor Maxim Fillingbroke. What Fillingbroke was unable to say was that the composer was of too low a birth for such a grand occasion and spoke with the trace of a common accent.

Stella was apoplectic with rage. 'That's it. I say we wash our hands of this stuck up country. They'll perform your work in Oz, no trouble.'

Much as Richard resented Fillingbroke, he had to calm Stella and stop her confronting the wretched little man in public. Now he seriously began to look at the Australian option. The post in Sydney was open for him at any time he chose to accept it. Then the final decision was made for him.

'Laura, that's good. You're well up to performance standard. My agent says you could perform that with the youth orchestra.'

Laura smiled up at him from the keyboard. Richard was pleased with the progress his pupil had made but she was beginning to trouble him. He had taught Laura ever since she was sixteen and she was now twenty-one. In that time she had become a mature performer. She had already given five classical recitals as well as being no mean jazz improviser. There really was nothing more that he could teach her.

'Laura, I want you to stay in touch but I think you'll have to be on your own from now on...'

Laura's expressive face turned from happiness to grief in a split second. She was on her feet burying her head in the front of his sports jacket and throwing her arms around him. 'Oh, no, I can't. You're my inspiration and...and...I love you.'

Richard was startled. He hadn't expected any of this. 'Laura, you are a fine pianist. You are long past the need for tuition. Just do the exercises and live for your music and you will be a success.'

'It's not that,' she wailed. 'I've told you. I can't do this without you help me. I love you.' The silly girl was clinging to him now and Richard was shocked. This was wholly unexpected. Worse much worse, Stella was standing in the doorway glaring. Gently he released the silly girl and pushed her away. 'Come on sit down and we'll talk rationally.'

'No, I won't.' Laura snatched her scores and stuffed them into the music case. Then with a sob she fled the apartment and ran down the stairs to the street.

Richard was aghast. He hadn't expected any of this.

Stella was in the room. She stood staring at him with an expression of anger mixed somehow with mild amusement. 'I heard all that,' she hissed at him.

'I can't help it,' he replied. 'The girl's a good pianist but I never knew there was this instability.'

'You never knew. Are you blind or something? I keep seeing this all the time and I'm fed up with it. I saw those girls in the Copenhagen orchestra; all doe eyes and giggling. Don't think I didn't see the way that friend of yours, Maria, looks at you. And there's a dozen more wherever we go.'

Richard was genuinely surprised. He knew Maria still had feelings for him, but Laura's outburst had come completely out of the blue. 'Stella, darling. I had no idea and I promise I've done nothing to encourage Laura. I like the girl and she is a good musician. I didn't know she was so highly strung. Can't we find her a nice young man of her own age?'

'I doubt that. I've been watching her. She's obsessed with you: world famous musician, top composer; dashing fighter pilot. That's what all these girls are thinking. Don't believe I haven't noticed.' She stood in front of him inches away. 'You must make a decision. If you really want to keep me you will accept the offer from Australia.'

Richard took his wife in his arms. 'Of course I want to keep you. There'll never be anyone else. If you want me to go with you to Australia, then I'll do it. It'll be an adventure.'

'Not for me,' Stella laughed happily now. 'I'm going home and I'll be bringing the world's finest young composer.'

'Tell me some more about this college.'

'It's the Con in Sydney.'

'The what?'

'It's the Sydney National Conservatorium.'

Richard sighed. 'That definitely sounds Australian – ghastly. Why do they want me – concerto for digeredoo – sonata for tin cans?'

'Dickie, I've told you before. The Con is part of the University of Sydney. It's rising fifty years old and it's got worldwide prestige. They wouldn't normally want to recruit another Pom, but you're regarded as special.'

'And I'm married to an Aussie and our next kid will be an Aussie born and bred.'

Stella flung her arms around his neck and kissed him. 'Now, mate, you're talking.'

CHAPTER 45

Sydney 1952–53

The six week trip was certainly a novelty. Such was the rush of British immigrants to reach Australia that extra ships had been converted from wartime troop carriers. One such was the dilapidated *Melbourne Castle.* Stella was not impressed. 'Since when has there been a castle in Melbourne?'

Apart from this, Richard qualified as a "ten pound Pom", whereas Stella was compelled to pay the entire one hundred and twenty pound fare. The ship was basic, although the food was tolerable. Entertainment was limited to the occasional film show. They watched the Third Man and others such as The African Queen. There was nothing that looked like a piano. Richard spent a lot of time reading music scores and running through performance in his head. Stella played her viola at dinner to the appreciation of the diners. Week after week of the same routine began to weary them, but in some strange way draw them even closer.

'Darling Stell, you say you're dragging me down under to get me away from girls. So, you're saying in fact that you are the only desirable girl in Australia. Are the others really that ugly?

'Jeez, no. There's thousands in Sydney alone and another few thousand in Melbourne. Not to mention all the naked lovelies on the beaches around Perth and Brisbane.'

'Oh, yes. So, why are you dragging me kicking and screaming into this paradise?'

'Well, for a start it gets you away from Laura and that Maria Corblimier or whatever.'

'I think you mean Maria Corbailier, Dowager Duchess of Hampshire.'

'Strewth, you Poms still haven't joined the real world. Don't get me wrong, I liked your Maria but she's still got her eyes on you. I'm a girl – I can tell. As for that Laura, she would've dragged you into bed pretty damned quick if I hadn't put my foot down.'

'You certainly did that.' He looked around. 'Is Tom still in that play nursery?'

'Yes, they'll be there for another half hour.'

'He talks English with an English accent. How long will that last?'

Stella laughed. 'He'll talk true blue Aussie within one hour of landing.'

Richard groaned. 'What have I done to deserve this?'

The Conservatorium was an impressive building and Richard's welcome would have suited royalty. Despite all his success he had never regarded himself as important. Now thousands of miles from home he began to realise that he was famous, in fact world famous. Yes, that little Sussex farm boy had come a long way, half way around the earth to be precise. He had a beautiful wife, a son to be proud of and another child due in a matter of weeks.

'You're professor of composition and we've some very promising piano students for you.' The college dean had shown Richard around his complex with pride. Although this man was the college chief he seemed to regard Richard with something near to hero worship. 'Am I right that you've got an unperformed symphony?'

'Yes, I've brought the score with me, but it was turned down for performance in London.'

The dean gave Richard a broad Aussie grin. 'We've heard all about it. That man Fillingbroke wasn't it? He'd better keep his poofter arse outa' here. Brits like him ain't welcome.'

'I'm a Brit.'

'No, Mr Dyer, or may I say Richard? You're different.'

'Richard, or Dick as my wife calls me.'

'That's good; we don't go much on surnames.'

Richard was beginning to feel relaxed. There was something about this city and country that appealed to him. Much was similar to London. The streets were filled with tramcars and some double deck buses as well as streams of busy traffic. Much of the architecture was recognizably British. Stella was happy and Richard was rapidly beginning to feel at home. Maybe when they were settled and in a year or two they could bring out his parents to join them. It had been so sad saying goodbye to them and to Alice. Alice was achieving in her acting career and had performed Shakespeare. She was confident that her company would be touring Australia sometime. Mr and Mrs Tenbury were talking of taking a holiday in Australia and visiting relatives in Queensland. Maybe after all home was not so far away. He couldn't help laughing when he remembered his father's face when he heard Alice speak. His sister had mastered an accent that would have rivalled Maria's for upper class enunciation.

'Your wife's Stella Barnes?' the dean broke into his thoughts.

‘Yes, she plays viola. Been in two orchestras and she’s done the Berlioz twice.’

‘They’re a musical family. Your wife’s mother was a fine contralto.’

‘Yes, she sang at our wedding.’

Stella and he had a new house in the Waverley district not far from Bondi and its beaches. It was certainly luxurious beyond anything Richard had lived in either in Sussex or London. It was furnished with a modern kitchen and fully stocked cupboards. In the living room was his piano that had been freighted out some weeks earlier. Stella and he deposited their luggage, explored the place and then hired a taxi to hit the town.

‘Well, what d’you think of Oz so far?’ Stella jabbed him with a finger.

‘It’s interesting. I mean you speak a sort of vague version of English and you drive on the left, so I think I’ll get on fine.’

‘What about the music?’

‘I like the college, very free and easy compared with the London Academy. I’m looking forward to it.’

They found a nice convenient restaurant near the city centre. Richard was even more surprised by the people around them. The girls were all dressed in stylish evening gowns and the men, though not over formal, were smart. And Stella was right about the girls. The three on the adjacent table were stunning and all dressed in off the shoulder gowns that showed their bronzed skin. Stella saw his ogling but didn’t seem unduly put out. They had brought little Tom with them and the restaurant did not seem to mind. They couldn’t have done that in fashionable London. Everything about this place was beginning to grow on Richard. He smiled at his wife; she too had put on a glamorous evening dress whose folds concealed her baby bump. She looked more beautiful than he had ever known. She was home after years of exile and she was happy and he was happy for her.

They finished their meal, drank their coffee and walked to a nearby dance hall. A twelve-piece dance band was playing to a floor crowded with couples, again all stylish in dress. Richard and Stella joined the floor and danced, both now relaxed and happy. The music worked through a number of popular dance numbers spanning the years and then without warning the band struck up the Sky Blues theme song: *I Live for Your Love,* the very same song that Richard had composed and written his own lyrics. It was Stella’s song. The band could not have known who they were. The surprise was total. They slowed their dance and narrowly avoided being bumped into by two other couples. 'What about that, sweetheart?' Stella smiled.

'I know, it's our song. I think that's an omen.'

These were exciting times for the pair. Richard began to enjoy the life of the Conservatorium in spite of, to his ears, its clumsy name. He didn't mention this. He was a new arrival Pom and it was extremely bad form for such as him to criticise anything. A newly arrived Englishman was a curiosity; a "whinging Pom" was despicable. He had six good piano students who could well go the distance and become performers. He had another six who tried hard and might make it into the dance halls or accompanists for singers.

Richard didn't care. He began to love the work and he could see his enthusiasm paying off. He had an academic function showing composition to a larger class of students. He could explain to them the construction of works by the great names of the past and the best of the present. The students all seemed to feel British as far as music went. He was able to point out the regional variations of the living composers. Vaughan Williams could show the warmth of the farmlands of East Anglia, while Britten was expressive of that land's bleak coast.

Inevitably they would question him about his own War Symphony. Yes, the third movement was his war experience but was inspired by his Sussex homeland. The Aussie-born students had little grasp of the geography of the old country but they all took the point and promised to reflect their own land in their work.

It was spring in Sydney, which meant autumn back home. In October Stella's time came. Australian men were not allowed anywhere near a delivery room so Richard spent an anxious four hours pacing around and then taking refuge in a bar with two other expectant fathers. At three o'clock in the morning of October 12th little Caroline was born. Three days later the pair were released and returned to the house in Waverley to begin the ritual of restless nights and breastfeeding. Stella's parents had arrived from Melbourne and doted on the new arrival as well as her big brother who had been in the care of a crèche. To Richard the name Caroline was dignified and right, had not the women instantly renamed her as Charlie. Well, he sighed, this was Australia and he'd better agree with the natives. It was nice to be able to go to the post office and send celebration telegrams to his parents, sister and, discreetly, to Maria.

Of course, like most migrants Richard was homesick for his own country, although he had no yearning to return home. He kept a photograph of his parents and sister on the bedside table. He was enjoying his new country. He loved the unstuffy Con and his students who responded to him and clearly loved music as much as he did. The summer was coming and the temperature was rising.

'I've applied to join the Middle Harbour Yacht Club,' he told Stella.

'That's fabulous,' she replied. 'It was sad moment when we had to leave our little *Dragonfly* on the water at Chichester. We've so many memories,'

The yacht club accepted them with enthusiasm and they both began sailing in racing events and on friends' boats, exploring the upper reaches of the harbour. Stella was still heavily involved in feeding and changing Charlie. It was typical of Australia that none of their new friends minded Charlie coming with Stella on a boat. Tom was already beginning to love the water. He was having swimming lessons, never asked about England and already had an Aussie twang to his voice. It was only during the big competitive racing events that Stella stayed ashore with the children. Heaving on lines and winding winches was not her forte and the ropes were rough on her music fingers.

Richard rapidly built a reputation as a racing helm and soon became in line to skipper one of the club yachts. The crews he sailed with always respected his need to guard his hands and fingers. It didn't matter as his skill as a tactician came naturally.

Richard replaced the telephone. 'I've got to be away for a week. They want me to play Tchaikovsky One in Perth. Funny, that's not the sort of place I'd expect a music scene.'

'Hey,' Stella shrieked. 'The way you pronounced "scene", you're beginning to talk Oz.'

'Crossed with Sussex – what a mismatch.'

'I don't think I can come with you, not with the two kids.'

'That's a pity. You see – there's an airline connection now. No four day train run any more.'

'You never wanted to be an airline pilot?'

Richard laughed. 'No thank you. I did all the flying I need in the war. By the way they've asked me to join the local Air Force Association. For a Pom that's quite an honour.'

'I keep telling you – you're special. You're Richard bloody Dyer, world famous musician and composer, and a famous fighter pilot on top of that is mega.' Stella assumed her severe expression. 'In Perth, you will keep your eyes off the beach lovelies and if you go in the sea watch out for sharks. Frankly I think the lovelies are the bigger menace.'

'I shall behave as an Englishman and a gentleman.'

'Oh, God, that's not much reassurance. Tell me: that Laura wrote to you; you tried to hide the letter but I saw it.'

'I don't mind, it's harmless. She's got a commission to play a recital in Bath and she thanks me for my help and apologises for the scene she made.'

Stella kissed him. 'Don't worry I'm not really a jealous type. Deep down I trust you.'

High summer in November seemed a contradiction. Richard was also puzzled by the genuine excitement that was building around the London coronation next year. Australia's vocal republican movement had become oddly muted. Everywhere flowed declarations of loyalty to the new Queen. Some light was shed for Richard by the Conservatorium's dean. 'No, Rich, the monarchy may be remote but it means stability. My ancestor was sent here for some minor crime, but there's tens of thousands of people of Brit descent, then there's all the migrants from UK and thousands from the likes of Greece and Italy. They're escaping to a better life. The Queen, God bless her, stands for stability, continuity, safety, whatever way you want to put it. I don't say this sentiment will last for ever, it won't, but right now it makes sense.'

Perth was an interesting city: remote and much hotter than Sydney. On the flight he was flattered to be invited into the cockpit to meet the crew. This flying was a long way from the frantic wartime combat. The captain, in a smart uniform and cap, showed him the controls and instruments. In high summer this was a bumpy ride but very much better than a sweltering trip by rail.

He was happy with his concert performance with a competent orchestra in an air-conditioned hall. The following day he had a chance to visit the yacht harbour at Fremantle and then swim from one of the beaches. Yes, there were gorgeous suntanned girls everywhere but none that could compete with Stella in her bikini. He returned to his hotel, took a shower and had a good night's sleep. The next morning he boarded the airliner for the return trip.

On arrival in Sydney it was already late evening. Richard hired a taxi to fetch him back to the house in Waverley. Stella had taken the two kids to see their grandparents in Melbourne, but by now they should be home. He let himself into the entry hall and now he had a shock. A violin was playing, and no ordinary violin. The instrument had a sweetness and refinement and it was playing the lovely slow movement of the Bruch violin concerto. He ran into the lounge and saw Stella. She put down the violin and smiled at him. 'How did it go in Perth?'

'It was good, but come on, where did you get that amazing violin?'

'You won't believe this but it was in a box in my old granddad's attic. When the poor old feller died, my mum cleared out his things and she found this. It's not a Stradivarius but it's from the same period in Italy and almost certainly from the same area by someone who saw old man Strad at work.'

'Well, all I can say is you do it justice. What a wonderful find.'

Stella put down the violin and reached up and kissed him. 'The thing is, I'm doing the Bruch concerto in Melbourne. The orchestra will be the Victoria state youth orchestra. They're all kids but they ain't half good. So, when I play I want you to conduct. The kids are right over the moon when they heard you might do it. So…?'

Richard hugged his wife. 'Well, I've always fought shy of conducting. Even with the Sky Blues I always wondered what the guys were thinking. But an orchestra of kids – all right I'll give it a go,'

Stella giggled again. 'Hey, give it a go! That's pure Aussie talk and your accent's coming on great.'

CHAPTER 46

Conducting the kids was rewarding. An orchestra composed of ages eight to eighteen was a new experience. If an adult band might regard a new conductor with cynicism, these youngsters looked at him with wide-eyed admiration.

'I wish you would get it into you thick head,' said Stella. 'You are famous.'

'Oh, yes. What about that taxi driver who refused to drive me? Said, "I don't take Poms". That's a fine welcome to your home city.'

'Don't worry, I've told you; one more year and you'll talk like a real Aussie.'

Richard worked with the orchestra for four evenings. He began to enjoy conducting. The children didn't argue; they accepted his interpretations without question. Stella had spent years playing the larger viola but she took to the beautifully crafted violin as if she had played it all her life. The concert was part of a festival of youth and youth culture. A year ago Richard would have laughed at such a concept in relation to Australia. His prejudice was all but gone now, although a proportion of the youth orchestra was of Italian and Mediterranean origin. It was Stella's big day, but he was satisfied that he and the band would not let her down.

They walked to the home of Stella's parents who were looking after the grandchildren. Stella was still clutching her violin case. 'I'm not letting this outa' my sight.'

'You nervous?' he asked.

'Yes and no. I just hope I'll remember the score as I go.'

'You'll be surprised. It'll take control of you, or the music will.'

Stella put an arm around him. 'That's what it does for you?'

'Every time I perform; the great concertos are locked in my brain and as soon as I sit down to play it's the music that takes over.'

'There's just one more thing. I've had a request from the director of the festival. Will you conduct the kids in movement three of the War Symphony?'

'He's been on to me already. I'm not sure. I mean it's a complicated score. I couldn't make it any easier and I don't want to.'

'No, don't run those kids down; they've been studying the score for months. The director says they're mad keen to do it.' Stella stopped walking and turned to face him. 'Dickie, you still don't realise what you've done. That music is one of the most important pieces this century. The director says lots of the dads and mums of the kids fought in the war and they want to hear it live with you conducting.'

'All right. It's your Bruch that matters but if they want me to do my bit I will.'

Richard rehearsed his symphony and Stella's concerto with the youth orchestra and was most gratified. These youngsters were raw material but they were keen and produced a wild version of his work in which the odd mistakes seemed to blend well in the final result. Stella enjoyed her violin performance and the applause was loud and long for everything played that night.

Following the performance they all stopped for a drink in the hotel by the concert hall with Grace and Ray Barnes, Stella's mum and dad.

'Stell, you were a bloody miracle,' said Grace. 'And Dickie those kids did you proud; that performance had something; much better than the gramo' record.'

'Did you tell them about that phone call?' asked Ray.

'Oh, no,' replied Grace. 'Dickie, a woman rang from Sydney, the janitor in your block gave her this number. I hope that's all right?'

'Who was it?'

'Well, she's a true blue Brit. Spoke exactly like Queen Liz. She's Mary something, funny surname, I couldn't catch.'

'Oh, not Maria?'

'Yes, that was it – Maria. Says she's here to find her relations. She'll be in for a shock if she thinks they'll talk like her.' Grace laughed while Richard and Stella exchanged glances.

'You don't look that thrilled,' said Grace. 'Who is she?'

'Dickie's ex. He couldn't marry her because she's too high-class. Am I right?' Stella grinned at Richard.

'We went to school together but you're right she's gentry and I was a farm boy. But I found a much better girl playing in an orchestra and that was love at first sight. Maria and I are just friends.'

'Christ,' said Stella. 'He does talk some bull. That girl would eat him and swallow him any time.'

Richard laughed. 'Only if I let her which I won't. I know her parents and they did say something about relations here, but they were in Queensland – not these parts.'

'Yes,' said Stella, 'So you tell me why Maria is in Sydney and not up there.'

'Well, I expect she thinks it's rude to come to Australia and not say hello.'

Stella blew a very unmusical raspberry.

As their taxi pulled up outside the house they saw Maria sitting on a park bench in the front garden in the shade of a palm tree. She stood up and waved.

'Strewth,' Stella muttered. 'Look at her: floppy hat, sundress and thong sandals.'

Richard groaned. 'That's exactly what you're wearing.'

'Well, I ain't a bleeding duchess.'

'And this is suburban Sydney, not Royal Ascot.'

They walked over and shook hands. Richard was amused to see that the two girls displayed friendship. 'Look Tom,' said Stella. 'Here's Auntie Maria. How are your two, the oldest must be eleven or so?'

'Actually James was twelve last September.'

'Are they with you?'

'No, they're with my mother and father. They're visiting relations near Brisbane.' She smiled. 'Sir Clement and Lady Flavia Tenbury. Baronet, but don't give that bit away if you're in those parts. This is Australia and to everyone they're Clem and Flav. They run a rather good vineyard.'

'Do they sound like Stella?' asked Richard.

Maria loosed her trademark giggle. 'I would say that Stella sounds quite refined compared to Flav's vowels.'

'Yes,' replied Stella. 'I expect you notice that Dickie is beginning to talk like a true Aussie.'

'A little bit,' said Maria. 'But there's still plenty of good honest Sussex there.'

Richard felt both disappointment and relief. He hoped he might have the chance to see his other two children, but not in front of Stella. James's resemblance to his true father would now be too blatant for Stella not to notice.

They took Maria indoors and Stella poured them all ice-cold drinks. 'You over here for long?' asked Stella.

Maria took a long sip of her drink. 'Making allowances for the sea trip, we've taken six months out to see your country; all of it from end to end.'

'You'll miss the coronation,' said Richard. 'You'd have a place in the Abbey?'

'No, I've had to miss out on that. My little James is the Duke now, but he's too young to stick his coronet on with the others.'

Richard laughed. 'So, he can't sit in the House of Lords?'

'Not until he's twenty one.'

'Look at Stella's face,' he said. 'Aussies don't go much on Lords.'

'I know. That's why Clem and Flav have to lead a double life.'

To see the two women in his life sitting amicably together was always a puzzle for Richard. He loved his wife: loved her sparkling personality, and her amusing. erratic lifestyle. Their family was complete and their lovemaking was still magic.

Maria was his childhood companion, the girl who had latched onto him in youth but could never be his. She too had given him two lovely children whom he could never acknowledge. Now he had both girls sitting in his house chatting away like old friends whatever the undercurrents.

A long-distant memory returned. 'Maria, I remember Miss Jeffries in the school with a big map of Australia and you said you'd like to go there. So, now you have.'

Once more Maria giggled. 'Fancy you remembering that. Stella, Miss Jeffries was our teacher. She thought all Australians were convicts.'

'Lots of Brits seem to think that,' Stella grinned. 'I'm not; my family are free settlers about eighty years ago. A lot of our top people, politicians and the like are descended from crims.'

'Politicians, that doesn't surprise me,' said Richard.

The coronation year passed by. They all watched the filmed record of the ceremony and the celebrations in London, Richard remembering how he and Maria had watched the last one in 1937. A few weeks later he went with the entire Tenbury family to see them board ship for home. Mr and Mrs Tenbury, both in their sixties, looked bronzed and well and had clearly enjoyed their Australian trip. Stella had tactfully let Richard be on his own with his friends. So he was able to say farewell to his two unrecognized children. It was sad that to them he still had to be Uncle Dick.

James, the young duke was a happy, cheerful lad with a taste for playing rugby. Richard was delighted to learn that Julia was already playing the piano. Maria promised she would keep in touch with regular reports on the children. The older Tenburys seemed unchanged from the earlier days. It was sad parting and he stayed watching as the ship left the dockside and moved towards the open sea.

CHAPTER 47

Sydney 1960s

The years passed and Richard and Stella both loved their new life. Richard's composed music was gaining enthusiasts worldwide. His original coronation symphony had been rewritten and was now the Sussex Symphony. It was a huge success both in its homeland and especially with its performances in Australia and New Zealand. Thousands of ex-patriot Brits related to it and praise was heaped on Richard from all directions. The War Symphony filled concert halls around the world, while Stella performed her Isle of Wight viola concerto in Sydney.

Sailing was his huge release from all this. Stella and he owned a small sailing cruiser on the harbour and Richard was in demand as an offshore skipper. He was now almost entirely absorbed into the culture of his adopted country. Stella marked his final crossover to one incident that never failed to delight her. It was a mid-nineteen sixties nightfall at the end of a January day of intense heat. The pair, dressed in shorts, sports shirts and walking barefoot, headed for home carrying between them a heavy coolbox stuffed with beer cans. On the last kilometre they had had enough and Richard hailed a passing taxi.

'Holiday season,' the driver complained. 'Don't get me wrong it's good money, but it is nice to give a ride to two genuine Aussies. Half my customers are bleeding Poms.'

'Too right, mate, you said it.' Richard replied, while Stella bravely tried to suppress hysterics.

'The Schwarz family want to take Tom to this concert,' said Stella one evening in 1962.

'What concert is that?' asked Richard.

Stella pulled a face. 'Johnny O'Keefe.'

'True Aussie culture,' Richard laughed.

'Well, he's very noisy if you can hear him above the screaming girls, but music – I don't think so.'

'I'm not a culture snob,' said Richard. 'I'm not against the new rock music. I've been told there's that young group in England called the Beatles. They sound innovative and are doing well. Then dear old Elvis has got a half decent voice, but our Johnny, sorry not for me.'

'Nor me.' Stella was grinning at him in that way he knew so well. 'You've had another letter from Laura Seydon.'

'Well, yes. She's played at the Albert Hall proms and she's ever so grateful; puts it all down to me.'

'Is she married?'

'Not that I gather, or she hasn't mentioned any attachments. And before you ask, Maria's not remarried and James, her eldest has left Eton and is studying at Oxford.' Richard paused. 'He's taking his seat in the Lords next year.'

'Jeez, that's Pomland for you.'

At the close of 1960 Richard had been in demand for a different reason. The new media, television, intended to celebrate the twentieth anniversary of the Battle of Britain. Richard was one of a dozen or so RAF veterans of the battle present in Australia and also a handful of Luftwaffe survivors. Richard spent three interesting days of filming and meeting his fellow airmen. It was pleasing to find that the Germans were very little different to himself. One of the Germans approached him with hand outstretched.

'I am Ernst Lidden. I think it is you who may have shot me down in 1940.'

Richard remembered the little German prisoner under guard in that police car.

'No,' Richard shook hands gladly. 'It wasn't our squadron. But I remember you.' He explained and the two of them had a surprisingly convivial reminiscence of those grim days,

The programme was broadcast on the anniversary and the Dyer War Symphony was played to an enthusiastic concert audience for three nights in a row. Then, near to Christmas, Richard and Stella went to their local town hall where Richard stood up and took the oath of allegiance to Australia. He was now a full citizen of his adopted country. Then they returned home to a celebratory barbecue in their garden with a gathering of neighbours, orchestral musicians and sailors from the yacht club. He still missed Sussex and England but this was now his home.

Richard was increasingly in demand to give piano recitals. Apart from the great classical composers he was invited to do re-workings of the Sky Blues numbers and in several of these he accompanied the singer Amanda Verriman who had originally performed with his wartime band at the age of twelve. Amanda, a New Zealander, was now nearly thirty and carving out a big name for herself in the world of folk-rock. After one of these recitals Richard found himself greeted by an elderly man who seemed familiar. He was Doctor Cotan the aeronautical designer whom Richard had worked for in the dying days of World War Two.

'Like you, Richard,' said Cotan, 'my Aussie wife dragged me to retirement in her home country.' Whether that was also a ploy to take the unworldly technician away from a female rival was not revealed. Richard was aware that his abandoning of his orchestra to go flying at the end of the war remained a sore point with Stella.

Richard was still reluctant to conduct his own work with mature orchestras, but found he had no problems with youth orchestras. He had already conducted a series of concerts with these both in Sydney and Melbourne, but in the early spring of 1963 he received an invitation to conduct his Sussex Symphony with the Youth Orchestra of Los Angeles. Air travel from Australia to the United States was sketchy. Richard and Stella decided to take the family for a long holiday in England and for Richard to fly to Los Angeles in the month in question.

CHAPTER 48

England 1963

This time their trip to England was not on a run down "ten pound Pom" transport but on a luxury liner. Richard's earnings, even after tax was paid, had been building slowly over the years while he was still receiving royalties from the Sky Blues. His royalties from his symphonic recordings were also growing, as were his recital fees. The family was not exactly wealthy but they had the status that went with first class travel. It was a long voyage but compared with outgoing trip this was an idyll. The food was sumptuous, the children had a pool to swim in and deck games to play. Their elders sunned themselves, noting the admiring glances for Stella in her latest and skimpiest bikini. The first class lounge had a piano and Richard gave several free performances.

It was on the second day out from Sydney that Richard picked up a four month-old copy of the London Times.

Coroner's court report.

The Coroner gave a verdict of suicide while the balance of the mind was disturbed.

Michael Lamingham, only son of the late Sir Rufus Lamingham was adjudged to have taken his own life by hanging. Michael Lamingham had been disinherited by his family for his membership of the pre-war British Union of Fascists for whom he was a brigade commander, before being detained under wartime regulations.

Richard handed the paper to Stella, 'He's the guy you replaced in the orchestra the night I first saw you. For that alone I suppose I must thank him, but he hated me.'

'I was a bit nervous that time,' she replied. 'Orchestras were a bit of an all male world then and I was a girl.'

'That's why I noticed.'

Day after day they settled into their luxurious routine. Richard tried his best to exercise running round the deck, but he knew he was putting on weight. Stella seemed to be able to eat as much a she liked and not lose her lissom figure. Richard noticed other mothers with young children who had been rewarded with stretch marks and podgy waistlines. The ship's administration had insisted they dine at the captain's table. Personally both Richard and Stella found the other celebrities a rather dull lot.

As they left the tropics behind the weather worsened with wind and cold rain. Stella's bikini had to be packed away for the remainder of the voyage. Finally they docked in Southampton and there on the quayside were Ted and Mabel with the Tenburys and Maria. Richard's parents were in their late sixties and the elder Tenburys were both over seventy. Maria greeted Richard with a kiss. She told him how she was now a partner in the London legal practice. James was taking his seat in the House of Lords and her brother Leo was a Catholic bishop somewhere in Thailand. Julia had spent three years at Roedean, the leading girls school, and had followed her brother to Oxford. She was reading classics and doing well with her music.

After everyone had hugged and greeted everyone, Mr and Mrs Tenbury drove them all to their old home village. They would stay one night at the manor and then they would take possession of a furnished cottage rented near the village of Chilgrove not far from Chichester. At the manor, Stella enthused over their bedroom, the Elgar room. Richard had vivid memories of the bed as the scene of his last wild night with Maria. Richard tried to push the memory away while they settled the two children in the old nursery.

Stella missed the autumn back home but Richard delighted in walking the Downs in the summer heat and revisiting his childhood secret places. It seemed they had missed the coldest and most snowbound winter for two hundred years. The Sussex countryside had ground to a halt amidst twenty foot walls of snow. Motorists had struggled to reach work; farmers had struggled to move feed for their stock. Only the Pockhampton children had enjoyed the experience although the local school had remained open for most days. Richard had been greeted by the sad news that his old labrador, Sam, had died three years previously at the grand old age of fifteen. His father had retired from active farm work but the Tenburys had let Mabel and he remain in their old farmhouse. Agriculture had changed since the crisis of war. Fewer people worked on the land and mechanization had taken over. Horses were no longer seen and the tractor was king. What had once been the old hay barn now contained a gigantic combine harvester mothballed for the winter. Ted Dyer grumbled about all this but accepted it.

Christmas came and the whole family sat down for a turkey dinner in the family home. Alice had joined them with her boyfriend, another actor; like Alice he spoke with a perfectly enunciated high-class accent. As he originally sprang from Birmingham that ability must have been learned, as with Alice, at acting school. This, along with Richard's acquired Australian speech was something his parents wondered at but in the end tolerated. Their children were now something in the outside world and that was a thing for pride.

Richard could not escape the clamour for him to play recitals and now to conduct. He had a happy evening conducting a local orchestra in the Petersfield Festival Hall, only a few miles from his rented home. They played a Mozart piano concerto and the pianist was Laura Seydon. Stella was with friends in London so he was able to take Laura for a post performance meal. They walked to her inn on the main street within a short distance of the concert hall and settled down for a meal and a long chat.

'You know I won that Paris piano competition,' said Laura.

'I know, you deserved it.'

'The LSO are touring Australia sometime next year and they've asked me to go with them. They want me to do the Rachmaninov second concerto. You Aussies are hooked on that film Brief Encounter.'

Richard was pleased. Laura had been his star pupil, disregarding her hysterics at the end. 'I think Brief Encounter is probably a bit dated. All this talk of liberation and all that...'

She interrupted him. 'Did Stella take you away to Australia because of me?'

Richard was shocked. What could be a tactful reply to this? 'Actually Stella likes you, but as for Australia, I'd been offered this teaching post in Sydney and Stella was very homesick. She'd been in the UK for fifteen years but never really settled here.'

'I know. I'll always regret that silly scene I made.'

'Don't worry, that's all past. Stella thinks she has a mission in life to protect me from beautiful women.'

'Does that include me?'

My God, he thought. She does have a really captivating smile.

'Well maybe.' He changed the subject. 'Is there anyone in your life?'

'Not really. I'm never in the same place long enough. It's all concerts three nights a week and living in hotels out of a suitcase.'

'That's a real shame. You are a pretty girl and you deserve a happy life and children.'

Now she was weeping, tears were flowing down her face and dropping into her soup. Richard was horrified. He had touched a sensitive nerve in the personality of this emotional girl. 'Please, Laura, I didn't mean to be tactless. I only want the best for you.' He handed her a large handkerchief. 'Go on, I haven't used it. It's clean.'

She wiped her face and eyes. 'I know, I'm a fool, but I'll never change…' She hesitated as the waitress interrupted her in mid sentence.

Laura let the incident pass. For the rest of the meal she chatted about her musical life and he gave her tips about Australia that could be useful during her visit. They said goodbye and she gave him a long passionate kiss. He walked back to his hired car outside the concert hall and drove back to Sussex. It had been a happy but disturbing occurrence and Stella must never know.

Richard had been involved in an expensive series of trans-Atlantic telephone calls. Everyone had been appalled by the assassination of President Kennedy. The tragedy had left the normally self-confident United States in grief and bewilderment. Richard was told that the Los Angeles concert was now to be a memorial event and Richard was asked to conduct the Sussex Symphony, but to conclude the concert by conducting movement three of his War Symphony. The audience would be asked to stand in respect, but not applaud.

In late January he went to Heathrow and boarded a Boeing 707 for the long flight across the Atlantic and on to California. The modern airliner was an experience, and once again he was invited to the cockpit. This jet engine powered aircraft was strangely quiet compared to the turboprop machines in Australia. Apart from this, it was a long and tedious experience. The seating felt cramped, the food indifferent, and the film show not to his taste. At last they were instructed to fix seat belts and the airliner touched down at Los Angeles airport. The door was opened and the gangway lowered and Richard with the crowd of fellow passengers stepped in to bright sunlight. This was January but noticeably warmer than in England even though a cool breeze blew off the Pacific. They entered the area where the customs and entry clearance officials worked. In those more innocent times clearance was quick and Richard emerged into the public areas to a shock. The hall was filled with news cameramen. He looked over his shoulder and around to see if he could recognize the film star, but no, to his surprise and dismay, the cameras were all pointed at him. 'Mr Dyer, Mr Dyer, this way, look this way...' Why the hell were they fixing on him?

Next, a film camera team caught him or rather trapped him in a corner near a newspaper stand. 'Mr Dyer, NBC News. Can you tell our viewers something about your work? Your War Symphony is huge all over our country.'

Richard did his best, but why should these people be remotely interested in a Limey, but adopted Australian piano player?

The explanation came minutes later. He had not expected a reception committee although he had been promised a guide to meet him off the plane and that guide he knew. His old friend David Goldstein was standing with a huge grin all over his face.

'David, wonderful to see you. Our people told me you were coming to the States.'

'Hi there, Dick. Can't say how proud we all are to have you with us for this concert.'

Richard was still baffled. 'David, tell me, why all this hubbub? All these cameras and interviews. No one told me about that.'

'Don't sell yourself short. This concert is a memorial for the late president. It's part of a whole series of same events all over the nation. Do you know that your War Symphony is listened to everywhere from the White House to every place where veterans live. I tell you straight. When I play those twenty bars for oboe alone I have to detach myself from my imagination. Those bars have a sort of Jewish intonation and I keep thinking of all those poor people in the death camps. It's the same with everyone else. There's passages for everyone that bring it all home again.'

Richard had heard much of this before especially in the performances in Australia. 'David, that third movement is very personal and it is based on things I remember but would like to forget. I saw a friend die in battle.'

'I know; you fought in that battle. You changed the course of the war while I was safe and protected code cracking.'

'No, David. You contributed to winning the war every bit as much as we did.'

David shook his head. 'Come on, grab your suitcase and we're outa' here. No hotel for, you we're going to my place. I want you to meet Donna and my two youngsters. I can tell you they'll be thrilled.'

Five days later was the big night. Originally Richard had been hired to conduct a children's orchestra. He had fulfilled that commitment the day before but now he was to be asked to conduct his own work with the Los Angeles Philharmonia Orchestra. He had been apprehensive but following two rehearsals all had been fine. He found he communicated well with the senior players and the younger musicians seemed to idolize him, which was embarrassing. The two performances were enjoyable.

His Sussex Symphony was by now his favourite work. It was wholly based on his early memories. The opening movement imagined the small boy running up the hill slope. The staccato rhythm of the melody represented nimble footsteps and gasps of breath. He had worked and reworked this until it switched in to a dramatic D Major, a sweeping lyrical expanse that painted the scene from the hilltop and the countryside stretching to the line of the sea. Two more movements each picturing different scenes of the English countryside: peaceful and then drenched with rain and blown with snow. It was to have been the Coronation symphony, had it not been rejected by the establishment for prejudice against himself. He was rather pleased with the way he had concealed bars of the national anthem as an enigma within the main work.

Then the orchestra had played the final movement of the War Symphony, the music that Richard had dreamed from his own experience. As ordained the audience stood in silent respect at the end. He did not have to respond, only to bring the orchestra to their feet and stand heads bowed for the two minutes. Somehow this seemed more fitting to this work than noisy applause.

That weekend he spent with the Goldstein family, or with David's American branch. David had played his oboe part in the symphony and the next evening he played the solo part in a performance of the Vaughan Williams Oboe Concerto. Now it was his turn to show his old friend something of the famous Los Angeles. Richard's name seemed to be a passport to everywhere. They visited Hollywood and the Disney complex and dined in the best restaurants. Richard felt guilty for having lost touch with the Goldsteins while in Australia. Naomi had married 'a nice Jewish boy,' said David. 'She's still working in music but for a recording company. Her man's an architect.'

Sadly the time came to say farewell and Richard boarded the 707 again heading for home. He had telephoned Stella to let her know his likely time of arrival, and the good news that his trip had swollen their funds by a thousand American dollars. This was all very satisfying, but would it last?

CHAPTER 49

Australia 1968

Life in Sydney was good and the opportunities to visit the whole of this vast nation were many. Richard had played piano in every city from Perth to Brisbane and from Adelaide to Darwin. As the children passed through school age, Stella had returned to playing in an orchestra. She too had carved out a modest career as a violin soloist.

Tom had passed through high school with distinction and was now at university reading medicine. Caroline or "Charlie" was fifteen and in her wilder teenage years with an even wilder circle of school friends. Both children loved the traditional outdoor life. That included sailing on the harbour, swimming at Bondi and the mandatory treks into the bush. Tom played cricket for his university and Charlie was a good netball player. Neither children were the most talented musicians, but Tom played confidently with the classical guitar while Charlie blew a spirited trombone part in her school band. But neither parent was going to force their children to any career. Time would tell.

Richard was still divided between his home country and his adopted nation. Stella had watched with amused expression as Richard and Tom had gone wild watching England win the 1966 football World Cup. Then, while watching the Mexico Olympic Games. 'Isn't it time you got yourselves a national anthem?' he grumbled to Stella. 'Just now the telly was on and I heard God Save the Queen. I jumped, thought, crickey, we've actually won an event. Then I ran into the room and it was a bunch of your bloody Aussie swimmers.'

Stella threw a mock punch. 'Yeah, you Poms ain't winning anything.'

'I know, don't tell me. Your secret; it's the climate, the diet and a complete lack of any intellectual stimulation.'

'Oh, come on. If we had no culture, you and me would be out of a job.'

'All right, you Aussies are musical. I've got to give you that. So, why can't you come up with a national anthem?'

'Maybe, I mean yours and ours is pretty dreary.'

'Well, Land of Hope and Glory then. That's Elgar. I told you I once met him when I was a kid.'

'Yes, many times,' Stella sighed. 'You played the piano for him and he said something patronizing.'

Richard was still teaching with his sixth batch of composition students and another four talented young pianists. He was working on a fourth symphony inspired by the bleak New South Wales landscape, plus an oboe concerto dedicated to his old friend David Goldstein who was now a noted conductor. He had an exciting new commission. He had been asked by the Australian poet Bob Jansen to write an opera. *Robin Hood and His Merry Men* was to be their collaboration. He decided at the start that the music, while matching the lyrics must reflect all the styles of the twentieth century. Bob Jansen was a cheerful outback Australian with an international reputation for his verse. He was an easy collaborator and the two worked well together. Bob's vision of Robin Hood was less Sherwood than "jolly swagman or wild colonial boy". In both cases it was the theme of defiance of authority. How historically accurate this was, no one could tell. Richard knew that during that period in Southern England there really had been the aristocratic robber, Adam Gurdon. Gurdon had taken from the rich and taken also from the poor but kept all the loot for himself.

Richard was busy working with two youth orchestras. It was the most rewarding experience. He was inspiring a generation of young people by enthusing them with music. By music he meant all music. In the Melbourne orchestra he had a brilliant young percussionist who also played in a rock group. Richard had written a work for percussion, taking in all the percussive instruments from triangle to xylophone, including a piano part that he played himself. The youngsters loved it, and it gave the percussionists their time of glory. In the case of the young drummer, Richard had written in thirty seconds for the boy to improvise with his rock drum kit. They had performed the whole work on television to the delight of the performers and their families.

Richard still missed England. His mother and father were rising seventy, but both steadfastly refused to join him in his new downunder life. They were adamant that they would live and die in their home village. Maria sent him regular reports of their children although she worded the letters carefully so that Stella might read them with no embarrassing implications. James had won an honours degree from Oxford and had begun to take an interest in the family's landed estates. Julia was now twenty-seven and back at Oxford studying for her PhD. She was a genuinely talented pianist who sometimes played the organ in Pockhampton church as well as the family's Catholic church in Chichester.

More embarrassing were the regular letters he received from Laura Seydon. These he did his best to conceal from Stella but not always with success.

'What's this,' Stella waved the letter at him. 'All my love? That's what it says.'

'It's only a form of words.'

'So you claim.' She laughed. 'All right, the woman behaved herself when she came here for that tour.'

'Well, she only came to play music. That concerto she played was good. After all she was and still is my best pupil.'

Life was not all work. Stella went for more outback treks and Richard had twice been part of a crew in the Sydney-Hobart yacht race. The second time he was appointed as skipper to the lovely ketch rigged *Purple Fox.* Richard, a Sussex country boy, had never seen a purple fox although he remembered the local hunt halooing after the brown variety. The yacht belonged to an Australian lawyer with a vivid imagination. The race was due to start on Boxing Day or, in Australia, the day after Christmas.

Richard always found Christmas in Australia a culture clash. The air temperature was over thirty but the media was still filled with winter carols and Father Christmas appeared in big stores just as he did at home in Sussex. The Aussies didn't like to admit it, but in some ways they were still very British. In early December, Richard boarded *Purple Fox* and met her crew. The yacht was a beautiful forty-five foot design with modern metal spars and terylene fibre sails. The crew were a cheerful bunch of mixed nationality with a shapely girl called Judy who was the navigator. Richard worried that they might resist their skipper for being a Pom piano basher, but his reputation as a seaman preceded him and it seemed this was good.

The start gun fired on a perfect summer day and the large fleet beat to windward, out through the harbour into the wide expanse of the Tasman Sea. The wind was light although the weather forecasters had predicted rising winds and rain. This region was always unpredictable and now they were heading south towards Antarctic regions. It was idyllic as the sun shone and the yacht sped south with all sail set including the biggest spinnaker. As the sun sank below the horizon they all noticed the buildup of cloud and with it flashes of lightning.

Judy the navigator appeared and she looked anxious 'Skipper, just been on the radio – severe weather alert.'

'All right, how severe and when will it reach us?'

'Dick, I don't like it. They're talking cyclone and that could be mega wind speed.'

Richard looked astern; the cloud had become menacing, the thunder and lightning closer and he could feel the first spots of rain. He called for Jake the sail trimmer and ordered an immediate sail reduction. Jake, a burly blond Queenslander also looked worried as he organised the retrieval of the spinnaker and a double reef in the main. Some of the younger crew grumbled but Richard was immovable; he knew Jake had seen all this before. Now the wind was rising and seas were building in a cold and menacing way. Blasts of wind slammed into the yacht at speeds off the scale of the wind meter and with these gusts came rain and then stinging driving hail, with quarter inch stones. The crew were all now in their oilskins and safety harnesses.

Then it happened; a massive gust of solid air slammed into them and *Purple Fox* heeled over until her starboard rail was buried in the sea. Richard saw two of the young crew hurled across the ship until they were brought up short by their harnesses. Jake bawled at the surviving crew and set about lowering sail. This done he worked his way back to where Richard was still on the wheel. 'Dick, guess this'll be worse before it gets better.'

Now Judy was shouting in his ear. 'Young Pete's got a broken arm. I've got him below and got him in a bunk but it's too rough to try and do a temporary splint.'

'OK, fill him up with pain killers and I'll try and smooth our passage.'

Richard turned to Jake and shouted. 'We could round up and lie hull on to the seas, but I think I'd rather run before it with bare poles.'

'Yeah, I second that. It's all we can do in these seas.'

'Good man, Jake. We'll share turns on the wheel.'

Jake nodded and began to work his way forward just as a huge wave hit them and washed over the whole ship. Jake was picked up and swept against the cabin top where he lay motionless. Judy crawled to him and turned the man onto his back. No mean feat from slender girl. Slowly she worked her way back to Richard as he struggled with the steering.

'Dick,' she yelled. 'Jake's out cold – hit his head. Gotta' get him below.'

'OK, Jude, mobilise some help and get him in a bunk.'

She crawled forward again, stopping and gripping a handhold as another wave swept over them. Richard couldn't leave the wheel for an instant, but could Judy manage to get help? The crew were young teens and twenties and this was their first big adventure. Gradually as Judy knelt by the cabin hatch, he saw one then two then three crew emerge and between them take the injured Jake below decks. Now he knew that the survival of the ship and all their lives would depend on him. Suddenly he was back as in war again; not strapped in his Hurricane cockpit but now held by his harness to a deck bolt.

He felt calm but anxious, resolved but apprehensive. This was as if he was in dispersal waiting for the squadron to scramble and again music began to flow. It was Mendelssohn, the Hebredian overture – Fingal's Cave. Originally a fair weather interpretation maybe, but the cadence, the rise and fall of the melody, helped him concentrate and somehow ride with the waves. He clung to the wheel as it fought back. The tackle working the rudder was below deck and out of sight. It must hold, it must. He was tired, he was cold, and the rain and hail slammed against his foulweather suit. The salt stung his eyes but he could still see. If that steering gear breaks we are lost. Mendelssohn was no more, now fresh music burned in his brain, exciting music and it was his music. He must survive now to score this and pass it to the wider world. He knew that without this music he could not have held his position at the yacht's helm for ten hours. Judy emerged from the cabin to report that those among the crew not injured where too seasick and frightened to help. Despite himself he was drawn to this girl: she was brave and beautiful, but he must be careful. Before the race Judy had given enough indications to show she would like to be a rival to Stella. Why did women do this to him? As the night passed the new music intensified, and with it he saw pictures of home in England and of Maria and little James and Julia. He wanted to see them again and that was reason enough to tough out this storm and win.

As daylight came it seemed the gale lessened although the huge seas remained. Richard was exhausted; he clung to the wheel while his eyes kept closing. A hand tapped him on the shoulder. 'Better let me give it a go, mate – you look crook.' It was Jake. The man had a heavy bandage swathed around his head and his right cheek was bruised.

'Jake, are you sure? You took one hell of a knock back there.'

'No, mate. I'm an Aussie born and bred.'

'Which I'm not,' Richard found himself grinning.

'Don't worry, Dickie. You did as well as any Aussie could ever have. You're one hell of a guy. Jude's been singing your praises.'

Richard handed Jake the wheel and sat watching for some minutes.

The wind was dropping now and Jake, although certainly concussed was coping well. Richard took a chance and left Jake to it and shuffled down below. He fell on his bunk and knew nothing more until he woke as Jake and the now revived crew took *Purple Fox* into harbour under power. They hadn't made it to Hobart but they had survived.

Richard could have done without the ensuing uproar. The unpredicted cyclone had taken its toll. Three yachts had been lost and some crews drowned. This race was, and is, a major Australian sporting event but that did not stop some carping critics from questioning whether it was safe to be run in future. His crew were fulsome in their praise and spoke freely to the newsmen and television reporters.

Great composer saves his ship...One man alone for ten hours saves his friends.

His family were shaken, relieved and proud. They had listened for hours to radio reports as the tragedy unfolded. There had been no mention of *Purple Fox* and they had feared the worst. Stella and the children had arrived at the obscure fishing harbour where the yacht had found sanctuary. Stella had hugged and kissed her husband while Caroline had wept. Richard was more worried by the look of deep suspicion with which Stella eyed Judy.

He still couldn't understand the fuss. Yes, he'd steered the yacht through that terrible night, but basically he had done it to save himself. If in the meantime he had saved the ship and her crew as well then – fine. He only hoped the uproar would subside and he could get on with some more music.

CHAPTER 50

1970
Australia and tragedy

Richard took a week off from the Conservatorium before he began work composing once more. He scored the music that had come to him at the height of the gale, but it was not enough for a full length work. It was only later in the wake of tragedy that he was able to use it.

When it came to Bob Jansen's opera lyrics he was pleased to work on the score with Stella. He would play his ideas on the piano and Stella would replicate the string section with her violin and viola. Every so often they had to call in Bob from his shack up country and persuade him to modify his lyrics, especially in the choral sections. Richard deliberately made the arias operatic while the remainder of the score had echoes of the Sky Blues. Eventually the work became enduringly popular with the public, but was criticized by the musical establishment, especially in Britain, for being neither an opera nor a stage musical. During composition all the family had fun when the children sang the arias, while their parents made the accompaniment.

Maid Marion's shrill aria was one of the show's climactic moments and was to be sung over the years by a variety of divas and artists worldwide. Whatever the merits of Robin Hood the public were to love it and it secured the Dyer family's fortune for the rest of their years. Bob Jansen became a wealthy man but remained in his outback shack until his death. The first performance in Sydney was a sell-out and earned rave reviews.

In February, Richard received an invitation to skipper a different racing yacht in a new event: an offshore race between Melbourne and Perth. He had been working harder than ever with performance and conducting. He had been sent on a tour of Japan, China and Singapore and had an enthusiastic reception everywhere. Stella had held the fort at home as well as playing her own instruments in the symphony orchestra. Tom was in his final years of training to become a doctor. Caroline, or Charlie, was seventeen and taking a gap year before going on to university. It was time for the whole family to take a break. Richard took ship with his yacht crew while Stella and Charlie went on a bush trek in Queensland. This sea trip was exactly what he needed to build his reserves for another busy autumn and winter. As always he would miss his wife and children, but the break gave them all a chance to relax with the outdoor challenges they loved.

'It's trek by Land Rover and walking in the outback and rain-forest,' Stella was gleeful. 'Wow, that's something I've dreamed of.'

Richard carried hers and Charlie's bags across the airport hall and then kissed them both goodbye. They walked towards the aircraft and then both turned, smiled and waved.

The yacht race was a marathon challenge of over two thousand miles before they found port. Apart from this there were very few places to put into. For once, the winds in the Tasman Sea were moderate and progress was slow for all the race entries. Ten days out from the start Richard was feeling uneasy. He was possessed with an irrational feeling that something was wrong. He couldn't quantify it; he only knew it was unconnected with the sea or music.

'Dickie, mate. You look real crook.' It was Jake; once again sail trimmer and also navigator.

'Jake, I don't know. I just feel something's wrong and I can't say what.'

Jake grinned. 'No worries. D'you know where we are?'

'I saw your last position, but that was hours back.'

Jake pointed to the horizon. 'Over there's Cape Catastrophe. Not a healthy place.'

For years to come Richard was to remember this – a horrible premonition.

After the best part of a month at sea they rounded Cape Leeuwin and picked up the famous Fremantle Doctor, the wind that blew them triumphantly into port. After thirty days at sea they passed south of Rottnest Island and headed for the finish line at Port Fremantle.

The lowered sail and floated securely into their appointed berth. Now Richard had a shock. On the dockside waited a group of his near family: Tom and Caroline were both there with Ray and Grace Barnes. He walked over to them, surprised to see them. and at once knew from the expression on all their faces that something had happened. Grace rushed to him and hugged him; her face was contorted and wet with tears.

'What's happened?' he felt sick and in his heart he thought he knew. 'It's Stella?'

Grace released him and walked away and Ray put an arm around Richard. 'Dick, I'm sorry but it's the worst news. Stella is dead.'

For Richard his world had ended and he could never come to terms with that. Stella had been the centre of his life. In peace and war she had been his soul mate, his love, his companion, the mother of his children. For weeks he could hardly sleep and if he did sleep; he was tormented with surreal dreams when he heard her voice, only to awake and find the bed empty beside him. Many times he wanted to take his own life and join his love, but each time he remembered his children and poor Grace and Ray who had lost such a precious only child. He knew that if life to date had been very kind to him, it had a sting.

It was another sort of sting that had been the cause of all their loss. Stella had been enjoying her jungle trek, only on the third day out to be bitten by a poisonous spider. As she slowly sank into a coma, a friendly truck driver had volunteered to rush her to hospital, but halfway on the trail the truck had swerved and fallen into a ravine. Both Stella and her driver had died instantly.

Accidental death had been the inquest verdict and the body had been released for burial. Then he had endured the terrible ordeal of her funeral. Tom, Caroline and himself with her family had walked behind the coffin into the little Anglican church near Stella's birthplace. He resolved to be strong but it was hopeless. Outside the church Stella's orchestra colleagues played the Indian's farewell, that haunting tune that he remembered from childhood. It was too much, he shook and the tears poured down his face. The service over, they took the short car ride to the cemetery. With his two children holding him tight he stumbled to the graveside and dropped a single red rose onto the coffin.

'Dad, I can't live in this house, not now, not any more,' Charlie was staring up into his face with her wide blue eyes; so very like her mother's. Stella's eyes had been closed in the funeral parlour and her face was one of sleep. It was a picture fixed in his mind for ever.

'Sorry, Charlie. I know how you feel. We need to start again.'

Yes, he thought; start again, but how can we?

Charlie stood up and stroked his hair. 'I'd like to go to England. I liked it when we went there that time when I was little. It would be a fresh start and you could work again.'

'Dad, she could have something there,' said Tom. 'I can't go; I'm near to qualifying as a doctor. But she's right, a fresh start. You could go back to Sussex and be near Gran and Granddad there.'

'Dad,' pleaded Charlie. 'Please think about it. It could be the best thing for all of us.'

'You were born here, Charlie. England is a very different country.' Suddenly Richard had a very small awakening. Could this really be a solution?

'Remember, Dad, there's an air route from here to there. We can always come back and see poor Mum's grave, and visit Gran and Granddad here.'

He sighed. 'All right, Charlie, sweetheart. You could for once in your life be right.'

For the first time in months Charlie smiled. 'Oh, Dad, let's go to England and please – yes please – would you write a requiem for Mum, she would like that.'

'Yes,' he spoke so softly the others hardly heard him. 'I must do that.'

No reception committee was waiting at Heathrow and for that Richard was grateful. Having cleared customs they saw the slim figure of Alice standing expectantly. She waved and then ran to them hugging and kissing both. 'Goodness, Caroline, what a big girl you are now.'

The trip had been both tiring and interesting. Richard and his daughter had been staggered by the heat of Singapore when their airliner had landed to refuel. The break had given them a chance for a meal in the city and a little bit of sight-seeing before their journey resumed. Richard could never conceal his grief, but as the prospect of England drew nearer a little bit of life awoke in him and just a scintilla of excitement, or could that be hope?

Caroline, or Carrie, as she would be hence forward, seemed excited at the prospect of a new country. Yes, she would forever mourn her mother. She would miss her old friends, but she would still keep in touch. She was a clever girl and had inherited both her father's high IQ and her mother's impulsiveness. Tom, now well on his way to qualifying as a doctor, had seriously considered coming to England to gain some experience in the NHS.

The bulk of their luggage would arrive later so they carried their overnight bags to Alice's car and took the road for Sussex. Alice, with the ageing Tenburys, had found them another furnished rented cottage not far from Pockhampton on the main road to Chichester. Although the place was a trifle musty and unlived in, it suited them. Richard felt at home and could live out his grief thousands of miles from his broken world.

'What'll your neighbours say,' Caroline giggled. 'You setting up home with a teenage Aussie girl?'

For the first time in months he actually laughed. 'We must all work hard to put the record straight. Anyway, have you got your certif.-icates?'

'Yep, I've gotta' see you safe and sound then I can start applying to universities here.'

'Oh, I shall be fine. Right now I need solitude if I'm going to work again.'

'You're a bloke, Dad. Blokes can't look after themselves. You'll have to find a woman.'

'Oh, I'll find a cleaner and cook, but I'm not marrying again if that's what you mean.'

'You wouldn't have to. This is the permissive society; you're a music man – nobody'll bat an eyelid.'

Once again and amazingly he laughed. 'Oh Carrie, you are all Aussie. Tell it as it is.'

'That's the only way.'

She was staring at him again, that oval face, fair hair and wide blue eyes, so like her mother. 'Dad, you must play piano again.'

'It'll be weeks before my piano arrives by sea.'

'Mrs Tenbury told Auntie Alice that they're having their piano specially tuned for you. I bet there'll be people wanting you to play concertos and all.'

'I've been away so long I doubt anyone will remember me.'

Caroline drew in a sharp breath and her eyes glinted; again so like her mother. 'Dad, you are world famous, everyone's heard of you. There'll be thousands wanting to hear you play.' She paused and her face softened. 'And you've got to compose a requiem for Mum.'

A week later he drove his newly-bought car to Pockhampton. Richard walked again his own solitary walk on Pockhampton Down, the walk he had taken so many times over so many years. It was the one place that Stella had never been and that was another reason why he wanted to walk here. It was like that old poem by William Barnes: Barnes the poet, no relation to Stella's family, but another born a farm boy.

Mourning The Lost Wife.

Below the darksome bough, my love

Where you did never dine.
And I don't grieve and miss you so
As I at home do pine.

Always, this place was his inspiration. Barnes wrote moving poetry for his dead wife; Richard would compose his own wife's requiem. And as before with the War Symphony, there came music, and he would never know from where. "Dies Irae, Dies Irae"; the words poured into his brain and with them superb music every bar burning with anger. All his sorrow, all the memories of his lovely Stella came back in fury for his cruel loss. He lay on the grass, his face wet with tears as the music took hold of his soul and his being. Then feeling shaken as never before, he limped down the steep track, found his car and drove the two miles to his new home.

Caroline was not there. He knew she was in the village, caring for her ageing grandparents. She would call him when it was time to come home. No, he needed to be alone. He rang the old farmhouse and asked Caroline to stay there overnight.

'That's OK, Dad. You're composing, am I right?'

'Yes, that's perceptive of you.'

'Is it…are you …?'

'Yes, sweetheart, it's the requiem.'

That night he couldn't sleep. Some force outside him had taken possession of body and soul. He scored the Dies Irae for orchestra and sketched in the choral voices. These he could perfect with an arranger in the unlikely event the work ever being performed. Suddenly he felt detached from everything as he scored the Lacrymosa, the Sanctus, Agnius Dei, then the opening requiem sequence. For the first time he was able to use the scored music that had come to him on the yacht in the gale. It was wild angry music that came from that terrifying night but in the context of the requiem it was exactly right. Finally he scored the triumphant conclusion – his Nunc Dimittis, the glorious anthem that would one day be sung in churches and concert halls throughout the world.

Richard had never been touched by religion but in an odd way as he scored this ultimate moment he felt some warm personality was riding with him. When eventually past six a.m. he stumbled into bed he dreamed and saw a vision of Stella's smiling face. "This was never the end. I will see you again."

CHAPTER 51

Sussex 1972

Very slowly life had returned for Richard. Six months after his arrival home in England he performed a piano recital in a hall in Reading. His Australian agent had transferred him to an associate in London who also had colleagues in New York, Toronto and San Francisco. Richard knew he couldn't slump in misery forever and he found performance was a salve to grief.

Everyone he knew had been helpful, and gradually he was settling to life in England. His old refined Sussex accent was returning and he was no longer mistaken for an Australian in shops. He wasn't sure if he was pleased or not that Maria had kept away. She had written to him a nice letter of condolence and then had given him news of the children. James was running the family lands, having taken a course in estate management at Cirencester College. He spent time in the House of Lords as a peer flying the flag for the younger generation and had held a junior minister's post. Much more important as far as Richard was concerned, James was married to a girl of not particularly high class, but they had a young daughter named Sophia or, as Maria called her, Sophie.

His, Richard's, daughter Julia was working in fashion journalism; although she was known for several high-profile affairs, she had not as yet married.

He had received a very brief note from Laura Seydon.

I'm so sorry, honestly I am, to hear about your loss. I know all in the world of music are thinking of you and wishing you well.

I'm playing the Greig at the London Proms and it's going to be on TV. Hope you will approve.

Laura xxx.

Caroline had picked up the letter. 'Mum told me about that lady. This could be a clever tactical move.'

Richard shook his head. 'Laura was my piano pupil. When I told her there was nothing more I could teach her she threw a teenage tantrum; just the sort of thing you used to do yourself. Unfortunately you mother overheard it and she had a warped idea about that girl for ever after.'

Caroline had gained a place in Birmingham University and was due there that autumn. 'Well, I can't look after you when I go to college. Would that lady be right for you? You can't stay moping for mum all your life.'

Richard sighed. 'That Laura is a professional performing pianist. She spends a life on the road travelling to all sorts of venues. Anyway, why on earth would you want a wicked stepmother?'

'I told you, this is the 1970s, you can have as many mistresses as you want. For a famous composer it's almost expected. We're in the permissive society. It's just I think you need looking after.'

'Oh. Come on, I've got the cleaner coming in four times a week and the other lady who cooks. I'm safe and secure as I'll ever be.'

'That all sounds very dull with no love life.'

'Carrie, you are a romantic. I'm a grizzled old war veteran and I'm over fifty. Not much of a catch there.'

'Oh yeah; well watch out for that Laura and maybe a dozen more.'

When finally Caroline did leave for college Richard settled to the solitary life. In fact he found that he rather enjoyed his own company. His piano had finally arrived by sea freight so he was able to put in hours of practice working through standard exercises and then his whole repertoire. Finally he was satisfied that he could perform at a proper standard and could inform his agent. That man had four playing engagements lined up. These would all help pay the bills but Richard did not want to be involved in non-stop touring. From now onwards composition was to be his life. His *Robin Hood* show was touring the provinces and pulling in the punters en-masse. The agent told him it would transfer to the West End after Christmas.

Peter Ross, his old head from the choir school was in his seventies and retired. He was still sailing his Chichester Harbour boat with Richard as occasional crew. Tentatively, Richard mentioned his now completed requiem and his need for advice on the choral settings. He had scored these himself for Robin Hood but the requiem was a religious work and for this he needed Ross's advice on the final arrangement.

'Yes, send the score to me,' Ross replied. 'This could be an exciting development for you. May we try it at Chichester?'

Richard felt apprehensive. 'Only if it's any good.'

Ross laughed. 'Not much doubt about that.'

Despite every resolution he found himself watching television and hearing Laura perform the Greig concerto at the proms. Her performance was a credit to herself and to his original tuition. He had to allow that to add to his ego. But for God's sake the girl, now at age forty, was stunning. She walked to the piano clad in a flowing halter-top dress that showed all her bare back and slim form. He felt that mixture of emotions: a man starved of physical love with the doubt that he himself could have bettered the emotion she poured into such a popular work.

Following the performance the presenter interviewed Laura. 'Miss Seydon,' the formality was a shock to Richard; Australians used first names. 'Miss Seydon; that was an amazing performance. Can you tell our viewers a little bit about your work? Is it true that you are largely self-taught?'

Laura tilted her head and smiled. 'I was taught by one of the finest musicians in the world: Richard Dyer. I owe everything to his tuition twenty years ago.'

The presenter looked surprised. 'Now that is a name to conjure with. You must be a very proud lady to have worked with Mr Dyer.'

Laura looked serious. 'He was a wonderful tutor and a very nice man. In my humble opinion he's one of the world's best composers.'

'That we can all agree with,' said the presenter.

The interview over, Laura smiled and walked away showing some more of her graceful bare back. Richard felt guilty. Poor Laura; he had treated her in that offhand, almost disdainful manner for years. He knew he had to if he was to quell Stella's suspicions. And those suspicions were groundless. Laura had been an emotional teenager, though one with special talents. He remembered her as a pretty girl, but more as the honorary niece or younger sister. Her hysterical declaration of love had been over twenty years ago. She had had those years to mature and she was a very fine musician. If he didn't owe her an apology, he should at least let her know that bygones were bygones.

At home again in England, Richard was able to attend his squadron reunion. He was curious to meet his old comrades, now over thirty years on. Twenty survivors of all ranks met in a hotel in Salisbury. Eight were pilots who had fought in the Battle of Britain, others he didn't know had served in North Africa, Malta and finally over

Europe in the final months. Richard was delighted to meet once more with his ground crew. These two now ageing men had played every bit as big a part in the victory as he had. Richard felt it was time historians and the general public alike knew this. It was a sad occasion and surprisingly nostalgic. After these years one forgot the terrors and tensions of war. Richard could never forget the horror of Tom Stacey's gruesome end. What could that poor boy have thought, as fully conscious, he plunged ten thousand feet to a watery death? At one point a hand had touched him on the shoulder. There stood a reporter from the local paper.

'My Dyer, we've been told that you scored your squadron's second highest total of shot down Lufwaffe planes. Can you tell us how many that would be?'

This wretched young man could have been talking about a footballer scoring goals. He could have no idea of the mental and physical toll all ranks had been through in those grim days.

'Well, I'm credited with eight kills, but remember men died at my hands; kills mean men killed even if our opponents were in a bad cause.'

Richard drove home slowly and reached Pockhamton in mid-evening. The post lay on the mat, a mix of advertising matter in buff envelopes and two letters with Australian post marks. These were both from old neighbours in Sydney with updates about their families and news of other friends. He must pass these on to Carrie. Lastly he opened an envelope with a glossy brochure. It appeared that Chichester Festival Theatre was holding a winter concert season. He flipped through the pages. It seemed the London Symphony Orchestra was performing a concert in late October. Next Richard had a shock. In their programme was the Beethoven 1st piano concerto, soloist Laura Seydon.

CHAPTER 52

As winter approached Richard was feeling more at ease. Stella's memory still haunted him, but he no longer had those days of misery when he was unable to leave the house. He could perform again and had already done three successful engagements. One morning he was sitting in the dentist's waiting room in Chichester. Not the most cheerful spot in the world. He picked up the current edition of the magazine Country Life and there it was: a portrait of the current gracious lady of that month.

The Honourable Julia Corbailier only daughter of the late Duke of Hampshire. MC. and Maria Dowager Duchess of Hampshire. Miss Corbailier is a fashion journalist who has announced her engagement to Mr Rory Rudgeon of Mayfair, West London and Salcombe Devonshire.

There she was, his Julia, facing the society photographer's camera with a self-confident half-smile. In her last letter Maria had hinted that Julia was leaving her wild life behind and settling down. Just who this Rudgeon could be was not clear but enjoying a Mayfair and Devon address he must be seriously wealthy; stockbroker or banker – who could say?

Richard examined the picture. His Julia was a good-looking young woman and he could see in her hair and features both his and Maria's mark. Now his emotions began to cut in. It was so wrong that he could never claim this lovely adorable girl as his own daughter. It was cruel as it was wrong. Once again he began to resent these snobbish Corbailiers. He felt angry, not with Maria but with these highborn families who had made a convenience of their secret love.

The telephone rang. 'Richard, it's Peter Ross.'

Richard's old school head had long since retired but Ross was still one of the finest choirmasters this century. 'Richard, I hope you don't mind but we've been trying out sequences of your requiem with the Chichester choir.'

'Oh, I don't mind. But is it any good? You see much of it is very personal…'

'Yes, you told me that. What I want to ask you is; can we perform it in the cathedral?'

'What!' Richard was genuinely startled. 'I mean it's personal to me as I said, but it's an experimental work. It's a requiem based on Roman Catholic ritual. Can you perform that in an Anglican Cathedral?'

'Oh, good heavens. We don't worry about that sort of thing these days. This is Sussex, not Ireland.'

'But, is it worth the effort, and do the choir mind?'

'Well, I've done the choral settings you asked for and it is most certainly worth doing. In fact we really want the credit for the first performance to the cathedral.'

Richard said goodbye and once more he worried as he had so many times before. He had this flashback to Beecham and the War Symphony. Had he overreached himself this time and would this be a dire failure? It was Stella's memorial and he couldn't bear the thought. It seemed that Ross and the choir were determined so he had no option than let them get on with it. Fate would decide.

Then the letter came with its intriguing if baffling message. Caroline was home from College for the weekend and sitting slumped lazily in an armchair.

'This must be a joke. "Most honourable Order of the British Empire..."

Carrie grabbed the letter. 'Yeah, you Poms haven't got much of an empire left, but we're still using this dated stuff in Oz. I gather that we're getting rid of it and bringing in our own gong. We'll put you in for that when the time comes.'

Richard was suspicious. 'What do you mean by "We"?'

Carrie had her best mocking look, so like her mother. 'If you must know, there's been an action group working away without you knowing. Don't you dare turn this down or that'll be very ungrateful.' She glared at him. 'Mum wouldn't like that.'

'I can't make a decision on that yet, but can you tell me about this alleged action group?'

'I've been kept in the loop as we say but...'

'What on earth does "in the loop mean"? I can't cope with all this garbage your generation talk.'

'It means I'm not in the group but they keep me posted. Anyway, about a dozen top people in music.' Carrie named several international musicians and one famous composer. 'Then there's the Corbailiers, plus your local MP and, God help us, the local bishop. This is only stage one. After this they're out to make you a Sir.''

Now Richard roared with laughter. 'I can't think the bishop needs God's help unless he's got a girl hid away in his palace. As for a knighthood, you've got to be joking.'

Carrie smiling flung her arms around him. 'And haven't I been a good girl. I was pledged to keep my mouth shut and that's a bloody hard task for an Aussie.'

'I can believe that.'

'And you will accept, won't you? This one, and the Sir that's coming next. It'll be a great day out and I can come with you to the palace both times. They said so.'

'All right. But I can't think why anyone picked on me. I'm just Dickie Dyer the Sussex yokel with a straw in his mouth.'

'Oh Dad, you're anything but. You are one of the world's finest composers.' Caroline changed the subject. 'You are going to Laura Seydon's recital?'

'That sounds a bit like an ultimatum. Anyway I am going. She was my best pupil and it would be rude to stay away.'

Now was the moment to tell her. 'Carrie, Chichester Cathedral are going to perform your Mum's requiem in the spring of next year. After that how about a trip back to Melbourne?'

'Wow, yes we must,'

Richard tried to digest this stuff about an honour but couldn't. He settled at the piano and began to play Dvorak's Humoresque. A few bars in and a soft soprano voice joined from the kitchen singing a highly ribald lyric to the same melody.

Once I've been inside your daughter
I've had trouble passing water
So I think that makes us quits all round.

'Carrie, what the hell is that?'

Her giggling voice replied. 'Sorry, Dad, you playing that tune – I couldn't resist it. The college rugby squad sing that in the showers.'

Richard laughed now. 'As long as you're not showering with them.'

She giggled again. 'They're some lovely hunks, but no.'

Richard grinned and switched to Liszt's Hungarian Rhapsody Two.

'We all want you to come to Julie's wedding,' Maria's voice rang down the telephone. She sounded just like the little girl of old.

'Yes, I would like to. I think I should. My congratulations of course. Who is this chap she's marrying?'

'Rory's a nice young man. Does something in the city. We've checked him out and he's financially secure. We all like him and I hope you do.'

'Well done, Julia. I really hope they'll be very happy.'

Maria sounded almost doleful. 'Oh, Dickie. I do wish you could give the bride away, but then people might ask questions.'

'I reckon they might and all.'

Maria shrieked with laughter. 'Oh. Dickie, you said "and all"; that's pure Sussex.

'I am Sussex, nothing can change that. When's the happy day?'

'May the sixteenth.'

'I'll look forward to it, but Maria, will your high-class friends mind a fellow guest being a Sussex yokel cross wild colonial oaf?'

'They will all be crazy to meet Richard Dyer OBE, world famous composer. They all like Sussex and we love Australians as long as they don't beat us at cricket.'

'Or rugby,' came a faint voice in the background.

'That's Julie. Shall I put her on.'

'Yes please.'

Julia's refined voice came on line. 'I'm so pleased you can be at my wedding.'

'I'll be delighted to be there. I'll look forward to meeting your young man.'

'And Rory wants to meet you. He wasn't old enough to be in the war, but he keeps playing your War Symphony on the record player. He's a tremendous fan of Bob Dylan. I wind him up and tell him I prefer the Stones.'

Richard laughed. 'They're all right, but personally I liked the Beatles, their Sergeant Pepper was really sophisticated stuff.'

'I'd better go now,' said Julia. Suddenly she whispered into the phone. 'Bye bye, Dad.'

Richard had been to the new Chichester theatre once before when Alice had played Ophelia. The theatre was a fine modern building, and thank goodness it had a large car park. Although a provincial theatre, the place had international repute and was associated with actors such as Olivier and many others. Tonight the London Symphony Orchestra was performing in concert with the Beethoven concerto played by Laura. Richard found he was looking forward to this event. It would be very interesting to hear his star pupil, and if he was honest, he wanted to see this glamorous girl in the flesh and very nice flesh it was. The theatre had a modern layout, a circular seating plan looking down on a stage that projected into the front of the auditorium. It was an excellent concert setting and far better than a theatre with a conventional stage. The orchestra's chairs and music stands were in place plus a rather fine piano.

The lights dimmed and the usual ritual began. The players filed in and took their places. Next, the leader walked on to applause and finally the conductor to louder applause. The conductor seemed a mere boy and Richard still couldn't see the point of applauding these people before they had proved they could play a note. The first item was the Mendelssohn violin concerto. The soloist was a wild looking Hungarian lady while the young conductor upped the tempo to a speed that Richard had never heard for this work. It was certainly a volatile performance and the audience loved it. Next came a rendering of Brahms Fourth. This time the young conductor returned to the normal tempo and produced a performance that won Richard's cautious approval.

During the interval, Richard in company with many others went into the foyer for a cup of tea while many went for something stronger. Next it was Laura's turn. Once again the lights dimmed and the conductor ushered Laura on stage with slightly over the top ceremony. She wore a flowing low-cut strapless dress. Her shoulders were still tanned and her dark hair shone in the spotlights. Even at forty the girl was gorgeous.

Richard was impressed. Laura's performance had resonance of his playing in that Australian recording. Once again he couldn't help feeling a scintilla of pride in his best pupil. The performance over, Laura stood smiling while the applause swept over her. She was a popular artist – no doubt of that. Richard, a few rows back from the front, stood with the rest. Laura, no more than twenty-five feet away seemed to be searching the rows of happy people. And then he caught her eye. She stiffened, and then smiling waved frantically. Richard grinned back and waved.

What happened next broke every rule of concert protocol. Laura pattered down the stage steps and rushed up the alleyway to his seat. Then in front of her colleagues and several hundred people, she grabbed his hand and pulled him towards the stage. The bemused audience had ceased applauding they were muttering now in puzzled interest.

'Ladies and gentlemen,' Laura's voice echoed around the theatre.

'I have with me Richard Dyer who taught me everything I know about the piano.'

Now the applause redoubled. Richard raised an arm in acknowledgement.

'I'm so glad you came to hear me,' said Laura. 'I so hoped you would and I was looking out for you.'

The young conductor came over and shook Richard's hand. 'Mr Dyer, I am so honoured to meet you. I've heard you play and your symphonies are magic.'

Richard grinned politely.

'We've rehearsed a little encore and with you here it's really appropriate.' He turned and addressed the house. 'Now, Ladies and gentlemen; a special orchestration of you local anthem. We give you: Sussex by the Sea.'

'We've got a lot to catch up on,' said Richard. 'Come and have dinner somewhere nice and you can tell me everything you've been doing.'

'Oh wow, yes let's'

'There's a nice pub out onto the road to Pockhampton. I've been there and the food's good. Have you got a car?'

Laura shook her head. 'Sorry, no. I came on the coach with the rest of them.'

'All right. I'll run you back to your hotel later.'

She pulled a face. 'Should I go and change my dress?'

'No, not likely. You look absolutely gorgeous in the one you're wearing.'

Laura grimaced. 'I'll keep my wrap on until I see how warm this pub is.'

Richard recovered his Rover and they climbed aboard.

The pub was one that Richard had known for years. He felt a little twinge of guilt when he remembered that Stella and he had been regular customers in their pre-Australian days. He had heard that the place still served excellent food and had a nice ambience. This was all still true. The dining room was comfortable and was warmed by a huge log fire. Laura slipped her wrap over the back of her chair. Her tanned shoulders glowed in the soft lighting and Richard could see the admiring glances of the male diners and he guessed the envious ones of their wives.

She smiled at him. No longer was she the highly-strung teenage prodigy. Both of them were much-travelled professional musicians and, my goodness, he thought; she really was the most attractive woman. Her voice had dropped from the shrill girlie whine of twenty-five years ago and her conversation, not just on music but about the world at large was entertaining. He knew too well that fate had had a hand in this meeting. He was already fond of this girl, maybe always had been, and he would strive to know her better and maybe ultimately keep her.

They ate their leisurely meal and talked until it was time to leave.

'It's after ten o'clock,' Richard was worried. 'Will your hotel still be open? We're over half-an-hour's drive away.'

'It'll be getting on for eleven by then and I don't think it will.'

Richard made a decision. Maybe it was unwise but he didn't care. 'Come on then. Into the car. My place is only three miles away and I've plenty of spare room.'

'Oh, Richard. That would be wonderful. I'll just see if the people in the pub will let me phone the hotel.' She ran back inside and emerged two minutes later. 'It's OK, they're going to do it for me.'

'That's a nice piano. Is that the one you work on,' Laura was poking around his living room with obvious interest.

'That's the one. I'm a good little boy I practice my exercises every day.'

'But, Richard, your symphonies – everyone raves about them. I can play a bit but I could never compose work like that.'

'It's an odd thing,' he replied. 'But I think everyone in the composing business would say the same. I walk on that hill over there and if the mood's right the music just comes, but from where I'll never know.'

She smiled. 'You know Elgar used to say that.'

'I know. Did I ever tell you I once met him?'

'No, when was that?'

Richard pointed at the fading monochrome framed photo on the wall: the old man with the small boy. 'That's us.'

'Gosh, how wonderful – what an honour.'

'Come on. Let's have a nightcap drink and then bed time.'

Laura looked at him with her most alluring smile. 'That spare room is a bit spooky and the bed's damp.' She had walked up to him and rested her hands gently on his shoulders. 'All my night things are in the hotel and I'm not sleeping in this dress. It's Paris design and rather valuable. So tonight I'll be naked.' Now she had placed her arms around his neck. 'Would you like to see me naked?'

Almost dreamlike he heard himself answer. 'Would you like to see me naked?'

She pressed herself against him. 'Oh, yes, yes, yes!'

CHAPTER 53

1974

The Pockhampton House Music Centre was an undoubted success, in spite of grumbles from the planners about congestion and roadside parking. Pockhampton House already had more than enough parking space. It was not music that caused villagers' tongues to wag. Richard "Dickie" Dyer was above himself. A village worker's son was setting up in the ancestral home of the Tenbury family. This was hardly the family's fault. Mr and Mrs Tenbury, both in their eighties, could no longer cope with the mansion and had moved into a small dower house on the edge of the estate. More sensible voices had pointed out that the big house would have been empty until some American millionaire took it on. Now they had an attraction, almost a rival to Glyndbourne, not far away and in a year of economic gloom the manor was providing some twenty new jobs.

Of course most of the village gossip was about the scandal. "Young Dickie" as he was known had moved from his proper abode in the cottage to the grand house and with him had gone his mistress: "that piano player – no better than she should be – mark my words". The permissive society might be all the rage in London but the old ways ruled in Pockhampton. The villagers were only slightly mollified when Richard married his second wife in a lavish ceremony in the cathedral. After a while the village grew to like the new mistress of the house. Mrs Laura was a kindly lady who took an interest in the WI and gave music lessons in the village school.

Richard's relationship with his new wife was very different from the way life had been with Stella. Laura was still tempestuous and the pair's disputes often led to furious exchanges that usually fizzled out into laughter and tears followed by delicious lovemaking. Richard was not in the least surprised to find his beloved second wife had Italian blood.

Laura was good for Richard in an important way. She was able to make her husband understand his place in the world. In the two years they had been together Richard's prestige had soared further. The *Requiem For a Departed Love* had been premiered in Chichester to huge acclaim. Thereafter Richard's world went mad. The work was performed worldwide from Paris to Australia by way of Carnegie Hall

New York and a performance in the Sistine Chapel attended by the Pope; a wonderful event combining the choirs of Westminster Abbey and Westminster cathedral with all the verses in Latin translated by Peter Ross. The symphonic works were gaining even more popularity. In the spring of 1974 Richard and Laura had been flown to Moscow for a lavish Soviet reception and to attend a packed concert hall for a performance of the War Symphony. The work had been acclaimed and the pair of them feted at a reception in the Kremlin. Richard wondered what the late Michael Lamingham would have said to that.

'Dickie,' said Laura. 'Will you once and for all get it into your head that you are the world's greatest living composer. You're a fine musician, apart from that you have a fine war record. That is why the world is beating a path to our door.'

Richard sighed. 'You may say that, but it's still *Robin Hood* that's bringing in the bacon.'

The opera or musical was packing in the audiences in the West End. The music establishment had been scathing about it from day one. Although Richard shared the royalties with his lyricist, the show provided fifty percent of his income. The Pockhampton Music Centre was Laura's project. The great house had been adapted. The old ballroom made an excellent concert hall for chamber orchestras. The Tenburys had presented their fine drawing room piano and Laura presided over a growing music school. The centre was not confined to the classics. Jazz and folk rock concerts were regular features with many big names from the popular music world performing. But as Laura wearily told her husband time and time again, the charity funding the centre would never have done so without the prestigious name of Richard Dyer.

He had been really happy to find that his children liked Laura. Caroline had been maid of honour at the cathedral wedding while Richard's old RAF comrade had repeated his role as best man. Tom was now in London training at Guy's to be a consultant. All three of them still mourned for Stella and Laura had accepted that.

Two events had livened the spring of 1971. Richard had gone with Laura and Caroline to Buckingham Palace to receive his OBE. The Queen had been gracious. She had reminisced briefly about the Sky Blues and the war before Richard had bowed and resumed his seat. A few days later both he and Laura attended Julia's wedding. It was a sumptuous occasion, as one would expect with the reception in the Corbailier town house, the same building that Richard remembered from 1937. He kept wondering how many of these people knew who the bride's real father was. Julia knew of course and he guessed her brother knew too. But pride of family, rank and inheritance prevented either from ever mentioning the Sussex farm boy and his lover. He chatted with Maria. The pair still had the same chemistry that Laura failed to notice. It was a relief to return home to their modest flat on the third floor of Pockhampton Manor.

Then in the autumn of 1974 Laura found she was pregnant at the age of forty-two: a matter of joy and concern. She was told to be cautious. She must give up long distance performing, alcohol was banned and strict medical observation ordered. Laura accepted all this cheerfully, but Richard had a small chill of fear. He remembered how his own mother had so nearly perished from middle age pregnancy.

Laura had flung herself into her piano tuition with promising students boarded in the house. Richard set out to compose his first piano concerto in honour of Laura. This time he didn't walk the Downs; he already had a three-movement theme that had been in his mind for a year. A poignant moment was the performance at the music centre of Stella's Isle of Wight viola concerto, the product of their sailing trip all those years ago. This work, with its beautiful melodic second movement was also gaining in popularity with chamber orchestras and viola players.

Under Laura's influence Richard's lifestyle was changing. The spruce ex-fighter pilot now had greying shoulder length hair and in summer wore lurid flowered shirts and knee length shorts. Likewise, in warmer weather Laura walked everywhere barefoot and wore floral headbands and full-length gowns decorated with chains of beads. The Pockhamton villagers were more amused than critical of: "them two hippies".

The outside world was depressing. The coalmine strikes leading to the three-day week had made life difficult for everyone. Power cuts had twice intruded on Pockhampton concerts. Richard had been required to race outside and wind the diesel generator until they installed an automatic switchover. He had to admire the famous folk rock group that had kept singing and playing in the pitch dark. The subsequent general election had returned the Wilson government. Richard had never admitted to his parents, let alone the Corbailiers, that he was a lifelong Labour voter. Life had been good to him, but he would never forget the nineteen thirties and the rural depression. Never forget the family's friends who had lost their farm through bankruptcy. That was as nothing compared with whole towns that had lost their only industries. He might be quietly well off and he might mix with the wealthy, but he would never forget where he came from.

Laura's pregnancy had called a halt to their plans to visit Australia. Stella's parents were still in good health but both in their late seventies. Richard was not happy for Caroline to make the trip on her own. There were too many lurid tales about unaccompanied girls in strange countries. Caroline was full of stories of her friends who had taken time off to tour and work in what the papers now called the Third World. She had to admit that these kids travelled in groups and often with an adult leader. It was now possible to telephone Australia and talk to Grace and Ray with voices as loud as if they were in the next town.

He looked up as Laura came into the room. 'Darling, all this stuff about the World's leading composer. It's got to be a load of crap hasn't it?'

Laura leaned down and kissed him followed by a playful slap. 'Work it out for yourself. 'No Elgar, no Vaughan Williams, no Holst, Delius, Sibelius, no Gershwin, Prokofiev, Rachmaninov, Stravinski, Mahler, no Beethoven, Tchaikovsky, Wagner, Bach, Handel, old Uncle Tom Cobley and all. So it's between little Dickie Dyer and Ben Britten. So until they dig up and resurrect Mozart it's going to be you who the public love.'

'Oh come on. What about Shostakovich?'

Laura kissed him again. 'I chatted to him at that reception in Moscow.' She laughed. 'I think he rather fancied me.'

'What, the man was in a wheelchair and coughing his guts out!'

'I know, he had lung cancer. Good thing you don't smoke. Did you ever?'

'No, never appealed, not even in war.'

'Anyway, he said he recognised that his Leningrad symphony might have influenced events, but then he said he could never create anything as dramatic as the third movement of your War Symphony.'

'Oh yeah, was he just flattering you?'

Laura sighed. 'He was praising you!'

'Not all Russians like my work. What about the great man that time in London?'

She laughed. 'Oh, yes. I remember he gave you a right ticking off because you've never written specially for the cello.' She laughed again. 'Then he pinched my bottom.'

'I'm sure that counts as an honour. But as for being a great composer. Are you saying that in an era of musical mediocrity, I'm the best of a bad bunch?'

Laura groaned. 'I just give up.'

CHAPTER 54

On June 15th 1975 little Rachel Dyer was born. She, who was to become another famous pianist, was no more than five pounds at birth, blue faced and breathing with difficulty. Laura came through her ordeal in good spirits to Richard's huge relief. He told the gynaecologist his tale of giving blood to save his mother.

'That was a bold move in those times,' said the doctor. 'Lucky you were a perfect match.'

Richard was still worried. 'The baby – what are her chances?'

'Well, she's little and underweight. We can't be definite but we'll do our best.'

Laura was kept in the maternity unit for ten days until mother and baby were allowed home. Richard hired a nurse to keep an eye on both and there followed an anxious month before all was declared well and the routine of nappies and sleepless nights returned. Richard now had five children by three different women. It made life complicated, but maybe it was par for the course for a composer.

Was he really a great composer? The first two symphonies and the viola concerto had been around for at least twenty-five years and the public bought the records in thousands and orchestras performed them from Moscow to Buenos Aires and Bombay to Seattle. An all-white orchestra in South Africa had wanted to play the War Symphony and at that Richard had drawn the line and registered his disapproval. The orchestra had gone ahead anyway and Richard had donated the royalties to charity. But huge orchestral works were no longer fashionable although the concert halls remained packed. The Isle of White viola concerto, the work he had dreamed up while on that boat trip with Stella, was probably his current favourite. It was Stella's very own piece and she had played at its premier. The requiem was sung everywhere in both concert and religious settings. The Sky Blues' repertoire, still popular years after the war, might almost be termed classical. He had been commissioned to write and had produced successful film scores.

He was now settling down to complete his piano concerto for Laura to perform. It was a classical setting but with a jazzy rock music theme. The piano passages that he worked at endlessly were complex but easily within Laura's range. He was determined that she would play the first performance so the work was put on hold while Laura breastfed her beloved baby Rachel. *Robin Hood* was transferring to Broadway, and that promised a huge shot of extra income. There was even talk of a Hollywood version. His accountant told him that in five years he might become a millionaire even after tax had been paid. That had to be crazy; Sussex farm boys did not aspire to be millionaires. He was not interested in the accountant's suggestion that he move himself and all assets to Jersey.

At least this money made certain he could give his parents a secure old age. Ted and Mabel were approaching eighty and finding life harder. Richard's intervention was not always welcome but between Alice and himself they had been persuaded to let him fit a stair lift and after all these years install a real bath in a bathroom with a mechanical lift. Ted absolutely refused to have a power shower fitted. 'Them things is for Yanks.'

Tom was doing well in his consultant training although he was nostalgic for his adopted home country. Caroline was still, thank goodness, working hard for her degree. In her spare time she played keyboard for the Oz Koalas an all-Australian student rock group who were cutting a bit of a dash on the Midlands pub circuit. Caroline had survived several boyfriends, all in Richard's opinion unsuitable. He was happy she was finding solace in music. Richard might be a classically trained musician but he had no prejudice against rock music. Any music that exuded quality was all right by him.

Country Life Magazine.

The Honourable Mrs Julia Rudgeon delighted guests at the house party with a short recital of pianoforte classical music...

Yes, he thought, snooty Country Life would blow a fuse if they ever found out the Honourable Julia's real dad was a Sussex farm yokel. He was amused as he remembered his eldest daughter's declared preference for The Rolling Stones. Did this highborn house party know that? Probably yes.

The telephone in the office rang. 'Hello, Dickie, mate. How you doing?'

'Ray,' Richard was surprised. In Australia it would be three o'clock in the morning. 'Is everything all right?'

'Couldn't be better. Me and the missus is in the UK right now and we're on a mission.'

'Mission?'

'That's it, and you're talking Brit again. Where's yer Aussie speech gone?'

Richard laughed. 'Back where it came from I imagine. I need people here to understand me. Anyway, what's this mission?'

'Tell you when I see you. Grace wants to see if your new girl passes muster.'

Richard couldn't help but laugh. He liked Ray and Grace. They'd always been the most relaxed in-laws. 'I will ignore that example of Aussie tact.'

He arranged for Ray and Grace to visit the following day and went and broke the news to Laura.

'Will they resent me?'

'No, they're not that sort of people. You and Stella are different personalities. Just be the graceful hostess.'

'I'll come straight to the point,' said Ray. 'The Government of Australia have mandated me to approach you and ask you to accept the new Order of Australia.'

'The what?'

'The OA. You said the Brits gave you the OBE, and you're up for a Sir. OBE, we've given up on all that. We said it stood for: "Other Bugger's Efforts". Anyway what bleeding empire?'

'But Ray, what's all this got to do with me?'

'You are still a citizen of Australia and will be until you croak. Grace is a big wheel in the music business back home. You are the world's number one composer.'

'That's what everybody says but I don't see it. Who'll listen to my stuff in a hundred years?'

'My guess is that Australians will be playing your stuff in two hundred years and from all we've heard that applies to most of the world. I'm telling you mate and I'm telling you it as Stella's dad. You will come to Australia and you will receive this gong.'

'Yes,' added Grace. 'And you will conduct your work.'

'May Laura come as well?'

Grace smiled at Laura. 'You've gotta' come as well, love. Support your hubbie.'

So they would be going to Australia. The long postponed trip was on again. Richard would once more be in Stella's home country and accompanying him would be Stella's wifely successor. Successor, yes: not replacement.

CHAPTER 55

1977

At Christmas 1977 the whole family travelled to Australia. Tom was returning anyway to take a post in a Brisbane hospital. Little Rachel was now two and Caroline had secured her degree. The medal ceremony in Canberra had been put on hold although Richard was already recorded as holding the honour. Once again came the shock as they felt the full heat of the Melbourne summer. The whole family went once more to Stella's grave. The Barnes, with Richard, Tom and Caroline stood at the graveside. Laura politely stood back some yards away, Rachel in her arms until Grace took her arm and led her to join them. 'Actually, Stell liked you. She didn't really see you as a rival but I guess she wouldn't mind you taking care of young Richard here.'

Choking back tears, Laura had hugged Grace. Suspicion was over – she was fully part of the extended family.

The medal ceremony in Canberra was in January. Richard and Laura had one big engagement to fulfil in Sydney. The premier of the Dyer piano concerto would take place in the new Opera House by the harbour with Laura as soloist. The work was for Laura but this was not revealed. Stella had been a popular figure around the Sydney music scene and Laura was still only a Pom. This work was in three movements. The first had a slow but traditional theme. The second movement took that theme and gave it a lilting wartime sound, with brass and woodwind, echoing the days of the Sky Blues. The third movement had a rock music intonation with syncopation piano and a strong beat. This was the most experimental work that Richard had so far attempted, but it worked. A predominately young audience loved it. Richard was satisfied. Let the critics and the musical establishment sneer. Laura now had her dedicated work to partner Stella's Isle of Wight concerto.

There was one last thing he needed to try. Richard had kept up his membership of the Yacht Club. Two days after the Sydney recital he took Laura sailing. She had sailed dinghies at home in Surrey on the famous Frensham Pond, but big boat sailing was a new world. It was a beautiful summer's day when, in their friend's forty foot yacht, they sailed down the harbour under the famous bridge and out to sea. These were not the conditions of the Sydney-Hobart race that he could never forget, but Laura, with Caroline and Tom and even little Rachel loved every minute. In recent years Richard and Laura had both been too busy travelling and performing, but now they had a settled life with the music centre, he could do what he had so long wanted to do. He would buy a comfortable boat for all the family and moor her on Chichester Harbour. That evening he wired the boatyard in Lymington and ordered a Contessa class yacht for the new English summer season.

The visit to the Governor General's Mansion was very different to the Palace in London. The ceremony was wholly Australian – laid back was their term. A band played the brand new anthem: *Advance Australia Fair.* Richard had tried to persuade his lyricist Bob Jansen to enter the new anthem competition with some sanitized words for *Waltzing Matilda.* Bob had been horrified at the suggestion of such sacrilege. Richard had been disappointed and felt the new anthem was as dreary as the old one. The Governor General was a genial Aussie about as far away as possible from the old style Imperial officer in an ostrich feathered hat. Richard was one of a handful of others being awarded the honour. He wished Stella could see him and that they could have shared this moment.

Next they were off to the airport for their flight to Queensland. Carefully secreted in a cool box was the film of Julia Rudgeon's wedding and Richard had promised Maria he would deliver it safely to Clement and Flavia Tenbury, or Clem and Flav as they were known. Very few of their friends and neighbours knew that Clem was a titled aristocrat, a baronet and Flav a Lady. That was definitely something one did not reveal down the pub in Australia. Tom was already working in a Brisbane hospital and had visited the exotically named Woodshack Creek. The name dated back to the early settlers and the Tenburys were stuck with it.

Nothing resembling a woodshack stood at Woodshack Creek. The estate was a two hundred acre vineyard at the centre of which stood a latter day Georgian house very similar to Pockhampton Manor. Flav had rushed out to greet them with a true Aussie shriek of welcome. She had ushered them into the delicious cool of the house to meet her husband. The titled Clem was now every inch the Australian business-man. With his newly-wed wife, both original ten pound Poms, they had arrived with his portion of family money and an invitation to work for a Brisbane wine merchant. Clem was clearly an astute operator. He had flung himself into the wine business and had been successful in popularizing wine drinking along the length of the Queensland holiday coast. From small beginnings he had created his vineyard, and through astute investments, had found the wealth to build this replica of an old family home. Clem and Flav were a shining example of what a British migrant couple could achieve in a lifetime of hard work and good sense.

'Dickie, mate, am I honoured to meet you,' Clem grinned. 'We went to your concert in Brisbane back in – when was it, Flav?'

'Sixty-six,' called Flav from the kitchen.

'Yes, that was it. Didn't know you'd been thick with our Maria then.'

This further example of Aussie tact made Richard look anxiously for Laura but she was already nattering with Nadine and Kellie; Flav and Clem's teenage daughters.

'Oh, mate – wish I could play like you do. I knock the old Joanna down the social a bit but that's my lot.'

My goodness, thought Richard: not a trace of the old Etonian left now.

'Yeah, I was just old enough to be called up at the end of the war,' Clem continued. 'Bloody guards officer if you'll believe it, but don't tell my neighbours that. But I remember listening to the Sky Blues. You really got the old feet tapping. Tell you something. I once played at a concert of yours.'

'Really when was this?'

'1946, Hampstead Heath, Tchaikovsky 1812.' He laughed. 'I commanded the big gun.'

'I remember and you were spot on with the timing – brilliant.'

Richard liked this man; an outspoken Australian, in a setting that could be rural England, or could be if the temperature hadn't been thirty-three Celsius.

'Sorry, Clem but I can't see you as a Guards officer.'

'That's why I have to play down that and the Bart. I've done my best to adapt, but down the social I'm still a Pom; still can't convince them we sometimes take a bath. But Dick, mate, this is a great country and you're a citizen even if you do reside in Britland. I saw on the news you've got our top gong.'

'I know. As a Pom myself I really feel honoured.'

They all sat down to lunch of steak with a glass of Woodshack

1971. Clem knew what Richard was thinking. 'No, mate, it's Woodshack. We don't want any airy-fairy names. We tell it as it is. Down south in Victoria there's a vineyard called Barbwireville Creek. Good old name but they've won prizes for their Shiraz in Europe.'

That evening Clem dug out the film projector and they watched Julia's wedding.

Their Australian hosts loved it and were wholly unfazed by the aristocratic Mayfair setting.

'Pretty kid that Julia,' said Flav. She grinned in a true Aussie sideways fashion. 'Guess you've got a bit of an interest in that one.'

With Laura sitting close by he couldn't ask her to amplify this. Flav was family and he supposed Maria must have told her.

Later Clem showed them the vineyard. It was vast, bigger than even than the vineyards they had seen in France. They inspected the modern winery, with a tasting of the vintages and after a tour of the visitor centre they retired to the garden for a traditional Aussie barbie. Richard was rapidly falling in love with this country for the second time, but without Stella he knew he could never settle here again. His future lay with Laura and their music project in England.

The Dyer *Requiem for a Departed Love,* was to be performed in the new Sydney opera house. The press and TV had finally discovered who the lost love was. Stella Dyer was fondly remembered as a virtuoso musician who had died tragically in the outback. The house was full. A fine choir and orchestra had assembled. Richard had declined an offer to conduct; he would always rather listen to a fresh interpretation and he knew he could never conceal his emotion. True to form, as the choir thundered the angry Dies Irae, his tears flowed. Once again he relived that awful meeting at Fremantle Harbour, the funeral and then the musical revelation on Pockhampton Down. Laura was always telling him he was over modest, but at that moment, as he sat listening, he knew that his requiem was a major work that would endure for centuries to come. He wasn't being conceited and there was no ego; he just knew. Once again as the triumphant anthem concluded the work, he had that vision of Stella's face smiling. I will see you again. I will always love you, he thought. I love all the three women in my life, but you were mine for so long.

CHAPTER 56

1985

The seven of them huddled together under the umbrellas as they watched the coffin bearers lower their burden into the open grave. Edward, "Ted" Dyer was joining his parents and grandparents in the quiet corner of Pockhampton churchyard. Mabel, Ted's frail widow, stood alone in the rain beside the grave. Mabel had been stoical throughout the funeral and her husband's last years. Dementia was the medical term for the deterioration of the mind that all his family had witnessed until the ageing farmer and war veteran failed to recognize his own children.

Richard was full of memories of the most decent kindly man he had ever known. Edward Dyer had lived by his principles, simple principles that guided an honest life of hard toil. His ageing children stood near the grave, Richard, had just qualified for the Old Age Pension, his fifty-two-year old sister Alice was a famous TV actress in what some people called a soap. The vicar spoke the final committal and now the whole family stood at the graveside to drop a handful of good Sussex earth or a flower on the wood below. Reconciliation was hardly the right term; but all five of Ted's grandchildren stood beside the grave: Tom, Caroline and Rachel with the Corbailiers, James and Julia, with their mother Maria. These latter could still never acknowledge their blood ties to Richard and Ted. They were present to represent the Tenbury family for whom Ted had worked for his whole lifetime.

Ted's decline had been speeded by the death of his old wartime captain, Leo Tenbury, ten years ago. Maria's brother, Leo, a victim of lung cancer had been interred in a humble monastic grave with minimal ceremony. The counterpoint to this had been later: the great service in Arundel Catholic Cathedral with the singing of the Richard Dyer requiem.

Leo and Maria's parents had passed away and were buried not far from Edward Dyer. This had to be life, Richard mused: a final levelling. First it was all weddings followed by christenings, now it was all funerals. *They grow not old as we that are left grow old,* the words of the poem for Remembrance Day came back to him. He was perhaps lucky to reach old age when so many of his wartime comrades had not.

Richard knew he had travelled one hell of a long way. How had he come from little farm boy Dickie Dyer to being today Sir Richard Dyer O.M. K.B.E. D.F.C. O.B.E. Order of Australia, recognised as a world composer, the subject of TV programmes and TV interviews from all over the world, patron of the Sussex Music Centre, and principal conductor of the National Youth Orchestra. He was old now, but he still had good health. He could walk to the summit of the Down; could still sail his boat. His bank balance was healthy and he drove a second-hand Mercedes. He dreamed of Stella, but he loved Laura, they had never been so close, and he still had feelings for Maria, his childhood sweetheart and later lover. Maria's children now covertly recognized him as their real father even though they could never admit it openly. He adored his four grandchildren. James's two: Sophie and Roger and Julia's Jonathan. His son Tom had married a fellow doctor and their son Richard was now at school. Caroline had set up home with what was known these days as a partner. She was still without children.

His real pride and joy had to be little Rachel who had inherited her parents musical gift. She was more advanced in her piano playing than either of her parents had been at the same age. Rachel, at ten, was a happy extrovert child; bubbly was the popular term. She found her elderly Mum and Dad embarrassing and sometimes tried to pass them off to her school friends as grandparents.

The funeral wake was in the village hall. Richard had to congratulate his sister Alice who with Laura and Maria had laid on a magnificent spread of food for over one hundred mourners and, further to this, had done so much to relieve the burden for Mabel. It was a nostalgic yet strangely happy occasion. Ted Dyer was free now from the torment of dementia and that had to be good.

Alice tapped him on the arm and awakened him from his dreamland. 'I think people would like you to pay a small tribute to Dad.'

'Of course. Could you call everyone to listen?'

Alice silenced the gathering and nodded to her brother.

'Ladies and gentlemen,' said Richard. 'We are here to remember my father. He was a countryman who gave his life service both in peace and war. In good times and bad he worked the land and grew the grain, meat, milk and wool that we all depend on. He never sought fame, money and honours. These may have been given to his children, but we, when all is said and done, are only entertainers. My father was in every way a worthier figure.'

For days afterwards Richard wondered if he could compose a tribute to his father. His inspiration had always been tragedy. For other historical composers it had been different. Poor Chopin had lost his inspiration through exhaustion as he tried to please his over-sexed mistress. Mozart composed some of his finest work through unrequited love for his future sister-in-law. Richard had written his best-regarded works inspired by grief and anger. The Sussex Symphony had grown out of the Coronation Symphony rejected unheard by that slimy, snobbish weasel, Fillingbroke. The wartime death of his school friend Tom Stacey still troubled him, but it had been the trigger for the third movement of the War Symphony. He had received thousands of letters of appreciation for it from all corners of the globe. Lastly his requiem, apparently held in awe everywhere, had resulted from the death of Stella. His piano and viola concertos were different; both had been inspired by love for his two wives and each work was in turn exclusively for them to play. Of course many thousands of other musicians had played them and he was pleased about that. He was resolved. He would compose a simple piano piece suited to a gifted child. They would premier it at the Pockhampton Music Centre and the soloist would be Rachel Dyer.

The Pockhampton concerts took place once a month throughout the year apart from the one occasion when the village was cut off by snow. Laura had resumed touring and had followed her husband with a stunning rendering of the Rachmaninov Three. Richard had found a new lease of life with his control of the National Youth Orchestra. What a difference to any other band he had worked with. None of the grumpy old performers he remembered in the Sky Blues days, nor the blasé opinionated players from some of the present day orchestras. These kids aged twelve to nineteen treated him with a sort of religious awe that sometimes made him uncomfortable. As they travelled around the country from Plymouth to Aberdeen and from Norwich to Cardiff, they performed a repertoire as complex as any adult orchestra.

Richard had been mildly shocked at the morbid glee the kids displayed when he explained the programme notes for Berlioz's March to the Scaffold. The boys laughed and the girls shrieked and giggled as he demonstrated the falling guillotine blade and the severing of the neck and the head held up by the executioner. The reward was in the eventual performance that had a wild quality quite unlike any heard before. There seemed no limits to what he could get away with; even a full performance of Beethoven's Ninth, with a largely youth choir in support, was a triumph.

It had its embarrassing moments. Laura had bought and framed a photograph of the youth orchestra rehearsing in a heatwave on the beach in Weymouth. A somewhat rotund Richard was standing on a wooden box, baton in hand, dressed in a floral shirt, Bermuda shorts and flipflops.

'Look at you,' said Laura with a mock glare. 'You're smiling at that flirtatious flautist in the mini-bikini and she's smiling back.'

'We were doing Tchaikovsky Four. I've just told her she's done a ten bar sequence rather well and as I am a pensioner and the flautist is only seventeen I don't think you've too much to worry about. That skinhead yob with the bassoon is her boyfriend.'

'You sound a wee bit envious,' she laughed.

'There was a lovely moment that day,' he recalled. 'We played Elgar Pomp and Circumstance and when we reached the chorus of *Land of Hope* we must have had a choir of a thousand. It seemed everyone on the seafront and the beaches joined in. It was totally unmusical but ever so moving.'

The most gratifying moment had been the international performance of Handel's Messiah in Berlin and the commentary of the distinguished critic in the Times.

Before this performance I worried that, even for Richard Dyer, this might prove a bridge too far. The South American youth orchestra had not played the work before and the singers comprised seven choirs of five different nationalities. I need not have worried. This performance had integrity and a fervour that I have never heard before. When it was over I made a point of asking the players, the soloists and the singers the secret of their performance. In every single case they simply didn't understand the question. They told me they were playing and singing for Richard Dyer. One day they could tell their children and grandchildren that they had performed for Richard Dyer. So of course, in their own terms, they had to raise their game above anything they had achieved before.

In June, Richard sailed his yacht *Harmony* in the annual Round the Isle of Wight race. With him as crew came Laura, Caroline and her boyfriend Mark plus two hefty lads from the local sailing club. They battled against the prevailing wind and breaking waves up to the Needles rocks. Richard remembered it from his sailing trips in *Dragonfly* with Stella and also in grimmer times seeing it from his cockpit in 1940. It was near here that Tom Stacey had fallen to his death. When would he ever shake that memory free? Once round the western tip of the island they could run free before the wind. This was a happy moment as they hoisted the spinnaker and the little yacht surged ahead, cutting through the waves and sometimes riding over them. There were a hundred other boats surrounding them, and they were not particularly well placed in the timed event race, but Richard felt the familiar sensation. He could feel music here. He could feel it, breathe it, and live it.

They finished their race somewhere mid-fleet on final timing. They moored opposite the famous Folly Inn and went ashore for a beer. 'Skipper's very quiet,' said one of the crew lads.

'Sorry,' said Richard. 'I've been dreaming.'

'No you're not,' Carrie was far too perceptive. 'You're creating. I've seen it before.'

He smiled at her. 'For once you are spot on.'

That night Richard lay restless in his bunk. He could not escape this extraordinary music that was taking over his mind and soul. Once again he had no idea where it had come from. He didn't need to score it on paper, or not yet. Someone had told him about gadgets being developed from computers, mini-versions of the machines in offices. With one of these, it was claimed the composer would no longer need reams of paper; just a dummy keyboard and monitor screen. This technology didn't appeal to Richard. Right now the score was firmly fixed in his head.

The following morning was cold and grey as they motored down the Medina river and past Cowes. Richard was at the helm as the whole crew kept a wary lookout for the big Solent ferries and, further out, the huge cargo carriers heading for Southampton. His only thought was to reach home and then set to work and score his music. Where had the spark come from? He didn't know and right now he didn't care. He only knew this was the culmination of a lifetime and he needed to set it down and then hear it performed.

At home in Pockhampton he worked on his symphony 3 for a month. Its premier was at the following year's London Proms. The reception was ecstatic. The reviewers said it secured the composer's place as the world's greatest. Richard was pleased but to him it was simply an old man's swansong.

CHAPTER 57

1990

The National Youth Orchestra with their conductor were invited to play three concerts in China during the school summer holidays. Rachel now fifteen and already an amazing pianist would go with them. She could already run off large chunks of Chopin and Bach as well as some jazz improvisation. Her parents had to agree that their little girl was at least as advanced as ever they were at her age. Rachel was enjoying her schooling not far away at Bedales near Petersfield from where she could come home at weekends.

Caroline had finally tied the knot with her long-term boyfriend, Mark, and now in her thirties had finally found herself pregnant. With his other children all with two each he would now have seven grandchildren to indulge him in his old age.

'I've been asked to take a position against this new poll tax.' Richard looked across the breakfast table to Laura. 'There's a petition going the rounds signed by people from the arts and sciences.'

'If you say so, but we come out of it rather well.'

'Yes. But that's not the point. All right, we pay the same rate as everyone but then so do the people on the council estate down the road and the farm workers. No wonder they've been rioting in Scotland.'

Laura grimaced. 'I don't think we should get mixed up in politics.'

'I don't think so either, but this isn't politics, not party politics. That woman's crazy if she thinks we'll put up with this.'

'It's nice to have a woman running things but I think you're probably right.' Laura's severe expression was turned on him. 'Why are you turning down the royal honour?'

'Absolutely no insult to the Sovereign. It's Master of the Queen's Music and judging by past holders I'd probably never compose another note.'

'Yesterday you were all on with this crap about humble birth and Sussex farm boy.'

'Well. Yes. There's that as well. It's a pity that man Fillingbroke is dead. I'd love to see his face if he knew.'

None of them would ever forget the Far East tour as long as they lived. Thirty young orchestral players and one very senior conductor plus wife and daughter arrived at Shanghai in July. They had forty-eight hours to settle in before they toured the city. Richard was most impressed by this hub of energy, bustling with its new industries and modern high-rise buildings: a capitalist stronghold in the midst of a communist nation.

Young Rachel was wide-eyed with wonder and excited by the promise of a master-class with Peng Ling, one of the world's outstanding young pianists. Following their week in Shanghai they would be off to Beijing to repeat their programme and to visit the Great Wall. The concert comprised standard works by Beethoven, Schubert and Dvorak. In the end the communist authorities even permitted some Gershwin. The last item on the programme was the Dyer Symphony No 1: The War Symphony.

Richard and the players had all been startled when the whole audience has risen to their feet for the last movement and had stood respectfully for its entire length. The applause had been long and wholly sincere. China, Richard mused, had been a nation ravaged by that terrible world war almost more than any other. There were still many long-lived veterans who had seen terrible things and he was happy if he could have brought them a little comfort through his work.

'Wow, Dad, Peng Ling says I'll be as good as him one day. I've just got to work at it and forget everything else.' Rachel was dancing up and down in delight.

'All right, all right,' her father replied. 'What about your A levels?'

'Oh, I'll be all right with them.'

'Well, you'll need all of them if you go to the Music Academy like I did.'

'You father is right,' said Laura. 'And all work and no play is not going to help you in the end. Get the balance right and you'll play a great performance. '

'As long as it's not an Eric Morecambe recital,' Richard laughed.

'A what?' Rachel looked blank.

Her mother laughed as well. 'He means all the right notes but not necessarily in the right order.'

'I still don't get it.' Rachel looked around. 'Those blokes who follow us, they're creepy. They're not perverts are they?'

'No, they're our minders. They watch out for us, and of course they stop us spreading any wicked pro-western propaganda.'

'Fat lot of good that would be,' Rachel giggled. 'None of us speak

Chinese except for Ellie the cellist. You're right they watch her all the time.'

Their success was repeated in Beijing in front of high party officials. The same moment came when the whole audience, including the top officials stood in respect for the War Symphony. Richard was much moved by this and was surprised when he was given some sort of People's Music award. The next day they were taken to the Great Wall and the youngsters spent a happy time running up and down its gradients. Then on to Hong Kong, and once again, they repeated their triumph with an audience standing for the War Symphony. There followed the long flight home and a happy but exhausted troupe of young musicians staggered back onto home soil.

The fiftieth anniversary of the Battle of Britain came around that autumn. Richard attended the special memorial service and took part in a fresh round of TV interviews along with surviving comrades. First he went to the cemetery in Chichester and laid a wreath on the grave of Tom Stacey. 'Tom, lad. I haven't forgotten you and I never will.'

Once more the War Symphony was played on Radio Three as well as Classic FM and Richard and his whole family attended a performance of the Dyer requiem in Chichester Cathedral. As the messages poured in from around the world he at last began to realize his status. He would never fully understand it: he was still Dickie Dyer the little farm boy. He had come a long way. Once again he felt this disbelief; how much further would he go before his fall?

In 1991 Rachel, like her mother before her, won the Paris young pianist award. She had performed the special pieces her father had written for her, then the Chopin preludes and finally a full rendering of Rubenstein Four, a work that should have been wholly beyond the scope of a sixteen-year-old. Nothing quite like this had been seen since her own father had performed Rachmaninov Three at the age of seventeen. Although his beloved daughter had made a few very minor glitches she performed far ahead of any rivals. So now, they had a household of three virtuoso pianists. Richard wondered if the place would explode with ego.

CHAPTER 58

2000

Richard was happy that at eighty he could still walk with his dog alongside to the top of Pockhampton Down. He had walked this path since childhood and it had been the place that had been the inspiration for much of his finest music. Once, long ago, he could have run up the final slope. Now with difficulty he limped the final hundred yards and stood once more by the stone trig-point. It was a murky overcast day and he could not see all the way to the coast and the sea. Had he any inspiration left? Maybe, but nothing was happening right now. His children were all married and he was now twice a great-grandfather. Rachel at twenty-five had married her fellow pianist, the Dane, Eric, and they had settled in an apartment not far away in Horsham. Rachel was still performed with the name Dyer. As yet they had no family but that was understandable as they both travelled Europe and further afield.

So much of his greatest work had been created in bitterness. Now this was less so. Pockhampton Music Centre had been honoured with a visit from a royal prince. It was Laura's remark that had caused the surprise. 'Richard's Sussex Symphony should have been the Coronation Symphony. I can't help thinking what might have been.'

The Prince had smiled and put a finger to his lips. 'Maybe we should think what may yet be to come.' Yes, thought Richard. Professor Fillingbroke, stuff you.

Like everyone in the world, they sat up to watch the arrival of the millennium on television. On the following evening of January the First, Richard had conducted the youth orchestra in a lively televised evening of music from the previous century. This included a medley of tunes from the Sky Blues, the Glen Miller orchestra and work by Vaughan Williams and Richard's old mentor William Walton. An intriguing dark haired girl singer took the stage and at the end gave him a smacking kiss on the cheek. It was a delight for an old man as long as the girl hadn't been covertly after his DNA. The discovery of this medical breakthrough could threaten to expose Maria's children to scandal and possible disinheritance. Of course few people survived to know the secret and not many cared about inherited titles these days. He gave orders to the music centre's security to keep out anyone from the tabloid press. The full implications had been revealed to him by Maria. They had met for a quiet dinner in a lovely secluded pub a few miles north of Petersfield.

'The pub with no name: well that's original,' Maria laughed. 'I've got a name now, you know.'

'Eh, what are you on about?'

Maria giggled. 'On about? You're talking Sussex again. It's this DNA. I know who my real father is. Mummy would never tell me, but when she died I vowed to do something about it. So I submitted my DNA and her background to a historical researcher.'

Richard was intrigued. 'And that told you what?'

'In the First War Mummy was working in Whitehall and she stayed on for a year or so after it ended.'

'So, how did that help you find your father?'

Now she giggled just like the little girl of long ago. 'Dickie, it seems I'm really Welsh and my real father is – or was world famous.'

'Oh wait a minute – Whitehall. I think I can guess where you're coming from. My old Dad used to sing that song he learned in the trenches. The man they were singing about was a lecherous old sod, by all accounts.'

'Well, the great man knew my Mum all right and the DNA has proved it.'

'I only wish we could acknowledge our children.' He sighed. 'I love them, we both love them.'

'Don't worry. They both know, but no one else does. Our secret is secure.' She looked up. 'Oh look, here comes our roast and it smells gorgeous.'

In April 2001 Laura and Richard with Caroline and her husband left Heathrow for Richard's final visit to Australia. A few of Stella's and his friends were still alive, but Stella's parents were not and both were buried in the cemetery near their daughter. Clem and Flav had been forced to resume ancestral ways with a houseful of Vietnamese domestics and a full-time nurse. They would die beside their vineyard before anyone put them in a care home. Richard couldn't help but be amused when the hotel was invaded by a group of smart-suited reporters who insisted that they were "cultural journalists". Australia was certainly changing.

'Sir Richard,' said one of the men, 'you'll always be an Australian in our eyes. Handel was a German but he's always reckoned an Englishman. You rate up there with him and you're an Australian.'

Richard laughed. 'I'd better remember that and I'm very happy to do so.'

'You're a serious composer, but is it true you like some modern rock music?'

Richard had been asked this before many times. It amused him. 'Oh, yes, any music of quality. I've always admired the Beatles. Roy Orbison: wonderful gift of singing pitch. I'd have signed him up for my wartime band if he'd been around. Then there's Queen, Bohemian Rhapsody, and Dire Straits, Brothers in Arms. That combines a lovely melody with genuine poetic words. I can tell you. if you'd ever fought in a war; that is exactly how we all felt.'

It was a nostalgic month when they travelled around that vast country visiting every part except Perth. Maybe he was being unfair to a fine city but the memory of that dockside revelation still cut him like a knife.

By June they had exchanged an Australian drought for a wet English summer. Then, one day in the summer of 2005 Richard had been invited to sit in the passenger seat of one of the Red Arrows display Hawk aircraft. He was put through a vigorous pre-medical something that he had been putting off for several years. He was pleased to be told his blood pressure was still normal. He was reassured that the pilot would not be putting in any high-G turns or violent aerobatics. That no doubt made medical sense. The Air Force did not wish any harm to one of their most famous ageing fighter pilots, but inwardly Richard felt a twinge of disappointment. He arrived at the air base, showed his day pass and parked his car. A gaggle of paparazzi and a TV crew were lying in wait.

'Sir Richard, how d'you feel? Sir Richard, how'd you like to fly jets today?'

In a crew room he was garbed in his flying suit, plus hard helmet and parachute. It was a long way from the days when he flew and fought in his everyday uniform. A cheerful Flight Lieutenant then escorted him to their aircraft. He could not believe how quiet the Hawk was, nor the force of the takeoff acceleration. The ground below vanished far quicker than he could ever remember from his Hurricane days.

'Hi there, Richard. How are you doing?' The pilot's voice came through in his helmet.

'I'm loving it.' That was true. Richard could feel music in his head and a feeling of wonder and exaltation.

'Fancy a quick roll?'

'You bet – go for it.' Just as in old times he saw the earth below rotate around him.

'See any 109s?' the pilot called.

'I think they must have all gone home,' he replied.

'Don't blame'em. They knew you were up here.'

His old Hurricane had floated down gently onto the runway. This aircraft rushed at the ground at well over one hundred and fifty knots and then touched down as lightly as a feather. Richard's estimation of these men rose even higher. They simply were the best of the best. The ground crew helped the lame old veteran down the ladder until he stood shakily on the tarmac.

The pilot shook his hand. 'My old granddad flew in Bomber Command. But all you blokes were heroes. I sometimes wonder how I'd shape up in a war.'

'From what I saw today, you'd be an ace.'

The Flight Lieutenant grinned. 'My daughter went to one of your daughter Rachel's concerts and your Rachel signed her autograph. My wife weeps buckets every time we play the CD of your War Symphony. It's magic.'

Richard drove home. At Pockhampton he was surprised to see a very smart BMW parked by the front entrance. As far as he knew no visitors were expected and none of Laura's piano pupils drove in that sort of style.

Laura was in the reception lounge with a large bald-headed man in his forties. Richard knew he had seen him before somewhere.

'Dick,' said Laura. 'This gentleman is Herman Hasselmein, the film director.'

Of course, now Richard knew him. The man who had directed that grim war film, but also the Hollywood version of Richard's own Robin Hood. Royalties from the latter had exploded their family fortune to millionaire status.

'What can I do for you, Mr Hasselmein?' Richard shook the director's hand.

'Say, Sir Richard, that's easy. We want to make a film of your life. It's called the Music Man.'

Richard was stunned. 'For God's sake – why me?' He was flattered, puzzled, but worried. He was a man with a well concealed double life.

'Why you, sir?' grinned the director. 'Well, you are Richard Dyer. Hey man, your music is playing somewhere right now this moment, somewhere in every continent on earth. You've an inspiring story to tell in peace and war. The world should know the truth.'

Richard felt a stab of real apprehension; the truth, does he mean the whole truth?

Laura was smiling happily. 'He wants Sherrie Joluant to play me, yes me! What about that?'

He knew he would have to give in. 'Look, it's my life. Do I get much input?'

'You betcha you do. You'll work with our script guys throughout.'

Richard sighed. He had truth he could reveal, but an awful lot that needed to be concealed. He remembered past Hollywood music epics. *The Glen Miller Story* and *Song of Norway.* He wondered what Miller or Greig would have made of these if they'd lived to watch them. It seemed likely that he would live to see his alleged epic and he was not sure he wanted to.

Once more he was baffled by all this public attention. It had increased five fold these last few years. On the radio Desert Island Discs he had startled everyone by declining to play any of his own music. Laura and Rachel had bullied him into going on TV chat programmes including that rather scary all female show. He had genuinely enjoyed being the oldest celebrity to race the reasonably priced car around the track for the TV motor show. He had felt something of his old flying days as he had put in a respectable time. Total strangers of numerous nationalities wrote to him. Others asked for his autograph, and a Chinese film company had made a programme about him. He was equally flattered and baffled to be told that next year an entire evening at the London Proms would be reserved for *The Music of Richard Dyer in Peace and War.* And why the hell should the Poles want a statue of him in their Warsaw music college? Now the local authority had renamed his old village school as the Richard Dyer Primary School. As far as Richard was concerned he was still the little Sussex farm boy who had travelled a long way by love of his profession and unlooked for good fortune.

CHAPTER 59

2010

The Music Man was launched on the world in 2008. Richard had been much relieved that none of his covert relationship with Maria emerged. A cheeky little extrovert lad, a modern cathedral choir boy, had depicted him in childhood and Richard was pleased that the boy could really play piano rather well. He loved the opening scene with the little lad running up the slope of the real Pockhampton Down as the Sussex Symphony rolled in with the opening titles. A debonair English soap actor played the Battle of Britain pilot and the subsequent band leader and composer.

'I'm from Sussex originally and there can be no greater honour for a Sussex man than to play Richard Dyer,' said the actor. Richard couldn't understand that. The fellow couldn't really mean it.

Best of all, Alice was cast as her own mother. The ageing comedian cast as Ted, Richard's father, did a passable imitation of the old man. The glamorous Sherrie Joluant did a reasonable depiction of Laura. Stella was played by an Aussie actress musician and Richard was relieved that the actress looked nothing like the real Stella. He was even more relieved that the film was built around music. The one and half hour epic was filled throughout with his own music. Why on earth these exotic film company people should want to record his life was a puzzle.

His War Symphony revelation on the Down was included and it was tasteful and moving. The script writer had respected Richard's memories. He wasn't certain about the imagined moment when a Spitfire swept overhead and metamorphosed into a flock of doves. It was acceptable if untrue. He really liked the final scene where the actor, now made up to look mature and middle-aged, stood once more on Pockhampton Down as sunlight flooded the landscape. The music that played was the triumphant conclusion to his requiem.

The film was premiered in New York and then in London. For a month his world went mad until he hired a tactful secretary to deal with the phone calls, emails and letters. Richard was mightily relieved that none of his secret life emerged either in the film or in the post-launch hysteria. The family was already sufficiently flush with money and he gave his royalties to charity.

Growing old gracefully was never easy. Richard was slowly slipping into a sedentary lifestyle. He sat in the garden with a pint of beer and ran back over his long life. It was a quieter life now. He had given up performing but still did the occasional conducting session with the youth orchestra. The children, never to his knowledge, mocked this greying old man. They still apparently idolized him. His composition was all short work including a very successful film score. Symphonies and concertos were no longer fashionable, although his work was still a regular feature of the concert circuit and the London Proms. His opera Robin Hood still packed in the crowds and a few years ago its lead soprano in the Hollywood version had won an Oscar. The royalties he shared with the children of the late Bob Jansen and his share had helped make him become a wealthy man. The short pieces he composed now also brought in good money but they were much more mundane film scores and even themes for TV shows.

An agent asked if the central melody in the second movement of Stella's Isle of Wight concerto could be adapted as an American Country ballad. Richard had always thought of this as a song without words anyway, but the personal nature of the piece made him wary. But when he saw the lyrics he was converted. The words were all about lost love and lost hope. Six months later the song was high in the pop music charts.

He mustn't complain, he was old and arthritic but life had treated him well. *Age shall not weary them nor the years condemn...*Yes, five of the greatest lines in the English language.

For God's sake he was ninety, a greater age than any of his hard-working ancestors had achieved. His children wanted him to make the century with a telegram from the sovereign and all that. Well, yes, but only if he could still walk a little way onto the Down. He didn't drive a car more than a few miles locally, but Rachel was coming down today to take him to her new house near Winchester. Rachel was still performing, as was her pianist husband Eric, but both now wanted to slow down and give the best years to their two children. He now had twelve grandchildren although only seven could be openly acknowledged. Roger, James' oldest was about to marry next spring. Roger's sister Sophie was married and awaiting her first child. He would become a great-grandfather; what a milestone that would be. James took a real hands-on interest in the Pockhampton estate and often asked Richard for information about the past. Both father and son had grown very close but were confident that no one else living knew their secret apart from James' mother. Maria was also ninety but bearing up well. She was confined to a battery-powered wheelchair, which she raced around as if she was still the child of long ago.

'Dad, are you ready?' Rachel called from the terrace. The same terrace that he had stood on the day he met Elgar. He had heard Rachel's bulky four-by-four grinding up the gravel drive. Painfully he lifted himself to his feet, grabbed his walking sticks and set off up the steps. He walked slowly to the car and Rachel helped him up into the passenger seat and fixed his belt. They set off along the twisting winding A272 road. How did Chesterton put it? *The rolling English drunkard made the rolling English road...*

Rachel was conscious that she must drive warily with her father there as passenger. It happened on the twisting stretch of road past the town of Petersfield. In a split second a flash of silver hurtled at her from the oncoming right hand side of the road. The other vehicle slammed into them and rolled over into the roadside verge. Both airbags had exploded with the impact. She was unhurt and she could see Dad slumped forward in his seat. 'Dad, are you OK – speak to me!'

'Gotta' get out. What was it, a 109?' His voice was slurred and unreal.

'Stay there, Dad. I'll go and look.' She climbed out of the car and walked around the front. The whole left side was smashed and the left front wheel was twisted around ninety degrees. The other vehicle was a silver sports car lying on its side; the single occupant was wailing with pain. He was a stocky young lad with red hair.

'Tom, Tom, you're alive and I saw your parachute catch fire.' Dad was now tottering around beside her before, to her horror, he collapsed on the ground with his left leg twitching.

'Lady, I saw it all happen, I was behind you.' It was the driver of the white van that had been in her mirror minutes ago. 'I've rung treble nine and the medics are on their way.'

Rachel had to hand it to the emergency services that arrived on the spot within fifteen minutes. An ambulance pulled up followed by the first police car. Rachel knelt tearfully beside her father. His speech was so slurred she could make little of it.

'What happened, love?' It was a policeman looking down at her.

'I don't know. That car came at me on the right hand side. I braked but he smashed into me.'

'All right, don't get upset. We've had a message. That other car was stolen.'

'Please,' Rachel was crying now. 'This is my father. He's ninety and he's had some sort of seizure.'

Now a paramedic was kneeling beside her. 'You say this gentleman is your father?'

'Yes.'

'He's certainly in advanced shock. We've sent for the air ambulance and they'll take both casualties to hospital.'

On cue they all heard the approaching helicopter. It circled for some minutes and landed in flat grass field not far away.

Rachel tried to comfort her father but he seemed oblivious. She turned to look at the red-haired boy who was lying moaning. The medics had cut away his trousers and she could see the compound fracture with the ugly bone sticking through the flesh in a pool of blood. Now the helicopter medics were at work strapping the leg as the patient screamed eerily. The pilot walked over to Rachel and looked down at Richard. 'They say your dad's badly shook up. How will he take a flight in our machine?'

'Oh, that'll be fine. He's a Second World War fighter pilot.'

'Goodness, you don't say. We'll take special care of him.'

Rachel watched as the helicopter lifted off and flew away towards the hospital in Southampton. 'Oh God, don't let Dad die, not yet and not in this way.'

She looked around. There were now six police cars on the scene plus the road ambulance. She suffered the humiliation of a breath-alyzer test which of course proved negative. She, in company with the van driver, had to repeat her statement. The senior copper came over to speak to her.

'You're Mrs Rachel Lindstrom?'

'Yes.'

'Right we've no quarrel with you. It seems the sports car was stolen in Alresford and the driver is an East European who seems to have forgotten or not known that here we drive on the left.'

'He was going much too fast.'

'I understand that the other casualty is your father. May we know his name.'

'He's Richard Dyer or rather Sir Richard Dyer.'

The copper stared open mouthed. 'Not the famous one?'

'The composer, yes, that's him.'

The copper shook his head. 'If anything happens to him there'll be all hell let loose.'

Rachel was annoyed. She was already tearful and she felt this man was callous. He seemed to think only of himself and the extra paper work he would be landed with. 'Do you know if he's all right?'

'The other driver's been labelled potentially life threatening but your father is only classified as stress resulting from shock.'

Richard had mentally relapsed seventy years. He was on a stretcher carried by four strong men. Of course he'd baled out, that was it. He faded away in semi-consciousness. He was in an aircraft. The motion was unmistakable but the engine was noisy and didn't sound like any he had flown with. He tried to sit up but his left leg was rigid and twitching. He felt a mask on his face. Yes, that would be his oxygen but where was his helmet?

'Lie still now,' said a gentle voice, a girl's voice. 'You've had a bit of a shock and we're taking you to hospital.'

'What's happened. Was I shot down?'

'No, you've been in a motor accident, but we're looking after you now.'

Famous composer injured in road crash.
Battle of Britain veteran injured in road accident.
World famous composer hurt in crash.

These were a selection of press headlines that hit the news-stands next day. The accident was reported soon afterwards in papers and news media the world over. Rachel was relieved that no one mentioned she was driving although all the reports stated that her father had been a passenger. *Not life threatening,* said all the reports. Rachel had been kept at the scene for two hours before the police allowed her to ring Eric her husband and allow him to take her away. All she cared about was her father, and straight away they drove to the hospital in Southampton.

'Sir Richard has suffered a mild seizure although the symptoms are similar to a stroke. He is a very elderly person and we will need to keep him here for some days.'

The young doctor seemed somewhat awe-struck to have been landed with such an important patient.

'Will he live?' This was all Rachel wanted to know.

'Oh yes, for his age your father is strong, but you must arrange careful nursing and observation when he is discharged.'

By now the whole world knew. The hospital was besieged by

reporters while the Dyer family, and not a few Corbailier family, gathered. Goodwill messages flooded in from musicians, from royalty and presidents, but so many also from ordinary people.

CHAPTER 60

2016

Richard Dyer never composed again and he never played the piano in public again.

The seizure that had gripped him on that Hampshire road did not kill him but its debilitating effect led to a slow decline with memory loss, low appetite and slurred speech. Richard's extended family and friends suffered almost as much as he did. Finally, there was relief when on March 3rd 2016 Richard Dyer passed away peacefully in the village where he had been born ninety-six years before.

THE DAY THE MUSIC DIED.

So shouted the headline in the Sun. The same was repeated in the Sydney Morning Herald and in different versions around the world. The truth was different. The Dyer music poured forth from every source, radio and television. Pictures reappeared: a very old man stands with a small boy. The boy, a young adult now, sits at a piano. The same young man dressed in Air Force uniform with pilot's wings standing beside a Hurricane, then conducting a dance band. Next a picture of the young man dressed in jacket and flannels. He stands beside another old man with the Albert Hall in the background. Then the man, with a pretty wife stands with the Sydney Harbour Bridge in the background.

The regular mid-afternoon TV broadcasts were interrupted. 'We have some breaking news. Buckingham Palace has announced that: *Her Majesty the Queen has been pleased to grant Sir Richard Dyer.OM. KBE. DFC. OBE. Order of Australia, an official state funeral.*

That evening the Prime Minister spoke to the nation.

In a week's time we will be celebrating the life of one of those fine Britons who, over the centuries, have enriched our culture and enriched the culture of the whole world. I speak of men and women such as Thomas Hardy, Edward Elgar, Charles Dickens, the Bronte family and so on all the way back to William Shakespeare. These were persons who started life without great wealth but advanced purely by talent and great natural gifts.

Such a one is Richard Dyer, a boy from a Sussex village, whose great music has brought such honour to our nation and to our sister nation of Australia, both in peace and war. Our parents and grandparents recall his Sky Blues orchestra that so cheered them in war. His famous War Symphony has moved millions around the world. When personal tragedy struck he composed his requiem, a work of such haunting quality. For those like myself who had the pleasure of hearing a live performance of his music it was a unique experience. Richard Dyer composed music that was accessible to everyone. It was music that went beyond beautiful melody into a haunting mode that moved a whole World. Richard Dyer was a man of humility who would never accept the truth that he was a genius. He was never a violent man; he hated war but learned to fight. In the desperate battle in the skies of 1940 he became one of our leading fighter pilots. When wounded in action, he returned to music and did so much to cheer our people through those harsh days. We will bury our departed friend with all the honour our nation can offer. This will be a symbolic moment, maybe the closing of a chapter, the end of an era.

That weekend a special concert was performed in the Albert Hall with the National Youth Orchestra. Every seat was taken. A grieving Rachel Dyer, performed her father's piano concerto. The orchestra played a medley of dance tunes from the days of the Sky Blues. Finally, the orchestra played the Dyer War Symphony. The whole audience stood in respect for the third movement. It was a haunting rendition. There was no conductor. A reporter asked the young orchestra leader how this had been achieved.

'It was weird, really weird,' she replied. 'There was no one on the podium but we all felt he was there.'

Anyone who questioned the wisdom of this funeral precedent was soon to be reassured by the public response. For a week the coffin lay on a dais in the Guild Hall. A steady stream of mourners passed it: famous faces and ordinary members of the public, ex-service veterans and iconic figures from both classical and popular music. The crowds that passed were both sad and respectful. As many commented; the creator was no more, but his music lived for ever.

The Prime Minister had been correct. The funeral had touched a nerve in his nation's consciousness. It was a symbolic closure. The working class boy made good. The pilot who had been part of their deliverance in 1940, remembered by millions who had loved his music in peace and war. It was a matter of intense national pride for two nations, and a time to mourn for millions around the world. The state funeral was a precedent, but not to the thousands who lined the streets nor for the millions watching worldwide. This time they were not honouring royalty or a president, but saying farewell to one of their own.

The Royal Air Force bearers carried the coffin up the wide steps of St Paul's and into the cathedral to the music of the Agnus Dei from the Richard Dyer requiem. It was escorted by the widow, Laura, his children and grandchildren. The cortege included many famous figures from the world of music with other dignitaries, including the Australian Prime Minister, the Chief of Air Staff and the Presidents of the Australian and British yachting associations, but everyone's attention was drawn to a very old and wizened man, the centenarian Group Captain Jones, Richard's wartime squadron leader who walked stiffly up the steps held by two of his grandchildren.

The service was dignified, the music stunning. Kathy Norlin, the international chart-topping popular singer led them all in a rendering of the beautiful *My Love is Not Lost*; the poignant song that Winston Churchill rescued from the war censorship. The crowds watching the big screen in Hyde Park joined in the chorus. So, according to the tabloid press next day, did the royalty and other dignitaries. Some criticism was levelled at the TV producers for playing their cameras on the faces of the assembled war widows both recent and past.

The address was by James, Duke of Hampshire the former Agriculture Minister. A strange choice but billed as an old family friend. His speech was the high moment of the service. It was moving, personal, amusing and emotional to the point where the speaker's voice momentarily broke; some commented that it could almost have been that of a son, bidding farewell to a father. Then his final words: *'We end our service today with the playing and singing of the triumphant concluding anthem of Richard Dyer's Requiem. It is that moment when the sadness and the poignancy of this work is blown away in a burst of optimism and hope. I have all Richard's family's permission and blessing to tell you this. Once he told me that this dramatic musical moment was inspired by a vision, a visitation even, of Stella his tragically departed wife and the intuition that he would one day see her again. I believe we can say that the sorrow of this day is relieved by the knowledge that now they are together again in reunion for ever...'*

Now the coffin was outside in the spring sunlight. The RAF band played the national anthems of Britain and Australia. Then they struck up William Walton's Spitfire Prelude and Fugue. Exactly on cue, the Battle of Britain Memorial Flight roared overhead. Onlookers covered their ears and others applauded. Seconds later, six Typhoon fighter jets flew over in diamond formation.

'These are from his squadron,' said the TV commentator. *'From Sir Richard Dyer's old battle squadron. We understand they have had their overseas deployment put back by forty eight hours because they insisted that they must take part today.'*

Last came the nine Red Arrows who soared skywards above the cathedral as they paid tribute, not just to their honorary member, also to the thousands of his comrades who had died in that war.

The following morning, at first light, the cortege with police escort left London almost unnoticed and travelled onto the M25 motorway. They left it and turned south into Sussex. Through every town and village crowds lined the roadside. Ex-service groups lowered their standards, schoolchildren scattered flower petals, adults applauded. Their famous son was coming home. In mid-afternoon the cortege reached Pockhampton. The police and security sealed off the churchyard. Among the family and friends who came to pay their last respects were the Prime Ministers of Britain and Australia. The choir of Chichester Cathedral sang *The day thou gavest,* as the coffin was carried to that quiet corner of the churchyard and lowered into the grave beside that of Richard's parents. The RAF guard fired a salute and family and friends in turn dropped handfuls of earth and flowers onto the wood below. Last of all, a very old lady was helped from her wheelchair and with her son supporting her on one side and Richard's sister Alice on the other, she shuffled to the graveside. Her supporters tactfully stood back while the old lady spoke a few words into the grave and then dropped a single red rose. She turned away and the onlookers saw Maria, ninety-six-year-old dowager Duchess of Hampshire reveal a face wet with tears and an expression of inconsolable grief.

THE END

By the same author

THE NEMESIS FILE

Professional yachtsman and Olympic medallist Steve Simpson has problems. His wife has died and his Chichester sail making business is under threat. When Steve and his daughter Sarah find the body of a young Dane in the sea off the Sussex coast they are inextricably sucked into an international blackmail and drugs conspiracy.

The story describes fourteen days in the late summer of 1990 that will change Steve's life. It is a test that leads him to new love and a rebirth of his hopes.

This tense mystery-thriller moves swiftly from Sussex to Copenhagen with interludes in Portsmouth, Italy and Scotland, and ends with a sea chase in a gale

ISBN 978-0-9548880-0-8 (0-9548880-0-6)

Available from Benhams Books
1 Fir Cottage, Greatham, Liss, Hampshire GU33 6BB

Reviews of *The Nemesis File*:

Journalist Pamela Payne: With locations as diverse as the South Coast of England, Naples and Denmark, *The Nemesis File*'s credible sailing scenes will either have you reaching for the seasickness-pills or signing on for a course; the sex scenes, however, are the most romantic I have read for along time. A great adventure story, which will delight both sexes – sailors or landlubbers."

Yachts and Yachting December 2004. "…Jim Morley is a sailor writing for sailors and his first novel is immersed in the South Coast yachting and dinghy scene…if somebody was going to write a novel for *Yachts and Yachting,* readers this would probably be it.

Yachting Monthly: 2006. Dell Quay based yachtsman Jim Morley has turned his hand to writing thrillers based on his sailing experiences of forty years. His first novel, *The Nemesis File,* is a murder mystery linking a Chichester sailmaker with a failing business, the corpse of a Dane found floating off Sussex and Nazi propaganda minister Josef Goebbels.

Reviews of *The Nemesis File* (continued):

Olympic sailor and coach: Cathy Foster, 11th Dec 2004

Rarely have I read such a racy book! It's carries you along at pace, and holds you fast until the very end. Just then, you think that maybe this is getting far-fetched, but the punch-line pulls you up short, and makes you re-assess the characters and their relationship to events. Suddenly the plot hangs together again in a very satisfactory way, just as good detective stories should.

Instead of long descriptions to 'paint a picture' of all the venues and situations, the writing is succinct and carefully crafted to give the maximum impression for the minimum words. This gives the book its fast tempo, yet nothing is lost because the accurate detailing of locations and action bonds the reader into plot. As a past Olympic sailor myself, I know the sailing venues described in both Chichester Harbour and Copenhagen well, and I can reassure any future reader that the author has definitely done his research. In addition, he's right – you do build life-long bonds with other British athletes and other countries' sailors when you are part of the Olympic team representing your country. It is a pleasure and highly unusual to read a book which describes the joys of sailing and racing so well. Yet it's not a book about sailing, full of technicalities of the sport. Sailing provides the background framework for a story of murder and blackmail where the investigation chases over four countries and three generations of lives. A thoroughly enjoyable read.

Cathy Foster went to the Olympics in 1984 (finished 7th and made history as the first woman helm since the 2nd World War) and competed in two other Olympic campaigns, the last being 2002/3. She's a freelance Coach who specialises in top level racing, including Olympic and Paralympic sailors

By the same author

ROCASTLE'S VENGEANCE

When out of work sea captain Peter Wilson takes a job as harbour master in the Dorset yacht harbour of Old Duddlestone, he is surprised to learn that his own father, James Wilson, was the harbour's wartime commander.

There are unsolved crimes involving this secretive community dating back fifty years. The deaths of the entire personnel of a research laboratory, then a rape and murder followed by a lynching.

Peter, aged ten, witnessed his father's suicide. Now he hears disquieting rumours about his father's dubious activities in Duddlestone. He forms a relationship with single-mother, Carol Stoneman. When Carol's ten-year-old son is abducted, Peter is forced into a situation that nearly bring his own destruction.

This mystery thriller is set on the Dorset coast in the summer of 1997, with a sailing background.

ISBN 978-0-9548880-1-5 (0-9548880-1-4)

Available from Benhams Books
1 Fir Cottage, Greatham, Liss, Hampshire GU33 6BB

Reviews of *Rocastle's Vengeance*:

Unsolicited comment on Amazon. *****
Wow! What a read. You know it is a good book when after a few pages you don't want to put it down, nor answer the phone, door or anything…

Bournemouth Echo, July 2006.
Novelist brings mystery to the coast.
Rocastle's Vengeance, James Morley's second novel, is brimming with references to Purbeck Poole and Bournemouth. The book recounts the tale of a harbour master who uncovers murky secrets when he takes a job in the imaginary village of Old Duddlestone…

Tim O'Kelly. Whitbread Prize judge southern region.
Jim Morley writes with skill and intelligence: a genuine storyteller in the finest tradition.

By the same author

MAGDALENA'S REDEMPTION

If an eight-year-old boy commits murder is he irredeemably evil? Can he ever be rehabilitated or will he kill again to preserve his secret?

Hampshire farmer, Tom O'Malley, finds the dead body of a young journalist. Not satisfied that she is a suicide he makes his own investigation.

Fed rumours about his friend and employer, Hollywood film director Gustav Fjortoft, he angrily rejects them. Yet all his inquiries into his friend's past seem to substantiate the rumours.

Following suspicious deaths in his own community, Tom's quest leads him the American West Coast, where he escapes abduction and near death.

Returning to England he finds the answers he seeks in a dramatic finale in his home village.

ISBN 978-0-9548880-2-2

EMILY'S HOUR

Everything changes for the Simpson family when the dead body of an internet millionaire is found in Branham Lake and a close friend is falsely accused of murder.

It is 2004 and Steve and Kirsten, the central characters in James Morley's first novel, The Nemesis File are now married and have settled in rural Sussex with their children Emily 13 and John-Kaj 8. Steve runs the family nautical business near Chichester but teaches sailing at Branham Lake on the Surrey Hampshire border.

When further deaths occur, a police inspector facing a mental breakdown is convinced of his suspect's guilt. While Steve and Kirsten fight to clear their friend's name they have no inkling of the nightmare that is to engulf them. When Emily, along with an elderly war veteran, is abducted by a sacrificial religious cult, the family become the centre of worldwide attention.

Emily's Hour is a tense thriller, with a background in sailing that will engage both adults and teenagers alike

ISBN 978-0-9548880-3-9

Available from Benhams Books
1 Fir Cottage, Greatham, Liss, Hampshire GU33 6BB

By the same author

OLYMPIC NEMESIS

Emily Simpson's Olympic dream is threatened by an internet gambling syndicate.

Emily and crewmates Chloë and Erin are selected to sail for Britain in games held in the mysterious South American country of Olifa. Emily's father, Steve, is sailing in the Paralympics. Speculation about a father/daughter double gold puts both under threat.

Former Olympian Steve recovers from a stroke to rediscover his love of sailing.

Emily's Danish mother, Kirsten, lives in the shadow of her family's wartime disgrace. Rumours circulating about Emily's ancestry bring her and partner, Tom, into danger from a deluded stalker.

ISBN 978-0-9548880-4-6

FLANAGAN'S LEGACY

An international conspiracy in 1919. The killing of children in a Spanish village in 1937. Distant events come back to haunt the lives of Clare O'Dwyer and Michael Walters a young couple unborn at the time of either.

It is the early summer of 1994. Clare has inherited the fortune of her grandfather: US Senator James O'Dwyer, war hero, rogue politician and last survivor of the Flanagan Plot. Even after seventy years the truth would cause a fatal breach in relations between the United States and Britain.

Clare has no knowledge of this plot but is not believed. She is threatened by both security services and terrorists. To escape the pair run away to sea in their sailing yacht *Quadra.* The voyage takes them from France, Dorset, Cornwall and finally West Cork. They are abducted by terrorists and survive a force ten gale off Southern Ireland. In a dramatic climax Michael narrowly escapes with his life and Clare discovers something about her grandfather that will change her life for ever.

ISBN 978-0-9548880-5-3

Available from Benhams Books
1 Fir Cottage, Greatham, Liss, Hampshire GU33 6BB